SMOKE CITY

SMOKE CITY

A NOVEL

KEITH ROSSON

Meerkat Press
Atlanta

ISBN-13 978-1-946154-16-3 (Hardcover)
ISBN-13 978-1-946154-05-7 (eBook)

Library of Congress Control Number: 2017916752

Cover design by Keith Rosson
Book design by Tricia Reeks
Author photo by Lindsay Beaumont

Printed in the United States of America

Published in the United States of America by
Meerkat Press, LLC, Atlanta, Georgia
www.meerkatpress.com

This haste, this crush of the crowd, these hundreds of English men-at-arms, this executioner—his name was Geoffroy Thérage—all for one young girl who in a high voice lamented and invoked God.

—Régine Pernoud and Marie-Véronique Clin
Joan of Arc: Her Story

SMOKE CITY

The first one appeared in May.

It happened in a wind-scoured canyon in a stretch of national forest, forty miles east of San Diego. Dusk laid its reds and golds against the canyon walls as the sun hung above the tree line. There was no grand sense of ceremony, no change in the surroundings—the thing simply appeared. An eye-blink's worth of time. Dim, but recognizable enough: a wavering form in the shape of a man.

Details swam in the vapor. Here was a hand with creased knuckles, there a faded patch at a knee. A pale eye. A downturned mouth. Threadbare jeans, a long-sleeved shirt frayed at the collar and cuffs. The figure, the *man,* could have been thirty years old or twice that. From this century or the one before it. It faded and snapped to sharpness and faded again, everything the color of old newsprint. A pair of kestrels wheeled in the sky and the sun sank lower and drew long shadows on the ground.

The figure staggered, gazing around at the terrain. As if lost. Afraid and bewildered, abandoned.

And then it disappeared just as quickly. Vanished. Ten, fifteen seconds from beginning to end.

The first one appeared in May, but nobody saw it, and then it was gone.

***The Quick And The Dead: Vale/Basquiat Show Wild Success
at Edwin Tanazzi Gallery***
(Excerpt from *American Artist,* vol. 32, no. 2, Feb. 1989)

Michael Vale—the young artist whose meteoric rise into the
blue-chip art world has left many people with their jaws (and
checkbooks) open—made history Friday night at the cavernous Edwin Tanazzi Gallery in downtown Los Angeles. The
exhibition has allowed Vale, not yet twenty, to become the first
living artist to garner equal representation in a two-person
gallery show with the iconic and recently deceased painter
Jean-Michel Basquiat.

   Despite the Tanazzi Gallery's insistence that no more than
two of Vale's paintings could be purchased by any individual
collector at the opening, his section of the show—thirty-two
new paintings, some of them upward of fifteen feet in length—
was sold out within the hour. Basquiat's work was on loan
from various collectors, as well as his estate—currently being
overseen by his father, Gerald Basquiat, who is embroiled in
several legal battles regarding ownership of many of the pieces
being shown . . .

• • •

***Controversial Artist Michael Vale Convicted of Public Drunk-
enness, Assault, Sentenced to Rehabilitation Center***
(Excerpt from *Outside the Lines: A Journal of Outsider Art,* no.
112, May 2008)

In a textbook example of the tenuous nature of the art world,
Michael Vale—who less than a decade ago was considered one
of the most renowned contemporary artists in America, with
early and mid-period canvasses still reaching six figures at auction—was sentenced to a 90-day treatment center in Portland,
Oregon today. He was convicted last December of DUII and

second degree assault after getting into a physical altercation with the driver of another vehicle involved in a collision.

Sources close to the artist hardly seem surprised. "Mike's really been going down a dark road for a while," says Jacob Burfine, a gallery curator who showed Vale's work when the two lived in Los Angeles. Years later, after both of them had moved to Portland, Burfine unsuccessfully attempted to arrange some exhibitions for Vale, despite the artist's marked drop in status and sales. "It's gotten to the point where he's so volatile it's hard to even talk to him sometimes. I don't think he's painted in years. Not that I can necessarily blame him, the way things have turned out. Hopefully this will make some kind of impact."

Vale was at one time married to mystery novelist Candice Hessler; Burfine and others say that Vale's recklessness has intensified since their divorce. "He's definitely stepped it up in the years since he and Candice split. Honestly, you hear the term 'loose cannon,' you think of Mike Vale. The fact that he doesn't even own his own paintings anymore probably doesn't help," says Burfine, referring to Vale's controversial decision to give exclusive rights and ownership to all work created before 1999 to his previous agent. The agent, Jared Brophy of the Brophy Agency in Los Angeles, claims that there was nothing disreputable or illegal about the contract, which gave him complete control over Vale's entire catalog of work up to that year, including percentages of resale prices at auction. "There's nothing hinky about it," Brophy insists. "I was trying to help him out. Mike needed some money badly and I was becoming unimpressed with the quality of his newer work; it was losing its vitality, its rage. The early and mid-period work has this fantastic, kinetic edge, but he'd just been phoning it in for a while. I gave him a flat fee, a very generous one, for contractual rights so he could pay off some debts. That's it." It's believed that Vale's paintings have fetched tens of millions of dollars since Brophy gained control over them, while Vale himself hasn't had a show of new work in years. The contract— which many insiders believe is a questionable one at best and would most likely be overturned by a judge should it ever be brought to court—won't be up for renewal for nearly another twenty years.

We were unable to contact Vale regarding his sentencing, and his lawyer declined to comment. It's unclear whether he will challenge the court's verdict or enter the rehabilitation program . . .

• • •

Drunks Do the Darnedest Things (When They're Totally Fucked Up): Has-Been Artist Turns Vigilante Against Evil, Evil Gallery Windows
(Excerpt from the *Portland Mercury*, July 31, 2013)

Looks like *somebody* can't handle their liquor. Police reports obtained by the *Mercury* indicate that painterly has-been Mike Vale got all Bruce Lee down in the Pearl District on Monday night, kicking and punching out the display windows of *seven galleries* before being apprehended by police. After being discharged from St. Vincent's for severe lacerations, he was arrested under a shitload of charges and taken to the drunk tank.

The galleries, including Tobias Chang Fine Art, Green Light Go! and Visions, refused to press charges after Vale's ex-wife, mystery writer Candice Hessler, paid for the damages. Vale's still looking at possible county time for being wasted in public, and maybe even a felony charge for tussling with the cops.

"In a way, I feel sorry for the guy," Tobias Chang said of Vale, who at one time had regularly sold out exhibitions in New York, LA, Milan and Paris. "I mean, he was bigger than God at one point, in terms of the art world. I'd still even be interested in looking at any new work that he's done, in spite of all this."

Yet it appears that Vale—who's now employed at a car wash and can regularly be seen getting eighty-sixed from local bars—is less interested in painting and more interested in property damage. Stay classy, Mike!

PART ONE

MY FATHER'S COAT

MONDAY

1

The years bled together. Each waking morning—or afternoon, truth be told, or evening—couched in a familiar bloom of panic. After that, after Vale realized where he was, who he was, came the rest: sickness, fear, assessment of damage, all of it stitched together with the fine red thread of guilt.

Art & Artists had once called him a "relentless avatar of our contemporary, post-nuclear unease."

He woke to the alarm, studded in fresh bruises. New scabs on his knees and his teeth loose in his mouth. His lack of memory familiar in itself. Sunlight fell in the room in fierce, distinct bands.

He stood shivering in the shower, the water lancing against him while lava, hot and malicious, compressed itself behind his optic nerves. This pulsing thunder in the skull, and moments from the Ace High the night before came to him slowly, like something spied through a fun house mirror. He bent over to pick up a sliver of soap and with his trembling hand batted a rust-dotted razor lying on the rim of the bathtub. The razor slid down the tub, luge-like, and Vale reached down for it, trying not to gag as dark spots burst like stars in his periphery. He stumbled and stepped on the razor. The crack of plastic, and thin threads of blood began to snake toward the drain. It was painless.

"Oh, come on," he croaked. "Shit's sake." He'd smoked nearly two packs of Camels the night before and sounded now like something pulled howling from a crypt. He tried to stand on his other foot to examine the cut and couldn't manage it. He put his foot back down and stepped on the broken razor *again*, and now the floor of the tub was awash in an idiot's Rorschach of red on white. He retched once and shut the water off, resigned to death—or at least collapse—at any second. The towel hanging from the back of the door reeked of mold, and he gagged against it and dropped it to the floor. He left bloody, shambling one-sided footprints to his bedroom.

Apart from the painting hanging above his bed (the sole Mike Vale original still in his possession), the fist-sized hole next to the light switch was the room's only decoration. There was a dresser pitted with cigarette burns and topped with a constellation of empty beer bottles. An unmade bed ringed with dirty sheets. The alarm clock on the floor. Plastic blinds rattled against the open window.

He dressed slowly and stepped to the kitchen. Flies dive-bombed bottles mounded in the sink, on the counters. The light on the answering machine was blinking. He pressed the Play button, already knowing who it would be—who else called him?—and there was Candice's voice.

"The only man in the country still using an answering machine," she said. "Okay. This is me saying hi. Give me a ring when you discover, you know, fire and the wheel." Her voice then became steeped in a cautious, thoughtful cadence, a measured quality he remembered more clearly from their marriage. "Richard and I should be heading up through there on tour for another Janey book soon. It'd be good to touch base, get dinner. Call me."

It was September, the last gasp of summer. The apartment was explosive with trapped heat. A swath of sunlight fell across the countertop. Just looking at that glare hurt his eyes, his entire body, made him feel as if rancid dishwater was shooting straight into his guts. A nameless sadness, *the* sadness, the exact opposite of the Moment and so much more insistent, tore through him like a torrent. Like a rip of lightning, there and gone, and Vale sobbed. Just once. One ragged, graceless gasp. Pathetic. He stood sweating over the answering machine, ashamed of himself.

He was out the door five minutes later, blood wetting his sock, cold coffee and aspirin hammering a bitter waltz somewhere below his heart.

Time had once called him "a shaman of America's apocalyptic incantations, one who catalogs our fears and thrusts them back at us in a ferocious Day-Glo palette."

On his way to the bus stop Mike Vale, the shaman, the avatar—looking down in his shirt pocket for a cigarette—ran directly into a telephone pole, hard enough to give himself a nosebleed.

2

From the journals of Marvin Deitz:

There's a grace inherent here. In writing things down. Like a confession signed, maybe. An admission. Nothing so lofty as a salve of the spirit, but at the very least it makes one feel a little better.

My earliest memory is of being in the marketplace in Rouen with my parents. I was probably three or four years old. I was walking with my parents amongst the stalls as fast as I could manage, amazed not at the flood of people, but at how the mass of them, the tide of them, parted for us. Because I'd thought at the time that it was *me*, right? My mother holding my hand, I thought it was *me* that made the people part ways for us.

I thought I was magic.

I did not notice at the time (but can imagine now, all too well) my mother's downcast gaze, the way we stepped hurriedly through the leering crowd. How we did not stop to look at the untold riches of food, the bolts of fabric, the tools for sale. Things we never saw in our own village. I didn't notice how my father gripped my mother's arm, nearly dragging her along, her belly huge and rounded as she was pregnant with my sister at the time.

Three, four years old. I noticed the people parting for us, I remember that, but not the revulsion in their eyes, the contempt.

I would realize later, of course, just what it was the townspeople had shied away from, had leered at: my father's coat, and the stitched image of the sword on the back.

The executioner's mark.

And as for Joan, those decades later?

She was not loved unequivocally. She just wasn't. At least not out loud. To do so was dangerous. But her victories, it was true, allowed some of us a rekindling of faith, a brief respite against death's constant stutter of war and plague and occupation. The hope that God was watching over us all. The idea of it, that He believed in France's sovereignty. That He might lift His face toward us again.

And thusly the order of her execution may as well have been passed down from the very day of her capture. The moment she was seized there outside the walls of Compiègne, it should have been clear to all that she would be put to death.

When Bishop Cauchon, toady of the English, bought her from the Burgundians after her capture, I knew the trial itself would be a hoax. A mockery. Yet I heard murmurings from serfs and landowners alike—from my darkened corner of the barroom, or on my way down the road to extract another bloody, weeping confession—and some of them hoped, *prayed,* that such a girl, who had served so obviously as the arm of God in the name of France, would not be allowed to die such a death. That God in His mercy would surely not allow such a thing. They prayed that Charles, their blessed King—after all Joan had done for him—would surely involve himself in the matter. That Burgundy would suddenly bend its allegiance like an arrow in the wind.

But I knew, there in the dim hallways of the heart, that men simply do what they want to do. Men do their darkness and misdeeds and later claim guidance under the banner of *God's will.*

Shouldn't I know that more than anyone? Didn't I traffic in such matters?

She would die and they would call it divinity, because that's what people do.

The trial was orchestrated by dozens of assessors and friars and clergymen, an ever-evolving assembly of men. The lot of them little more than castrated politicians hiding behind the guise of theology. English stormtroopers practically leaning over the benches with swords drawn throughout the entire sorry thing.

And Cauchon, ah, you should have seen him. Christ, that man. So puffed up with wine and his own righteousness and the quaking fear of an English blade suddenly tickling his balls in bed some night. Terrified, but paid well for his work, too. He would later die inexplicably in his barber's chair, and the vengeful part of me still hopes the barber was paid to bleed him. And that it hurt terribly.

I dream of Cauchon nearly as often as I dream of Joan.

But *Joan.* Every avenue circles back. Everything returns to the mysterious and martyred Joan of Orléans. The young peasant girl who for a brief heartbeat of time was believed to have felt God's lips pressed to her ear.

What of Joan of Arc?

For all of my grief and heartache and guilt, the truth is I only met her once, and that was the day I burned her alive.

• • •

"I turn fifty-seven next Monday," I said. "One week. Which means I'll be dead in six days or less. Or so history dictates."

Julia crossed her legs, cleared her throat. She said, "I know, Marvin. Would you like to talk about it?"

I smiled, pleased with myself, my hands laced across my chest. My sessions with Julia were generally the high point of my week. "Well, to tell you the truth? The fact that I've survived this long surprises me."

Within the periphery of my good eye, I could see Julia set her pen and yellow legal pad on her desk. She uncrossed her legs and smoothed her skirt—her version, I knew, of an exasperated sigh.

"Because you don't always," she said.

"Live this long? God, no. Hardly ever, in fact. I've died anywhere from a few weeks old to my mid-fifties. But this long? A *week* before my birthday? Nope, this is a record."

Julia waited for me to keep talking. When I didn't, she said, "And what do you think that means?"

I had thrown any amount of incendiary, outlandish trivia Julia's way in our sessions, and she always managed the same impassive, impenetrable veneer. That wonderful amalgam of detachment and polite, professional interest.

My relationship with my therapist, distilled: I confessed my sins and she tried, through dogged perseverance dense with silences, to convince me my truth was fiction. I bemused her; I confounded her. I was her high-functioning, erringly pleasant pet lunatic. I was her act of charity. I impressed her with the depth and seamlessness of my delusion. I paid her in jazz records.

Julia's office was in a strip mall on Eighty-second Avenue, amid a string of used car dealerships, apartment complexes with parking lots of buckled concrete, and fast food outlets with typos on their marquees. Eighty-second stretched for miles, a stitched scar running north to south, the city's class-dividing Cesarean. The traffic was ceaseless and deafening, and on a hot summer day like today, the stench of exhaust and melting blacktop was like a fist to the nose. Julia's office was couched between a tanning salon called Life's A Beach and an oft-darkened dry cleaners that I was convinced was some kind of front.

During our first session, I'd gone into her office and been surprised when she actually wanted me to lie on a couch, like in the movies.

"Is this really necessary?" I'd asked.

"It relaxes me," she'd said.

"It relaxes *you*?"

But now I couldn't imagine telling Julia the things I told her while sitting upright, hands planted on my knees in some office chair. In Julia's office, the couch—a lumbering leather beast the width of a twin mattress—sat flanked against one wall. She rarely sat at her desk; it seemed like something she kept around to throw her notepad on. A potted fern stood quietly dying in the corner. On the wall, Julia's diplomas and licenses hung amid a drawing her son Adam had done when he was either a toddler or very, very drunk. It was about what you'd expect of a therapist's office whose neighbor was a tanning salon with a dead starfish in the window display. And yet my profound disinterest in living—my outright contempt of it, actually—seemed to dissipate during the fifty minutes I sank into those vast, dark cushions. Seriously, I loved that fucking couch.

Finally, I shrugged—the couch gave a little squeak of protest— and said, "I don't know what it means. I don't think it means anything."

"Really? It seems like it might be an improvement."

Another pause. "Well, it's not," I said. "It's the same old shit, Julia, believe me."

Julia picked up her pad and wrote something on it and asked if I was still volunteering.

I nodded. "I have another shift later today."

"Do you have any different feelings about it?"

I smiled. "Besides a black and ceaseless disdain for any kind of supposed 'guiding force' in the world?"

A smile, humoring me. "I suppose, yes."

"No," I said. "No different feelings about it. I'm grateful for the opportunity to help there, and at the same time it makes me feel so powerless that I want to hit something until that something breaks. I want to rail against God."

"Well, honestly, that seems like a pretty normal response, Marvin. I mean we're all powerless in the face of death, aren't we? And they're children. It's got to be hard."

I turned and looked at her. Julia was a pretty woman, maybe ten years younger than me, with a glossy wing of auburn hair that covered one eye as she wrote and that particular softness that some people get when they reach the point where exercise becomes a luxury and not a lifestyle. It worked very well for her. A lovely scattering of freckles beneath her eyes. She wore dark hose and a brown skirt, a black blouse. I felt a surprising tenderness for her when I saw a chafe mark on her ankle, the cost of some ill-fitting sandal.

"You think I'm just afraid of dying. Is that it?"

"Aren't you?"

"Julia, come on. It would be clichéd to say I've died a hundred times, but it wouldn't be that far from the truth. Dying is nothing new."

Chimes sounded in her desk drawer. The alarm going off, like some ethereal angel breaking wind. Our time was up.

I could see her dilemma. She was torn between calling me out on what she undoubtedly believed was my bullshit—the guilt over my made-up stories about Joan of Arc and Pierre Cauchon and all the rest were clearly, she felt, masking some other very real guilt. And yet she struggled with her education, her profession's standards and base practices, perhaps even her own beliefs and value system, all which staunchly noted that change must come from within.

I appreciated her for that, for that struggle. Because if she ever had actually called me out in the year I'd been seeing her, I'd have beat feet. Going and gone. I'd have promptly left her office and never spoken to her again. Our relationship was contingent on that structure: I confessed and she listened, no matter how ludicrous my tales. She could doubt but she could not refute. I needed to tell someone.

I extricated myself from the arms of the couch. A thinning, pot-bellied old man with a pair of prescription glasses, one lens transparent and the other ink-black. I felt relaxed. My Post-Confession High, I called it. I leaned over and handed Julia a paper bag that had been leaning against the couch.

She opened it and gently, picking it up from the edges the way I had showed her, extracted the record and laid it on her desk. A sealed copy, a 1959 original of John Coltrane's *Giant Steps* LP.

"Adam should be able to get at least a few hundred dollars for that," I said. "At least. Tell him to try the jazz auction sites first, then Discogs, and eBay as a last resort." She sat looking down at the record as if it were some kind of rune, some glyph to figure out. Coltrane's long fingers loomed on the cover, ratcheted around his sax. When she looked up at me there was a flatness to her expression, a blankness that surprised me.

"Are you in danger of hurting yourself, Marvin? I really need to know that."

I looked at Adam's childhood drawing on the wall—Jesus, was it a man surfing? A dog attack? I couldn't tell. "This is just how it is, Julia. I live and then I die and then I live again."

"You didn't answer my question."

"No. I'm not a danger to myself."

"Well, Marvin," she said, "I'd like to schedule one more appointment with you before you die." I laughed. Julia didn't. She thumbed through her planner, frowning. "Considering the fact that you believe you'll be dead by next Monday and reincarnated as . . . How does it go again?"

"As penance for my past transgressions. For what I did to Joan."

Julia nodded, still with the frown. "That's right. For your sins against Joan of Arc."

"Julia, you're being glib."

"I'm really not, Marvin. How does tomorrow at three sound? Can you fit that in? I know it's short notice."

"Is sarcasm a popular method in psychiatry today?"

Julia looked up from her planner. She raised her eyebrows and smiled, but there was a coldness to it—I realized that I'd hurt her, that she'd allowed herself to finally be frustrated; she was taking it personally, the steadfastness of my delusion. "I'm not a psychiatrist, Marvin, remember? I'm a psychologist. A therapist. If I *was* a psychiatrist, we'd be having a very different conversation right now, believe me."

"Why is that?" I said. Knowing what was coming.

"Because I think you would greatly benefit from medication, Marvin. Because I'm worried about your safety."

I gently rapped on the doorframe with two knuckles. "There's nothing to worry about," I said. Meaning, of course, that some bad things happen whether we worry about them or not. "I'll see you at three tomorrow."

Outside, the world was the same as I'd left it. Hot, the sun winking off the chrome of passing cars, that stink of melting blacktop.

My birthday was in a week, but I'd be dead before then. Some terrible death in the next seven days. And then on to the next life. So it had been, so it would be.

Honestly? It was hard to get excited about much.

3

Oh, there were so many reasons to clock the guy.

As Vale leapt from the countertop, as he watched the man's mouth move and curl but heard nothing besides the howl of his own blood in his ears, he ran through them. The list came fluidly and easily to mind:

1) Blood had by then hardened to a dark crust inside his sock.
2) His last two cigarettes had busted in half after he ran into the telephone pole.
3) The blood spatter from his nosebleed on his last clean work shirt.
4) Having to borrow one of Mario's extra work shirts, the humiliation being compounded when said shirt was so small on him it felt like Vale was wearing a fucking wet suit.
5) A hazy memory of the bartender at the Ace High laughingly cutting him off last night, and Vale realizing he may have literally *cried in his beer* before the bartender had taken his empty glass away.
6) Throwing up in the employee bathroom as soon as he got to work, his retching undoubtedly loud enough for both customers and coworkers to hear.
7) The fact that the other employees at Bean There, Bun That—loud, gum-chewing teenagers and solemn, tight-lipped Latinos, all of them twenty years his junior—perpetually avoided

him, as if, every day, he'd just strolled into work after his early morning shift of gleefully fellating irradiated warthogs outside the Fukushima reactor.

He was airborne, weightless. The overhead lights gleamed on the shaved dome of the guy's skull. Also:

8) The fact that Candice already had a new book out. He'd seen it in line at the grocery store the other day. Another Janey Delancy thriller. What was this, her twelfth novel? Thirteenth? The woman wrote like a goddamned metronome.
9) His hangover was brutal, but that was hardly an excuse anymore. That was like blaming nearsightedness, or being buck-toothed, or circumcised.

But mostly?

10) A sudden and terrible clarity: none of it meant anything. None of it meant shit. He was nearly fifty years old and had his ex-wife's name tattooed on his hands and seventeen dollars in his wallet. He was wearing a paper hat shaped like a hot dog and was pretty sure that he'd splashed a fair amount of vomit on his pants during his little bathroom visit. Nothing mattered.

So when the bald guy in the muumuu-like jersey had stepped through the doors with his phone pressed to his ear, practically shoulder-checking an old, curmudgeonly, wobbly-kneed regular that Vale actually kind of liked, that was it. Then when Purple Jersey Guy didn't even apologize on top of that, it was a done deal. Vale might as well have turned his lettuce leaf–shaped apron in right there.

"Oh," the guy practically bellowed into the phone once he got to the counter, "she was a total bitch, dude," drawing out the word *total* as if it were a piece of taffy. "I mean, she had that look already, but then she started talking, you know?"

Vale tightened his hands on the sides of the register and steeled himself for a new chapter of his life. "And what can I get for you, sir?" he said brightly.

The guy held up a finger as he looked above Vale's head, nodding.

He laughed—no, Vale thought, he *chortled*—and said, "That's what I *told* her, dude. I said, 'Dinner and a movie? Well, I'm gonna be straight with you. If I'm paying for dinner and a movie, I expect some *reciprocation.*'"

Out on the floor, bleary-eyed mothers sat at tables festooned with howling children, flying hot dogs into their mouths like plummeting airplanes, begging them to eat. Clusters of old men read day-old newspapers, men who remembered war rationing and could stoically nurse a bean and cheese burrito and a cup of ice for three hours.

"Grass, gas or ass, bro, that's right," the guy said. "That's exactly what I told her. Yeah." A pause, another chortle. "What do *you* think? We came to an agreement." The guy's eyes flitted over Vale's for just a moment. The sum total of the man's decorum seemed to be summed up by the fact that he minutely turned away from Vale before he said, "Oh hell yeah, I blew my nut. *Hell* yeah. Alright, lates." And then he hung up.

Vale could sometimes *feel* Mario, his boss, on the line behind him, doing bun counts in the kitchen and checking employee shirt tucks and whatever the fuck else a tight-assed twenty-year-old kid had to do to become a Senior Manager, while Vale took countless orders for flash-frozen burritos and hot dogs as wrinkled as a toddler's fingers in a bathtub. This was one of those times. Mario and his laser focus.

"Yeah," the guy finally rumbled, looking up at the menu now with his jaw hinged open. "Give me two TacoBurger specials with Chili King Fries. Extra jalapeño cheese. Two chocolate Devil Dogs. And a large Coke."

Vale gently set his hot dog hat on the counter. The guy was still in thrall to the Great Menu Above, so slack-jawed Vale could see his fillings. Mario suddenly appeared at Vale's side, his headset perched in his ear like some cyborg grasshopper. "Everything okay here, Mike?" he chirped nervously. Mario was good like that, some managerial spider-sense that warned him of impending fuckups. Vale ignored him.

Instead, he leaned over the counter and pressed a finger into the guy's chest. He said, "You fucking suck, man." It was all he could come up with. The inside of his head was a red cloud.

The guy looked down slowly, from the menu to Vale's finger and then up to his face. "What? What did you say to me?"

Vale said, "You suck, man. You totally suck. You're seriously a worthless human being. Flat-out." He slapped his hand on the counter. Heads turned. "Grass, gas or ass? I'll bet you a hundred bucks you've never said 'Grass, gas or ass' to a woman in your entire life. And if you have, I guaran-fucking-*tee* they recognized you for the petrified, misogynist dumbfuck that you are and ran the other way." His voice had risen. He was yelling, and it felt evangelical, redemptive. It felt *good* to yell at someone. "I call *bullshit on you,* you purple-shirted, rap-rock-loving, tribal tattoo-and-goatee, TacoBurger-eating motherfucker."

It was the guy's turn to point a stubby finger at Vale. Looking at Mario, he said, "So this is the guy you want, like, manning your register? This is the face of your business? This asshole?"

Mario had his hands out in front of him. "I am very sorry, sir. Really." He turned to Vale, grinning and terrified. "Mike, why don't you go work on the Tater-Totaler for a bit, and Brittany can relieve you here at the register. Sound good, Mike?"

Mario put a hand on his shoulder. Vale shrugged it off and suddenly leaned across the counter and seized the man's nipples in each hand. He twisted, hard. "I expect some *reciprocation,*" he snarled.

"Ow," the man said. The two of them stayed that way for a moment, Vale's hands on the man's breasts, and then the man's lips pulled back and he was slapping at Vale's hands, trying to grab them, and Mario said something like, "Pardon me, folks, hey guys, I'm the manager," trying to get between them, and things were finally, finally moving.

Vale hiked his leg up on the counter and he had already begun crafting the list of reasons why he was going to hit this man, it took no time at all, and it was only when he was mid-leap, when he was actually in the air, that Vale realized he was smiling for the first time in days.

4

Excerpt from *Sound on Sound: An Oral History of Jazz*, 1978:

Alan Coates, Columbia Studios session engineer: "Who, Bill Creswell? Yeah, I remember him. We used to call him Dollar Bill. A regular at the Blue Door, the Hi Hat, all those places. Tall, gangly white dude, real shy. Always wore long sleeve shirts 'cause you could see he had burn scars all up and down his arms. He was a jazzman for sure. Ate it up, man. Loved it. One time John [Coltrane] and some others was over at his loft—he had this place on Avenue B—and the motherfucker just had stacks of records, man, just *stacks* of them. I mean, like, ten copies of this album, twenty of that one. *'Round About Midnight* had just come out, and John said Dollar Bill had about *fifty copies* of that son of a bitch just sitting there untouched. Just right there in a box. So after that, he was Dollar Bill from then on. I don't know what he ever did with all those records, but they go for some money now, you know."

• • •

I was dumping inventory in the computer while Adam walked around the store stocking records. Even with his glasses on, Adam had to hold the album covers close up to his face. We were listening to the Dead Boys and dust motes hung motionless in the window's sunlight. "Listen," I said. "Hypothetical question. If you had a choice, would you rather own ten amazing records, or a hundred mediocre ones?"

"Genre?" Adam said, having moved over to the *Dead Punks* section. (A bonus of owning your own record store: you could file them any goddamned way you wanted to.)

"All kinds. The gamut. Good, bad. Mediocre."

"Collectible?"

"Doesn't matter."

"I don't know."

I said, "Mostly mediocre, actually."

I was fishing, trying to gauge Adam's interest. I'd made up my will six months before and had left Adam the shop, and now I was having second thoughts about it. He was my only friend, it was true, but he was also twenty years old. A kid. Julia didn't really count as a friend, since there was that troublesome issue of her doubting my sanity, as well as the fact I paid her, even if it was in store inventory. So, Adam. But the more I'd thought about it, the more I'd begun doubting myself. What college sophomore would want to be saddled with a business like this? With thousands of dusty albums and a monthly lease? Was that even fair of me? The kid couldn't even drink yet.

Still, Adam was majoring in philosophy; I might have been doing him a favor. The age-old quandary: it wasn't like I could come right out and say, "Adam, I will be dying a violent death within the next week. And I have no other friends. Shall I leave the record store to you, good chap?"

Adam said, "I'd probably go for the bigger one, the hundred piece lot."

"Okay. Why?"

He squinted at a record. "Because an album that seems mediocre today may be incredible a year later. People change." Spoken, I thought, with all the certainty of youth. Where a year can seem another lifetime.

The bell above the door chimed and Randy Noonan squeezed his wheezing girth through the doorway. Now my landlord, I'd known Randy since he was a teenager, when he'd been sullen and quiet. Now in his forties, he exuded impatience and a kind of jolly menace that hung like dank potpourri around him. He coughed and ran a handkerchief down his face. "Hotter than a pyromaniac's snatch out there."

He wore cargo shorts and a turquoise Hawaiian shirt unbuttoned low enough to show damp whorls of chest hair.

He had moved to Boston not long after I had leased the space from his mother all those years ago, and then moved back to town when his mom died. Since then I'd listened to his thinly-disguised tales of Bostonian gunrunning and strong-arming every time he came in to collect his rent. Always with the insinuation of mob connections. The way he made it sound, it was as if he and Whitey Bulger had scratched each other's lottery tickets, tucked each other in at night.

Personally, I believed very little of it; Randy drove a thirty-year-old Nissan hatchback and wore sandals and socks. He carried a key ring the size of a tennis ball. I found it difficult to be afraid of him. But I'd also begun wondering just how it was I'd be meeting my demise over the next week. It had to happen sometime, so why not at Randy's hands? You never knew; that was the thing about the Curse.

"The fuck is this?" he said, pointing at the speakers. I'd heard punk for the first time in 1977. This exact record, actually: the Dead Boys *Young, Loud and Snotty* LP. Before that I'd been a disciple of Coltrane and Miles, but I'd given it up as soon as I heard those chords. Jazz had been for my previous life as Bill Creswell and all of Bill's trappings. Nowadays punk rattled me, propped the me-as-Marvin up on two legs like nothing else did. It was sneering and ugly and vacillated between not giving a shit and caring so much it hurt.

I put the computer to sleep and smiled over the monitor. "What can I do for you, Randy?"

He fixed a thumb at the door and said to Adam, "Hey, kid. Beat it. I got to talk to this guy about something." That affected accent, so Boston it made your teeth ache.

Adam turned and looked at me, his eyes big and worried behind his glasses.

"He's fine," I said.

Randy looked from me to Adam and back, smirking. "I don't think you're gonna want him to hear this, Deitz."

Adam had been a regular at the store for years, since he was in junior high. He didn't know the particulars of my situation—unless Julia had told him, which hadn't happened as far as I could tell—but we'd managed any number of conversations about guilt, regret, the concepts of sin and redemption. He was a philosophy major, remember? That and music was the backbone of our relationship. Adam, without knowing the particulars, had listened to me prattle on and been perceptive enough to suggest that I arrange some sessions with his mother. He'd even gone so far as to help us work out our particular payment arrangement. (I was grateful; while Bill Creswell had managed to insure that inventory, records stacked upon records, would never be a problem, money itself was usually tight.) There are some people you meet, regardless of age, and an earnestness shines through. Adam was like that. It didn't happen often, but when it did, you latched on. Like I said, he was my friend.

I said, "He's staying, Randy."

Randy shrugged, and a reddened tube of skin wobbled around his neck. He was one of those guys who seemed almost pitiable until his mouth started moving. "No skin off these balls," he said.

He pulled a sheaf of papers out of his back pocket and slapped them onto the counter. "Here's the deal. I got some investors flying in here from Southie in three days, bud." He held up one finger and twirled it in a circle. "We're razing the building, putting up condos. All you people are out of here." He pointed at the papers curled on the counter. "You in particular? You're being evicted due to a blatant disregard of noise ordinances, complaints spanning a period of over three years."

"What? What noise complaints?"

Randy shook his head ruefully, holding his hands up. "It's out of my hands, Deitz. I tried to work with you. The cops are sick of you refusing to turn the goddamned music down. All hours of the day and night. Look in the papers there. Turns out the city's kept extensive records of your infractions."

"This is total bullshit," Adam said. "There's rules about no-cause evictions."

Randy grinned, wiped his face again. "Noise complaints. Three years' worth. This is cause, little fella." He slowly turned back to me.

"You've got seventy-two hours to get all your shit packed, Deitz. All this wonderful music you're listening to."

Adam said, "Call the cops, Marvin."

Randy laughed. "The cops *signed* those papers, you dumb shit." He hooked a thumb toward Adam. "This kid. You got a mouth on you, you know that? You want to be careful with that mouth of yours."

I stood there at the counter. I shouldn't have cared about any of it, I knew that. In less than a week I'd be gone anyway, thrown headlong into some other life. And *yet*. You wake up and the world keeps insisting you move in it.

I said, "So that's it? You and your mob buddies are just edging everyone in the building out? You've seen Portland in the last couple years, right, Randy? The whole city's becoming just one big condo at this point. There's legal ways you can do this."

Randy ran his handkerchief around his neck as he stood in the doorway. It was a tight fit; he was limned in sunlight, a dark shape blocking the brightly lit world beyond. When he spoke, he sounded sad, bereft. "There's no time for that, bud. You've got seventy-two hours. You're a nice enough guy, Deitz. But you're dead weight. You got to go."

5

Vale bled into a towel wrapped around a handful of frozen Where Have You Bean? Mini-Bites while Mario filled out paperwork. The manager's office was a cinder block supply closet with just enough room for a desk, two chairs, and a few company-issued inspirational posters gummed onto the pocked walls. Vale's last check sat on the desk between them.

Mario muttered to himself while he worked through the report. Vale had taken the guy to the ground, but after that, the guy had simply pinned him with one meaty arm and punched him with the other. Vale's body thrummed with that post-adrenaline sickness that always came after an ass-kicking. Mario, ever the peacemaker, had managed to calm things only after frantically waving gift cards in the guy's face. Eventually—amid a chorus of crying, frightened children and old men risen to their feet, yelling with newly rediscovered bloodlust—the guy had been talked out of the restaurant and Vale had stood, joyous and blood-spattered, his shirt ripped like a gladiator. He had followed Mario into his office without another word, both of them knowing what was coming next.

Mario signed his incident report and leaned back in his chair. He looked at the rips at the armpits, the blood dotting Mike's shirt—which was actually Mario's shirt—and his expression was parked somewhere between contempt and pity. The fluorescents in the ceiling quietly hummed and popped. Mario looked sallow and ghoulish under the light, and Vale assumed he himself looked much, much worse.

"Dude, how old are you?"

Vale rolled his eyes. "Fuck you, Mario."

Mario, Vale could just tell, would own his own franchise within ten years and retire at forty a millionaire. He was that guy. He'd raise a family. Shyly put dollar bills into the hands of homeless men at stoplights. He wore a safety strap on his glasses and spoke machine-gun Spanish to employees and customers alike. There was a delicate, nearly invisible crucifix on a chain around his neck. Vale could not remember a time that Mario had not smiled like he was honestly happy to be there. He couldn't understand it.

"No, seriously," Mario said. "Picking fights with customers? You could have gone to jail, boom, just like that. You don't want to be here? Just quit. Why the big show?"

Vale, enjoying himself now, held his hands open as if imploring the ceiling. "It's the drama, Mario. I'm addicted to the drama."

Mario shook his head. "You're an asshole, dude."

Vale nodded solemnly. "That is the truth."

Mario picked up Vale's check, tapped it against the edge of his desk. "I looked you up on the internet a while back. I couldn't figure out why my brother-in-law would want me to hire this old, tattoo-covered dude, you know? Then I looked you up and couldn't figure out why you'd *want* to work here."

"I *don't* want to work here, Mario. I mean, I thought we just established that."

Mario shook his head again. "I saw online, one of your paintings went for over half a million dollars, man. Like six months ago that happened."

"I don't get any of that money."

"I read about that, too."

"My agent got me on a three-day blackout and I signed everything over to him. All my rights."

Quietly, not unkindly, Mario looked away and said, "Maybe you shouldn't drink so much then."

And oh the anger came so fast these days, didn't it? He went from a kind of lighthearted joviality to just . . . *rage*. He suddenly wanted to hit Mario, sweet little Mario, in the mouth so badly that the back of his hands itched. He pulled the towel away from his mouth and said flatly, "And maybe you should give me my check and shut your mouth."

Mario shrugged and pushed the check across the desk. "That's what I mean. It's like you want to burn all your bridges up so you can never come back to them. You're too old to do that, man. You won't have anything left."

Vale leaned forward grinning, anger sparking off him like static. He could feel it barreling into Mario, their eyes locked, this snapping, unwavering line of contempt that connected them together.

He said, "Hey, Mario. Guess what? I've got pieces in the MOMA. Okay? I made *millions*. I was in *Time, Rolling Stone, Spin*. From painting. What are you, a level ten burrito master? Lord of the Tater Tots? Huh? Sucking on that Bean There teat. Who the fuck do you think you are, talking to me like that?"

Mario shrugged one last time and looked down, pushing Vale's check across the desk. When he looked back up, Vale could see the hurt and anger in his face, the kid's eyes starting to go wet and misty. He said, "I'm the guy that's firing you, Mike."

6

From the journals of Marvin Deitz:

The Five Rules:

1) I must always honor Joan.
2) I must confess my sins.
3) I must expect little.
4) I must refute violence whenever possible.
5) I must be aware of portents and signs.

Additionally, the Three Parameters of the Curse:

1) I will die sometime between infancy and my fifty-sixth birth-day. I have never, ever lived to my fifty-seventh birthday, in any of my lives.
2) I will always suffer some significant disfigurement or phys-iognomic alteration sometime between infancy and my first two decades of life. Generally pretty early on. The disfig-urement will be something that, to some degree, alters and dictates the pathway of my existence. Loss of limb, birth defect, etc. Losing an eye, as I did in this life, is actually somewhat mundane.
3) When I die, I will without fail die a violent death. No going peacefully in my sleep for this guy.

Sometimes, it's just good to remind myself. Like I said, writing it down makes me feel better sometimes.

• • •

I volunteered once a week in the pediatric oncology ward at Seward's Children's Hospital.

I couldn't fault Julia's idea that being of service to others would be valuable. It's the cornerstone of thousands of years of experience in both civics and religion. Alcoholics Anonymous is adamant that service to others is a gigantic part of keeping alcoholics sober. Buddhists talk about expecting less, and charities bank on the good feelings that arise from making donations. Julia hoped volunteering would get me outside of myself, put things in perspective. And it had.

My seething contempt toward God was *much* more finely tuned now.

Seward's Children's Hospital was in Northeast Portland. Eight stories tall, a box of glass that beautifully reflected the setting sun against its face. I got off the bus ten minutes early for my shift and stopped in the cafeteria for a cup of coffee.

I got my lanyard from the woman at the reception desk. My shoes squeaked on the marbled floor. I stepped into the elevator. The oncology unit was on the fourth floor.

I stepped out of the elevator and waved at Velma, the grizzled septuagenarian of a receptionist. In spite of the fact that I had been volunteering for a year now, Velma made a great show of inspecting my visitor's badge. I loved Velma and her wrinkled scowl, her crisp gray mustache. Her dour stolidity, and how she brooked no shit from staff and yet remained resolutely gentle with patients and their families. Sometimes, I daydreamed about Velma being present at Joan's trial—fantasized that she would've planted her gnarled hands on her hips and said to Cauchon in that gravelly, no-nonsense growl, "Are you an idiot? Are you *trying* to get this girl killed?"

The fourth floor was painted in warm pastels, bracketed with big panes of glass. A mural of animals danced on a far wall. I sat down behind the horseshoe of the reception desk and Velma pointed to a stack of envelopes and a sheaf of papers. The monthly newsletter that went out to donors and board members. She handed me one of those little water tubes with the swab at the end.

"Stuff, swab and stamp."

I bowed my head. "Yes, m'lord."

I stuffed, swabbed and stamped. I fell evenly into the rhythm of it as I always did, grateful this time for the distraction from Randy, from time's inevitability.

I'd done it all at Seward's. There was a garden on the roof, and a greenhouse, and those children well enough to go would tend and care for the plants up there. Smiling, pale, green-veined children, their hands dusted with earth. I had tilled soil with them, helped them repot those plants grown too large for their containers. Helped them hoist water cans. I had run the beverage cart up and down the halls, escorted dazed, grief-blasted grandparents to the appropriate wing, filed papers. Read stories to the brothers and sisters of sick children. Cold-called previous donors. Stuffed envelopes.

Once a week, four hours a day.

I was intimately familiar with death and its equations. I had long been intimate with the stilled architecture of the corpse. The decay, the sugary-sweet stink of it all, the odor like a mixture of shit and rotten fruit. The primacy of rotted meat. The simple subtraction of animation pulled from a body, a face. Doing all I had done throughout the centuries, I knew death. I wanted it. I sought it, courted it. And yet none of that mattered when I stepped onto the fourth floor. There, I raged against death, I leaned snarling against it.

I was stuffing envelopes and Velma was on the phone when a woman walked up to our counter holding a little girl's hand. You could tell a parent: they carried a kind of psychic weight, like an invisible hand seizing the throat, that aunts or uncles or grandparents usually did not; there was no *distance* afforded parents. The looks on their faces were beyond knowing. I have seen my own children die before, and it is a kind of flat murder of the soul. It's beyond words. With cancer and its incremental diminishments, where death is afforded the luxury of small bites, parents invariably come to look hollowed out, as if it's happening to them as well.

Heart and lungs are all that is propelling them, these parents—
everything else is reserved for ache and worry and terror.

The mother offered me a tired smile and began speaking to
Velma. She was most likely pretty once, and attuned to the world,
reaching for its possibilities. But now, with bruised gray rings
beneath her eyes, her grief was turning her skeletal. Exhausted.
She looked at us without really seeing us, and I couldn't blame her
for that. The little girl peered at me from around the corner of the
counter. I smiled. Her shirt was yellow, with an embroidered cat
on it. She put her chin on the countertop.

"What's your name?" she whispered.

I ducked my head down a little. "My name's Marvin," I whispered back. "What's your name?"

"Mellie. It's short for Amelia."

"Hi, Mellie."

She looked at her mother for a moment and then turned back
to me. "My little brother's really sick," she said.

"I'm very, very sorry to hear that."

"Something's wrong with him. With his little baby bones."

These moments. You want to rend worlds apart in moments
like these.

I said, "Well, I want you to know we have very good doctors
here."

"His bones have holes in them. Our whole church is praying
for him."

Osteosarcoma? Rhabdomyosarcoma? The patois of the dead
sang in my skull. And yet what thing named is ever robbed of its
power simply by the naming?

"Why are part of your glasses black?"

"I can't see out of this eye very well," I said, pointing. "So the
doctor put a black lens in. I can only see out of my good eye."

"Is it icky?"

"My eye?"

She nodded, pointing at the lens. "Is it icky in there?"

I nodded, grimacing. "It is pretty icky."

She was poised, I knew, to ask to see it—the idea of an icky
eyeball all too tempting—when her mother finished her business
with Velma.

"Come on, Mellie," her mother said, and Mellie took her mother's hand and gave me a small wave as they walked away. Her mother smiled at me and nodded and didn't see me at all. I was vapor, a mirage. The totality of her world was held in her hand and in a room down the hall. Her heart was a vessel, I knew by experience, but one incapable of being filled. The heart's capacity for grief seemed boundless. Mellie's boots clacked down the hall and I thought of her brother, a little boy inculpable of sin beyond the most original and banal—that of being born. And yet still dying for it, his devastation piecemealed out.

But me? Amidst all the blood I've spilled through the centuries? Me, you can't get rid of. I've visited horror upon horror on the world and what happens? A violent death, yes, sure.

But then a rebirth, my memory intact.

The oncology ward is one of the few places I *feel* anything, the only time I can muster up anything beyond a profound indifference. My palette consists of lethargy and rage, and when I am here in these rooms I hold that rage next to my heart like a gift.

7

"So what are you gonna do, then?" Raph asked.

Vale looked around at the dark red walls of the Ace High, heard the crack and clack of pool balls kissing each other behind him.

"First I'm going to finish this beer," he said. "And then I'm going to get another one."

"Shit," Raph said, shaking his head above his crossed forearms. "Dumb, man. Really dumb. You know how much I had to kiss Mario's ass to get you that job? Larissa's little brother, man, and there I am practically blowing him to get you that job."

They sat next to each other at the bar, their faces in the mirror dented and distorted. Vale waved a hand. "Yeah, so I could dress up in a paper hat and sell hot dogs to shitbags? Forget it."

Raph leaned back, both hands wrapped around his glass. "There's some gratitude for you."

"I *do* appreciate it, man. Seriously. I'm just saying there's plenty of shit jobs out there."

"Listen. I don't want to disagree with you. I've worked plenty of shit jobs in my life, you know? But shit jobs for a dude like you? No disrespect. Forty-whatever years old? Tattoos on his hands? A record? I don't know."

The bartender, Nate, wore matching sleeves of blurred tattoos and a t-shirt mounded tight around his gut. Nate had always despised him, for no particular reason Vale could discern. The man would be jovial and yelling over the jukebox to other patrons, his eyes shining, and when it came Vale's turn at the bar he would wind down like a clock. Vale couldn't quite remember if it had been Nate who'd kicked him out the night before.

Vale made a *V* with his fingers. "Two more IPAs, Jeeves."

"Hey. Big spender," Raph said. "Thanks, man."

Nate poured, set the glasses down. Vale, knowing he would regret it, gave him a five dollar tip just to see what would happen. Nate took it without comment, face like a stone idol. "You're welcome," Vale called out bitterly. And yet in spite of it, he felt the stirrings of a Moment.

The definition of a Moment: those periods—always drunk, always brief—when Vale was awarded a savage, tumbling happiness. A smoothing out of the world's sharp edges. The goal of drinking—beyond the drunkenness itself—was the culmination, if he could manage it, of a Moment. He'd lived so long with hangovers by now, was intimate with shaking hands, night tremors. Occasional lacings of blood in his shit. Loose teeth, insomnia. All rote by now. But there were also the Moments, those times in which he was purely joyous, and the sacrifices and ravages to his body seemed a fair trade for these. If there was one thing Vale knew, it was that nothing was free. Ever.

And as if just by thinking of it, he realized it had arrived. As if he'd conjured it. That perfect balance of intoxication that he would for the rest of the night attempt to maintain. It took an alchemist's precision. At stake: the shimmering way the light haloed itself over the hanging lamps above the pool tables. How the girls half his age were so achingly beautiful, how *free* they seemed, how the pure quicksilver joy of life leapt inside them. It was like lust but more—what? Clean? Distanced? In the Moment, yes. And also how the young men surrounded each other, their rough laughter and small kindnesses to each other, pool chalk passed wordlessly from one to the other, commiserations on missed shots even amid a kind of offhanded cruelty.

He loved even more the Ace High itself: the cement walls painted a crimson red, the Christmas lights strung up in the windows, the threadbare carpet laced inexplicably here and there in duct tape. If only his *life* was like the floor of this fucking bar! Something so grievously used but—look!—still functional! With purpose! Music from the jukebox rattled his heart like a stone in a glass.

"How I feel right now?" Vale said, rolling his head on his shoulders. "This good feeling I have in me? Painting used to make me feel like this."

He bought another round. He looked into Nate's eyes as he handed him exact change this time, and Nate looked right through him.

And the evening wound around them. Two vultures curled on their stools as the bar wailed electric around them. They were of a different world than the other patrons—full-blown barflies, the two of them—and as such were hardly visible. He was an awkward piece of furniture that brayed laughter at odd times, got sloppy, fell off his stool. And the shame of this? The knowledge of what he was? It was all lessened when he was in the Moment.

They watched the television hanging above the bar. Tanks trundling down a smoking, cratered highway in the Middle East. Someone was shot outside a convenience store in Gresham. Then grainy footage of yet another smoke sighting in Southern California. Somewhere in Orange County, according to the closed captioning. This one showed a smoke standing in some mini-mall parking lot, wringing its hands, looking down at the pavement. It was bearded, in suspenders, looking for all the world like some woeful, shit-luck lumberjack. Yellowed as an old photograph. They never interacted with the living. Just stood there, locked in their own repetition, their own little worlds. And then, of course, the newscast cut to the familiar footage of the Bride there on her golf course, her hands buried in the fabric of her dress as she ran one way on the putting green and then the other.

The sightings had begun appearing at the beginning of summer. Footage of the Bride, as she came to be called, aired first. She went viral in a day, and then news crews began getting others on film. Things escalated, flared. Chain of authority ran up and down the pipeline until the CDC, of all organizations, was tasked with leading the investigation.

Various committees were appointed at the federal, state, county and local level. The economy had nearly collapsed and was now ballooning with a kind of joyous panic. There was Congressional talk of a curfew throughout heavily populated areas like LA, San Diego, something the President denied would happen. So far the spirits had only appeared in Southern California and Northern Mexico—everything else had proven to be hoaxes. No one, of course, could explain any of it. Some people were saying it was somehow a Russian hoax, that they were—somehow—satellite-controlled holograms. Others were saying it was End Times. That Western decadence would soon be laid to waste. Some people were rapturous when they said it. Curbside prophets sang and threatened and prophesied, would thrust crazed, disjointed pamphlets into your hand as you passed. You couldn't walk a block without getting accosted. Suicide cults had bloomed.

Two weeks previous, a Southwest Airlines pilot died of a heart attack after a smoke, a little ghost boy, appeared in the cockpit, thirty thousand feet in the air. The plane had almost crashed into downtown Pasadena; the FAA had imposed a flight ban throughout Washington, Oregon, and California that was still in effect. Some people were moving away from the west coast entirely, while hot spots like Los Angeles and Tijuana exploded with visitors. In the space of a few months, and despite the constraints on the airlines, the smokes had become a multimillion dollar industry. California was packed, in spite of the supposed exodus. Everyone wanted to see for themselves.

And all the while, that global murmur: This Is Quite Likely the End of the World, People. Capitals for emphasis.

Vale didn't know. He couldn't get his head around it. He believed in ghosts the way he believed in space travel; he didn't understand the mechanics of it, but why not? He lifted his glass to light; he was drunk now, expansive, worldly. Benevolent now that he was in the Moment. Let the ghosts have Los Angeles! They could have California, who gave a shit? Raph got more Catholic the more he drank and insisted the whole thing was a sham. "Because otherwise," he said, "it's the Reckoning, man." He pointed at the television, his eyes wide with sincerity. "It means those are souls trapped on earth and who wants to think that, you know? Because why? What would that mean? Heaven is full or something?"

The two of them went out to smoke and when they came back had missed last call. Nate turned the lights on. "What the fuck,"

Raph hissed, and everyone in the bar shrank down into themselves like vampires, murmuring.

"Pick 'em up, boys and girls," Nate yelled. "You can go anywhere you want but you can't stay here."

Outside, the night was cloudless. Vale nearly rolled his ankle walking down the steps and Raph grabbed the back of his shirt before he could do a face-plant on the pavement. Just like that, the Moment faded into tatters.

"I'll see you later, man," Raph said, grinning, standing with his bicycle between his legs, his eyes half-lidded.

Staggering in place on the sidewalk, Vale snarled, "You won't see me later," but they both knew this was meaningless, just Vale sad and drunk and leaning against the walls of the world.

"Fuckin' Nate," he said, gazing at the bar.

"Forget about it. See you tomorrow."

"Yeah, okay."

Vale staggered toward his apartment, raging with inner proclamations, promises to himself. When he got home, he would do a hundred push-ups, drink a dozen glasses of water until he was sober. He would wait and sober up through the dawn until the sunrise colored the wall behind him. He would sleep for days and when he rose he would be cleansed. He would be calm. He would listen to talk radio for the sound of people's voices. He would drink tea and read history books. He would find a job that didn't seem to kill him an inch at a time, something he liked. He would get a library card! Yes, a library card. He'd meet a nice woman who worked in a coffee shop and she would learn his name and his order by heart because he came in so often. He would come in one day and she would ask him what he was reading, because he had gotten a book at the library and brought it with him, and that's how it would start between them. She would realize that he was a nice man, a man who had been haunted at one time but had managed to move beyond it, and he was calm now, and good. He had been one person and now he was someone else, someone better.

He fell into someone's rose bushes and cursed as the thorns snared themselves in his shirt, as they cut traceries in his arms, across his face. It didn't hurt. He'd taken a wrong turn somewhere and pulled himself up from the bushes and crossed the street. He found himself with his hands laced around the cool metal bars of a fence. He saw the gray shapes a few feet away and realized they were gravestones, that he was looking into a cemetery, the entire thing surrounded by a two-foot concrete retaining wall and, above that, the black iron-wrought bars he gripped in his hands.

Vale's arms were beaded with blood and there was no breeze, none. A litany of regrets flared white-hot in his heart, and he held a bar of the fence in each fist and shook them as hard as he could. He tried to pull the fence apart. Odd guttural keenings loosed themselves from his throat.

Vale sank to his knees, his hands still locked around the bars. He began running his forehead along the lip of the cement wall, back and forth, back and forth, growling. There was no bravery in him anywhere. Only a great nameless ache. Nearly fifty and feeling like this. Busted. Hurt. Like some young kid who'd let the world take a bite out of him. There would be no sobering up, there would be no calming life. There would be, Jesus Christ, no woman in a coffee shop.

There would be only him and his own trappings, forever: this man lost, his hands laced around the bars of a graveyard fence. This man growling and weeping, grinding the curve of his skull against the edge of a concrete wall over and over again, the name of his ex-wife tattooed on his knuckles.

TUESDAY

1

From the journals of Marvin Deitz:

I was born Geoffroy Thérage in a mud-hewn village called Moineau, only a few miles outside of Rouen, where Joan the Maid would be put to death all those decades later. The date of my birth is of some dispute, even to me, but the few theologians and historians interested in such things (and yes, there are a few) seem to generally agree on the year of 1381. This seems right: it would make me fifty years old when I lit Joan's pyre, an old man for those times, and fifty-six when I died, which obviously fits the Curse's parameters.

Moineau was a cluster of maybe sixty scattered shops and homes, the whole thing ringed with fields and skirted with random huts and outbuildings (including our home; given my father's occupation, we were considered unclean and not allowed to live within the village proper). The whole affair was laced through with the mudded ruts of roads, the comforting bleat of animals, leaning fences and the constant smell of shit.

I was the oldest of four children. (There had been three before me, all of whom had died by the time I was a young boy—enough so that I hardly remembered them. There had been two sisters, twins felled by the plague within the same year, and a baby brother who lived for a week sickly and tiny and had hardly seemed to be there at all. A tiny breath on the surface of the world, a feather let loose in the wind.)

So I was the oldest and had three younger sisters. I would find my mother looking at me sometimes, her jaw at work for just a moment, as if gauging when or where I would be taken. Death was like that, casual with its cruelty. We slept huddled together on mats stuffed with straw, our animals tethered against the open entrance of our home, to block the chill, to keep us safe from marauders and animals both. Rats were limned shapes on the hardpacked dirt floor, chattering like gossips in the night. Fleas, those envoys of death and plague, were constant. My sister Esme, a sweet blonde girl three years younger than me, had been born with a cleft palate. At night she loosed a high, pinched snore that I waited for; it was a comfort to me. It let me know that we were all safe. My father was gone on his rounds for weeks at a time and when he was home took heavily to the wine to quell his own visions, his own weighted demons. I had long realized I would need to be the one to protect them all, and Esme's night sounds were my signal that I could sleep.

Life was lived lean against the bone. We received little quarter from our neighbors. They traveled to our hut only when an animal needed butchering (my father) or, sometimes, when clothes needed mending (my mother). Given the nature of my father's employment, we did not need to work the fields. We weren't allowed to. Doing so would have been to invite even more blight upon the crops. We kept our personal garden, our animals for milk and meat.

The idea of a salary was ludicrous for an executioner; my father was paid by the killing. We lived on the land rent-free, and my father, when he remembered it, was allowed a portion of produce at the market. (Though he was not allowed to *touch* the produce, and instead used a long handled spoon the vendors kept nearby for such matters. Which probably played a large part in why he so often forgot to bring any home.)

Honestly, we were better off than most in many ways. Still, even when things were going well, we were all at the mercy of another cold winter or damp spring.

I was ten when the trajectory of my own damnation began. That evening we sat, the five of us, around our table. I remember the supper: rock-hard bread, heavy with the mealy taste of the acorns my mother had cut the flour with. Greens from the garden. A particular treat; my father had shot a hart with his bow the week before and we had deer meat, a luxury. I was a well-fed child compared to many. I remember Esme and Riva giggling across the table at each other, some invented game, when my father wiped the grease from his beard and said to me in that voice that brooked no argument, "Tomorrow, Geoffroy, you'll come with me."

I felt it inside me. My life turning like a wheel.

"Jean, no," my mother said. My father raised his cup to candlelight and quieted her with a glance and my mother pressed her knuckles to her mouth, silenced. She must have known it was coming: what else was there for me? As the son of an executioner, there seemed no other avenue left, save crime or begging.

"Death comes for us all," my father said. He would never be mistaken for a kind man—he was too haunted for that, brutality being his trade—but it was the softest I had ever heard him speak. "I will not walk here forever. He's needed."

"Jean."

"Don't worry, woman," he smirked. "*God provides.*" He drained his cup so high I could see the workings of his pale throat. He said, "Tomorrow, you'll come with me," and poured more wine in his cup.

I smelled raw earth, burning tallow from the candles, meat, the animal tang of shit. A spider climbed up the ridged candle in front of me and crawled directly into the sputtering flame. Its tiny husk, shrunken and black, tumbled to the table.

Esme's snoring did not lull me to sleep that night. The very night that the trajectory of my life had been set—I was an executioner's son, and so would be an executioner—was also the night my world became unmoored. Who could sleep? I heard the skittering of rats in the dark, and the slumbering lexicon of my family on their mats next to me, the night murmurings of our animals. The bites of the fleas you never noticed until you suddenly did, all at once, to the point where it became maddening. At some point, sleep did come. I woke at one point to the pale dawn at the mouth of our hut. Little Riva clutched me for warmth. She seemed angelic in sleep despite the ring of grime around her mouth, her matted hair. I closed my eyes again.

Sometime later, my father kicked my foot and I opened my eyes. The light was brighter and I heard my mother at work near the hearth. On a normal day, my sisters and I would have long since done the milking, would have gathered wood, checked for frost in the garden. Yet this morning I had slept—my mother's doing, I was sure. *Give him a little more time. Let him rest.*

The rain had gone but the morning was dew-heavy, the sky an iron gray. My mother kissed me and gave my father a look that at the time was unreadable but I now realize was couched between reproach and a resentful understanding. Esme started crying, and like a chorus, so began Riva and Jehanne. My mother ushered them inside.

We had two little mules to pull my father's cart. Ancient, leather-tough creatures my sisters had named a dozen times over, something my father forbade—they were tools and nothing more. My sisters would whisper the names to each other and I thought *Pierre and Nicolas! Graisse and Maigre!* as we tethered them to their traces.

"Boy," my father snapped. I hoisted myself into the cart; he clicked at the mules and slapped the reins and we started on our way. He reached beneath him and then pushed a woolen coat and leather gloves into my lap. "Put these on," he said. He'd long since put on his own tunic.

I saw Alain Lelong, the widower who lived nearest us, as we left the village behind and rounded a bend in the road. He had once made me a wooden horse, when I was little, and sometimes made my sisters laugh with his impressions. Never when my father was near, of course, but his wife had died two years before and had bore him no children, and he was kinder to us than most. But as we rounded the curve in the road and he saw that I rode in the cart with my father, that the both of us wore tunics and gloves and were about our business, a cloud walked across his face. He said nothing as we passed him, only clicked the reins of his horse, his head cast down as if he had not seen us at all.

My father looked at me and sneered. Spat over the side of the cart. "Get used to it," he said.

• • •

The next day I went to the Noise Control Office in City Hall, a windowless, single-room affair on the third floor, and smaller than my studio apartment. The officer who had signed off on Randy's noise complaints, all nine of them, had a brilliant cap of white hair and a sandwich that he was just about to tuck into. It was like a wig, that hair, like a Q-Tip come to life. He coughed extensively, looked longingly at the sandwich on his desk, and insisted the documents were legal.

I laid a finger on the papers next to his sandwich. "You've signed all nine of these complaints. So apparently you've been there. What does the inside of my store look like?"

The guy sighed. "That's not how this works, sir. The officers write the reports. I sign them."

I said, "How much is Randy Noonan paying you to falsify city documents?" and some color crept into his cheeks.

He hoisted a thumb over his shoulder and blithely informed me that there were police right down the hall and I would be arrested if I didn't leave immediately. Part of me was furious, but mostly I was just tired. Of everything. I tossed the papers on his sandwich and walked out.

An hour later, I stepped off the bus and the day's grit covered me like a film. Eighty-second was sweltering. I was in front of the dry cleaners next to Julia's office when my cell phone rang.

"How fucking eager are you to get capped, Marvin? Huh? Is that your intention with me?"

"Hey, Randy. How's things?"

"The fuck is the matter with you? You go to Bud Keating's office and try to strong-arm him? Are you kidding me with this? When he's eating *lunch*?"

"I was just doing a little investigating," I said innocently, feeling the loose skittering of emotions that always surged toward the ending of one of my lives: fury, resentment, bafflement. Hopelessness. Mostly fury, though. I was smiling into the phone.

"I got something you can investigate, Marvin. You hear me? It's nine inches long and looks like a python, okay?"

I shook my head. "Jesus, Randy."

"I'm not messing with you. I don't mess around."

"Right. Listen, I was thinking. How interested would the mayor be if I brought her proof of graft and corruption in the Bureau of City Services? That's worth at least a *little* of the commissioner's time. Don't you think? That might put a damper on your plans, huh?"

Randy laughed. It sounded like sheets tearing. He said, "You can't shake me down, Marvin. It's cute, what you're doing, and I almost respect it, but you need to take a step back and pull my dick out of your ear for a minute. You don't have the guts required. You're suffering from a severe lack of balls, is what I'm saying. So hire some movers and get a U-Haul and pull all those Charlie Manson eight-tracks out of your little store there. You got two days now. It's not worth getting in a dick-swinging contest with me."

"Good lord. Enough with the dicks, Randy."

"You've lost," he said. "You've already lost. And if you bother Bud Keating again, I will put you in a world of hurt without a second thought. It'll be bad, Marvin."

I couldn't think of anything to say. The best I could manage was, "Your mother would be so proud of you."

In Julia's waiting room my limbs were heavy and loose, like my bones were coming unhinged. Would my will even be in effect with Randy's eviction hanging over me? And Jesus, if I was going to be dead in a week and rebirthed in some other corner of the planet, how much did I really want to give a shit? Was any of this even worth it? That was the one question that I could never get past: if every life was immediately followed by another one, who *cared*?

"It's been a hell of a day, Julia," I called out. I could see Adam's drawing through the open doorway, and the idea of sinking into that couch again was a soothing one. Lie down and live with Joan for a while, wallow in the surf of my guilt. Even if it was the last time in the foreseeable future.

"All I want," I said as I walked through the lobby and into her office, tracing the arm of the couch with the same adoration as a game show model, "is to just sit here for a minute. Can we do that? Before we start talking? I'd just like to sit."

Julia was seated behind her desk, her hands clasped so tight her knuckles were white. She exhaled and said in a shaky voice, "Marvin, I'm sorry, but no."

I stood there in an odd half-crouch over the couch. "No? Why are you sitting at your desk?"

"Marvin—"

"You never sit at your desk, Julia."

She laid her hands flat on her desk and lifted her chin toward me. Her mouth was a thin line. "Marvin. I've arranged for a pair of officers to check you into a mental health facility. They are on their way. Nobody, and I mean this with total sincerity, nobody will hurt you."

I could see a vein throbbing in Julia's neck. I turned my head and looked at her with my good eye. I could feel an odd half-smile on my lips, rubbery and strange. "Say what?" I sat on the couch, felt the cushion cool against my palms.

She pushed hair out of her eyes with one hand, and then brought her hands back together on her desktop. "Marvin, I'm sorry if you feel that I betrayed your trust. I care about your welfare very much, and I believe you're a danger to yourself. The perseverance of your delusion—and it *is* a delusion, Marvin—is dangerous."

My chest felt loose and hot. I slowly stood up. "Are you . . . wait, are you kidding me with this?"

"I'm concerned for your safety. Please understand, this is based out of concern."

I laughed, looked around the room. "I'm not pissed, necessarily. I don't think I am. Disappointed, yeah. I've enjoyed my time here, talking to you."

"Again, Marvin—"

"But listen, Julia. You listen to me. *I have carved men from the inside out.* Living men. Living people. To the point where it took days for them to die. Where I *extended* their pain. Where they had gratitude in their eyes by the time I laid their fucking heads on the block. Do you understand that?"

Julia licked her lips. "It's clear that you're hurting, Marvin. I believe that with everything fiber of my—"

"*I burned her alive.*"

"There are so many people that want to help you."

Her eyes kept jumping to the doorway. I was scaring her.

"It's nothing that a shrink with a hard-on for Klonopin and touch therapy is going to fix, Julia."

"Marvin. Joan of Arc and Pierre Cauchon have been dead for six hundred years. I don't know what this is about, but it's not about them."

I smiled, sad a little, at the way she clipped his name, brutalized it. *Couch-On.* That, and that she had called me out. We were truly done.

"But there's no moving forward, Julia. There isn't. I've been telling you that. There's just the same goddamned thing endlessly repeated."

I turned and walked out.

There was nothing left. I'd be dead soon enough—amid all my questioning, the surety of *that* still rocketed toward me like a bullet train—but I'd be damned if I'd spend my last days in a lockup of any kind.

I spared a glance back. Julia was standing now, still behind her desk. Watching me, her hands cinched together in front of her.

2

A second before the phone started ringing, Vale opened his eyes.

A thin scrum of watery sunlight fell across his hand, the hair on his knuckles edged in light. He blinked once and the phone began ringing. *The only man in the city with a landline.* His eyes settled on the hole in the wall above him and beside it, his last canvas. His head felt compressed in a strange, unfamiliar heat. It wasn't pain exactly. A tightness.

The phone rang and rang.

He thought, *Don't answer that. Do anything but answer that.*

He thought, *Whatever that is, it's nothing good.*

He sat up and his pillow came with him. Dried blood cinched his face tight to the pillowcase from hairline to jaw. The shade rattled in a sparse breeze. The top third of his bedsheet was the color of rust. The phone kept ringing.

He hoisted his legs over the bed and leaned over, gagging between his splayed knees. He rose and walked down the hall, holding the pillow to his face, laughing a little at the ridiculousness.

He picked up the phone. "Hello?" he said, his throat paved in dry coals. The pillow was warm against his face, as if holding the summer's heat. It hurt his head to keep his eyes open.

"Mike. It's Richard."

Vale's legs threatened to give out: that watery, built-out-of-sticks feeling he used to get before an opening. He sank slowly to the kitchen floor, feeling bits of garbage sticking to the back of his legs.

The room was hot. He sat there, the phone in one hand, the pillow still glued to his skull. He saw threads of dried blood scattered over his pale legs, dotting his underwear, driven into the creases at the bends in his arms and legs. He was covered in it.

"Hey, Richard," he said brightly, fear skittering in him like oil in a pan, knowing even then, trying to disavow it even then, trying to keep the horror out of his voice. Richard was Candice's husband and Vale heard everything in the man's delivery. Just in saying his name. He knew what was coming. "I hope everything's okay."

A pause. "Mike, I have a moral obligation to tell you this," Richard said, "if not a legal one."

Vale rocked forward, peering down at his legs. "Okay, but Candy's alright, right? Right, Richard? Did menopause strike early or something? She having a hot flash?" He let out a shaky laugh—so false he could practically see *HA HA* floating out of his mouth and shattering in the air—and the inside of his skull pulsed so fiercely that he nearly vomited. He and Candice talked like this. It had become the bedrock of their post-marriage relationship, how Vale bracketed his truths and fears within this cynicism, this sarcasm. Candice had matched him there, but she'd also been able to find *him* within it, the truths of him within that armor of speech. She had allowed him that weakness. But when he said it to Richard, it sounded jarring and fucked up, a dark mockery. The refrigerator kicked on next to him and he flinched.

"There was a . . . It was a clot, Mike. I guess. She'd been complaining of headaches recently . . . I don't know."

"Yeah," Vale said hurriedly, stepping over Richard's voice on the other end, "oh man, she would get some bad migraines when she was in school, sure."

Outside, a car alarm started bleating. Richard was silent.

"So how bad is she? Is she going to be okay?"

The moment stretched out. "No," Richard said. "She died yesterday, Mike."

The blood caked in the whorls of his skin was as complicated as parchment, as the topography of riverbeds.

Richard exhaled again, slow and trembling. "It was an aneurysm, I guess. By the time they got her to the hospital . . ." His voice trailed off again and Vale could almost see the vague, helpless shrug that accompanied it. On the other end of the line, Richard honked into a tissue. The forced intimacy of it, hearing that, felt somehow obscene.

The corners of his kitchen floor were edged in grime. He pulled the pillow away from his face slowly, felt the skin of his cheek pull taut. The pain was in his forehead, layered and brutal: bright and glass-like on top, dull and rhythmic underneath, in time with the cadence of his heartbeat. He flung the pillow away like some bloodied, maladroit tumor and felt the warmth of fresh blood creep down his face.

The memory came back to him then, running his head along the cement edge of the graveyard wall, and he shut his eyes as if he could keep the memory at bay.

"Mike? You okay?"

"Yeah," his voice thick. "Sorry." He tried to picture Richard in his sun-washed house in LA, a place he'd never stepped foot in. He pictured a lawn like a vicious emerald sea outside the windows, the haze of the city's smog a brown, half-translucent band on the horizon. Richard, he imagined, would be in board shorts and a short-sleeved button-up. Sandals. Call it Douchebag Casual. Or would he be wearing a suit? The day after his wife died, making phone calls to ex-husbands, what would a smug, self-righteous entertainment lawyer wear?

Richard said, "It was a hemorrhage, an aneurysm . . . a fucking, I don't know, a *brain thing*. I'm not getting a straight answer from any doctors. She was there one second and gone the next." He let out a jagged little caw of laughter. "She died having lunch with Lisa Coletti, if you can believe that."

"I have no fucking clue who Lisa Coletti is, Richard."

A pause. "Her editor. She was eating lunch with her editor."

"Okay."

"I just . . ." Richard's voice almost cracked then, and Vale opened his eyes. If Richard wept, it would signify something, some collusion with death, some finality. Some admittance. More than that, an intimacy between the two of them. There was no way Vale could handle that.

But he was saved—Richard cleared his throat and said, "I know we haven't always seen eye to eye, Mike. To put it bluntly. And I know it might be tough to get down here, with the airline situation being what it is. But the funeral's on Thursday and if you can make it down here, well, you're welcome to."

"Thursday?" Vale said.

"Yeah."

"Down there?"

"Yeah. We'll have the memorial at the house here. I know it's not much time." He paused. "Do you have the address?"

Vale touched his forehead. "Let me get a pen." He stood up, feeling like he was on a ship, sea-wobbly like that, and took a pen from the coffee cup by the phone. He couldn't find any paper and wrote the address on his hand. Richard started to give him directions and Vale cut him off. "I'll find it."

"Okay. Services start at two. With all the sightings and stuff, traffic has been insane. I'd get here as early as possible, just to make sure."

A moment of silence between them then; a rerouting. Richard cleared his throat again. "Listen," he said, quieter. "I don't know how to say this other than to just come out with it. Okay? I don't know what your situation is like this days, but no drinking please, Mike. Alright? This will be tough enough for all of us as it is."

"Of course," Vale said. "Yes."

"I mean, she would definitely want you here, you know? She would." His voice threatened to crack again and Vale said goodbye and hung up and gently unfolded himself onto the dirty kitchen floor. The sun fell across his white belly in one bright wing of light and his head throbbed like some dolorous animal. He could feel blood inching down his temple into his hair. There was no grief, not yet, only a sense of dark wonderment, a falling.

He stood some time later and walked gingerly to the bathroom and looked in the mirror. His forehead was a raw pocket of pinked flesh peppered with black bits of grit and gravel. The wound was still beading blood. Beneath his eyes was a red mask, blood in rusty spatters all down his pale chest. All over him.

3

The first smoke to actually be witnessed by people appeared on Sepulveda and West Centinela at 3:13 on a Thursday afternoon. First week in June, right in the heart of Los Angeles. Right there between the Howard Hughes Center and the foot-high Culver City letters in homage to the Hollywood sign. It was a rare afternoon of rain that day, and at a four-way intersection, with well over a dozen lanes of active traffic. The gutters ran and rain beaded on windshields, with fantails of water arcing beyond the wheels of vehicles.

And then—in an eye blink, less—someone appeared in one of the westbound lanes.

Hazy, then solid, then hazy again, like the filament in a light bulb cooling and snapping back. But he was visible enough: a beard, a button-up shirt with the pattern showing when he flared bright. Pants tucked into scuffed boots. A gaze so distant and lost as to hardly be there at all. An Esplanade drove right through him, veering sharply much too late, and finally coming to rest after plowing through a pair of bus stop benches.

Various other collisions ensued as well, multi-vehicle pileups. The moment between the last pebbles of safety glass tumbling to the pavement and the first screams was a heavy one, pregnant with that silence that comes seconds before injuries become apparent. Drivers behind the sight-lines of the wreckage lay on their horns, oblivious, cursing the rain, other drivers, the city itself.

The smoke pivoted in the roadway, his hands laced around his head as if it was all too much for him, his frenzy and fear obvious to those few able to see him. And then he, like the Bride, like all those to come, disappeared.

He would follow a familiar pattern: He was there, he was lost, and then he was gone.

4

Portland's Pearl District had long been a breathing dichotomy, a place moored in a willful schizophrenia.

The Pearl today: boxy, monolithic lofts, upscale bars, and dance clubs with lines out the door and wrapped around the corner on weekend nights. Overpriced salons and restaurants espousing menus that were local, cruelty-free, organic, vegan. The luxury of the well-to-do: the choice of morality when coupled with commerce. And yet the Pearl District has grown from the roots of the city's skid row.

Outside the doors of the coffee shop with its biodegradable cups and green-garden roof, the homeless stand smoking on street corners in loose clusters. Businessmen bark into ear buds as they wend through these men, on their way to the nearby financial district, another loosely delegated name for what is the complex, interwoven, organic beast of Portland's downtown. Food carts line parking lots where women in business suits and Reeboks order lunch, their office shoes poking out of their purses like shy little pets. Ten feet away men sleep in doorways, huddled beneath garbage bags and flattened moving boxes.

This dichotomy, old as Rome.

Fuel Gallery sat at Broadway and Glisan. It was a large, two-story storefront couched between a boutique full of nearly naked glass mannequins and a gelato shop with a fetish for brushed steel. Even this place was an anomaly: so much of the Pearl had been reduced to condos, luxury high-rises for the massive influx of new money into the city. Vale walked down Glisan carrying something wrapped beneath a blue tarp. He nodded at a man in a wheelchair holding a scorched teddy bear.

"What's up, brother," the man crowed. His palsy gave him the air of one tuned to some interior music.

"Hey," Vale said.

The man winked, held up the bear. "You got a cigarette for my friend here?"

Vale passed him and without breaking stride said, "I look like the guy that's handing out cigarettes today?"

He hit Broadway and leaned into the storefront window of Fuel, his hand over his brow to block the glare. Abstract works lined the walls. Warm pastel panels—peach, vermilion, sherbet—fused atop bands of oxidized, blowtorched metal. He tried the doors but they were locked. As he peered in again, he could see someone leaning over a computer at the reception desk near the back of the room. Vale knocked and the man looked up and shook his head. He pointed at his wrist, annoyed.

Vale leaned the tarp against the window and was fishing his cigarettes out of his pocket when someone said his name.

He turned. Jacob Burfine was standing there on the pavement, his jaw hanging open.

"Mike *Vale?*"

Burfine stood there in his skinny black jeans, his button-up. A pair of sunglasses perched on his forehead. The surprise seemed genuine: to say they no longer ran in the same circles was an understatement.

"Jake," Vale said brightly. "Looking pretty slick, man."

Burfine, meanwhile, looked like he was trying to grin through a bout of food poisoning. "Yeah, hey. Mike. Wow. You're looking pretty . . . wow." He patted Vale on the shoulder and managed, "It's been a while. It's great to see you." The vast falsity of that statement hung in the air, awkward as a fart in church. They were both embarrassed by its obviousness.

In the bathroom earlier that morning, Vale had taken a shower, gingerly rinsing his devastated forehead with as much delicacy as he could manage. He'd bought gauze pads, alcohol, and an elastic bandage at a Walgreen's. The cashier had openly gaped; blood was still beading up from the wound.

Now, he stood before Burfine with his untrimmed beard, the gauze cinched around his head and a bloodied bandage poking out. His tarp rustling where it leaned against the window. He looked like he belonged there in the Pearl, another castaway member of downtown in the middle of a housing and homeless crisis. Just another piece of the class-collision jigsaw puzzle that made up the neighborhood, the city.

Vale shook his head, smiling. He lit a cigarette. "Don't bullshit me, Jake. I get it."

Burfine laughed uncomfortably and jammed his hands in his pockets.

"But I want to talk to you about something. I need to make some money," Vale said. At the mention of the word *money,* a certain dullness fell over Burfine's eyes.

Vale could read that look in a heartbeat. He'd been seeing variants of it countless times since he'd signed that damning contract all those years ago. Seen it every time he paid for a pack of smokes with change, laying coins down and pushing them across the counter; every time he asked Nick at the Ace High, or some variant of Nick, to let him sign over a check for his tab. There were varying degrees of that look, but they all meant the same: Go fuck yourself, Mike. No handouts for you.

"I said I need to *make* some money, Jake. I'll be the first to tell you—I understand that nothing's for free."

Burfine winced and moved past him, again with the delicate shoulder pat. He kept looking at Vale's gauze. "I'm sorry, Mike. I am. I just . . . I don't know how I can help you." He knocked on the gallery's glass door and Vale saw the assistant rise from the computer.

Vale walked over, pulled the tarp away. He dropped it to the cement and stepped on it so it wouldn't flit away down the street. He hoisted the painting up and said to Burfine's back, "I want to sell this painting to you, Jake. At a very significant discount."

Burfine turned.

Vale had painted *This Great and Permanent Unraveling* in 1994, and in his protracted decline it had been seen by very few people; mostly by those few lost and drunken women he could wrangle into his bed. It measured two by five feet and had been Brophy's supposed "gift" to him: he'd allowed Vale to keep one painting of his choice after signing the contract. A single painting, provided he, Brophy, could photograph it beforehand.

In 2005, Sotheby's had published an estimated auction price for the painting, amid dozens of other Vale originals Brophy had flipped to collectors over the years. Vale had read about it online. *This Great and Permanent Unraveling*, Sotheby's estimated, would probably go at auction for $350,000–400,000. Especially considering it had only been in Vale's possession since its completion. And that had been back in 2005, a lifetime ago.

"I need some money," Vale said flatly. "I have to get to a funeral."

Burfine looked at the painting, looked at the mess that made up Vale's head, took a deep breath and said, "Come inside."

• • •

The assistant hovered around like a fretful bird until Burfine leveled his gaze and said, "Chadwick, why don't you go make Mike some espresso." The assistant nodded and spun on one heel and Burfine turned back to the painting. They were playing the game, curator and artist. Vale's skull throbbed.

They stood in the back room of the gallery. A gigantic butcher-block table in the center of the room held a computer, shipping boxes, giant coils of Bubble Wrap, containers of Styrofoam peanuts. Huge shipping pallets stood stacked against one wall. A latticework of vertical shelves took up another, most of it filled with inventory waiting to be cycled through or shown to visiting collectors: paintings, drawings, lithographs and prints from Burfine's roster of gallery artists. *This Great and Permanent Unraveling* hung unceremoniously from a nail. Burfine had taken everything else down around it.

"It's a beautiful painting," he admitted, his knuckles mashed against his lips as he stared.

It was. And Vale held a slim pride in the fact that he'd held onto it for all these years. Through evictions and catastrophe and hundreds of sad, knife-edged mornings, he'd held onto this one painting, this last vestige of what he had once been capable of.

"I'm willing to cut you a deal," Vale said. "Provided you can give me some cash up front. That's the trade."

Burfine snorted. "Just how much of a deal are we talking about, Mike?"

"I'll sell it to you for ten percent of market value."

Burfine nodded, considering. Trying not to show his excitement. But Vale had caught the eye-bulge: *Holy shit.* "I have no idea what the market value for this piece is. Like I said, we'd need to involve Brophy in this, because of that shitty contract you signed."

Vale felt a stitch of anger work its way through him. "Uh-huh."

"It complicates things, is all."

"Two things: This is *my* piece. I've got the paperwork for it. And don't bullshit me. You know exactly which painting this is. Sotheby's quoted it between three-fifty and four, and that was fifteen fucking years ago."

Burfine shrugged. "You know how things go. Market's fickle. Prices fluctuate."

"Give me a break," Vale said.

The assistant came back with a tiny porcelain cup of espresso, a tiny saucer. Vale's hands trembled as he reached for it. It was so sweet it made Vale's teeth ache. "Look. If you can get me twenty thousand dollars today," he said, "I'll write you a bill of sale for the fucking thing right here. I'll sign it in blood if you want. I don't care. That's an insane deal."

Around his knuckles, still staring at the painting, Burfine said, "I don't have that kind of cash around, Mike."

Vale sighed, walked out onto the gallery floor. Pieces of distorted, painfully twisted metalwork sat on pedestals around the room. Five-digit price tags. He wanted to pick one up and hurl it through the window. He thought, *Every minute I'm here is one I'm not using to get to there.*

He called out, "I need to get to LA, Jake. You buy that painting, everyone from the *New York Times* to *Art & Artists* is gonna be running a piece on Fuel. It's a deal."

Silence from the back room. Vale drank from his little cup.

A minute later, Burfine called his name. He was standing at the butcher-block table. He exhaled as if it pained him and pushed pieces of paper and a pen across the table at Vale. He'd printed out a bill of a sale and a certificate of authenticity. The assistant stood nearby with a digital camera.

"I can juggle some things around. I'll need to run a few errands."

"Okay," Vale said. "How long?"

"I can get you the money in an hour."

"That's fine."

He leaned over to sign, the ache in his head flaring in tandem with the pulse of his heart.

He signed it and thought, I'm moving toward you, Candice. Years too late, but still.

Try to forgive me, yeah?

I'm on my way.

5

From the journals of Marvin Deitz:

The fog had deepened by the time we entered the gates of Rouen, the sun above a glittering coin in the pale sky. The hoofbeats of our mules were damped and muted in the heavy air, and the city's turrets and parapets above the wall rose like something from a dream. I heard the town well before I saw it. The cries of the barkers, the market already thrumming early in the morning. I smelled horse shit and rotten vegetables and the brine of fish in the air. I found myself trying to meet peoples' eyes, but everyone passed us as if we were invisible. It was the first inkling into who my father was, what he had been molded into by time and circumstance.

The constabulary was a squat stone building in the center of the city, the lip of its roof peppered in crows shouldering each other for space. We tethered the mules and stepped inside and my father greeted the crag-faced man seated behind a great oaken desk. The room was dank, moisture seeping from the cracks between the stones, the stink of mold in the air.

Wordlessly the man pushed a small sack across the desk and my father put it in the pocket of his coat.

"You can count it," the man said.

"You say that every time," my father said. "To cheat me . . ."

"Is as likely as cheating the gallows itself," the man finished in pompous mockery, and my father seemed to take some grim satisfaction from it. "I hear you, Jean."

The man squinted then, holding a scrap of foolscap far from his face, his lips moving beneath his grayed, drooping mustache. "Two of them downstairs. Luc knows the details. After that, there's two cows died over at Jon the Black's farm, northeast of town."

My father sighed. (I would later find that beyond the executions and sessions of torture to extract confession, a large part of my father's job constituted the removal and interment of dead animals and men who had died in nearby prisons.)

"Who's this?" the man said, lifting his chin at me. He had dirt in the wrinkles of his neck.

"My boy, come to learn the trade," my father said, and with that the man leaned back on his stool and laughed and laughed, clapping a bony hand against his knee. When we stepped past the desk and down an arched hallway, the smell of rot growing heavier, he was still laughing.

Down a flight of slick stone stairs, water pooling in the seams between wall and floor. Down another flight, we came to a hallway studded with torches that dripped tallow, the wall blackened behind them. Half a dozen oaken doors lined each side of the hall. The occasional moans of men came from behind the doors. A rat ran bold over my foot. My knees trembled, went watery.

One of the doors hung open and inside it stood a boy whipcord thin—presumably the constable's apprentice—and an emaciated man chained to the wall. The boy turned and grinned at us and it was a terrible thing to see. His teeth looked as if they'd been flung into his mouth by someone with questionable aim. That and the flat, obvious madness in his eyes are the two things I will always remember most about Luc. I tried not to look at the man on the wall.

"Why are we here, Luc?" My father already sounded tired.

The boy hooked a thumb at the hanging man. "He was caught stealing both bread and coin from a baker. And then, at the time of his arrest, he fought the constable." Luc turned to the man and crowed, "Didn't you, good sir?" He held a broad spike in one hand, and a small mallet in the other. He stepped forward, traced the hanging man's jawline with the spike, but the man didn't seem to notice. He was already covered in suppurating sores and terrible red and white blooms ran up his legs. His head sagged on the stem of his neck. I had to put my fist over my mouth as we stood there; the stench was unreal, beyond words, the rot of it. The prisoner was rotting alive.

Still with his spike against the man's chin, Luc said, "Across the hall, that one's been accused of heresy."

"The bishops have been informed?"

"The bishops sent him here."

Pointing at the man in chains, my father said. "How long has he been here, Luc?"

"Not long enough, clearly." He tapped the spike in a downward arc with every word: chin, throat, chest, navel.

"Has he confessed?"

"Oh, a hundred times over."

My father sighed. "Get a signed confession and oath of repayment. Brand him for a thief on the hand and let him go."

"But—"

"Let him go, Luc."

Luc exhaled, his eyes glittering with fury. "Of course," he said.

My father put his hand on my shoulder and with his other hand removed a key ring bristling with keys from beneath his coat. We stepped across the hall to the other man, the wet stones glimmering in torchlight.

• • •

I walked down Eighty-second Avenue, keeping my eyes open for Julia's officers. A lowrider blared past me, strobing bass and gas fumes. I passed a restaurant with a gigantic plaster bucket of chicken on top. I was embarrassed. Ashamed, really: I'd overreacted.

I had set up the perimeters of my relationship with Julia. *I* had placed myself in a position to be hurt. She was doing what she thought was best.

I saw a police cruiser among the northbound lanes a block or two up and I veered, as discreetly as I could, from the sidewalk toward a low-slung bar with scabbed yellow paint and one red door. Tiny windows like an afterthought. Neon cursive hung in red script in two of them, the word halved: *Dest iny's.*

I walked through the door and a scattering of regulars looked up, squinting like moles against the light. The door wheezed shut behind me and they turned back wordlessly to the mouths of their drinks.

I straddled a stool and ordered a beer. The place was full of muted televisions and the rattle of the AC. The half dozen men lining the bar were roughly my age, and one would occasionally lean over and murmur something to another and then chuckle wetly. The slow traffic of a game of eight ball unfolded in the back of the room.

"What can I get you?"

The bartender's cleavage belonged to a twenty-year-old, and her eyes were a beautiful, fierce green, ringed in clots of mascara. The rest of her seemed sun-blasted, and fiercely red. Skin hung loose at her throat—old as I was. The man beside me coughed and coughed like he was drowning in his own lungs.

I ordered a beer, wondered if the cruiser had been for me, if Julia actually had called anyone. It seemed against her sense of propriety to lie. What purpose would it serve? The bartender set my beer down.

I took out my wallet and absently looked up at one of the televisions. When I did, my heart stuttered, galloped. Felt suddenly like it was about to burst through the fabric of my shirt.

"You okay, hon?" the bartender asked, frowning. Beside me the man rattled phlegm into his fist. She scowled at him. "Jesus wept, Bill, hit the john and cough it up if you have to. Sounds like you're about to pull a lung."

I pointed to the television. "Can you turn this up? Please?"

She turned up the volume from a remote under the bar and for a moment all of the men's heads rose like flowers. The man next to me cleared his throat and spoke into his glass. "Trash," he said. "Shows like this. Pure trash."

"Oh hush your mouth, Bill," the bartender said, leaning back and propping one elbow on the bar.

It was a talk show; a banner at the bottom of the screen said that it was called *To the Point with Jesse Pamona*. The title of this particular show was "Bad Girls Gone Really, Really Good."

The host stood before her audience. They had just laughed

at something she'd said. Then she said something else and the audience jeered, pumped their fists. Then it cut back to her guests.

A man and a woman. The man was a hulking, tanned monstrosity in a dark suit. His gelled hair was cropped close enough on the sides to see his pale scalp underneath, the little rivers of bunched veins at his temples. The woman was young, blonde, pretty. She wore a smartly-cut black business suit and a severe ponytail, very little makeup. Collagen lips and wide blue eyes.

The banner beneath her read: *Lyla, 23. Adult Entertainer, Claims She's Possessed by Joan of Arc.*

"So," Jesse Pamona said, panning to her audience once more before facing her guests, "*who* did you say you were again?"

The man leaned forward and tucked his chin in—he was clearly used to ducking down to speak to people. The marquee at the bottom of the screen read: *Louis: Personal trainer/Joan of Arc's "Chaperone?"*

"Jesse, I'm just the bodyguard," he said. This got a warm ripple of laughter from the audience.

"Oooookay," Jesse purred, winking to the camera. Then she turned her attention to the woman. "And what about *you*, my dear? What is it you do for a living again?"

"Well, I used to be a dancer." High-pitched voice, a little worn. Smoker. A knowing groan spread throughout the audience. The men at the bar chortled like trolls. My body seemed then a separate thing from my mind, my vision. I felt like I was looking out at myself, at some other Marvin Dietz looking at the television.

Jesse winked at Lyla. "A *dancer* dancer or a *pole* dancer? An *adult* dancer?"

Lyla squared her shoulders. "I was an adult entertainer, yes. Since these . . . realizations have come to light, all that's changed. My whole life has changed."

"Okay," Jesse said again. "And when did these realizations take place again?"

"Three weeks ago."

Jesse leaned forward, intimate. Two girlfriends sharing secrets. "And what happened exactly? Can you tell me, Lyla?"

A close-up of Lyla's face then, and my hand tightened around my glass. I was looking for Joan's face in hers somewhere, some hint of the same knowledge, some sliver of recognition of the woman I had seen on that overcast day in Rouen. I didn't see it, but that didn't mean anything, did it? What did I bear of Geoffroy these days? How much of that vessel remained in this one? How much did I really even remember of Joan as she'd actually been? Memory's as faceted as a shattered mirror.

"It wasn't gradual," Lyla said. "It happened all at once." She snapped her fingers. "Joan's entire history, her entire life, came to me all at once." She smiled bashfully. "I was shopping with my mom when it happened."

"Joan's life came to you all at once?"

"Yes."

Again Jesse performed her half-twist to face her audience. *Get a load of her, people.* "So, you're saying you've got, what, split personalities? That you're simultaneously a—pardon the expression, but isn't it true?—a stripper and a *martyred saint?* Is that what you're telling us?"

Next to me, Bill mournfully said, "All the good ones are crazier than hell." He ate some peanuts.

"It's not really split personalities, Jesse. I don't know how to explain it, honestly." She paused. "I don't really know how much I *should* tell you, honestly."

Jesse frowned. Her audience frowned with her, on the verge of turning on Lyla. The bodyguard winced, sensing their polarity. "Why is that?" Jesse asked.

Lyla lifted her slim shoulders, defiant. "Because I was told to wait. I was in a dressing room and everything—her childhood, her voices, King Charles, the English soldiers, everything—came to me all at once, like a flood. I fell down, just freaking out, and a voice told me that I was supposed to wait. That more . . . that more would be revealed." She paused, seemed ready to say more, and then shrugged. "I don't know *why* I was chosen, but I believe there was a purpose for it."

"Good God," Bill said bitterly. He turned and looked at me with his bulbous reddened nose, his doomed and bloodshot eyes. He shook his head and raised a hand toward the bartender and said, "Darlin', I'm gonna need another drink if I'm to partake in such otherworldly horseshit as this. Between blondie there and the supposed goddamned haints down in *California,* I've had just about enough of the whole sorry mess."

"World's a strange place, Bill," the bartender said, putting another beer in front of him.

"Horseshit is what it is," he said. "Horseshit or the devil at work." He started coughing again.

6

Vale walked down Glisan with the sun in his eyes.

He was carrying twenty thousand dollars in a taped-up Nike shoebox.

He'd counted it twice in spite of Burfine's insistence that it was all there. Brophy, much too late, had taught him to forevermore count the money and read the small print. While he waited for Burfine to return with the cash, his assistant had plied Vale with espressos and a kind of skittering deference, as if Vale was a half-tamed creature capable of a strange intelligence: a pit bull that did quadratic equations, something like that. Vale had no idea how Burfine had come up with that much cash so quickly, what kind of ungodly favors had been called in, and he didn't give a shit.

He raised his face to the sun, the thunder in his skull loosening a bit with the caffeine, the movement. Sweating joggers in span-dex ran by him, clots of hipsters in tight-fitting clothes smoking outside their condos, tech-industry people taking a break from their remote positions in Silicon Valley or wherever the hell they were from. Gutter punks peppered the curbs, spitting at people's feet as they passed. Candice was a sadness rattling inside him that he had sloughed off for the time being. Just for now. Look at all of these people! There was so much goddamned relentless living going on around him!

He headed toward Burnside, that artery that divided the city north and south. The world around him was dense with movement, the glassed high-rises flinging knives of light back at him. There was a car dealership across the river, right at the foot of the bridge, and the plan was rough-hewn but at least present: buy the cheapest car they had and drive to Los Angeles. Point A to Point B. And then the thought came to him: would a legitimate dealership even *sell* him a car? With his rime of beard and jittery, tattooed hands? Stinking of last night's booze and paying cash with a ring of blood-darkened gauze wrapped around his head? He looked like he'd busted out of a prison hospital.

He passed the twin golden lions that flanked Chinatown. The Rescue Mission was two blocks ahead, loose knots of homeless men and women camping out front. Old Town had the clearest demarcations: people sleeping with cardboard boxes folded over them, sleeping at the foot of luxury housing.

He passed a pair of legs jutting out from the sliding door of a green minivan parked at the curb, the rest of the man's body lost in the gloom. He passed, and then looked back—it was as close to a hunch as Vale had ever felt in his life—and saw the words *FOR SALE* soaped in the rear window. *'98 CHRYSLER RUNS GOOD $2500.* A phone number. Just like that.

He walked back to the van, where the shirtless man in black jeans, his long red hair wrapped in sweaty whorls around his neck, was in the process of lighting a cigarette.

"Hey," Vale said, and the man jumped and hit his head on the roof of the van.

"Dang, guy," the man hissed, rubbing the crown of his skull. There were no backseats; instead the back of the van held maybe another dozen cardboard boxes, a few folded blankets. A dress shirt and tie hung over the headrest of the passenger seat.

"Sorry," Vale said. "Is this your van?"

"Sure is," the man said, looking him over. An incalculable look on his face, part shrewdness, part suspicion.

"Well," Vale said, opening his shoebox. "I'm interested."

7

From the journals of Marvin Deitz:

"Do not speak," my father called out as we stepped into the chamber across the hall from the first man, from Luc. "Stand over there. No matter what you see, do not speak, and do not cry out."

My father knew the intricacies of theater and the manner in which it related to confession. Half of the work was theater, really. The cultivation of fear, the steady distillation of terror. The meting out of it. The other half, of course, was finely ritualized violence and bloodshed. A distinct understanding of anatomy.

I would later come to understand just how malleable the body is, to darkly marvel at just how many variants for ruination there are. How there is finally a tipping point for every body, every shell we inhabit, before it allows its dim light to be extinguished. But also how *strong* the body is! How stubbornly capable of enduring punishment!

Compared to the man across the hall, this one was kingly. Pale, his hands cinched and shackled above his head, his legs tethered by irons on the floor. His body was sheathed in muscle, his belly a pronounced little bullethead of fat. There was a table in the center of the room, shackles on the wall for a half dozen more men, though he was the only prisoner. Luc, or someone, had cut his undershirt from him. It hung in rags around his waist, still tucked into his pants.

"You're no stranger to the dinner table," my father said absently. The man's eyes followed him as he went to the wooden cabinet against one wall and, from there, removed an oilcloth bound with twine. He left the cabinet doors open. Dark instruments hung on pegs, their shapes dim, their purposes unfathomable. He placed the oilcloth on the table in the center of the room. Lamps sputtered and hissed.

"Can you see this?" my father asked. "Can you see me over here?" The man was silent.

My father undid the knot on the twine and slowly unrolled the cloth. Within came the dense clank of metal against metal.

And that was all it took; the man's resolve gave way. "Please," he breathed.

Another rat ran across my foot, heavy and warm. I kicked it away. For a moment, they both looked at me, and then my father's eyes fell upon the man again.

"What is your name?"

"Simon. I'm a smithy in Provins. Please."

My father still stood behind the table, his instruments spread out before him. "You have been accused of heresy, Simon," he said.

"I know it. It's a falsehood."

"A falsehood?"

"It's my neighbor, Andre Mauvoisin. He covets my wife, slandered my name to the priests. I am faithful to the Lord God."

My father nodded, pensive. Seemed to consider it. "How do we prove this, Simon?"

"Isn't my saying it enough? Please. If I were a heretic, would I be so quick to claim my allegiance to the Almighty?"

I knew my father was strong, but I had never before seen him move that fast. In a second he was in front of the man and held a rust-clotted spike in one hand and Simon's jaw in the other, hard enough to wrest it open. Simon made an animal gargling sound and I heard his piss patter to the floor as my father lay the spike beneath one bulging eye. I began weeping.

"Simon of Provins," my father said with great dark cheer, holding the point of that spike under the man's madly wavering eye, "it's the unfaithful ones, the godless ones, who will say anything to stop the turning of the screws. *Stop* crying, Geoffroy." He said this last without turning his head.

The man burbled, wept. *"Please—"*

"The soul's greatest gift, Simon: If you are guilty and confess your crimes, you shall be granted entrance to heaven. If you are innocent and it is a false confession and an unjust death? Your entrance is assured as well. Tidy, is it not?"

I slid against the wet wall. I drew my knees to my chest and buried my eyes there.

"The body is but a shell, Simon. Do you confess?"

"Please, I—"

When I looked up, my father was pressing the point of the spike delicately against the lid of Simon's closed eye. He quivered against his chains. Even in the poor light I saw this. I was riveted, rooted to the floor.

"Simon of Provins, do you confess to the charges of heresy?"

"Praise God, yes! Anything! Just—"

My father looked at me over his shoulder then, took the spike away as the man thrummed and sobbed against his bonds.

"See this, Geoffroy. Know it," my father said. *"No one protects us."*

He turned back to the man chained to the wall, and any number of terrible things happened after that.

• • •

My apartment above the record store was practically monk-like in its utility. After my life as Bill Creswell, I was tired of collecting things. The record store and its ceaseless accumulations, the volume of artifacts there, exhausted me sometimes. Here I had a bed and a dresser. Warped wooden floors that creaked with every step. A small writing desk with a lamp and a coffee cup full of pens.

I shoved handfuls of clothes and my journals into a duffel bag. The charger for my cell phone. I looked around and realized there was nothing more that I needed. I'd spent *years* here, years sleeping in this small room with its clanging pipes and finicky radiator.

I believed her. Lyla.

No, I *wanted* to believe her.

How Joan came to her like a shotgun blast—another's lifetime opened upon her all at once. I could relate.

How often had I found myself hoping throughout the years? How diligently had I petitioned some mechanism of the holy world for an answer? And nothing had come of it, until now.

I went downstairs to the store. After five minutes on the laptop, I had the address of the Los Angeles studio where *To the Point* was filmed. Nothing on Lyla beyond the little I'd learned from the show. I resisted the urge to rifle through the dozens of YouTube clips of the show, to rewatch her episode. I was almost fearful of how excited I was.

I wrote a quick letter to Adam, outlining the fact that I'd left him the store, included the number of the lawyer who'd drafted the will for me. My day for grand gestures, apparently. I put the letter in an envelope and wrote his name on the front and left it on the counter. He had a key. If—when—I died, on my way to LA or otherwise, someone would find it. I hoped it was the right choice.

Half an hour later, I was on the southbound off-ramp of I-5, hot wind buffeting my clothes, my thumb held out. A dozen cars passed, maybe less, when a green minivan with a *For Sale* sign in one of the side windows slowed and pulled onto the soft shoulder ahead of me, hazards blinking. Simple as that. I dared to harbor the idea, just for a moment, that destiny—or something—was bending to accommodate me.

I ran, could actually feel the asphalt give a little in the heat. My eyeglasses threatened to slip off. I opened the passenger door and threw my bag on the floorboard.

The driver was bearded, wore an oversized pair of women's sunglasses. A sweat-stained t-shirt, tattoos on his fingers. His head was ringed in a bloody, flesh-colored bandage.

"Heading south, chief?" he asked, ashing a cigarette. "Hop in. Let's get to it."

8

The caffeine from Chadwick's espressos had faded. Vale was crashing. The sale had gone fine; the owner had claimed to have been going through a divorce, and the boxes, empty leftovers from his move. No back seats, but who would he need to be carting around? The man had scrawled a bill of sale on the back of envelope he'd taken from the glove box, Vale had paid him in cash, and that was that.

Meanwhile, he was already lamenting picking up this new guy, this portly old man with his duffel bag and weird eyeglasses. That good feeling he'd had managed to stay with him even as he'd driven home and quickly packed a backpack and gotten on the freeway; that sense that he was doing exactly what he should be. How often did that ever happen? When was the last time he'd felt that? It had lasted another ten miles or so down the freeway, enough for his passenger to throw a few bones of conversation Vale's way and then to stop once he realized it just wasn't going to happen. Vale was already drawing back into himself, thinking about Candice again.

Couched in the arms of his hangover, the day's lasting heat, the wink and snarl of sunlight off the chrome of passing cars. Would he ever be able to feel something for more than ten minutes at a stretch?

His passenger stuck out a hand. "My name's Marvin, by the way."

"Hi, Marvin. Mike Vale." Perfunctory. They shook without Vale taking his eyes from the road.

"I appreciate the ride."

Vale shrugged. They drove in silence. Beyond town now. Office parks and auto dealerships and the start of farmlands, the visual stutter of mini-malls and outlet stores wedged among rolling hills.

Marvin took another stab at it. "So, uh, what do you do, Mike? What brings you on the road?"

Vale sighed, irritated. Picking this guy up had been a mistake. Spur of the moment. "Well, I used to feed obese children deep-fried burritos, Marvin, but then I got fired for punching a customer." He looked over, expecting the man to be taken aback, maybe a little scared. Something. But the guy just nodded sagely, as if this was a perfectly reasonable answer. This actually endeared him to Vale, at least a little. "What about you?" he asked.

Marvin took out his wallet and handed Vale a business card. Vale squinted to read it. "*Sounds Good?* What is that?"

"That's the name of my record store."

Vale flipped the card onto the dashboard. "That's kind of a sucky name, Marvin. No offense."

Marvin laughed, nodded. "None at all," he said.

There was Mount Hood, blue in the distance. The day was still hot, shot through with clouds, the heat pressing down. An hour and a half later, Vale pulled into the lot of a convenience store. The store was called the Pumpin' Pig; its sign was thirty feet tall and showed a bright pink pig holding a gas nozzle, tears of near-orgasmic joy leaping from its eyes.

Vale stepped inside the store while Marvin stayed in the van. His head ached so badly by now it made his eyes flutter. He stepped up to the counter with two six-packs of microbrews—living large!—and realized he had just left a taped-up shoebox with nearly eighteen thousand dollars in the van with a complete stranger. He paid and asked the teenaged clerk for a bathroom key.

"There's no key," she said, putting his beers in a sack. "It's just around back. Listen, do you need an ambulance or something?"

Vale stared at her. "A what? No. Why?"

She waved her hand in front of her own face, frowning. "You're kind of messed up a little bit. Bleeding."

Vale stepped outside, saw Marvin standing at the side of the van, his hands in the back pockets of his chinos, his face held up to the sun. He looked like a low-level office manager gone to seed, and Vale sighed with relief. He nodded at Marvin, making some inscrutable gesture as he walked around to the back of the building with his paper sack. Air horns from semis drifted low from the highway.

The bathroom was a concrete box with a drain in the middle of the floor, a little room that smelled of bleach-vapor and piss. Vale's face was a pocked and dented ruin in the warped metal mirror above the sink, and he drained his first beer in one tilt of the bottle and then stared at his splayed hand in front of him, willing the tremors out of it. The teeth of his hangover loosened almost immediately. He set the bottle on the toilet tank and tilted a second bottle up to the sputtering florescent light. With that, relief flooded through him like someone had flipped a switch. He left the two bottles in there and walked back to the van, his nerves suddenly as evened out as a surgeon's. Marvin was already in the van, his seatbelt back on.

"Ready to hit the road, boss?" Vale cried cheerily. "You one-eyed bastard." He winked at Marvin and set the bag of beers on the floorboard at his feet. He checked the shoebox—brazen about it, too—then shoved it back under the seat. He cranked the radio. John Mellencamp, loud enough to vibrate the dashboard. He gazed in the rearview; you really couldn't see shit, all those boxes stacked and tiered in the back.

Marvin looked at him a moment and then nodded, smiling. He tucked his hands over his belly and said, almost to himself, "Ready is one thing I am, yeah."

Vale whooped, tore ass out of the parking lot.

9

The Bride was famous.

A bottled water sales rep, getting in nine holes at a course in La Jolla, California, caught the Bride on film. And nothing was the same after that.

In two minutes and three seconds, the Bride changed the world.

Her fame was two-fold: she was the first smoke to be caught on tape, and her story was classic. The whole tale was right there, digestible and frame-ready and still resonant with a certain mystery. *An anguished bride? What* happened *to her?* It was her footage they used when rounding out a news update about the smokes, even though she'd appeared all the way back in June and there were now hundreds of filmed and verified sightings throughout Southern California and Northern Mexico.

The footage of the Bride lasts for one hundred and twenty three seconds and what remained so striking about it, beyond the obvious, was the fact that the film was rolling *before* she appeared; the sales rep was using his smartphone to film his partner sink an eagle. His camerawork was steady enough and the man himself, the rep, who would be interviewed incessantly over the coming months, gained a certain ironic fame for his first words to the apparition.

The shot was of his buddy from the waist down, sunlight flaring off the putter and the buddy's watch, and then both men back-pedaled and one of them—the rep insisted it was his pal—gave out a little high-pitched scream, because there she was. The Bride.

Like they all did, she just winked into existence: suddenly there, no fading in slowly, none of that. Just *bam*. Her back to them, her train trailing behind her on the green.

"Can I help you with anything?" the sales rep said, his voice surprisingly calm, and that line alone would inspire untold amounts of merchandising—t-shirts, pillow covers, phone cases, temporary tattoos—over the next three months. The Bride ignored him—*par for the course* was a joke that would eventually be run into the ground by any number of late night talk show hosts—and continued to walk a slow and seemingly aimless perimeter around the spot from which she had originally appeared.

Historians assessing the footage, when she snapped from haze to sharpness, said the fabric of the Bride's dress was a kind of silver tissue and lace common with dresses of the early to mid-nineteenth century. Her eyes were dark with tears and she managed, somehow, to spend the entire one hundred twenty-three seconds without seeming to lock on to any common landmark: not the two men who backpedaled to stay out of her way, nor the bag of clubs that she drifted right through, and beyond that the clubhouse and phalanx of trees bracing the edge of the course. She seemed to see none of it.

And after two minutes and three seconds, she vanished.

10

From the journals of Marvin Deitz:

When we stepped out from the constabulary, the air was cool on my reddened cheeks. All was as we had left it: the shops still thronged with people, the bleat of animals, the calls and laughter, the streets churned to mud. But the world had changed irrevocably for me. How could it not?

It is right that they turn their faces from us, I remember thinking. It is right that they shun us, mark us. My father in short order had reduced Simon of Provins to the keening sounds a child would make, an animal stuck in a trap. A bloody thumbprint had served as signature on a confession of heresy the bishops had drawn up. My father would oversee Simon's execution the following week.

"Any problems?" the man upstairs had asked. His eyes had taken on a slow, glassy look; a tankard of wine stood on his desk.

"None," my father said. My father removed his gloves and threw them in the hearth. Heavy things, they lay there and smoked for a time before catching.

"There's a fire for burning that shit out back," the man yelled as he dropped his feet from his desk. "Don't burn those unholy goddamned things in here, fool."

My father's face darkened, but he nodded. The two of them looked at each other, gauging each other in ways I could not understand. Finally, the man drew another pull from his wine and the moment passed. He and my father sat about drawing up a bill the constable would present to the lord overseeing Simon's estate. You paid for your own execution, I would come to learn.

My father had always been unknowable to me. Always full of strange pockets of silence, a propensity for impatience and drink. I had always loved him and feared him both. But now, after I had seen him and Luc walk down that dark hallway and up the stairs, their jobs done? My father's gloves dark with Simon's blood? His willingness to do that to another man, who howled and screamed and tried to pull away? Love, it could be said, had taken a backseat. The fear, though. That bloomed.

We got back on our cart and started on our way. "Now to the Black farm," my father said. "You remember that place? We went there once; we bought a sheep there. Do you remember?"

I turned my face away, my vision trembling as tears threatened.

My father clicked his tongue, pulled the reins. The mules stopped. I saw thousands of tiny droplets of dew studding their manes. I seemed to see everything with this terrible clarity.

He pulled the woolen cap from his head, gripped it in his hands. He looked down at his boots on the buckboard of our cart. "You'll need to get used to it, Geoffroy."

"He said he didn't do it," I said. "His neighbor—"

My father shook his head. "He might as well have been on the wheel as soon as the bishop sent word to elicit a confession. There's no escape from a charge of heresy, Geoffroy. Not in these times."

"But you said—"

My father put his hand over mine, and put his other hand over the back of my neck. He leaned in close to me. He smelled ripe and awful, a rich, long-seated dankness we all carried and hardly noticed until someone else got close. His hands were rough and warm. It was the gentlest he had ever touched me in my life.

"Geoffroy, listen to me. There is no Almighty. There isn't. Were there, I'd have been struck a hundred times dead for what I have wrought on the world. What God is it, Geoffroy, that lets a plague pass over the executioner while the priests rot and die as young men? What God is that? No, Geoffroy, we are alone. *Men* cast judgment on our deeds, and those doing the judging are blood-mad themselves."

I took my hand from his and tucked my chin to my chest. "I'll never," I said. "*Never.*"

My father's smile was small and sad. There was a delicate stippling of blood next to his eye. He snapped the reins and the mules took foot.

• • •

Driving with Vale, it seemed doubtful we'd make it to the California border, much less to Los Angeles. At one point he very nearly kissed the mud flaps of a semi during an abrupt lane switch. The horns of terrified motorists dopplered past us. The speedometer jittered around eighty, the chassis of the van groaning beneath the radio. The wind roared through Vale's open window.

Things had gotten complicated. With the notion of Lyla, I was suddenly invested in the business of living. I *cared* all of a sudden, and in doing so put myself at risk.

Vale turned to me and cried, "I just bought this car." It was clear he'd drunk a few beers at the gas station. Now that he was buzzed, he was talkative, cheerful. With his matted beard, bloody bandages and gigantic old-lady sunglasses, the man looked absolutely insane. "There's no backseats," he bellowed, "but what the shit, right? The guy who sold it to me was a tweaker. Bought it right off the street, man."

"Well, again," I said drily, my fingernails practically embedded in the dashboard, "thanks for picking me up."

Vale shrugged. "Not a big deal." He turned the dial on the radio station and we started drifting toward the shoulder. Vale settled on the Kinks—"Lola"—and finally, thankfully, put his hands back on the wheel.

One of my Five Rules: *Look for portents and signs.* Lola, I thought—close enough to Lyla? I was reaching.

Vale, meanwhile, was oblivious. Trying to light his cigarette going eighty with the window rolled down. "What brings you out on the road, Marvin?" His cigarette wagged as he spoke.

"I'm, uh, heading down south to visit a friend."

"Yeah? Heading down for a funeral, unfortunately."

"Sorry to hear that," I said. "How far south do you think you'll be going?"

"The funeral's in LA. I'm just doing a straight shot down there."

My heart did a clumsy stutter. *Portents and signs.* "So you're going straight to Los Angeles?"

Beyond the ceaseless repetition of my death and rebirths, I'd quit searching for any *meaning* a while back. How does one find meaning in a maelstrom? Order in a cyclone? The parameters of the Curse had made themselves clear long ago. It was like a palindrome, the repetition of it. But I believed in coincidence no more than I believed in benevolence. This was the problem with searching for portents and signs: once you found them, once they revealed themselves, what did you *do* with the goddamned things? How did you read them?

What were the odds that the man who picked me up in Portland would be taking a straight shot to Los Angeles, where Lyla was?

Vale finally got part of his cigarette lit, an inch-long section of ash running down one side of it. "Indeedy I am, Marvin. Straight there. I am heading to Los Angeles like a fucking bullet train, buddy."

"Wow," I said, my voice heavy and strange in my own ears. "That's crazy. That's where I'm going too."

Vale turned and looked at me—much longer than he should have, we started veering again—and said, "You should ride with me, Marvin. I could use the company." He sounded joyous, happy. A dark coin of blood had seeped through the gauze wrapped around his head. "To be honest, it's been a rough day."

11

Even if there wasn't a flight ban, Vale wouldn't be flying to LA.

Because after Paris, Vale didn't fly anymore. Not a chance.

He and Candice had been married for three years. He was in his mid-twenties, at the apex of his trajectory. He'd already grown accustomed to the life, the pressure and benefits both. So, Paris. He'd been invited to participate in a Brut art exhibition at the Museum d'Orsay; something Brophy had talked him into.

"Sounds like a fucking pain," Vale had said when they talked about it over the phone. "Paris drivers, all that. I mean, I've never even heard of this museum, man." Trying to sound so worldly. When he thought about it now, it made him want to puke.

Brophy had laughed at him. He was used to indulging Vale, smoothing the rough edges over with some ego-stroking. "It *guarantees* a spike in overseas sales, Mike. Get on the plane and go. You're the star of the show. We both know it."

Vale had been more amused than anything when no less than four of Brophy's assistants came to his studio the next day and cherry-picked half a dozen canvasses from a folder full of photographs they'd brought with them.

He'd just convinced Candice to move to Portland with him; after a few years of living there, Los Angeles had just grown too filthy and fake for him, and just felt too goddamned *big*. He liked Portland's compactness, its earnestness. And cheap? Christ, it'd been cheap then.

Vale had stood in his massive studio—he rented a warehouse down in the industrial section by the river—drinking vodka cran from a water bottle and laughing as the assistants moved through the space with the efficiency and coordination of a hit squad. They hardly said a word to him, just conferred with the photos and then packed them out to a truck.

The day he left for Paris, Vale leaned out the kitchen window of their apartment, smoking and looking for Brophy's limo that would take him to the airport. Candice washed the dishes, everything telegraphed by the sound of plates and glasses clinking against each other in the suds.

"Come on," he said over his shoulder. "Don't be like this."

"You could've gotten me tickets," she said.

Vale laughed. "You're working on your *book*. You need time to write, remember? Well," he said, twirling his cigarette in the air, little curlicues of smoke, "here's time to write." This old argument of theirs.

The clatter of silverware. The faucet.

Vale said, "First you ask for something, Candice, then you complain about it when you get it."

She dropped the sponge in the sink. "That is so shitty," she said. "That is such a shitty thing to say, Mike. Aren't we in this together? I mean, Jesus."

"Candy," he said. "Babe." Just like that, he was gracious and consoling as he saw the limo pull to a stop downstairs, "I'm sorry." He went over to her and kissed her forehead, her eyes, her lips. "I'm not even going to be *doing* anything. I'm just going to be hanging around the museum, nodding at a bunch of French bankers. I'll be back in three days."

She sighed and leaned against him. She'd graduated from UCLA a few months before and was editing yet another draft of her novel, *The Weeping Trees*. Her professor there, a cadaverous man prone to wearing bow ties, a man who had won a National Book Award around the time Johnny-fucking-Appleseed was gallivanting around the countryside and who Vale knew wanted to bang her, had raved about it, urged her to seek a publisher. But she was frozen, insisted it wasn't done. She hadn't even let Vale read it yet.

They stood in the kitchen and she laced her hands around his neck and steadied him. She looked him in the eye and said, "Don't do anything stupid. Don't drink all the wine."

He rolled his eyes and smiled. "Come on. I have to go."

She yanked on his hair, that incendiary mixture of the plaintive and sultry. "I'm serious."

"I know," he said. "I won't drink all the wine. I'll be good." And that was the thing: he'd meant it.

He'd meant it, hadn't he?

But what happens when you paint every ugly thing inside yourself and they laud you for it? What happens when a sketch you give a taxi driver as a tip for a ride to the bar fetches *sixty grand* at a Christie's auction a year later? What happens when you're twenty-four and surrounded by yes-men, shitwads with dollar-sign eyeballs, at every turn? When your agent says, "Fuck it, you're going to Paris, Mike. Live a little." What happens then?

The world eats you for breakfast, that's what. You think you own the world but the world owns you. You're a sucker.

You're a sucker because you're young and you don't know any better. You're a sucker because the painting comes easy, because the painting's a salve, because the painting lights you up. But the big reason, the main reason you're a sucker?

Because you've started to believe what they say about you.

The limo had a bar. The airport had a bar. The airplane had a bar. By the time they were in the air, he'd lost count of how many drinks he'd had.

"Another rum and Coke, madam," Vale said to the stewardess. He made a gun with his finger and shot her. She rolled her eyes, brought him another one.

Twelve hours later he stepped through the terminal at Charles de Gaulle International, nearly blind with intoxication after drinking his way across an ocean. He wandered the airport, enjoying himself immensely, drunkenly pawing magazine racks and peering at his reflection in the windows of overpriced restaurants. Fixing his hair, smiling at people, ensconced in the sexy, ambient din of a language he couldn't speak. He bought a corkscrew key chain in a gift shop that had the Eiffel Tower on it and after an hour or so returned to the concord he'd exited from, where he staggered into a man holding a placard bearing his name. Vale had stared at the man with his jaw hanging open as if he'd just materialized there.

"Victory!" he crowed, slobbering. People passing by had stared, traded looks with each other. He threw a shoulder around the man with the placard like they'd caught shrapnel in Normandy together.

The man's name, he found out, was François. A representative of the museum, he said. He would be Vale's guide and chauffeur throughout his stay in Paris. François was a short, blunt-featured man in an impeccable suit. He had an obvious toupee and nothing that came remotely near a sense of humor. None. A screaming void where François's funny resided. He drove them through a series of rainswept, winding streets and dropped Vale off in front of his hotel.

Vale spent most of the next day ordering from room service and nursing his hangover. He called Candice, told her he'd made it through fine. She was curt and Vale hung up on her, angry.

That evening, François came to his door. Vale's hangover was finally in remission; he had just started his second bottle of champagne. It was six o'clock.

"Frankie!" he cried cheerfully. "Have a drink!"

François's nose curled and he said in his heavily accented English, "We go now, Michael, okay? We check that the art is good for the show tomorrow, okay?" They stepped out into a fog-heavy night and he felt impervious to death; transcendent. He was in Paris! His handler had a toupee and no joy in his life! Yes! Life was good. François cursed under his breath when Vale spent most of the ride leaning out the window and gleefully yelling lewd suggestions at Parisian pedestrians.

The Museum d'Orsay was madness. A columned monstrosity, huge. It was a testament to his ignorance that he hadn't heard of the place. He was frisked by slab-faced guards who noted his drunkenness and were clearly reluctant to let him in. François argued with them while Vale grinned at the exchange of spitfire French like it was a tennis match. They finally let him through, François leaving curses in their wake.

The museum thrummed with activity, a hundred different artists and their handlers and assistants. Curators and staff. Reporters. A few collectors calling in favors, getting to see the show early.

People barked into walkie-talkies or stood on stepladders, hanging eyelets and holding electronic levels against the walls as others below them barked orders.

"If this was New York, the show would have been ready days ago," Vale said. It wasn't necessarily true, but the truth had never stopped him before. He waved at a group of bejowled men in *ghutras*, who frowned at him and walked on.

François pursed his lips and said, "This is not New York, Michael, okay?"

Everyone was trying to eye each other's work, size it up. After traveling the length of the museum twice they still hadn't located Vale's paintings. Nobody knew where the museum director was, or the curator in charge of this wing. People with handheld recorders and notepads kept brightening with recognition and tugging at Vale's sleeve as he passed, but François kept them at bay until he abruptly spun around in a circle, cursing. He put a hand gently against Vale's chest.

"You stay here, Michael." He wagged his finger. "I will look for David. You stay, please, okay? Just stay to the ground."

"Who's David?"

"The—" François sputtered, seesawed his hand in a circle, impatient. "Museum man, you know."

"The head of the museum? To find my paintings?"

"*Oui.*"

"Got it, Frankie. No problem." Vale's buzz was wearing thin by then, but the hum and snap of the room held him aloft for the time being. He was still cruising.

He immediately walked the rooms again. A few reporters asked him questions. He tried his best.

He nodded at Kenny Scharf and his bad haircut; Scharf had pieced together an installation using cartoon transparencies and television sets. It was crap, Vale knew, and he was sure Scharf would soon enough convince himself of the same about Vale's paintings. There was a Basquiat triptych on loan from the museum's permanent collection. Four of Judith Scott's carapace-like weavings took up an entire wall of one room; they were braced by three of Jeffrey Koons's meticulously painted wax casts of people in mundane repose.

If Brophy's little gestapo assistants had fucking *lost* a half dozen of his paintings in transit to Paris, heads would roll.

He stood beneath one of Scott's weavings and didn't realize until he'd put his lighter back in his pocket that he'd lit a cigarette inside the museum. People turned, scowling.

"Mister Vale? I'm sorry, but it is a no smoking building."

The woman held a clipboard in one hand and a clasp of keys in the other. Blonde, her hair cut jagged at the jawline. His age? Green-flecked eyes and the slightest overbite. She bowed slightly when he turned to face her.

"*Je suis désolé*," she said, nearly curtsying again, and waved a hand at the room. "The exhibition is an important event for the museum. The work is fragile." She took the cigarette from his fingers and dropped it to the floor, which garnered a smattering of applause from those around them. A bridge sparked between them. He recognized it for what it was.

"My name is Mike," he said, and held out his hand. He sounded leering, buffoonish, in his own ears.

She'd picked the crushed cigarette back up, awkwardly between her thumb and middle finger. She switched it to her other hand and shook. Her hand was tiny. "Oh, I know who you are. I have loved your paintings since I was in school, you know?" She laughed, and when she did showed one crooked tooth. She saw him looking and covered her mouth. He asked her what her name was.

"Olivia," she said.

"Olivia." Vale said. He gazed around the room, looked back at her. "Olivia, I'd like to have a drink with you."

"Yes," she said immediately. "Me too."

They left. Olivia held his wrist as they wended through the museum and stepped through a door marked *Privé* that turned out to be a filing room with an even smaller door behind it. They ran through that as well, the cacophony dimming behind them, and they laughed and he wanted to kiss her then, but his blooming sobriety held him back—which was what he would only later understand to be, of course, his sense of loyalty. His propriety, sense of justice. Rightness. His *love*.

He would only later understand—years later, long after he had split with Candice—that some part of him would always seek to sink lower, would only feel good when he tried to claw himself up from further and further depths. It was fucked.

But for now, her car was in the back parking lot. A tiny thing, the bed he shared with Candice was larger. Olivia sped from the lot and they wheeled down rue Saint Dominique and rue de l'Université with the river threading like a slash of ink along beside them, and she talked about *him*, about how she loved his paintings, how he was a hero to her and her friends, his paintings spoke to her, the *emblematic accuracy* of them—such a thing to say, and *Christ,* with a French accent!—and his heart was lifted. His great and ceaseless vanity.

They passed a shop that sold wine and Vale made her stop. They ran in and he threw a handful of money at the proprietor and Olivia laughed and said, "No, no, it's too much," and took some of the money and handed it back to him. They stepped out with bottles pressed tight against them, as many as they could carry.

Just within that minute or two in the wine shop, it had begun to rain again. He dropped a bottle on the ground and it broke with a sound like coughing and he cursed and laughed. He was suddenly sure that Candice was looking out the window thinking about him at that moment, he could imagine it: she would have a book open and slices of apple on a saucer, and when they got back to Olivia's car he opened a bottle of wine in the passenger seat with his new corkscrew key chain. He did a bad job of it and savaged the cork until it crumbled in pieces into the bottle.

He drank and the wine spilled down the sides of his face, darkening his collar. He was in a panic to finish the thing, to quell the image of Candice from his mind, to drink more.

Olivia lived in a tiny flat at the top of a brownstone. There was a winding staircase with a flimsy, ornate railing. At her door a black cat entwined itself around her legs and she gently pushed it away with her foot. She opened the door and they stepped inside and she turned suddenly shy again, setting the bottles on the counter in her cramped kitchen and smoothing her skirt. He felt like an animal loosed in there, something too big for the room, churlish and awkward. This American beast with his wine bottle and his false bravado and his bullshit. He drank from the bottle again and looked at her and she blushed. She took a bottle opener from a drawer and a glass and said, "I guess you don't need one of these."

"I do not," he agreed. She turned her back to him and poured a glass and he felt it all on the verge of dissipating.

He stepped through the kitchen into the small living room. A bookshelf full of monographs and art history texts on one wall, a CD player and mismatched wingback chairs. Traffic down at street level, a little white dog tied up outside of a café, barking at people that passed. It was still early. There was a coffee table covered in medieval maps and glossed in Lucite. He walked over to it.

On the maps, the unknown edges of the world were populated by blue, unfathomable beasts with scales and many heads. It hurt his heart a little to see: it was something a girl in college would make. He almost left then. Above the love seat was a reproduction of Pollock's *Number 7, 1951*, the right half of it always seeming to him like a face in profile, a playful caricature.

He stood there in her small apartment, saw through the doorway the dried herbs hanging above the kitchen sink. The photos of strangers on the refrigerator, Olivia in front of a tree, silly and cross-eyed with her arm slung around the neck of another girl, the sun flung on her like paint. Only a teenager in that one.

She stepped into the living room, her eyes fixed at a point beyond his seeing. Determined. He finished his bottle of wine and dropped it where it rang hollowly against the floor. She cringed: the neighbors. He put her at twenty-one, twenty-two. Olivia raised her glass to her mouth and then held it in front of her birdlike chest and he wrapped his hands in her hair and kissed her first.

Afterward, after they were done, Olivia pulled a comforter from the love seat and lay wrapped in his arms on the floor while the cat continued to ingratiate itself against their legs. His heart clanged in his chest with a fear that would eventually char its way down into a fine silt of shame. A silt that he would eventually inure himself to, that he would over the years grow, if not comfortable, at least familiar with. He would do this again and again.

He cradled another bottle of wine to his chest, like an infant, waiting for his heart to slow.

"I have to get back to the hotel," he said. "I have to call my guard dog. François."

"Oh," she said, raising her head so he could pull his arm free. "I can drive you," she offered, her voice bright with hurt, and he could see that he had of course failed her too.

"No," he said. "That's okay, thanks."

And then the graceless act of the drunken adulterer clumsily pulling his pants on. Maybe nine o'clock at night. Olivia lay on the floor, her blonde hair fanned out on a pillow, one hand pinning the comforter to her chest as he staggered about the room for his clothes. She stared at the ceiling.

He stood at her doorway—a shithead enough to take another bottle of wine with him—and said, "It was nice meeting you, Olivia. I had a nice time."

A tight smile flitted across her face, her eyes hard as stones.

"You're beautiful," he managed.

She laughed and pressed both of her hands against the floor, pinning the blanket down at her sides. "*Poltron*," she said, and flitted her hand at him as if her were an insect. His fear clanged like a stone against the ladder of his ribs.

"Maybe I'll see you at the show tomorrow," he ventured, and cried out as his empty wine bottle struck him above the eye.

Fifteen minutes later, his own wine bottle emptied and abandoned on a bench, he managed to hail a cab. The driver slowed and peered at him through the rain-beaded window. He was a hawk-nosed man who began to accelerate until Vale slapped the window and held a wad of francs against the glass. Toy money, colorful and brash. The driver slowed and unlocked the door.

"*Où?* Where to, my friend?" His reluctance was obvious. Vale pressed his hand to his eye, trying to stem the blood.

Vale got in, the wine roaring inside him. He knew little besides that in failing Candice, he had failed any vestige of probity or morality within himself. He also understood that grievous errors required great proclamations. And that he had drunk three bottles of wine in two hours.

Still, most importantly: he had committed adultery. Something needed to be done. Atonement.

"Tattoo parlor," he burbled.

"You're bleeding, my friend."

"A definitive statement is needed," Vale said, slapping the back of the driver's seat. "Tattoo *motherfucking* parlor, please."

"Where is your hotel?"

"*Tattoo parlor,* goddamnit."

"Of course, the drunk American is in my cab," the driver said, sighing and edging his way into traffic. He bit a thumbnail and spit the clipping out. "The drunk, bleeding American. A tattoo is exactly what you need."

Vale handed him the wad of money and the driver shook his head. He took the roll from Vale, thumbed half of it out bill by bill. He paused, took one more bill and handed the rest back.

Vale leaned his head against the seat. Touched his eye. The blood on his fingers was black and then bloomed into color when they passed beneath a streetlight.

The driver muttered to himself and pulled a U-turn. Car horns sang out, headlights ran across the interior of the cab. He tossed a newspaper over his shoulder onto the backseat.

"I don't need to read the paper right now," Vale said.

The driver shook his head, readjusted his cap. "Sit on it. I don't want you bleeding on my seat."

• • •

It was in a basement somewhere. A tiny, brick room with a drain set in the checkered floor. The walls were painted red and covered in tiny, framed illustrations. The room caged in drawings of pirates, broken hearts impaled by swords, screaming panthers, blue-eyed women with roses in their hair. The tattooist wore a leather vest over skinny arms and a vast gut. A torpedo-breasted demon glowered over his bellybutton. He sighed when he saw Vale stumble in with the driver.

The two of them laughed and talked in French while Vale swayed in front of the art. Finally the driver left, jovially clapping Vale on the back as he walked out. "You are a fucking idiot, my friend. You're on your own."

"I know it," Vale said.

The tattooist didn't understand what he wanted. His English

was worse than the driver's. "The word of candy?" he kept asking. He lit a cigarette and scratched his armpit with his thumb. "Why the word like that, my friend?"

"No," Mike slurred, "my wife. My wife's name. Here." He took a piece of paper and a blue pencil from the man's table of supplies.

"Ah, okay," the man said. He thought for a moment. "But they do not match, okay? No . . . no *balancing.*"

The man waggled his fingers in front of Mike's face as if he were showing off rings. "You see? C-A-N-D on this hand. I-C-E on *this* hand. Does not match, my friend. No balance."

"Fuck it," Mike said. "Put an exclamation point at the end."

The tattooist's eyebrows rose.

Vale drew it on the scrap paper:

C-A-N-D on his right hand.

I-C-E-! on the left.

The man laughed. "You are an idiot." He grinned and clapped Vale on the shoulder.

It was a brotherly gesture, friendly, and it made remorse rise like bile in his throat. He remembered the feel of Olivia's ass in his hands, the knobs of her spine like topography. And then came the images of Candice: walking around their room in only her socks as she talked on the telephone. How she always held a book by its top half. That dimple of a scar on her ribs from some forgotten childhood wound. Her back to him as she'd washed dishes the day before, as if already aware of his transgressions.

"Let's go," Vale said. "Let's get this done."

• • •

François was furious with him—"We nearly called the police," he hissed—and then seemed strangely satisfied when he saw Vale's bandaged hands and cut eyebrow. A man who could do such things within the space of a few hours, François seemed to think, was clearly one who could not be reasoned with. After that, François mostly left him alone.

His paintings had been located. Two collectors bought them all for roughly a quarter of a million dollars. Vale stayed sober throughout the opening the next night, shaking hands and posing for photographs. His shame was like a bed of coals; it banked and glowed on its own whim, its own current. He didn't see Olivia anywhere and wondered if she'd gotten in trouble for leaving the museum the day before.

The day after the opening, François met him in the lobby of his hotel and put him in a cab without another word spoken between them. In the airport bathroom, the letters on his fingers were a fine and depthless black.

They almost died crossing the Atlantic.

He'd been about to ask the stewardess for a menu when the plane suddenly dipped—lurched really—the overhead lights dimming, and a sickening angle of blue-green sea pivoting toward them outside the windows. The engines actually seemed to sputter and catch, a strange and coughing sound that made his balls crawl and his asshole tighten up in animal terror. The oxygen masks dropped and unspooled from their housings, bobbing playful things with their yellow mouthpieces. Screams popped like party favors up and down the aisles. The whole thing lasted maybe twenty seconds and then the plane righted itself, the engines returning.

They did an emergency landing at JFK, the landing strip lined with ambulances and fire engines even though the captain had spent much of the rest of the flight reassuring everyone that things were fine.

Still, Vale had seen the faces of the stewardesses, and the immutable blankness of the sea rising to meet them.

It was punishment, he knew. Or at the very least, his guilt made physical. His transgressions courting disaster.

So yeah, Vale doesn't fly.

12

From the journals of Marvin Deitz:

Years passed.

I was my father's son.

We ate supper with rain falling in strings outside our hut. The poultice my mother had wrapped around my hand stank of sulfur, garlic.

My father coughed, awful wet rattles that vibrated in his chest. He'd been ill for months. We had sought out three healers before one agreed to visit our home. Her fee for such a visit was astronomical. She refused to actually touch my father, called his illness a sickness of the spirit and prescribed prayer and a satchel of herbs to be buried in the ground for a week and then laid on his chest. To no avail, of course; his cough worsened. No one was surprised. Thunder boomed outside.

"How was it?" father asked, wincing against the grit that inevitably settled like silt in his mouth after a drink of wine. He motioned for my mother to fill his cup again.

I held up my hand in its bandage as way of explanation.

"He cut you?"

"A bite," I said.

My father nodded, scooped more potatoes into his mouth. "The toothless man can't bite, Geoffroy. Remember that." He had long since ceased his rounds; I had replaced him. And yet in his retellings of tales, his constant unsolicited advice, he would recast himself in a nobler or more vicious light, depending on the situation. He'd grown fat on such proclamations. We all listened in silence.

I remember thinking I would never get old like my father.

I said, "He was afraid. That's all." My father snorted, lifted his cup.

The year was 1400. I was—what? Twenty years old? I had replaced my father at the gallows, the dungeon. Luc had become my superior. In Rouen, I answered to him; elsewhere my rounds took me days away from home. My father, with time on his hands, had tried his hand at growing a small crop or two, but they seemed inured to his past and were meager things, or blighted. He mostly spent his afternoons and evenings drinking wine and browbeating my mother about her own chores. This dwindling down of a man.

Esme, as the daughter of an executioner and disfigured on top of it, remained unmarried. The four of us lived together still, with Riva and Jehanne having gained husbands by moving to cities on the coast. We had heard nothing of them in months. There was always the gnawing worry they had passed on from famine, war, pestilence. I slept nearest the hearth now, my one increase in stature as provider for the family.

Here is what I had learned since watching my father pry his confession from Simon of Provins those years ago: The prisoners themselves became interchangeable. *Bodies* were interchangeable. There was little to differentiate one man from the next; such was the raw honesty of the flesh.

They were all the same: Fragile sacks of gristle and shit and yellow bone. Blood and howls. The faces blurred together into one indistinct face. A non-face, almost.

I would sometimes find myself walking down the avenue or a country road and in passing someone think of the latticework of their ribs, the spongy pale fat couched beneath the skin, what their gibbering pleas would sound like. It became natural, the course of how my mind worked. This is what had happened to me: everyone had been distilled to simple flesh. There was little I hadn't done to a person.

Esme, once my guide into sleep, my ship in the darkness, looked at me now as if I was some kind of animal. I spent days away on my travels and was sullen and silent when home.

I wore my father's coat now, the sword stitched on my back.

The turn of the century had brought with it any amount of doomsaying. Even steady, faithful people had fallen prey to it. The end of the world was drawing near, they said. Some rejoiced. Others lamented. Roving bands of flagellants traveled from town to town, loudly praying and whipping themselves bloody. Punishing themselves for the earthly sins of man. Still, such people were afforded room, board and gifts by benevolent citizens of the towns they passed through, all three a scarcity in a nation wracked with plague and occupation.

A band of them had been passing through the village of L'Houmeau and a man, a serf known only as Jean, had thrown a stone at them, called them opportunists. That'd been enough; he'd been beaten, jailed and brought to the constabulary at Rouen. There were rumors at this time that King Charles had gone mad; somehow he had heard of Jean of L'Houmeau's charges and the order had traveled down from the King's advisors to the bailiff of Rouen: the man, this Jean, was to be publicly quartered for his heresy. The bailiff passed word to Luc, who'd chortled like a fool and assigned the job to me.

The market had been opened to all and citizens were ordered to bear witness. A dais was built in the center of the square. Jean of L'Houmeau was placed flat on his back, the bonds at his arms and legs knotted with heavy leather straps that led to the traces on the horses' backs. Like most of what we did, it had the terrible showmanship of theater.

The priest had performed his meager ministrations over the man as another monk waved incense around the platform. Luc and I stood at the rear, I with my hands crossed before me and a short sword in a scabbard at my side. The man had wept and pulled at his bonds. Between Luc and I, while searching for an admission of guilt, he had lost fingernails, teeth. I had shattered the bones of his feet with a mallet. Luc had removed long peels of flesh from his ribs with a curved knife. The layers beneath shone scabrous now, red and pink, dense with writhing maggots.

Throughout it all, Jean of L'Houmeau had refused to claim guilt.

I had found myself more than once angry at his recalcitrance, his lack of fealty.

The priest looked at me and nodded with his watery eyes. I had stepped forward and went to lash Jean's neck with the last remaining bond and he'd bitten me, his remaining teeth yellow and bright among the grime and blood caked on his face.

"Damn you," I'd said, and struck him. Behind me, Luc laughed. Someone threw a rotten lettuce and it exploded like a bomb on the wooden platform. Boos and murmurings began from the crowd, and the ragged line of men-at-arms below exchanged glances, tightened the grips on their pikes and mallets.

"All these trappings of men," Jean hissed through his broken mouth as I lashed the strap around his neck, "do obfuscate the word of God."

"Oh, prattle on, heretic," I said, and gave the signal.

The men stationed at the five points whipped the flanks of their horses, urging them forward, and soon enough Jean of L'Houmeau was done talking.

My father looked at me over the smoking candle in our little hut. His eyes glittered in his great shaggy head. "He was just afraid," I said again. "It's all a bad business."

My father stopped chewing. Sick as he was, pale as he was, the fire quickened in his eyes at that.

"*I know* what it is, boy. I *know* what kind of business. Don't ever doubt it."

Esme, always sensitive and attuned to the workings of the house in ways the rest of us were not, struggled with tears. My mother told her to hush.

"You weren't built for this," my father said.

I shrugged. Why fight it? "It's true," I said. "I grew angry with him at times."

"Why?"

"Because he made me hurt him. Because he cared more about being right then being alive."

My father shook his head. "You don't have the backbone for it."

"Perhaps not." I looked down at my plate. The thought hung precarious there, unspoken. Finally I said, "To be truthful, I fear for my soul at times."

And with that my father leaned his head back and roared laughter, the rain hissing in the fields outside.

• • •

Blue sky, patchy green fields beyond the windows, fields scattered with huge circular mounds of lashed hay. Traffic had thinned significantly. Vale sounded darkly cheerful when he peered at the temperature gauge and said, "You hear that?"

"What?"

"That knocking? That knocking sound?"

Said sound had been coming from the engine for the past forty miles or more. I'd just assumed that Vale knew about it. "Well, well, well," he muttered. "That didn't take long. Goddamnit." He pulled a beer from the sack on the floorboard.

"Marvin," he said, pointing the beer bottle at me as he talked. "What I'm going to do is I'm going to pull over at the next exit. This van is about to shit the bed." He handed me the bottle. "Meanwhile, I would greatly appreciate it if you could open this fellow for me."

I looked down at the bottle. "I don't think that's a particularly good idea, Mike."

Vale nodded as if he understood. "I've known you for about an hour and a half, Marvin. Please don't be upset when I tell you I don't give much of a shit if you think it's a good idea or not."

"And what happens if we get pulled over?"

Vale shook his head, took his beer back. A flap of bandage had come loose at the back of his head and hung there like a filthy, blood-spotted ponytail. "Marvin, I just *said* I'm pulling over, man. Look," and he pointed the beer at a passing sign, "says there's a gas station coming up in a mile and a half. Just open this fucking beer in the meanwhile."

"I can't do that, Mike."

"Goddamnit." He dropped it back into the bag.

The van began giving odd bucks and lurches, other drivers giving us commiserating *I'm sorry* looks as they flew past us. We made it to the off-ramp and pulled into the parking lot of yet another gas station. Vale slammed the door and stormed inside the convenience store. On all sides of us lay rolling hills burned brown by summer. I got out, wondering what Lyla was doing right then.

Vale came back out a minute later and poured a jug of water into the open hood of the van. Somewhere in its guts, things gurgled and hissed.

"Mike," I said.

Vale held up a hand. He'd retied his bandage in the back with a knot and now looked like some kind of dirty, half-crazed Rambo cosplayer. "Fuck you, Marvin. You weird one-eyed motherfucker."

"What? Jesus. What's the matter with you?"

"The matter with *me?*" He slammed the hood down, shot a seething glare my way. "Where do you get the nerve, man? I just *met* you."

Anger flared, quick as a match. "Yeah, I know. I understand that."

"This is my van. *I'm* the driver."

Grown men, talking to each other like this. I held up my hands. "Have you ever seen a human body that's been in a sixty-mile-an-hour collision?"

"It's not about that."

"Yeah? What's it about then?"

He peered into the mouth of the water jug and then banged it against his leg. The van gurgled and croaked. "If I need any kind of imposed morality, I'll go fall on my knees in some church. I'll go call my ex-wife, okay? I don't need your one-eyed moon face casting judgment on me."

"I wasn't judging you."

Vale laughed, pushed his big sunglasses up on his nose.

No one spoke. We spent a few moments looking out at the hills. Customers again gave Vale the once-over, kept on their way.

"Okay," I said, "I was judging you. Fine. But listen. The shittiness of being even remotely drunk and driving aside"—Vale opened his mouth to speak, and I held up a hand—"the danger you're putting other drivers and their families in, all that aside, open containers are a death-kiss. You really want to go to jail on a DUI charge in some piss-ass town on 101? It's just a bad move."

Even before I was done talking, Vale was nodding in agreement. Acquiescence. Even with the bandage and the sunglasses on, the beard, I recognized the look he gave me. I recognized shrewdness when I saw it. This man so desperate for companionship, camaraderie. And I, so desperate to believe I was being *guided* somewhere that I would stick with him in spite of this idiocy. Portents and signs.

A hell of a pairing, the two of us.

13

The gauge continued to tremble, the temperature continued to climb. The van sputtered and moaned, its shuddering visible to other cars. "Thank you," Vale said, smiling and waving his hand in mock cheer as another driver made frantic motions beside them. "I had no idea what was going on. You drive a hybrid. A real steward of the earth, thank you."

Marvin looked out his mirror. "Well, we're leaking water. We're leaving a big stripe of water behind us."

Vale took the next exit and they pulled into the parking lot of a Walmart. Stop and start and stop again. "My entire fucking life is going to be gas stations and parking lots," he said. The town was named Roseburg and seemed to be populated mostly by sullen, overweight rednecks and tanned retirees in bright pastel.

They stepped into the cavernous building, Vale's shoes clomping on the cement floor, and went to the customer service desk. He asked to use a phone book.

The customer service guy wore a red vest and a bow tie and looked like he should have a pet monkey next to him clapping a pair of cymbals together. Vale could see the guy processing what the hell a phone book even was, and then he looked them over—brazenly and pretty haughtily for a man in a bow tie, Vale thought—and asked if they were customers.

"Our van broke down," Marvin said.

The guy's smile was so fake, it looked like he was passing a kidney stone. "I'm sorry to hear that, sir. But I'll need a sales receipt for you guys to use our phone."

Vale put his hands on the counter. "That doesn't even make sense."

The smile, a tilt of his head. The leer. "It's policy, sir."

A few minutes later Vale came back to the customer service desk with a twelve pack and a receipt. The guy pulled a Yellow Pages from beneath the counter and pushed it over to him. There were a half dozen pages of listings for *Auto Repair*.

Vale looked up. "I probably have to invest in company stock to use your phone, right?"

"Here." Marvin handed him his cell phone.

Vale picked the listing for Gary's Authentic Automotive and Towing because it sounded backwoods as hell. Why not? Go for the whole experience. How shittier could things get?

The tow truck driver said he'd be there in fifteen minutes. Easy enough.

"Thanks so much for your help," Vale said to the customer service guy. Then he pushed the phone book off the counter with one finger and walked away.

• • •

The driver wore oil-stained coveralls and had a band of green barbed wire tattooed around his bicep, a bulb of chew fattening his lip. He lifted up the hood and stared thoughtfully at the engine for a grand total of roughly five seconds. "Tell you right now, guys, your water pump's gone tits up. Hear that hissing? Shit's done for." He honked laughter and seconds later turned grim, eyeing the two of them, catching the vibe they were throwing out. "We'll get you down to the shop and try to get it fixed up real quick."

Vale winced. "We're in a bit of a rush."

The guy worked his chew around to another pocket of his mouth and winked at Marvin. He turned to Vale. "No worries. We ain't exactly got water pumps for a '98 Town and Country fallin' out of our ass cracks over there, but I bet we can line something up. Can't do a thing in the parking lot of the Walmart, though."

Vale and Marvin traded looks. "Okay," Vale finally said. "Whatever."

"Okey doke. Let's hook 'er up."

The driver slammed the hood shut and leaned over, releasing a terrific jet of black tobacco juice onto the pavement. The sun was beginning to sink below the lip of the valley. It was coming on dusk and they'd managed less than two hundred miles.

14

Jared Brophy was having a drink after his checkup. He was in some shithole in Silver Lake drinking with a bunch of kids thirty years younger than him. The news had been about what he'd expected—bad—so with a sense, this sudden urge, to just do one goddamned thing that didn't seem preordained or inevitable, he'd driven around until he found a bar and ordered a G&T from a bartender with a straight-up bull ring through her nose. The alcohol supposedly wasn't good for him but did it really matter at this point? Really?

The bar was a faux-redneck deal called Lu-Lu's. Wood paneling, a gigantic stuffed black bear on its hind legs in one corner. Singing bass on the walls. Framed posters of *The Dukes of Hazzard* and Jeff Foxworthy. They served—Jesus Christ—they served shots of mystery booze in spent shotgun shells, which had to be against some kind of code. And yet cans of PBR were still seven dollars.

His gin and tonic could've fed his parents for two weeks when they were growing up. He marveled at this city, sometimes. At the very least, you had to have a trust fund or be a fucking executive to get drunk anywhere besides your own home. Where did these kids get the money? They all looked like they were skipping social studies to be here.

Still, the booze helped, buoyed him a little. *It's not good, no,* the doctor'd told him today, a gravity to his voice that had thus far been held in check. What he meant was obvious. The doctor might as well have been a singing fish himself, his one tune belted out again and again: *You're dying.*

"Hit me again, madam," Brophy said. The bartender picked up his empty glass and then, her eyes widening, dropped it to the floor. It didn't break, but clattered to the floor, rolling. Behind him, someone screamed.

Brophy turned. Not ten feet away, a smoke—he recognized it immediately for what it was—stood in the middle of the room. This one stayed hazy for a few seconds and then snapped to a solidity that hadn't really been present on any of the videos Brophy had watched. Certainly the Bride remained more transparent than this.

It was a weightlifter, a bodybuilder of some kind. At least, that's what Brophy assumed, because the motherfucker was huge. African-American guy—it was the vernacular now, but given the nature of these things, the guy could have just as easily actually been from Africa, could have been from fucking anywhere, right? Being a *ghost* and all?—who stood with his arms stretched wide at his sides, taking big gulps of air through his nose, terrified, and then he went all hazy again, colorless as a cloud of pulp smoke.

"I'm going to pump you up," some kid bellowed in a terrible Schwarzenegger impression. A few people laughed, nervous laughter that bounced around the room like ricochets.

The smoke took a few steps to the left and someone flipped a drink coaster at him like a Frisbee. It sailed above the smoke's shoulder. Someone else threw a plastic cup and it went, of course, right through him. Within seconds the air was full of projectiles— napkins, glasses, menus, shotgun shells, a bowl full of peanuts—and had taken on a fevered, carnival quality as people began shrieking, laughing. The smoke just kept looking around like they all did. None of it seemed to register.

Watching the people around him, Brophy's sickness felt coiled inside him, a small dark animal waiting to spring. Claws hooked and snarled in his blood, his organs. Candice Hessler's death had hit him harder than he thought it would. Surprised him, yeah, and scared him only a little more than he already was; he'd become well versed lately in the body's fragility. But mostly it made him sad.

Nostalgia was a shithead like that. The contract he'd saddled Vale with all those years ago, God. Flimsy as a cardboard shithouse and he'd become undeniably rich because of it. But Vale had needed cash and had become so volatile. Such a pain in the ass to work with. Brophy knew it was a smart move, business-wise. He still believed it. But in the long run? What had been the point of any of it? Rich, not rich? He'd never been Candice's favorite person, even when things were good, but it shamed him now to think that she, this woman he hadn't thought of in years, had gone to her grave most likely thinking him an asshole. A cheat. Which, let's face it, he kind of had been.

He stood and walked to the door but before he opened it something hit him in the back, some missile gone off course. He turned to see everyone in the bar standing, still jeering at the smoke in the center of the room, which still had not acknowledged that it even knew where the hell it was.

"Hey," he said to a young lady standing next to the door. She had on a pair of those acid-splattered jeans hiked up past her navel, the kind that'd been popular when Vale and Candice were just starting out, all those years ago. Everything circular.

"Yeah," she said without looking away. She threw a napkin. "What?"

He coughed once against the back of his hand.

"You're all idiots," he said. "You know that? Okay? Just because you can doesn't mean you have to."

He stepped outside into shards of sunlight and the air surprised him with its sweetness.

15

From the journals of Marvin Deitz:

Time passed, took all. Time was free of allegiance or enemy.

It had been another dark winter full of rain all throughout France; the crops would be sparse again. Starvation would continue to stipple the countryside. Taxes would be raised once more, the English would commandeer the bulk of the food and supplies for themselves, plague would move from one pocket of the country to another like a drunkard on an evening stroll.

This was our province of life, this morning damp and nightly chill. To find an entire family dead at the side of the road—that deadly coupling of starvation and exposure—became common enough. We were familiar with it by now.

I was fifty years old when word came of Joan's capture outside of Compiègne. Esme was kneading dough on the table near the hearth when I told her, her arms dusted in flour. Logs hissed wet in the fire, gave little warmth.

"The Burgundians got her," I said. "She surrendered. There's talk that she was abandoned there by her own men. A trap."

"Good," Esme said, tucking a lock of hair behind her ear. She had in recent years found an uncharted pool of bitterness within herself; its depth would sometimes surprise me. There had been no word from Riva or Jehanne in years; our mother had died from pneumonia the previous winter, a heavy cough that hollowed her from the inside out. Esme spent those last weeks with her as our father continued taking walks into the countryside with his tankards of wine. As my mother's illness grew, my father's walks became longer and longer until one dismal gray afternoon Esme had pronounced her gone, and my father bore the news wordlessly as he tottered in the doorway.

"You and Geoffroy will dig a grave," Esme said to him, her eyes glinting with fury. I'd knelt next to my mother on her thin pallet next to the hearth; she had grown birdlike in her thinness, so brittle in her ending days. I found it incredible that either she or my father had survived as long as they had. "I have some coins for the priest to say some words," Esme said, her voice growing thick.

"Small use," my father slurred, unable to look at us.

"Use enough," Esme hissed.

We buried her in the field beyond and the priest took our money and said some words. We hoped to purchase her some kind of entry into a world kinder than this one.

Even Luc was gone now, he of the bloodlust and teeth like magician's dice, having been knifed in a tavern dispute a decade before. Esme and I were all that was left now. I was a busy man, the only seasoned executioner for a hundred miles in any direction.

"They're saying that this Cauchon's in Paris shitting himself," I said, grinning and furious. "That he's gleeful with it. There is talk of paying a ransom and trying her for her crimes."

"Of course they will. And of course they'll lord it over us."

"Unless the King intercedes."

Esme with her little fists against the dough. "Charles? Will he?"

I shrugged. "With the English already here? Sleeping in our beds? No. No, I doubt it." A wing of hunger fluttered in me. Even now, with just Esme and me, we still knew paucity. We knew the taste of broth and bread that surprised with its flavors: acorn, thyme, dandelion. Wheat and bread had grown monstrously expensive: Esme cut it with whatever ground meal could be found. The joints in her wrists were pronounced knobs, the veins blue and winding beneath her skin. Both of us were riddled by then with arthritis. This was our province.

She turned back to the hearth. "They left another one," she said quietly.

I stiffened, my hand unconsciously going to the scabbard on my thigh. "When? Where?"

"Outside. Out back."

"What was it this time?"

"A hen. Spiked to the butcher's block."

My first thought, in spite of it all, was of food. Esme read the look immediately and shook her head.

"It was long rotted, Geoffroy."

I laughed, incredulous. "And you heard nothing? A rotting fowl nailed to the cutting block? *Pounded* in?"

Esme turned on me then. She had become so thin; the blades of her cheekbones, hair listless as straw. "There are things, Geoffroy, to be done here. Every day. The garden. The cooking. Sewing. A fence post leaned and *I* fixed that. I'm well versed by now in the constant difficulty of making *something*"—she slammed a bowl of stew down in front of me—"from *nothing!*"

There was a time where I might have said a word and all might have been well, but that time had passed. We had both curled into the shells of ourselves. She said, "Your job is the torture and murder of men, Geoffroy. Mine, it seems, is all else."

I rose and drew my hand back, already sick of myself, and Esme flinched and brushed her hand against the simmering cookpot. She hissed in pain, held her fist to her narrow chest. I lowered my hand, ashamed.

"I'm sorry," I said.

"*They don't want us here,*" she cried.

"We've lived here our entire lives, sister. This is the life we were handed."

I looked out at the dim palette of night. A log popped. The crops would flood, I was sure the English would continue to come, and what little food there was would continue to rise in price and scarcity. We were already fighting and dying over scraps, rats seeking the highest point in a sinking ship.

I strode out, grateful for the rain's chill, the water cool down the back of my neck.

My father had not been sighted since the day of my mother's

death. We had buried her, he and I, and returned home. He'd taken a walk later that evening with his wine and had never returned. Gone like smoke. Leaving me to my legacy.

• • •

We rode three to a seat in the tow truck, the van hooked and trailing on two wheels behind us. Roseburg seemed couched in a valley of fields and grasses so dry they could ignite with a hard stare.

"Just so you know," Vale said, his hands locked around his knees as he sat between us. "We're on a time schedule. I need to be in Los Angeles in two days."

"Pain in the ass flying these days," Gary nodded. "That's for sure."

Gary's shop was a weathered two-bay garage on a gravel lot outside of town. Behind the shop were knots of crabgrass growing into the links of cyclone fencing, blackberry bushes scattered amid clots of rusted cars.

Across the road was an A-frame building called the Tip-Top Lounge, its lettering fashioned to look like sawn logs. Next to that was a two-story motel built with a 1950s bomb shelter aesthetic in mind, equal parts concrete and corrugated tin. Nothing else but the tidal roar of the freeway. Valley grasses so crisp and pale they looked nearly white. A ragtag armada of pickups sat around the parking lot of the restaurant. The motel seemed desolate, possibly abandoned.

Gary backed the tow truck up, maneuvered the van into one of the garage bays. Stepping out of the truck into the dimness, I was struck with how quiet things were. A man across the road came out of the Tip-Top and ambled toward his truck and I could hear every footfall on the gravel.

Gary took another plug of chewing tobacco from a tin in his back pocket. He spat into a coffee can in the corner and stood there in front of the van, his hands on his hips. Surveying. Finally he said, "You guys feel free to go on over and get some dinner. I'll find that pump and get to work."

Vale started to say something and I put my hand on his arm. "Let's let him get to work, Mike."

We trudged across the road toward the restaurant, Vale cursing under his breath. Crickets had by then begun their whirring in the grass. Vale had his shoebox tucked under one arm. He looked angry, but more than that he looked pale and used up, sick.

The Tip-Top had lace doilies under the sugar shakers. At the register, a pie wheel sat next to a coffee cup full of American flags. Booths lined three walls of the restaurant, with a scattering of tables in the middle. A counter faced the kitchen, and upon entry, Vale and I were soundly ignored by the half dozen old men perched there. Opposite the booths was a doorway marked *Lounge*. Vale saw that and swiped a hand down his mouth.

"Order me some pie, Marvin. I'll be out in a sec."

I felt time running down the hourglass, but what else could I do? Vale in the lounge seemed like a bad idea, but obviously trying to commandeer my destiny had never worked out particularly well. Vale, I knew, wouldn't veer. He was locked into something bigger than himself. I took a seat at a booth and the waitress walked over with a menu and a pot of coffee, watching Vale push his way through the lounge doors. "Anything to drink while you look at the menu, hon?" She sounded catgut-tough, forty years of Pall Malls working their magic.

"Water's fine."

"Your friend joining you, or is he drinking his dinner tonight?"

"That's a good question. I'm not sure."

"I'll check back in a minute."

When she did, Vale had yet to come out of the lounge. I ordered blackberry pie. Out the window the last bit of daylight was thumbed pink and orange against the crest of the hills. I could dimly see the van in Gary's garage across the road. It'd been a long time since I'd felt this way, *wanting* to live. Felt anything beyond contempt and those few invigorating moments of righteous fury.

A pair of headlights wound themselves up the road and a truck spackled in gray primer screeched into the parking lot, hitting the brakes so close that I could hear a spattering of gravel thunk against the side of the restaurant.

The driver of the truck jumped down from the cab. He was wearing cowboy boots and, chubby as he was, had packed himself into a pair of crisp blue jeans that looked like they'd been vacuum-sealed on him. He reached into the truck, showing a generous cleft of plumber's crack, and came out with an aluminum baseball bat from the floorboard. With his baseball cap and patchy red beard, he might have graduated high school a few hours before. He certainly looked dumb enough.

The waitress stormed out from behind the counter and threw open the door, pointing a finger at him. "Don't you dare, Casper. Don't you do it."

The guy hiked up as much of his jeans as he could. Through the door I heard him say, "If he wants to come out and talk about it like a man, I'm all ears." He spat out an impressive jet of tobacco juice onto the gravel. "Otherwise, I'm going in there and cooking up a nice shitkicking soufflé."

16

Vale didn't know shit about bull markets or hyperinflation or collectors hoarding and flipping paintings when he headed to Los Angeles the summer after high school. He didn't know anything, really: just that Jasper Johns and Mark Rothko left paint on the canvas is if they'd laid it there with their palette knives and then went out and got drunk. That Rauschenberg seemed like he was fucking with you half the time. That Gary Panter's comic panels seemed the thing of glorious dope-dreams. He knew Jean-Michel Basquiat made painting look both kinetic and effortless, a kind of languid threat, a layman's fury coupled with an innate, genius sense of color and composition.

He knew there were two oases for painters in the US: Los Angeles and New York. Art teachers had buoyed him up for years about his supposed talent, his eye, his creativity. He'd been buoyed further by a newfound companion in alcohol, the way it stitched up all the loose ends inside him. The profound egotism of it all: he packed his pens and watercolors, a stack of small paintings on illustration board, some ink drawings into a backpack.

He brought one extra pair of pants, socks, and underwear, his Walkman and some tapes. He kept his money in his shoes. He had the address of Edwin Tanazzi's gallery tucked in his wallet. It had started raining as soon as he stepped onto I-5 and stuck out his thumb, and all along the way he'd held onto the same sense of certainty that he'd left with. In retrospect, he'd been too dumb to be afraid.

He hitchhiked to Los Angeles without incident; he told his parents he was going camping with friends for the weekend. He wouldn't see them again for eleven months, and that would be at his first solo show at Edwin's gallery, where his father would accept a cigar, goggle-eyed and silent, from Dennis Hopper. The only moment of concern came around the California border when the man who'd picked him up, slowly—so slowly it almost seemed like a joke—crept his hand along the seat and onto Vale's leg. Vale's heart had galloped in his chest as he'd gently lifted the man's hand and put it back on the seat. And that had been that. They spoke nothing of it, and the man later bought him lunch at a diner in Redding and seemed almost grateful to have been rebuffed.

He made it to LA quickly enough. It took him another day of hitching, asking directions, taking the wrong buses, and getting lost before he made it to Beverly Hills. So much walking. Miles upon miles. He'd earlier taken what appeared to be the last bus of the evening and, having gone the wrong way, he'd had to walk back the way he'd come. Nothing appeared open by the time he arrived at the gallery, not on this stretch of street.

Traffic was steady, but all the cars, streetlights twining off their hoods, drove by with their windows cinched tight. There were no other pedestrians. Bored, he walked around the neighborhood but turned back when two separate police cars saw him and slowed. Palm trees bowed in the dark, the breeze rich with eucalyptus and exhaust. He was in the heart of something, clearly, but this part of the city seemed to close up like a fist at night. The Tanazzi Gallery was all crisp cement edges and old bay doors paneled in glass.

There was a loading dock behind the gallery stacked with pallets and folded cardboard boxes. He made a bed from the boxes and slept poorly. He rose at dawn, stiff and tired, and sat on the loading dock with his pens and Bristol board. He drew until the sky filled with some color and he could hear the bleat and honk of morning traffic on the street.

He walked around to the front of the gallery and did what was undoubtedly a bug-eyed double take. It was a moment he would always remember: Jean-Michel Basquiat and another man stepped out of the gallery and began walking toward him. Basquiat was hunched and small. Vale's legs went watery but he managed to call out the man's name after they passed him.

Basquiat turned to him stiffly, like an old man. His face was gray and terrible-looking and he wore a voluminous green parka that hung to his knees. His Afro was flattened on one side and sores were scattered on his face. He picked at one, his eyes half-lidded. He was clearly high.

"It's an honor to meet you," Vale managed, his voice sounded high and feminine to his own ears.

Basquiat nodded, looking somewhere around Vale's chest. The other man put his hand on Basquiat's arm. "Let's go," he said. "Let's go, man."

Vale was eighteen years old. He'd been so *dumb.* "Your paintings," he said, "are . . . brilliant. Regal. Ferocious and . . . studious at the same time. You know? They're incredible." Yammering.

Basquiat nodded and put his hands in his pockets and with a kind of steadied, indefatigable sadness pulled his fists out and held them in front of Vale. Vale held his hands out palm up and Basquiat dropped into the nest of his hands crumpled receipts, a book of rolling papers, a cassette tape, a gold money clip with a sheaf of hundreds showing.

"Goddamnit, Jean. Don't do that. Don't give him that," the other man said.

"They'll take every ounce, man," Basquiat said. It was nearly a whisper. "They'll take everything in there. Edwin owes me money." He was missing a tooth, Vale saw.

Basquiat abruptly turned then and the man with him said softly to Vale, "Sorry, man," and scooped the items from his hands.

He watched as the man led Basquiat to a blue sedan parked down the street.

"Where're we going?" Basquiat called querulously, his voice high and plaintive. He sounded like a young boy, a child.

The man opened the passenger door for him. "We're going to Larry's."

"Larry's? I don't want to go to Larry's."

"We're going to Larry's, Jean," the man said, and helped him inside. Less than a year later, Basquiat would be dead and Vale himself would be on his own howling trajectory to stardom. He watched the car pull into traffic and felt a clear arrow of sorrow for the man take flight, his diminishment. Vale vowed then, a vow cast out with the great impetuousness and surety of youth: *Never me. No fucking way.*

He stepped then into the open door of the gallery, buoyed and emboldened. Sunlight fell in pale squares on the cement floor. The place was made up of two gigantic rooms braced by track lighting and moveable paneling; a random doorway here and there. He called out a hello and a moment later heard the clack of heels on the floor.

She stepped from the other room wearing a brisk charcoal suit and a cap of dark red hair that curled at her temples. High cheekbones, green eyes bright as stones. Vale found himself almost unable to speak for the second time in as many minutes.

Finally he managed, "Uh, is Mr. Tanazzi here?" His voice cracked on the last word.

She took one look at him and the boards in his hands and rolled her eyes. When she did that, he realized she was probably only a few years older than him. It was 1987: the shoulders of her suit were padded like a linebacker's; she wobbled on her heels and seemed dedicated to moving as little as possible. He felt like they were both children playing dress-up.

"You're a painter, right?" she said drily.

"Right."

She sighed. "Do you have slides?"

"Slides? No. I have these drawings." He held them out to her.

The way she looked at him—was it curiosity? Condescension? Christ, *pity?* "I'm just the assistant," she murmured, but she took the boards and slowly shuffled through them. She went through them again. A moment later she raised her face to his and he knew—without doubt—that his trajectory and talent was assured. At least with her, this girl.

Mark his arriving: September of 1987, the day he met Candice Hessler in Los Angeles.

"How old are you?"

"Eighteen," he said.

She looked back down at the boards. "When did you do these?"

"Last night," Vale said. "This morning." He decided to risk it. "I slept on the loading dock back there."

She lifted her eyes again, stared at him. "You did these today."

"And last night."

"You people." She smiled grimly and shook her head. "I hate painters, do you know that?"

Candice, he would find out, was twenty-two, in her last year at UCLA, trudging through an art history degree, a minor in English. There was no sense of collision or collusion, no sense of predestination between them. He had no idea. He had come all this way to instigate his own destiny. She was alluring, but at first, honestly, she was simply a doorway. That was all. And truth be told, the pantsuit had been an unlovely thing.

"Mr. Tanazzi will probably be in about an hour from now. I can show him these then." She shuffled through the boards once more and then handed them back. "I hardly ever say this, but you should wait for him to show up. Those are really good. Do you want some coffee?"

If Vale was gifted a legacy, it rested wire-thin on so many things. Most of them reliant on Candice and how she had looked through his early Bristol board drawings and opened the door for him. She had made it so easy for him. How his life would've been different if she'd turned him away.

He would think many times in the years that followed: *Candice, goddamn, I owed you for every good thing, didn't I?*

And to what did he owe the bad? His own limitations? The drinking? But that was the thing about drinking, about how far he'd fallen: Drinking, even then, constantly diminished and renewed Vale's world. Daily. It was a constant do-over. Tomorrow's road would simultaneously be paved in soul-death and possibility. Alcohol's greatest gift and simultaneous curse, then as now: there would always be another chance to get it right. Tomorrow was a new day to atone for grievances and walk straight in the world. Tomorrow was the day he would manage the grace to go about drinking less and moving more throughout the world. Tomorrow he would banish heartache and open his arms.

And so on and so forth.

But tonight?

Tonight he was in the Tip-Top Lounge in Roseburg, Oregon, waiting for his van to get fixed.

Thinking about Candice.

The bartender poured him another whiskey, generous. "Anything else?"

Tomorrow I'll do better, he thought, and shook his head.

When he'd gotten back from Paris, Candice had wanted to pick him up from the airport but he'd begged off and said he'd meet her at home. He'd taken a taxi, angry at the way guilt slung itself into his bones, made him hunch over with its weight, its obviousness. And then he was angry for being angry. And on and on.

She knew, of course, the moment he walked into the kitchen and set his bag down.

Not the specifics, clearly, but the depth of it. The scope. That look of clarity on her face. She was holding a blue mug of tea and she told him later that if he'd taken a step toward her, just one, that she would have thrown it at him. And that might have been enough, might have made it a little easier to forgive him. But he didn't do anything. He just stood there.

Candice looked from his face to his bag and back to his face. He couldn't meet her eyes and kept looking to the stove where the teakettle sat clicking above the coils. She had a clip in her hair and was barefoot and the recognition of his betrayal became clear on her own face, like a wound trying to close. The light threw strands of copper in her hair and she would never be more beautiful or more lost to him. Candice scratched one foot with the other and sucked her teeth and turned to the sink.

"I'm sorry," he said.

She turned her back to him. She turned the faucet on and rinsed out her cup, set it gently in the sink. She said, "Your shit's already packed. Go somewhere else for a while."

"Candice."

She lifted her head, held up one hand. "I'm serious, Mike. Go. Drink up. Fuck some starlets. Go live the dream."

"*Candy.*"

"Get. The fuck. Out."

"Candy, please." He went to her and put a hand on her shoulder and she flung her arm loose like some thing grown blood-maddened just by his nearness. She wouldn't turn to him. Her shoulders hitched up and down as she wept silently. He stood there a moment longer and then took his bag and stepped back through their doorway and down the stairs.

And that had pretty much been that. The doorway that lead to his many transgressions. If he thought of Olivia at all afterward—and he rarely had—she was a figure outlined behind a screen. Her color dimmed. The first in a series. Just some blonde French girl. It got easier, the falsehoods.

He thought of Candice often. All the time. They divorced a year after Paris. She had actually been willing to walk through it at first. Counseling was brought up, but Vale had refused. He worked in absolutes. Broken or fixed. No in-between. Why bother? He moved out. Some kind of dam inside him had broken.

His guilt and drunkenness and shame were all at odds with each other; and also that ceaseless ugly urge for gluttony. And he found there was no shortage of interested women.

The year after Paris was the last year he would paint anything of any strength. Anything that was worth a shit. Candice moved back to LA after the divorce. She wanted nothing from him financially, only his agreement that he would sign the divorce papers without fanfare, which he did.

The Weeping Trees was published soon after, and received decent reviews and low sales. Six months after the move to LA, she was broke and out of desperation wrote a mystery novel about a newly divorced female private investigator. She signed a three-book deal—her first advance was sizeable—and hung up on him when he, drunk and repentant, would call her at night.

He coasted on sales and reputation for a few years more, painting less and less, painting muddied shit. No draftsmanship to them. No vigor. No ache to them. Started painting blackout drunk. Then not painting at all. Reviews went from mixed to bad in short order. He started getting turned down for shows. Collectors started paying less, then just wanted the early work.

Brophy hired assistants for him, supposedly there to help do the shitwork, stretching canvasses, prep-painting the bigger works. Even Vale could read between the lines: they were guard dogs. Babysitters and bottle-stoppers.

He found himself looking for her in restaurant windows and taxicabs, in the strut and arch of a woman walking down the street ahead of him. He was living in his studio at that point, relying on his dwindling savings and the generosity of women young enough to still be starstruck by his name.

He was thirty-three years old when Brophy had a case of bourbon delivered and then came to the studio uninvited with a gram of cocaine and a sophomore from Pratt named Mindy who paid her tuition by stripping. It was like a bad joke.

Vale and Mindy did lines until it felt like someone had pressed shaved ice into his sinuses and he could feel his heartbeat in his teeth. That was when Brophy pulled out the contract and started talking. One million dollars for the early paintings. One lump sum. Get your head on straight, Mike. Get back to work. It seemed like an answer of some kind. He signed it and Brophy cut a check and the earbud assistants came by the next day and took everything from the early days. Everything, except the one painting. Afterward, there was hardly anything left. A few shitty leaning canvasses, muddy and dark.

He spent entire days in blackouts. He came to once in the back of a detox van, held down by a rubber-gloved cop as he howled obscenities into the air. Blood everywhere. He'd shit himself. It scared him straight for a little bit. But then he lost the studio and got an apartment out on 128th and Stark, way the hell out there in the dead zone, and every time he even saw a paintbrush he got scared.

Only alcohol seemed to thaw him. Only the Moment. Then came the time he'd gone berserk on the gallery windows down in the Pearl, with rage unfurling in him like someone snapping a sheet off a laundry line.

How long, a wise man once asked, does it take to drink up a million dollars?

The answer: Years. It takes fucking years.

They were able to reconnect, years after the divorce. There was a gentleness there that seemed to surprise them both; Candice had already married Richard by then, which allowed her a certain distance. It was due in no small part to that, to her grace. When he spoke to her, Vale was not surprised; able to find parts of himself that he thought had long since atrophied or been scorched away.

Decades later, he pined for her like a schoolboy but knew everything had been ruined.

And now here he was. Long since bankrupt, his last card played. Sitting in the Tip-Top Lounge with a broken down van and a one-eyed hitchhiker. A dead ex-wife, the only woman he'd ever loved. Again, it was like a joke. His entire life. As if aliens had written the lyrics to a country and western song.

He ordered another shot and lifted it toward the hanging lights, and it went down burning and glorious, like drinking jet fuel is glorious.

He watched the bartender pour him another. Tomorrow, he thought. Tomorrow he would shake hands with Richard on their emerald lawn. He would grieve Candice honorably.

But tonight?

Tonight the liver gets an acid bath, my dear.

"One more," Vale said.

"You're the boss," the bartender said, grinning and shaking his head. Vale's shoebox sat on the stool next to him. He and the bartender were the only living things in the room, though dozens of animal heads studded the walls. Deer, elk, big cats; everything blued by the television and the lottery machines. Vale eyed a moose mounted on a plank of glossy wood, its eyes a deep and fathomless black. *Grim.*

"My uncle hit a cougar once," Vale said. "With his truck. It was an accident. He had a buddy who was a taxidermist, so he had the thing mounted. Made the thing look so fierce in death, you know? Jaws open like this, all ready to pounce. But really he'd just run over the fucking thing."

The bartender nodded. He hooked a thumb over his shoulder toward something that looked a little like a fox. "I shot that one," he said. It was a tiny and sad-looking little thing, whorls of dirty red fur. Each ear was as big as its skull.

"Is that a baby?" Vale couldn't imagine shooting such a thing—a bullet would disintegrate it. "Is that a little baby fox?" He could feel the booze starting to warm him, sand off the angles of things.

"It's a kit fox," the bartender said. "They're actually endangered as hell, turns out. All I knew was it was getting in the old lady's tomatoes." He laughed.

"Did the rest of it disappear? When you shot it? I bet it just about evaporated."

"Oh yeah, pert near," the bartender said, happily enough. "Pretty much all that was *left* was the head, you know? Speaking of which, the hell happened to *your* head, bud?"

Vale leaned forward, angry at the bartender, angry at the off-handed ease with which he discussed shooting the little fox. Sick with the world. "I gave the Tasmanian Devil a blowjob," he sneered, holding his shot in front of his mouth. "I really *slobbed his knob,* man. Things got out of hand."

The bartender frowned and opened his mouth to say something—their friendship was clearly in danger—when from the restaurant came a chorus of bellows and one high-pitched scream, sounding for a moment like some truly awful a cappella group.

Vale staggered off his stool and into the restaurant. He saw a pair of men circling each other around a table in the middle of the room. Marvin stood at the front door, his hands on his hips. The waitress wrung her hands while the old men at the counter gazed from their stools, interested enough. The man holding the bat—a pot-bellied kid in a goofy shirt and a pair of jeans that looked like they'd been spray-painted on—pivoted to the right. The other kid, gaunt and sore-pocked, juked left.

"Goddamnit, Casper," the waitress said, "I am for real calling the police this time."

"Call whoever you want, Janelle," the kid with baseball bat snarled, feinting to the left again, not breaking eye contact with the other guy. "Me and Dunk need to get something straight between us." This prompted one of the men at the counter to bug out his eyes and hold his hand out in front of his pants, followed by a lot of laughter and knee-slapping.

"Oh, it'll be real hilarious when I bust all y'all's asses," Casper called out.

"Hell, son," one of the men said. "Looks like you couldn't bust your own ass with that thing."

With that, Casper took a half-hearted swing at Dunk over the table top. Dunk backpedaled and then toppled when he hooked a boot around a chair leg. The waitress screamed.

Casper scrambled around the table and raised the bat.

17

From the journals of Marvin Deitz:

Joan of Arc's execution took place on the morning of May 31st, 1431. She was, most historians agree, probably nineteen years old. She had been sold by the Duke of Burgundy and judged guilty by a room full of terrified theologians for, long story short, dressing as a man.

As English mercenaries watched over her day and night, leering and suggestive and brazen in their threats of assaulting and raping her during her imprisonment, she dressed as a man to dispel their advances. And was thusly judged a witch for it. She was brilliant and frequently acidic during Cauchon's interrogations, and always adamant in her faithfulness, even as he tried incessantly to verbally trip her up. I think Cauchon was afraid of her.

Joan of Arc, judged guilty of heresy and witchcraft. For dressing as a man to fend off advances from captors who should never have served as her guards in the first place. Had it been a proper trial she would have been placed in an ecclesiastical prison, had nuns as her guards. But not with Cauchon and the English involved, no way. There was a lot at stake here.

The execution took place at the Vieux-Marché in Rouen, not far at all from the marketplace where I had chased the tails of my father's coat those many years ago. So much of my life took place within the walls of that city, and so little of it worth anything.

The fug of horse shit and rotten vegetables still hung in the air amid the same clamor of voices. The air that particular morning was heavy with the stink of thousands of unwashed bodies, all of us packed together, vying for space.

Lines of English men-at-arms leered at the crowd, occasionally calling them names and brandishing swords if they got too close. Thousands of people. I heard a soldier tell Cauchon, who was gathered beyond the pyre with a clutch of his assessors, to hasten it up, lest his men grow impatient and do the deed themselves.

I have been participant to executions where the crowd had a kind of inexplicable joviality, as if it were a celebration. Blankets laid out, lunches unpacked. Children had played games while the gallows stood within arm's reach. But there was none of that today.

Joan was brought forth eventually and led the half dozen steps up the scaffold. Bracketing her was a pair of men I knew from their visits of mercy to the constabulary: the Fathers Isambart de la Pierre and Martin Ladvenu. Pious men. Good men, as far as those of their kind went. Joan was a diminutive girl no taller than Lavendu's shoulder. Her hair had been shorn, badly. She was dungeon-pale and murmured prayers to herself, her eyes closed tight.

"*Witch!*" someone in the crowd screamed in a voice shrill as scree loosing itself along a cliff side. No one took up the call. I saw more than a few English gloves tighten on the hafts of swords.

Lavendu took quiet counsel with Joan as she was lashed to the pillar and Cauchon, sweating in his cassock, ordered his men to lay the mounds of tinder beneath the scaffold on which she stood. Bitterly dry wood, stove-lengths of it, bleached white by the sun somewhere.

After some minutes of this, and disagreements among the men as to the best manner in which to stack the wood, Cauchon walked onto the scaffold and held a scroll before him. His judgment began with the words, "In the Name of the Lord: Amen," and his voice was high and reedy, wind whistling through the cracks in a wall.

I loathed him. He was little more than a bully hiding behind the impenetrable armor of Godliness, and it was beyond true that I had had my fill of bullies by then. Of course, I was one too, a monstrous one. A murderous one. It was our similarity, I realized, that drove me to hate him.

Cauchon pronounced Joan a relapsed heretic and it was read that we as a people would act as witness; we would see her cast off from the Church and she would be put to death. There was nothing beyond the sound of Cauchon's pitched voice and the occasional burst of wind soughing along the city walls. Crows cawed their dumb flap-winged amusements from the garrets.

Cauchon stepped down and Joan's lashings were adjusted again. Then the crowd grew still when she cast her gaze upon us and implored us all to pray for her and begged our pardon. She pardoned us for any harm we had done her. Her voice was high but without tremor and she asked Lavendu for a cross that she might pray with. Like I said, she was a pale girl, and her eyes were dusted with fatigue but also fiercely bright.

And I stood amazed when I saw an English soldier with a cross hanging loose in his tunic take it and, without a second glance, hand it to Father Lavendu. The father held it dumbly in his hand and looked back at the man, and I thought, *maybe.*

But then Lavendu stepped up the scaffold and placed it in the folds of Joan's tunic so that she could look down at it, and I felt then the terrible velocity with which we were moving, this end that we were all moving toward. Some great and untenable act from which we would not be able to come back.

And I understood then, looking out at those faces, how sometimes people feel a strident desire to finish a thing, even if it is the wrong thing. Even if it's terrible.

Another Englishman turned to Cauchon and cried, "What, priest, you'll keep us here until suppertime?" A scattering of laughter among them. An English captain turned to me with teeth like dark beads in his mouth and said, grinning, "That's right. Do it soon, harrier, or we will."

Joan prayed, gazing down at that ragged, twine-lashed cross leaning crooked in the folds of her clothing. The sky was flat and white above us all and I felt the nearness of God for the first time in my life.

No, that's wrong. Not the nearness of God.

What I felt was Joan's perfect, impervious belief in God.

Joan's belief.

I looked at her up there on the scaffold, and her faith was

like a living thing nearly coruscating around her. In all my days of leading men toward death, cajoling them toward it, hurtling them, all of my days in which a mere glance from me was enough to set them rambling and begging for their lives, I had never seen anyone approach death like this. And I looked around and there were those in the crowd now openly weeping, studied men and layman alike with eyes streaming tears under that frank iron sky. People of both countries, of supposedly different Gods, armed with different intentions. Openly weeping.

Cauchon was in meeting now with the Englishmen and his judges and there was another glimmer of hope then, of possibility, but then Cauchon's eyes found mine across the throng of people and I saw nothing there but a thirst to slake, a fear to quell, and he sent a runner to me who told me in a husky voice rife with bitterness, "The Bishop orders the pyre lit."

And I have sometimes permitted myself the luxury of wondering what would have happened had I not? Had I strode up the scaffolding and loosened Joan's bonds with the halberd in my belt? Would we have risen up against the English with their axes and swords? Eight hundred Englishmen against two thousand unarmed villagers, farmers?

Would that slaughter have been any more just or righteous or Godly than what I did instead?

I walked to where the torch was held for me, and Cauchon then would not turn his eyes my way. I held the torch, its sputtering flame, its dripping sparks and little globs of tumbling fire, and the English captain laughed again.

Joan's faith was like a radiance around her, but me? I was only myself. I was the grand summation of the things I had done.

"Hold a cross in your hand that I might see it," Joan pleaded, and Lavendu, weeping, pushed past me and placed himself in the crowd where she could see him, another cross in his hand now. She looked at the sky for a moment. The torch I held narrowed and flared against a flurry of wind.

She looked down at me then. The floor of the scaffold stood level with my chest, the wood piled beneath it. The look in her eyes was terrible, a thing beyond my understanding.

It was clear she pitied me.

"God be with you," she said kindly.

"And with you," I said, and turned my face away as I lowered the torch to the tinder.

The flames leapt, roared, wood blackening and soon glowing white and pink at their cores in hardly a minute, the smoke and heat rising in a shimmering funnel. The scaffolding lit then. The first flames licked her. Joan leaned her head against the pillar and cried Jesus's name. Her form wavered in the haze. The heat pulled my skin tight.

The flames ate her form, swallowed her. She cried Jesus's name again.

The world was a roaring cavalcade of fire and the faces around me, warped and shimmered, dark faces, and I looked to the sky for respite and this—oh!—*this* is what I saw near the end: I saw a white curl of smoke leave the flames and rise in the sky and take on the shape of a dove. It flew into the sky, wings beating, and vanished.

It was her soul, I knew. Joan's soul. Leaving her body, ascending to the heavens.

I dropped to my knees right there.

I had damned myself.

• • •

Truth be told, I had centuries of terrible violence to draw from. Even after my life as Geoffroy, there had been any number of horrors I had seen and taken part in. A willful participant.

All that's to say the fight that unfolded before us in the dining room of the Tip-Top was a little anticlimactic.

"Well, do it if you're gonna do it, boy," one of the counter men said to Casper, who stood there with his bat aloft.

Another sighed and said, "Go ahead and get your string up, son. My God."

"Couple of limp dicks," muttered a third, and turned back to his coffee cup. It was this that seemed to inspire both of the combatants toward some kind of action. The skinny one, Dunk, crab-walked across the floor, and Casper finally swung. I couldn't help but wince when the bat connected to the floor with a hollow *thwock* that you could see run all the way up his arms. Vale stood looking confused and very drunk in front of the lounge door.

Casper said, "You owe me an EMF meter, Dunk. Among other things."

"You're living a lie, man," Dunk cried out, still on his ass, arms raised in front of him.

"What about *Specter Detectives?* Huh?"

"No one's gonna watch your stupid show, idiot! *Rectum Detectives* is more like it."

"Why would you *say* that?" Casper lunged again, and now Dunk was scuttling *around* the table on his hands and knees. Casper lurched behind him, his hands choked up around the bat. We could all see he didn't have it in him.

"This is one sad deal," one of the men said, disgusted. He turned back to his plate.

"I want my money," Casper said. "My money or my gear. You pick."

"Jesus wept," the last counterman said before wheeling around on his stool.

Then Gary, our mechanic, walked past me and threaded his way though the tables. He laid his hand on the end of the bat. Casper turned and looked at him. What little fight there was deflated out of him like a balloon. Almost lovingly, Gary put him in a headlock.

"Casper, Duncan sold your meter for a bag of crank days ago. Give it a break. Getting money from him is like getting Thousand Island from a basset hound's tits, man. You can squeeze all you want, but it ain't happening."

From beneath the table, Dunk said, "Screw you, Gary."

Gary said, "You better stay down there you're gonna talk that way to me, you dickless wonder."

Gary pushed Casper over my way. He held the bat in his other hand. "Got a big heart, this one, but a little short on guts. Anyway I got your van all prepped and jacked up, but it's pushing nine o'clock and my old lady's gonna shit a brick if I don't get home soon. I'm gonna have to get the pump done in the morning." Conversational, as if stopping an assault was just another thing that was done in the Tip-Top.

Vale had heard Gary from across the room and threw up his

hands in disgust. He said, "Jesus Christ," and without another word pushed his way back into the lounge. Dunk stood up and made a show of dusting off his clothes, and then slunk into the nearest booth and sat down.

Gary hooked a thumb over his shoulder. "Motel next door's always got vacancies. I'll see you over at the shop at seven o'clock sharp. Won't take long to put that water pump in. I just gotta get home; the wife gets pissed otherwise."

"Thank you," I said.

"No biggie."

"Let me go, Gary," Casper said, his voice muffled.

"Shut up," Gary said, his bicep rising like a pool ball as he gave Casper a good shake. "You're gonna go over and apologize to Janelle for making a scene. You ought to know better."

Casper said, "I ain't going over there. Not a chance. Dunk's right there."

Gary shook his head and gave me a *What are you going to do?* kind of look. "Dunk doesn't care, Casper. He doesn't have your ghost meter thing but he doesn't have any shame, either." Gary spun around with Casper's head still buried in his armpit. "Dunk," Gary said, "you care if Casper heads over there?"

"Hell, I don't care," Dunk said glumly, spinning a coffee cup around.

Gary let him go. "See that?"

Casper ran his hands over his hair and spent quite a while putting his baseball cap on just right. Then he went over and quietly apologized to Janelle the waitress. He got a fair amount of ribbing from the men at the counter.

Janelle brought my pie.

Just a normal night at the Tip-Top.

18

There were accidents.

Quite a lot of them.

Congress eventually needed to devise a term for them, if only to appease the insurance industry, and so smoke-related accidents and injuries generally fell under the heading of *Unintended Collateral Results.*

For instance.

A Town Hall meeting was held in Encinitas, California in July. There'd been a marked increase in looting and crime downtown since the smokes had appeared; several shops had had their windows broken and a jewelry store, nearly its entire inventory taken. The city council and the sheriff, begrudgingly, came up with a rotating roster of officers to patrol the downtown area twenty-four hours a day.

"It's a stop-gap measure," the sheriff said, but the people didn't care. The town's biggest industry was poinsettias, for God's sake; let someone else, let *San Diego* have its jewelry heists and crime. People lived in goddamned Encinitas to get away from that.

During the town's Classic Car Cruise Night a week later, loads of purring, finned Corvettes and low-slung Mustangs cruised up and down the town's stretch of 101, the air heady with the scent of exhaust and cotton candy, mothers pushing babies in strollers, sticky-faced toddlers being pulled alongside, with couples in sunglasses walking arm in arm.

A monthly affair, Cruise Night, and the usual sense of frivolity and raucousness was tampered only slightly by the pairs of police officers stationed every few blocks.

It was a beautiful evening, the purr of the surf heard beneath the rumbling of the cars, the laughter and clamor of the kids. The moon hung fat over the sea. The police felt prepared, pairs of men glancing steel-eyed among the pedestrians. Prepped for anything: any one of these people could be the mastermind behind a jewelry heist, could be poised to burn down a poinsettia farm for kicks or deface the side of Swami's. They were ready for anything.

Anything except the ghost of a Viet Cong soldier appearing in the middle of 101.

Wearing sandals and dark fatigues that faded to nothingness. A ghost man brandishing a ghost AK-47. Right there in the highway, his eyes wide white *O*'s.

Bedlam ensued. People bolted, single flip-flops lay scattered on the sidewalks like strange carapaces. People dropped water bottles, iPhones. Someone ran their Barracuda into a fire hydrant. Car alarms blared. Babies crying.

The nearest deputies, both terrified—neither having seen a smoke in person before, both of them thinking more than a little bit that it was all probably some kind of joke—ordered the VC to drop to his knees and release his weapon.

When the man did not comply, did not even seem to hear them, one of the deputies opened fire. He fired eleven rounds, all the rounds in his pistol, none of which had any effect on the apparition.

Two rounds, however, entered the chest cavity and exited the back of an eight-year-old boy who had been watching the cars with his father before they were to meet the boy's mother at a nearby restaurant.

These things happened. These and more.

Unintended Collateral Results.

19

Marvin went to the motel to get them rooms. Vale invited him to come back for a drink but Marvin begged off. Vale himself was surprised to find that on a Tuesday night, the lounge of the Tip-Top apparently attracted every alcoholic, dope fiend and wanting-to-party redneck within a fifty mile radius. The fox-killing bartender, who everyone called Jimmy Two (or was it Jimmy Too?), muted all the televisions and turned on the jukebox. A nauseating flow of auto-tuned country songs rattled forth.

Vale ordered shot after shot of whiskey with beer backs. Cowboy hats and mesh-back baseball caps were the only constants throughout the room, and cans of chewing tobacco whitened the back pockets of many a pair of jeans.

A woman sat down next to Vale at the bar. She had a tsunami of gelled hair and a pair of gigantic breasts that struggled against the constraints of her top and seemed, like everyone else in the bar, infused with a kind of unwitting melancholy, the result, Vale assumed, of having spent your entire life in a thirty-mile radius.

"Hon," she said, "you look about like how I feel." She laughed shrilly and rubbed the bar with one hand as if she had a rag.

Vale sat silent and petrified. Decades of bravado had vanished with his fleeting fame. He was suddenly vastly interested in the television playing in front of him. He lifted his bottle up, that reassuring clink of glass against his teeth.

She turned to him and planted an elbow on the bar. "What happened to your head?"

He couldn't help it—his eyes skittered up her cleavage like a mole rat up a cliffside. She winked at him and pressed her knee against his leg.

"Motorcycle accident," he said, the first thing that came to him.

"Oooh," the woman said.

A man stepped up to the bar on Vale's other side. He slugged back his drink and exhaled, shook his head like a mastiff sloughing off water. He was possibly the hairiest man Vale had ever seen, with a beard that crept up nearly to his eyes. Into the mouth of his glass he said, "Don't do it, Maura."

"I'll do what I want, Robby," the woman snapped. "You little two-pump chump."

Robby sighed and motioned to Jimmy Two for another drink.

"Hit me again too," Maura said, leaning over on her elbows. Jimmy Two shared an uncomfortable glance with Robby and said, "It's on Robby's card, Maura. And he says no. Sorry."

"I'll buy her a drink," Vale said. Maura beamed.

Jimmy Two looked at all of them, sad and uncomfortable. Vale was too, but here was something—if not the Moment, then at least something else. Some feeling. Robby leaned his massive sagging face toward Vale's ear and said, almost kindly, "Don't write a check that your ass can't cash, mister man."

"Whatever he's saying," Maura said, "don't listen to him."

Robby peered at her over Vale's shoulder. "We aren't divorced yet, Maura."

"Consider it done," she said, waving her hand like she was writing something in the air. "You've been infidelitous on me for the last time."

Vale pushed a twenty toward the bartender, who said, "I wish you wouldn't, bud."

Vale said, "Get her a drink, Jimmy. Jimmy Two. Can I call you Jimmy Two?"

Jimmy Two said, "You can't." Then he said to Maura, "You know this guy gave a blowjob to the Tasmanian Devil, right?" He walked off with Vale's money.

Maura laughed and slapped her hand on the bar like Jimmy Two had told the best joke ever. Vale's head was full of light and fog.

Robby drank and fumed beside him. His glass looked tiny inside his gigantic furry hand. Vale couldn't be sure, but it looked like he had hair on every knuckle on his finger, right down to the fingernail. Like a werewolf redneck in a plaid shirt. On the jukebox some cowgirl drawled in a voice heavy as syrup, *"He's my truck-drivin, fly-fishin, straight-shootin maaaaaaan. Uh-huh! And he knows just how I like it."*

"You're buying yourself a world of hurt," Robby said. "One shit storm bought and paid for. Not even on layaway." Vale turned to him and smiled. The Moment would not be making an appearance tonight. But yes, *something* would be happening, he was sure of it. He felt loose-boned and impervious to harm. Robby could throw him against the wall and he would bounce off, not hurt until tomorrow. He would either sleep tonight in the glorious hammock of Maura's breasts or be beaten to a pulp in a gravel parking lot by her monstrous, furry, estranged husband. Either one would work because either one was beyond where he was now. His head wobbled on his shoulders.

"This one cheated on me," Maura said. "With that fat-assed Becky Tomlinson down at the Stihl outlet. 'I gotta go get oil for the chainsaw, honey,'" she said in a shockingly good imitation of Robby's baritone. "Coming home ten o'clock at night, reeking of poontang and motor oil, good God."

"A man has needs," Robby said petulantly, and Vale laughed.

Maura leaned over onto the bar again—a breathtaking spill of cleavage in his peripheral, and Vale's eyes rabbited up to the television again—and said, "Yeah, well, you ain't the only one. I know you're hearing me over there."

Jimmy came back and reluctantly pushed Maura's drink across the bar. It was some cloudy pink thing that looked like he had poured some evil combination of liquor over a can of fruit cocktail. It emboldened her, and she put her arm around Vale's neck, pushed her breasts against him. Jimmy Two did not give him any change.

"I might just take this buck right here," Maura said.

Robby shook his head, wounded and shocked. "This dirty, scabbed-up motherfucker? You wouldn't."

Maura sucked some of her drink through a swirly red straw that lay shipwrecked in the fruity island of her glass. "You keep telling me what I will and won't do, Robby. See what happens."

"Maura—"

"How's Becky these days? How's your *chainsaw,* stud?"

"I told you I was sorry about it."

"You told me *one time* you were sorry about it, and then you *went and did it again!*"

"What do you want me to do? Get down on my fuckin' knees?"

"I want you to get the hell out of here. I'm on a date." Maura cinched her arm tighter around Vale's neck; he couldn't help but think of Casper in a headlock a few hours before. She smelled like gin and hairspray and a perfume that reminded him of magazine samples. Her fingernails were painted turquoise, and he saw a line where her pale scalp met her orange spray-on tan and even in his embattled state felt the stirrings of an erection.

Vale grinned and placed his hand on the small of Maura's back. "You blew it, Robby."

Robby pushed himself off the bar and pulled Maura's arm off of him. Then he put his own hand on the back of Vale's neck. His fingers almost met at Vale's throat, he was that big. "I don't know what weird-ass, liberal Portland hobo camp you came out of, but it's time for you to go back there, asshole."

"Hell," Maura said, leaning over and licking Vale's ear. "Me and him might even put that shit up on YouTube, you never know."

Robby, still with one hand around Vale's neck, drew his other hand into a fist, held it out in front of Vale. He couldn't help it, it was so silly: he laughed, and so did Maura.

And then someone behind them said, "Excuse me," and Robby turned, bringing Vale along with him. And there was Marvin, whose head came roughly to Robby's midsection. "I was wondering," Marvin said absently, as if to begin some long-winded question about directions, and he struck his fingertips to the inside of Robby's free arm, a little jab. It didn't seem like much.

Robby promptly sank to his knees, his face opening up in a soundless scream.

Marvin looked up and said, "I got us a couple rooms, Mike."

"Jesus fudge mothershit that hurts so bad oh my God—"

"We should get going," Marvin said, as Robby gasped and pawed weakly at their knees with his good arm. "Lot of driving to do tomorrow." Vale let himself be led away.

20

From the journals of Marvin Deitz:

The English ordered the body burned three times. After they raked through the remains, a rumor wove through the stunned crowd: Joan's heart lay uncharred among the ruins. Much of the crowd had vanished by then, but not all of them. Those that remained looked reproachful, dazed. Sick at what we'd done.

I heard a man cry out that there, there was her heart! Her heart! Though it was simply a bulb of red coal that glowed when revealed to the open air. Inside me whirled a funnel cloud of fear, the blooming certainty of damnation.

The ashes were burned again, men adding fresh tinder and hunks of wood to the ashes and char. We stood tending it throughout the rest of the day and then in the growing gloom.

It was dusk, and I could smell only woodsmoke by the time I was bid to rake the ash and gather it up in a wagon for transport to the Seine. I had already burned my gloves, the torchwood itself, all the things that were considered soiled and unusable. Night blued the building tops around us.

We dissipated without word, Cauchon's appointed men and the English soldiers told to keep watch over us. I wandered the streets of Rouen in a daze as a dense rain began to fall, persistent but warm as whirling ash. All eyes, I was convinced, were upon me. I felt as if Death himself rode at my side. A boy passed by carrying a tankard of wine for delivery. I took it from him and flung some coins at his feet.

"Give it back!" he crowed, reaching for me.

I touched the halberd at my side and said, "Take your coins and run. Persist and it's the gallows for you, boy." He saw my coat, the maelstrom in my eyes, and fled. The stars wheeled above and the walls of the city pulsed with torchlight. I drank the wine. Few people were out that night.

The tavern quieted when I entered. I'd finished the tankard.

"Why the gloom," I cried, toppling into the barman's counter. "Why the silence when Death's messenger enters?" Men shrank from me. I staggered to the hearth—my life seemed dedicated to flame this day—and pulled my blade from its scabbard. I waved it around, like a fool. "A pox upon us all!" I bellowed, wine-drunk and mad, when I felt a hand on my shoulder. It shocked me. I could not remember the last time I'd been touched.

"Monsieur Thérage."

Father Lavendu stood there with red-rimmed eyes. I knew him those few times we'd passed in the constabulary; he was more than once called in for sacraments and last rites among my prisoners.

I grinned. "I have damned myself, father. Make no mistake. It was me, lit the pyre of Joan of Orléans today."

Lavendu's smile was sad. Still his hand rested on my shoulder. "If you weren't the flame-bearer today, someone else would have been."

"I saw her soul leave her body," I said, my voice wavering. I sank to a chair and wept, laying my cheek against the rough-hewn wood of the table.

My history of torture, my livelihood of ruination and murder, had culminated in this moment: broken down, drunk, weeping in front of a priest amid a roomful of men who loathed and feared me.

The barkeep came around the counter and stepped close, nervously eyeing the blade still in my hand. "Father, beg pardon, but he needs to leave. Paying folks should be close to the fire, not the likes of him. Men here are just as like to kill him right now anyway."

"I understand," Lavendu said.

I gripped the table with those killer's hands and watched the barman flinch as I raised my head and howled in that dim room. Drunks cowered at the sound, pulled their shoulders to their ears. Six hundred years later I cringe at the unabashed melodrama of it, but at the time? I meant it. I was anguished. I howled for myself, and for Joan, for what had been taken from us both. I'd hoped it would rend something inside me, change somehow the immutable fact of her death.

• • •

Vale stomped along beside me, slack-jawed, his footsteps heavy on the gravel. The air was heavy with night sounds, moths battering the lights along the motel eaves.

"How did you do that?" Vale slurred.

"Do what?"

"The thing with that guy's arm. He was crying like a baby." Vale belched, squinting his eyes shut and then opening them wide. "Like a gigantic, hairy, stupid baby that was full of shit."

"You're very drunk," I said.

An odd byproduct of the Curse: muscle memory lived a surprising half-life. I'd sometimes find myself the recipient of blips and bursts of centuries-old information. Brushing my teeth above the record store, I'd suddenly remember the protocol for dissecting a cadaver in the seventeenth century or, I don't know, how to operate a steam-powered printing press. I had a rudimentary, working remembrance of eight or ten languages.

When I stepped into the bar, one of those whispers had slipped in, some ghostly framework of jujitsu coming back to me. It wasn't something I could control, and I probably couldn't even do it again. It was like getting a melody stuck in your head for a bit.

Vale walked behind me, his chin dipped into breastbone, shoebox like a pillow tucked under his arm, weaving in the gravel.

I handed him the key to his room. He stabbed it toward the doorknob a few times. I took it back from him, let him in. His room was the same as mine: burnt-orange carpeting, faux wood paneling that would buckle against a toddler's tantrum. I opened the drawer next to the bed and the corpse of a mosquito sat on top of a Bible, its wingspan almost as large as my hand.

Vale fell onto the bed face-first. "Forgot my backpack in the van," he croaked, his face mashed into the pillow, his shoebox beside him.

"I'm not undressing you," I said. "You're on your own."

"G'night, Marvin," Vale slurred. "Thank you for saving me from the Hairy Shit Baby." When I touched the doorknob, he said with an aching clarity and sounding entirely sober, "I really do miss my wife."

I said, "Your wife?" but he was already out.

I turned out the lights and left. Then I went back in and put the wastebasket next to his head. In my own room, it took me a long time to get to sleep. I listened to the rattle of the pipes in the walls, the bursts of laughter and yelling and country music from the bar across the road. I thought of Joan and how she might have moved through a world like this, what she would have done here.

WEDNESDAY

1

They made their way down to the garage, Vale's guts still twisted from his morning heave. The fields shone golden beyond the road, each blade of grass spotted with dew, the deep blue sky above flecked with a few ragged tatters of cloud.

It was gorgeous, and nausea clutched Vale like a jealous lover. Through the window of the Tip-Top they could see a few countermen drinking coffee, leafing through the morning paper, trading lies. Marvin walked with his face cast up toward the sun, the black lens of his glasses kicking back sparks from its reflection. The stride of the smug and sober, Vale thought, thumbing sweat from his eye. His hands were brick-like with cold, thrumming with tremors. His guts felt watery and loose, and some minor demon had clearly taken a shit inside his eye sockets in the middle of the night. The hangovers seemed to be getting worse.

"You want to get something to eat before we go? Might be a good idea."

"Food? Christ, Marvin, you're going to make me puke again."

Gary greeted them in the dim cavern of the garage, the bay doors open to the day. He cast a shrewd eye at Vale, who stood with his hands jammed in his pockets, shivering; his ever-present shoebox tucked under one arm.

"God dang, somebody had some beers, looks like," Gary said, clapping him on the shoulder. Vale grunted. The van sat there in the gloom, silent and grimy with dust. It was impossible to tell what had or had not been done to it.

"Well," Gary said, packing a plug of chew into his bottom lip, "she's ready to rip."

Vale lifted his head. "It's ready to go?"

"I fixed the ever-loving shit out of it, man."

"We're not going to get fifty miles down the road," Vale said, "and some other piece of the engine seizes up or something."

"I don't believe so, bud, no. I fixed it, is what I'm saying."

"Awesome. What do I owe you?"

"I'll tell you what," Gary said, looking thoughtfully at the dust-wracked van. "Don't worry about it."

Marvin frowned. "What do you mean, don't worry about it?"

Gary walked out into the sunlight and spat on the gravel, his hands in his back pockets. "Listen, you guys seem nice enough." He lifted his chin toward Vale. "You got a lot of stuff going on." Vale couldn't tell if Gary specifically meant his injury or just the general, overall mess that he was. "How about you just get down there to LA and we'll call it good. Follow your dreams and all that shit."

"No, really," Vale said, beginning to pull back the taped flap of the shoebox. Any act of goodwill was one housed in treachery and deceit; Brophy had taught him that. No, he'd taught *himself* that. Life had taught him that. Nothing was free. This would inevitably bite him in the ass somewhere down the road. "I'm happy to pay you."

"Seriously, keep your money," Gary said.

"What's the catch, man?"

Gary held out his hands, shrugged. "No catch. That pump was doing jack shit around here anyway. Like I said, if it isn't built Ford tough, we don't have much use for it around here." Vale and Marvin traded glances. Marvin shrugged.

Back on the highway the day opened up blue and wide in front of them. Vale gripped his hands tight to the wheel to stop their shaking. He felt chilled beads of sweat on his forehead, the small of his back. The bottles beneath his seat sang out to him like sirens, cruel little brown-glassed mermaids calling out to this shipwreck of his body, his heart.

Marvin said, "You want me to drive?"

"I'm good," he said. The bottles clinked against each other.

Let's just shut up about it and get there, he thought. *Let's just do this one thing well.*

2

From the journals of Marvin Deitz:

After Joan came the winding down of my life.

While I still performed executions, still pulled corpses from the prisons and dispatched diseased animals at surrounding farms, I hired no apprentice to take my place. Word got around regarding my behavior at Rouen and in the tavern following. If it was possible, I became even more of a pariah.

I honestly, truly believed I was damned, heedless of what I did with my remaining days.

This alone made me a fearsome man for the first time in my life.

What had been cruelty measured with theater before now became staunch heartlessness. I lacked compunction. Joan's death—and seeing her soul take flight through the smoke—had carved that from me. There would be no pardon from God.

In Rouen, in the hallways and stinking chambers beneath the constabulary, I would speak at length of my own damnation to the prisoners, my fear of it, my assuredness, as I performed any number of atrocities upon them. I've wondered since if this is where the seedling of my need to confess was planted. Christ, I hope not.

It horrified them, of course—my confession stacked upon what I did to their bodies, their minds.

I became wraithlike in my terror, my disregard.

Those last five years of my life, word spread throughout France:

Fear the executioner, the old man Geoffroy Thérage, who believed himself the murderer of a saint. He's crazy, and there's nothing— absolutely nothing—he won't do to a man.

I sought out Father Lavendu once, but he had moved to another parish farther south, hoping assumedly to cast the pall of Joan's killing from his eyes. The English stayed on and the war continued with victories for each swaying like the tide, the only constants being the ceaseless and unnecessary death of men and the dying of the crops. I, for my part, crossed the road whenever a holy man came near. I wanted no truck with it: Lavendu was the only religious man I'd have spoken to.

I dreamt of Joan, Cauchon, and damnation, all in equal measure.

My death came in 1436. Esme had died the year before of pneumonia, and as such, the home had fallen into great misuse. I paid a priest an astonishing sum to deliver last rites over her body. The desire to mourn was inside me, the idea of it, some small flower of grief that wanted to bloom, but it would not take root. I dug a grave and buried her next to our mother.

I slept solitary on a bed of damp straw and, alone now, felt the rats skitter over my legs in the night. Sections of the roof fell in. I spent my nights at home wrapped in rags, staring into the hissing hearth, my unwashed hands frequently darkened in the gore of recalcitrant men. I hardly ate. I looked for sigils of my future in the wavering coals.

My death, when it arrived, came from my horse. Of all things! Laughable. This was something I was to learn about death—how many ways besides war there are in which to die, the majority of them graceless and terrible, and so many of them full of a kind of dark mirth.

The mules, of course, had decades ago been butchered, and I had no use for a wagon anymore, as I needed little more than a simple blade and a gaze to extract confession or perform executions.

I had purchased a mare, old when I bought her; she had seemed a steady and diffident animal. I did not mistreat or abuse her: I could take the fingers off a man as if sawing through a rind of dry bread and I would feel nothing save my own impending doom, but the idea of ever hurting an animal simply did not cross my mind. The mare slept tethered in the house, her own sets of rags bundled over her for warmth.

Even now I feel I had done nothing to elicit her resentment or mistrust.

And yet the kick came one windswept rainy morning as I leaned behind her, reaching for that very coat my father had worn before me. I had cast it to the floor the night before, a stinking and blood-soaked thing. I reached for it, and the kick came from an animal who had never shown me any inkling of ill will, an animal so old I hardly thought her capable of kicking at all.

It's enough to make you wonder, isn't it?

• • •

We were nearly at the California border. The van was infused with Vale's rancid sweat and deep sense of melancholy. I was trying to write in one of my journals, the words wavering, while quelling a bout of nausea. I've never quite gotten the hang of cars, even as a passenger.

The wind roared through Vale's open window. Outside were vistas of grape fields and mountains dim and snow-shot in the distance, wineries and their tasting rooms like gaudy toys flung on the hills—but next to the highway itself were the boxy outlets, the strip malls, the parking lots and gas stations.

I had just put my journal in my duffel bag when someone in the back of the van said, "Hey, you guys are still going to LA, right?"

Vale screamed and swerved to the left, very nearly collid-ing with a rust-battered Camaro that appeared to be leaking pot smoke from its windows. The Camaro swerved toward the shoulder, fishtailed and swerved back toward us. A hand with its middle finger extended rose from the window's smoky depths. Well, I thought, this is how I'm going. Highway collision. Damn. But the Camaro smoothed out and drove ahead of us. It was a close thing.

"*Motherfucker!*" Vale bellowed into the rear view mirror, then lashed his head over his shoulder, trying to look through the for-tress of stacked boxes in the back.

And that's when Casper's head and shoulders rose up; he'd built himself a little fort back there, hidden himself amid the boxes and blankets. Vale had his hangover, but what was my excuse? How in God's name had I missed *that*?

"Better pull over," I said.

3

They stood on the shoulder of the highway, the passing traffic flattening their clothes against them. Casper refused to come out from behind the boxes. Vale leaned in the open sliding door and yelled at him.

"I'm not coming out when you're like this," Casper said. He sat there, cross-legged and resolute.

Vale was incredulous. His mouth hung open, his dirty bandage waving behind his head. "When *I'm* like this? You're in my van, man. You're like, *inside* it."

Casper held up his palms. "I'm just trying to get a ride to LA. Just like you guys. Gary told me to hop in, keep my head down. Come on, Marvin. It's just a ride"

Vale pointed. "I'm Mike. He's Marvin. And you're a stowaway."

"Well, this explains why Gary was so generous," Marvin said quietly.

"He's looking out for me. You know? Listen," Casper said, "I really have to pee. But how do I know you guys won't drive away if I come outside?"

A semi passed, the van rocking in its wake.

"Drive away? I should kick your ass," Vale said.

Marvin hiked an arm up on the roof and leaned in the van's doorway. "Get out of the van, Casper."

Casper sighed and pushed his way past the boxes. He clambered out and held up one finger. "I'll be right back," he said. "Don't leave." He trotted down into the trash-strewn ditch, below the sight line of passing traffic.

"Jesus," Vale said. "I am not turning back and taking that kid back to Hicksville. I'm already late."

Marvin nodded. "I don't want to go back either."

Vale blew smoke, looked down at Casper pissing into the weeds. "What a mess."

"Could've been worse."

"That Camaro?" Vale said.

"Yeah, that was close."

Vale sighed. "Should just leave the dipshit right here."

"Too late," Marvin said. "He's coming back."

• • •

The tails of Vale's bandages snapped in the breeze. He was full of a bubbling, jovial fury. Marvin was back to writing in his notebook, and Casper had pushed some boxes aside and now sat behind the two seats and peered out the windshield.

Vale was sweating for a beer, smoking furiously. He kept thinking about pulling over and putting the sack of unopened bottles on the side of the road and couldn't bring himself to do it. He kept thinking of picking Casper up by the collar of his dumb shirt and throwing him out onto the shoulder of the highway and couldn't do that either. He stared at the kid in the rearview mirror and said, "So tell me, what is it that's going to keep you afloat in Kodiak chew and ironic shirts when you're in Los Angeles? My new friend Casper?"

Casper peered down at his chest. "What do you mean, ironic shirts?"

Vale's eyebrows arched up. "I mean your shirt, man. The bald eagle holding the beer? Driving the truck? It's ridiculous."

"How is it ironic?"

"You mean it's *not* ironic?"

Casper shrugged. "I don't know. I like trucks. I like beer. Eagles are cool. I like it."

Marvin laughed into his notebook.

"Okay," Vale said, rolling his shoulders. "Whatever. Let me rephrase. Why are you going to LA, Casper?"

"Truth?"

"Sure," Vale said. "Yeah."

"I want to do a show about the ghosts. *Specter Detectives*. I've got the whole thing planned out."

Sagging fence posts ticked past like metronomes. Vale sat with it for a moment. "You want to do a show. About the smokes," he said slowly.

Marvin turned around in his seat. "You want to make, what? A documentary?"

"Reality show." Casper drummed his fingers on a box beside him. "Me and Dunk were filming the pilot."

"Dunk being the guy in the restaurant," Vale said, changing lanes, "that you kind of pussed out on going after with a baseball bat."

"Dunk," Casper said, "being the guy that quit going to his NA meetings a few months back and sold all of our gear for crystal. We've been friends since sixth grade, me and him. I should've seen it coming. He's had a tough time with it."

"So you're going to go to LA to become a movie star." He looked over at Marvin. "Nothing clichéd about that."

"Come on, Mike," Marvin said.

"Man, I'm a *paranormal investigator*. There's a science involved."

"God help us," Vale said, switching lanes again.

As if in response, the bottles beneath his seat clinked. He felt the warmth of the sun on his arms, the breeze, heard the static roar of the open window. If he could stay living in every single moment and just not move from there, always stay poised in that specific millisecond, he might have half a chance. Beyond that was where everything got screwed. A lifetime ago, such a notion would have made a decent painting. The reality of that, the simple loss of it, the ghost of that *love* of something, hit him like a blow to the chest.

"There's ten thousand people," he said acidly, "who'll knife you in the ass before you even get started, Casper. That's the entertainment world. Trust me. I know. That's the world for you."

"Whatever, man."

Candice would have loved this, he thought. She'd have welcomed the ridiculousness of it all, even his vitriol directed at this sweet kid. He could practically hear her: *Nice work, Mike. Even though you're an asshole, it's nice to see you getting out of the house.*

4

Some people argued there were certain hot spots. Geographic focal points. Scientists weren't offering up all that much information yet; the country still seemed restricted to a bevy of talking heads and unfounded speculation—but if there was one thing Brophy knew, it was that every layman wanted his opinion heard.

So people argued. Incessantly. Callers on radio shows, the girls in his office, whoever. And Brophy listened. People were saying that there were particular places with a commonality, where smokes seemed to gather, to appear more frequently. *Heavy traffic,* one guy on his sports show had said, and that stuck with him. What people couldn't fathom was why some of them appeared in the most goddamned inopportune places. Was it just the law of averages or what?

A perfect example: where Brophy was right now. Sun heavy in the sky, late morning. Traffic should be reasonably light. Right there where Highway 10 and Highway 60 joined together, right before the river, and a radio station's traffic report had just called in another sighting, claiming that it was a "point of repeated apparition appearances" and to expect heavy delays. The highway shoulders were bracketed with the now-familiar fleets of cop cars flanking CDC vehicles, the dicks in their hazmat suits wandering around, yellow lights painting the air. All for a single smoke a mile up the road, an apparition morose and distraught and oblivious, one who would most likely walk around in circles for a minute or an hour and hurt nobody, and then vanish.

Meanwhile, an hour-long commute got stretched to two, three. More.

But why there? Why so often in that spot? It was a question—one among many—worth asking. No one could say for sure, but everyone had an opinion. One of the guys in Brophy's office argued that sites with heavy traffic could be places where great violence had occurred. Like hauntings.

There'd been talk of investigations in certain areas, looking for mass graves, perhaps. Some kind of evidence, which Brophy thought was hilarious. If people thought the President, the Governor of California and anybody at Caltrans were going to unanimously green-light digging up the ground beneath the 10 and the 60 and potentially exhume a bunch of bones, they were fucking nuts.

A lot of people took it as a sign of a flat-out gleeful malevolence on the part of the spirits—the smokes making standstill traffic even more choked up—that they were sentient, at least to that extent. Like gremlins, rooted in mischief, getting off on humanity's discomfort and irritation.

Brophy, who was, in his doctor's words, *terminally ill,* and who felt his own mortality perilously crouched on his shoulders like an animal about to jump off, thought that was a pretty lofty and self-centered view of humanity's desperate need to get home and watch reruns of *New Girl.*

And still others argued the "if a tree falls" theory: Yes, the smokes were seen repeatedly on freeways, and in the stands at Dodger Stadium, at bus benches in Irvine, in a particular hospital emergency room in Ensenada, Mexico, yes. But it was at least arguable: it wasn't because there were more of them coming through in those particular spots, but there were just more people around to see them. There were more of the living there to lay witness. *What about the forests?* someone posed on one of the call-in shows, and Brophy had nodded, felt this minute sense of vindication. It was exactly right. What about the deserts? How many smokes were wandering right this minute through the dusty, broiling expanses of Death Valley? Or alone among the rock-strewn gorges outside of Cananea? If there was no one there to see them, did they still appear?

Traffic surged forward a few car lengths and Brophy found himself idling next to one of the CDC trucks, a safety-orange beast festooned in whirling lights and stencil fonts proclaiming people to keep their distance. The guy inside had his hazmat hood off and was eating a sandwich, his eyes glassy as he chewed. The guy on the radio said, "Just doesn't look like there's any end in sight, folks," and Brophy changed the station.

5

From the journals of Marvin Deitz:

What comes after death?
     For me, I mean.
     Yup: birth. Right.
     The Curse works like this: Memory arrives in lockstep with sentience, with self-awareness. It arrives all at once, *boom*. A detonation. I'm a newborn handed this sudden bomb-blast of identity, this explosive memory of all previous lives lived all at once. Even as synapses struggle to form, neurons connecting with muscle cells.
     I'm not sure specifically when this detonation occurs, this awareness, but I'd say it generally happens before my first birthday. Certainly before I'm crawling. There's probably, like my deaths, never a specific time—or at least one that I've yet to discern.
     Let me put it like this: I died as Geoffroy Thérage from a kick from my horse, a graceless and laughable death, and was reborn. So much of that first rebirth is thankfully lost to me. I do remember the physicality of it, brief shutter-clicks of imagery as my memory came back to me: howling until my tiny throat rent itself hoarse, trying to scratch at my own body with those hands that would not, could not, act out my desires—a simple issue of motor control. I lay there roiling inside my own skin.
     I had no idea where I was, of course, and sanity was a fleeting thing that first time around—I'm sorry, but how could it *not* be?

Time was elastic, malevolent. They put little swatches of fabric over my hands to protect me from myself. Blurred swatches of color slowly became tapestries that hung against stone walls, as rugs on the floor.

Dark-skinned women cooed over me in no language I had ever heard. I was eventually aware of the sputtering candles clustered around my crib, their falling flames marking the passage of my hours, my days. Sleep came stealthily and often, an interloper I was grateful for.

I would dream of Esme and Riva giggling as they tried to fit my father's hood around the head of one of the mules until my mother came out and scolded them, a twinkle in her eye. I would awaken smiling at this and for a moment the face hovering over me would brighten—*He's smiling!*—until the understanding of my circumstances returned to me and I would begin howling again.

It was not the damnation I'd expected, of course, but the simple memory of the atrocities was enough.

Sometimes, one of the women would set me on the floor, make sounds to encourage me to crawl to her. I felt the smooth purl of the tapestry's weave beneath my little hands, the baying wolfhounds and knighted men emblazoned across it. I crawled toward her.

Soon I began using the walls and banisters of my crib to pull myself upright: my first shuffling, stumbling steps. It felt like perhaps seconds had passed—that this was simply a nightmare I was locked into.

The woman would laugh and clap as I crawled, until the day I rose on my little stilted legs and, her back momentarily turned, pulled myself to the lip of my crib and spilled myself upon the stone floor of the nursery.

Picture it, the texture of any given moment: the slats of a crib around your tiny, kicking legs, broad swaths of coarse fabric against you, voices in the hall speaking in unknowable tongues. But also in your mind: Esme's face, and your father pressing the clotted spike against a man's eye, and Luc, and Joan the Maid's pyre turned to glowing ash, and all the terrible things you had wrought upon men.

And that was just the first life, right?

Imagine that three dozen times—four—each with its own set of requisite horrors.

What do you *think* happened?

What do you think happened when death had become simply a brief moment of silence between lives?

After I cast myself to that stone floor, dashing my skull upon the stone, I woke again to *that* memory—the tapestries, the nurse-maids—as well as my life as Geoffroy.

My world the third time was a hut of some kind, a hole in the roof for the smoke to climb, the blazing, dripping green of a jungle outside.

I remembered it all. I always did.

So this is what happened to me. My post-Geoffroy biography:

I lived and died and lived again, and centuries of madness followed.

• • •

We stopped at a rest area just short of the state line where a man stood in front of the cinder block restrooms proselytizing with a box of tracts at his feet. Vale went into the restroom, and Casper stood and stretched and listened to the man's sermon. I sat in the van watching him.

He was a strange one, Casper, but mostly in the fact that he seemed open and unharmed in ways that Vale and I clearly had been harmed. I watched him walk up and speak to the preacher while everyone else hustled in and out with their heads down, trying their best to avoid contact.

After a while, the man reached down and thumbed through the box at his feet, handing Casper a stack of pamphlets. They shook hands. Casper came back and sat in the open door of the van, thumbing through them.

"You made a friend."

"I'll be honest, guy made about as much sense as jumbo shrimp, man."

"It's a strange world these days," I said. "A cult?"

"Definitely," Casper said. In a stiff, formal voice, not too loud to catch the preacher's attention, he read, "*From Static to Signal: Discovering the Almighty's Resonance in a Time of Sin. Issued by the Transmittal Foundation for Eternal Life.* These guys apparently think that God's next instructions will come through radio frequencies."

"Not even the internet, huh?"

"Guess not."

"Points for creativity, at least."

"Maybe," Casper said. We saw Vale stomp out of the restroom and Casper tucked his feet in and slid the door shut. "I feel like ghosts appearing? That kind of levels the field. You know? I mean, I think he's a kook, but he could be as right as anyone, seems like. Like you said, it's a strange world."

As science stumbled to find a reason for the ghosts, religion had strode forth and laid claim. Cults bloomed. Most sat squarely in the field of doom, hellfire and the end of days. Like most people, the idea that they could be right—that we were counting down to some kind of oblivion—scared me. I mean, I had lived for centuries and never seen them. This was different. But Casper was also right—the world was up for grabs.

Maybe, somehow, this was something good. Who knew?

Maybe, ultimately, it was just something that was happening, and people ascribed good or bad to it.

Casper mock-roared when we passed the California border, shaking his fists, and we gassed up in Mount Shasta, a town as close to a medieval village as you could probably get in America today.

In front of the police headquarters an old man sat smoking a pipe and wearing suspenders, an American flag jutting waggishly from the handle of his walker. "Asshole," Vale muttered. Apart from the town's abundance of crystal shops, Norman Rockwell would have spasmed with the quaintness of it all.

In the parking lot of a gas station, I watched as Vale got out and pulled a beer from the bag beneath his seat and just stared at it, holding it in his hand.

"Stop looking at me, Marvin, okay? I'm going to have a beer tonight, after I park the van. One beer."

"Whatever you say," I said, my palms up. "No judgment, remember?"

"Yeah, right." He stormed over and set the sack down next to a garbage can. He went in to pay for the gas and came out with a two-liter jug of soda and a box of doughnuts. He set the stuff down in his seat, then pivoted on his heels and ran back and grabbed the sack of beer, shoved it back under his seat.

"You okay, dude?" Casper called out from his spot waiting for the bathroom.

Vale's hands trembled. He lit a cigarette like he was mad at it and jammed his lighter in his pocket. His bandages were sweat-stained, grimy. "Shut the fuck up, Casper."

We hit Sacramento at rush hour, the sun falling bloody behind the skyline. We threaded our way through stop and go traffic, with Vale glaring and occasionally tracking a passing car with his middle finger jammed out the window.

"That's a good way to get shot these days," I said.

"Suck it," Vale said. "Suck it." I didn't know if he was talking to me or another driver. Eventually we rolled our windows up; the city smelled inexplicably of burning plastic.

It was full dark by the time we made it out of there, back to sere hills and billboards. I kept feeling these flurries, these constrictions in my chest: *I have to find her. Lyla. Joan. Whatever her name is. Put your goddamned cigarettes and doughnuts down, Vale, and let's move.*

Hours ticking down. But I kept it in check—he was doing okay, all things considered. He was growing on me, Vale.

PART TWO

ALL THE TUMBLING WORLD

THURSDAY

1

He was the last bright and shining comet the art world would ever produce.

He held root to majesty in a singular, fixed point in time.

He had been a painter, maybe the last certifiable *famous painter* that America would give the world. His bullet ascended simultaneously with the death knell of the art inflation and excess of the 1980s. *Still* he survived, *still* he bloomed, even as the market itself took a shit. In an art movement so muddled and self-conscious and feasting on its own newfound sense of irony, its own self-awareness, he *exploded.*

The critics saw it as his *morality*—and it was, but it was also his own ache for revelation, a need to admit to his guilt and rage and fear. Lust. Greed. All arrows were double-tipped: inward and outward. All of those canvasses laid waste to the excess and impiety and fecundity of man, of capitalism, of society. But they were, at their core, internal immolations of the self. And it was freedom, purging himself like that.

His fame had partly been a matter of being in the right place at the right time—even Vale could admit that—but it was also *the work.* These huge, seething, allegorical things that he made. He was technically gifted, blessed with that innate eye.

There was a period there, four or five years probably, where he painted every day, and the paintings were *good.* His life then had a joyous momentum to it, this rocket-fuel mixture of luck, ambition, guile and perseverance. Paintings sold as quickly as he signed his name on them. Ideas came to him loose and free-form, and he filled notebooks up with sketches. Critics begged for appointments to meet him so they could write fawning articles. Candice was his anchor, a steadying light guiding him through unfamiliar rooms.

There was a time when the world bent toward him like a flower.

God, he'd loved painting so much. *He'd loved it.* He'd seethed with that love. It had snapped off of him like electricity, that love.

And then came the unraveling. Paris. Olivia. Brophy's stupid contract, the cocaine, the stripper. MindyfromPratt, as he thought of her now, all one word like that.

How do you pinpoint the beginnings of a cyclone, or measure the fallout of a man's failings? What's the first step in a downward spiral?

The last time he'd seen Candice had been three months ago. Right before the first ghost sightings. She'd taken him to a restaurant in the Pearl, only a few blocks from where he had smashed all those gallery windows years before. It had been a sunny, crisp spring day and he'd been only mildly hungover. Summer peeking around the curtain.

He'd passed the restaurant a hundred times before and never paid it a second glance, but Candice had called him up and invited him, and as recently as three months ago, he would have done anything for her except the things that would've helped him the most.

He'd stepped inside and the maître d' had seen him and smirked.

Candice had been in town touring for another Janey book. She was one of those authors who would stay perpetually in the mid-level range of the *New York Times* bestseller lists; her books were read by millions of people and then generally forgotten about until the next one came along. They were pleasant and comfortable and well-written: the trials and tribulations of Janey Delancy, the reluctant PI with the tattered love life.

He'd read the new book the night before—this one was titled *Night's Claws*—and saw flashes of pure Candice in it, where she allowed her bravery as a writer to shine through the formula. Every one of her books cleaved him in half with heartache and he devoured them all.

Candice had waited for him before being seated. "Jesus, Mike. Nice of you to get dressed up," she said when she saw him.

She looked amazing: She wore a dark suit with that red hair pinned up. An arc of black pearls traced her collarbone. Vale saw a hint of cleavage and looked away as lust reared up brutish inside him, a little surprising in its fierceness.

It made him feel sad and old—not the lust itself, but the shame that came with it. The tremors had not been as bad that day but after they hugged, Vale kept his hands in his pockets. His feet felt like cold hunks of river rock. The waiter gave them menus, walked them to their table, professional again once he saw who Vale was with.

"Nice haircut. You must be an artist," Candice said. An old joke of theirs.

"You look beautiful," he said honestly. "Very pretty."

They talked. He felt, as always, profoundly grateful for her company. He drank water and held her gaze and smiled in the right places. He gave very little of himself as they traveled across well-trod subjects, things previously cleared of emotional land mines through years of careful cultivation. She was his last friend, after all. There was Raph, but he and Raph were like conjoined twins connected by a barstool and a litany of bad ideas. No, there was only Candice. The waiter came and asked if they'd like to start with drinks. Vale weakened and ordered a Bloody Mary and a cup of coffee. Candice didn't say a word but watched him with an eye that caught everything and always had.

"So you're still at the burrito place," she said, unable to hide the tartness from her voice, as if she'd bitten into something mealy.

"It's a job," he'd said. "I make rent."

She looked at him and Vale sighed and suddenly felt his throat swell up; crying jags rocked him with such ease these days, he was like a teenager. And then a woman was suddenly standing over Candice. Leaning over discreetly, respectfully, holding a copy of *Night's Claws,* that foil cover showing a rose amid a scattering of bullets. Of course she was the biggest fan and could Candice possibly sign this? It would mean so much. The people around them stole glances.

Candice was gracious and radiant. She pulled a pen from a suit pocket—prepared, he was sure—for such things.

Their drinks came and the waiter took their order, and Vale ate a full meal for the first time in days and struggled to hold it down. Candice stirred a tiny spoonful of sugar into her coffee cup and then pointed the spoon at him. It was a gesture he was used to and again he felt that swelling in his chest, his throat. He knew what she was going to say before she said it because she always prefaced it with that pointing that she did. They knew each other.

She said, "Brophy."

"Stop," he said, smiling, his palm held up.

"I'm serious, Mike. That contract? That contract is illegal."

"Dee, forget about it."

"Do you know how much *The Dissipation* went for? Do you have any idea? Brophy just sold that to Keith Richards, okay? It made the *Times*."

"I don't even remember which painting that is."

"I don't even remember which painting that is," she mocked, a vicious, mincing lilt. Vale laughed. She said, "It's the one with the wolves on the ground and all the priests and businessmen and people, like, floating in the air, holding onto bundles of balloons. *That* one. Don't be an asshole."

He remembered it. He'd probably done his best paintings those few years in LA while Candice was in school. *Dissipation* had been one of them. He'd been shit-faced drunk for the opening, of course—a solo show that Tanazzi and Brophy had worked out together. Thirty paintings. He'd thrown up on Cheech Marin's shoes.

Candice said, "Brophy sold that painting to Keith Richards for four hundred and eighty thousand dollars, Mike."

Vale shook his head and tilted his Bloody Mary back until the glass clicked against his teeth. "You know I don't get any of that money," he said around a mouthful of ice.

"Let me get you a lawyer. Your stuff still sells, clearly. That contract is shit."

"Honestly, Dee. I'm really not interested."

Candice started to say to something and then pursed her lips. She looked to the left, the right, as if they were spies in some Cold War saga. She hissed, "How can you not be interested? *How?* What are you afraid of?"

"Dee. Candice. Please." Smiling, still trying to hold on to some semblance of conversation. Feeling the heat of shame crawl up his neck as he stared into his lap.

"You make corn dogs for a living, and you probably suck at it. I can name half a dozen lawyers who would *wreck* him, Mike, I swear to God. Half a dozen off the top of my head."

"Do you always talk like the bad guys in your books?"

She stared at him and then looked down at the table, took a breath. She opened her mouth to say something, closed it. Finally she said, "At least think about doing another show. I could give you a loan for supplies. Whatever. Get you an assistant part-time. I'd be happy to."

He sighed.

"You'd make a killing easily," she said, "enough to get back on your feet. Any gallery would be happy to have you."

"I'm not even close to ready for that."

She held out a hand. "Look at you, man. You're not even *eating.*" She was near tears.

Afterward, Mike walked her to her rental car. Candice offered to drive him home. He hugged her, held her perhaps a moment too long. The familiar press and weight of her body against his, the ghost of it. The drink had smoothed the edges of things but left his body crying out for more. She opened the car door and tried to hand him a hundred dollar bill. Mike took a step back.

"Take it, you idiot," she said, and shoved it into his shirt pocket.

"This is enabling behavior," he said, and there was a danger there of having said too much. He could see it on her face.

"Call me when you get a life." The same line she said every time they parted.

It was the last time he saw her.

2

From the journals of Marvin Deitz:

I gathered years, lives. Sloughed off any steadfast notions of mortality. Both suicide and death by "exterior sources," I discovered, bore the same result: rebirth and rebirth again. I was always disfigured in childhood some way, and always with my memories an anchor around me. Lives of virtue and lives of greed were met with the same results: I came back, heartsick and heavy with Geoffroy's dismantlement and all that had followed. Do it enough times and you mold yourself to madness eventually—how else to accept it?

Because you keep living and dying whether you accept it or not.

It was my seventh or eighth way through the world when I simply stopped petitioning God for help. My continued lives and their accompanying disfigurements were their own strange response to that. After that I sought solace in confession, but a confession among the world of men. I began simply cataloging my regrets, like I'm doing now.

By the seventh or eighth time, I'd gathered around me a basic understanding of how the Curse worked, the machinations of it. In one of those early lives I'd been born to brutal, solemn parents in a small village in Hungary (for a time my reincarnations were very heavily centered around Europe—the better to cycle me through a few dozen deaths by plague, famine and war, I imagined) and it was there that I told a village priest my tale. This marked the first time I'd spoken to a holy man since Father Lavendu.

I was twelve years old and my father had inexplicably beaten me earlier that day, and I felt furious and trapped. After speaking to the Hungarian priest, he'd taken me by the arm and marched me home and repeated to my father my ludicrous tale, and my father had simply beaten me again. The priest, however, *also* told the magistrates and the local bishop, who sensed a whiff of dark magic about me and promptly gathered a mob.

So there was that.

At twelve years old they had me weighted with stones and drowned in the Tisza River for a warlock.

Lesson learned and learned again: *no one will save you.*

So what happens?

You live and live and live again. You become a summation of your disparate histories. Terror comes in waves, bookended in mundanities. You grow to have fifty parents, a hundred siblings, a thousand lovers, enemies beyond number.

All of these relationships cheapened and lessened by the *sameness* of it all, the machinelike quality of death and life.

You heart breaks in the knowledge that all of your children through all of your years are now dry husks in the earth. Your heart is so used and careworn it becomes dry as straw, useless. Love wears you down like water on rock.

Your name is Geoffroy Thérage and also Marvin Deitz. And in between that your name is Sa'am, Lila, Matilda Jean, Cristina, Pilar, Agu, Sachdev, Alfonse, Damiáo, Eliot, Matthew, Haru, Mohammed, Edward, Little Foot, Terrence, Bhumika, Stephen, Than, Gavan, Ula, Malik, Jose, Changpu, Arjana, Ata'haine, Stefan, Pedro, John, Pazit, Elizabeth, Jordan, Richard, Fethee, and more and more and more.

All of these names trailing streaks of blood in the dust of your life—the knowledge of the loss that came before. You practically come out from every womb, out of every poor mother, already filling your lungs, trailing heartbreak behind you.

Sometimes you do not live long enough to even become named, your life too short to be written on the backs of people's tongues.

Sometimes you have a name and try deliberately to forget it because it is just too sad to remember.

There's no gift in living when nothing you do can take such a gift away.

• • •

I woke from a dream in which Joan sacrificed herself by leaning her chest on a flaming sword and sinking down onto it, all the time imploring me with her dark and depthless gaze. The crowd crushed and pressed around us, jockeying for a look. I kept reaching for her and missing, again and again, all the while the crowd pressing behind me.

I woke with the sheets lying tangled around my legs, the room stiflingly hot. The bed felt peppered in dirt, unclean. I could hear Casper quietly weeping on his own bed.

"Casper. You okay?"

He pulled in a ragged hitch of breath, sputtered it out.

"Sorry for waking you up, Marvin."

I ran a hand down my face, heard the brittle rasp of stubble, Joan's face still burned like an afterimage against my eyes. We were in some hotel room on I-5, still a good ways from Los Angeles. There would be some driving to be done tomorrow. I felt that moment of panic again: I had less than a week, just a few days, to find Lyla, to find some answers—if there were any at all. I could leave this life at any time.

"You didn't wake me up," I said. "What's the matter? You alright?"

He didn't speak for a while. Then he said, sounding bashful, embarrassed, "I'm just worried. I don't know what . . . I don't know what the hell I'm doing here. Gary said I'd never leave Roseburg if I didn't have someone with me. That this was an opportunity and I should grab it."

"I still can't believe you hid in the van. And that we didn't see you."

"For real. I thought you guys would find me right away."

We lay there in our beds, the occasional pair of headlights sneaking under the curtain and roving across the wall as people pulled out of the parking lot.

"You'll be okay, Casper."

"I guess." He coughed. "Sorry for making a big deal about it. I know I should be stoked."

"It's okay," I said. "It's not like Mike and I know each other, you know? All three of us are just stumbling forward. California, the Land of Opportunity, and all that."

"The Western nest of sin and fornication," Casper quoted.

I laughed. "Right."

"Those pamphlets are nuts," he said. "The Transmittal Foundation or whatever it's called."

"Yeah."

We were quiet a while. It was like any moment throughout time, two people bullshitting in the dark. The walls were thin enough that I heard Vale moan in his sleep in his own room, a haunted noise that ran a finger of ice down my spine.

Quietly, Casper said, "I was just afraid to go by myself, Marvin."

"Don't worry about it," I said. "You're with us. We're all going to the same place."

It took me a long time to fall asleep, to get Joan's face out of my mind. To get that picture of her spreading her arms and falling onto her sword to turn into something else.

3

"I bet it's a ghost," Casper said.

"It's not a ghost." Vale leaned back—he'd let Marvin drive, finally—and folded his arms behind his head. He put his sunglasses back on. "It's a fender bender."

Vale had drunk eight beers in his motel room the night before. Eight exactly. Not a horrible night, all told. The hangover was not bad today and he'd quickly downed another bottle in the bathroom before they left. It settled his nerves, smoothed out his guts, and now with Marvin at the wheel he felt like this was good, this was a good thing.

He'd left the rest of the beers on the dresser along with a fifty. A blessed tip for the cleaning staff. He was doing okay. He was petitioning the universe's good fortune with hard cash.

Today was the funeral and he would make it there. Anything beyond that was cake, unnecessary. They'd left early and were making good time but by the time they passed a little town called Volta, traffic had slowed down greatly, moving forward grudgingly only after long periods of stillness. Now they'd reached more sun-blasted fields, hills blue in the distance. You could hear stereos through the open windows of other cars as emergency vehicles sped past them on the shoulder, lights pulsing.

"Nah," said Casper from the back. "Ghost."

"Bull."

"See," said Casper, slapping the back of Vale's headrest as a truck passed on the shoulder. "CDC, not the Highway Department."

It was like that for an hour. Everyone was getting edgy. But he found an atlas and a map of the West Coast in the glove box, and was able at least to figure out which freeways they'd need to take and the exit to get off at to reach Richard and Candice's place. No small feat, navigating that. Casper read them snippets of the Foundation pamphlets for entertainment.

And then they rounded a curve of the highway and it turned out it was both things, that they were both right.

Two of the southbound lanes were blocked by a jackknifed semi—those lanes and again the shoulder were thronged with fire trucks, police cruisers, an ambulance. All those spinning lights so robbed of their power in the light of day. But aside from that, down past the shoulder in a field of knee high grass, maybe a hundred yards away—

"Holy mother," Casper said, rolling onto his knees and pressing his face to the passenger window of the van like a child.

A trio of CDC panel trucks were parked further in the grass and a half dozen men in hooded hazmat suits were setting up a perimeter, a half circle of bright orange sawhorses, DANGER stenciled across them in black. Traffic oozed, stopped, oozed. A mustached cop spoke into a bullhorn: "Do not exit your vehicle. Do not take photographs. If you exit your vehicle you may be charged with obstructing traffic and endangering a federal investigation. The appropriate authorities are on the scene. Do not exit your vehicle . . ."

Within the cordon of the orange sawhorses, a ghost child stood pale and smoke-rimmed in the dry grass.

They all looked as they passed, even Marvin, who craned his neck to see, the van rolling along at five miles an hour or so, the cop himself flinching at a *bloop* of the bullhorn's feedback, and there it fucking was, Vale couldn't believe it. It was right there, this thing, this remnant. A little girl.

"Prime footage right there," he murmured.

"I don't have a camera," Casper said.

"What about your phone?"

"I've just got a burner," he said, enrapt.

"Jesus, man."

"I know."

It was a young girl—impossible to tell how old from this distance—and there was that sense about her, about *it*. A sense of shifting; how the form stayed the same but the opacity, its *thereness,* seemed to waver, to bend and snap at the mercy of something the living weren't privy to.

It stepped one way in the grass, turned, looked the other way. Its hair was dark, pulled back in a bun, its dress bone-colored and falling to its ankles. The thing's color wavered between smoke and aged newspaper. It stood in the grass and raised its chin as if testing the air for fire or as if it heard something calling to it, and then turned around again. And then its hands went to its face and they saw, everyone saw, this tide of people, they all saw its shoulders rise and fall as it stood alone in the yellow grass of a shadowed foothill by the side of the highway.

"It's lost," said Vale.

Casper said, "That's a girl, Mike. That's a little kid."

Vale said nothing, and Casper said it again, "That's a person," and something inside Vale, something that had nothing to do with the smoke, or at least not much to do with it, something way down inside him broke clean as a piece of glass.

4

Excerpts from the twenty-seven articles drafted on May 4, 1456, and used as a basis of Joan's nullification trial. Original witnesses were asked to verbally confirm or deny the truth of each charge in regards to their questioning during Joan's original trial in 1431:

4) That neither judges, confessors, or consultants, nor the promoter and others intervening in the trial, dared to exercise free judgment because of the severe threats made against them by the terrorizing English; but that they were forced to suit their actions to their fear and to the pressure of the English if they wished to avoid grave perils and even the peril of death. And so it was and that is the truth . . .

8) That they kept Joan in a secular prison, her feet fettered with irons and chains; and that they forbade anyone to speak to her so that she might not be able to defend herself in any way, and they even placed English guards over her. And so it was and that is the truth . . .

25) That Joan continuously, and notably at the moment of her death, behaved in a saintly and Catholic manner; commending her soul to God and invoking Jesus aloud even with her last breath in such a manner as to draw from all those present, and even from her English enemies, effusions and tears. And so it was and that is the truth.

• • •

"I just have to do this," Vale croaked. "I have to get to Los Angeles, man. Can we just hurry the fuck up, please?" He put his foot up on the dashboard and tucked his hands into his armpits. Sitting there like that, with his posture and his bandages and sunglasses, he looked like history's most ravaged and sullen teenager.

Traffic had picked up. "We're going," I said. "We're on our way."

"Dude," Casper said, leaning over our seats, getting in Vale's face, "we just saw a *ghost,* Mike."

"I know, Casper," Vale said. He sounded miserable. "It's just . . . I have to get to LA for a funeral. My wife's funeral. I *have* to. Do you get that?" He took his sunglasses off and pressed his heels to his eyes. He might've been crying, but it was clear you'd have to be an idiot to ask him about it.

"Hey, it's cool," Casper said. "We're moving again. We're on our way."

Vale put his sunglasses back on. "It's not *cool,* Casper. There's nothing *cool* about it. Name one fucking thing that's cool."

I watched Casper shrug in the rearview mirror and sit back on his knees. "My shirt's cool, remember? Bald eagles and shit? Beers? You're cool, Mike. You look like a really shitty extra from *The Road Warrior.* That's cool."

Vale nodded once. "Thanks." I watched a small smile creep across his face.

Casper leaned over the seat again. "Don't worry about it, dude. I totally cried last night. Didn't I, Marvin? I figure if there's little ghost kids lost in random fields by the side of the road? Dead and lost? Things are weird enough that it's no big deal if guys like me and you freak out every once in a while. We're the last ones anyone's gonna care about. Go ahead and melt down, I say."

5

By the time they hit Santa Clarita, Vale remembered why he had grown to despise Southern California in general and LA specifically. The ceaseless traffic, the noise, the phalanxes of single occupancy vehicles stretching as far as the eye could see. The ball-of-yarn confusion of the freeways. The great and callous waste of it all, just the sheer volume of shit being taken and used and irrevocably thrown away. It was the same everywhere, of course, all over the planet, but nowhere did it seem as pronounced as it did here. Los Angeles. Christ.

He thought for approximately three seconds about calling someone he knew, and then realized there was absolutely no one he wanted to see. What was he going to do, go hang out with Edwin Tanazzi? Get a cappuccino with Jared Brophy? See if Mindyfrom-Pratt wanted to do a few more lines of blow? No. There'd been one good thing about Los Angeles, one good thing left to him at all, and she was gone now.

• • •

Vale only had to ask directions once to find the place. The familiarity of the city coming back to him. Memory, that old reluctant ghost.

Candice and Richard's home was a sprawling one-level sandstone in Culver City. There was a half circle of a driveway and an iron fence laced around the property. Beyond the fence the sloping lawn was just as Vale had imagined it, emerald-green and lush as carpet. In front of the house was an island of raked gravel studded with blooming cactuses. Cars filled the driveway and lined the street. Nice cars. They found parking a few blocks away.

Casper and Marvin stood awkwardly on the sidewalk, squinting in the dazzling sunlight as Vale unwound his bandage in the front seat, peering into the rearview mirror. He probed gingerly at his scab. It was about as bad as he expected, which was pretty bad. *My God,* he thought. *It looks like I've got fruit leather on my forehead.* This was compounded by that fact that the flesh around his eyes looked bruised and purple, and his hair, filthy and wind-blown, had formed a kind of stringy, blown-back pompadour.

He turned to Marvin. "Be honest. Does it look better with the bandage or without it?"

Marvin winced and tilted his hand back and forth. "That's kind of a tough question, Mike."

They walked back to the house. Wide stone steps led up to the front door, which was braced by a pair of huge picture windows. Two men stood there in dark suits. One had a clipboard. They both had the jaws of comic book superheroes and, as they watched the three approach, were clearly telegraphing fuck off vibes. Casper took his baseball cap off and wrung it in his hands.

Vale said, "I'm Michael Vale."

The doorman looked at his clipboard and then looked up. He looked at the other guy. For a moment, nobody said anything.

"I'm sober," Vale said flatly.

The second doorman looked over Vale's shoulder. "These gentlemen are your guests?"

Vale turned to him. He'd decided to leave the bandage off and could feel the scab tighten when he made certain expressions. Like when he scowled, which he did now. "Yes. They are. These gentlemen are my guests."

The one with the clipboard nodded and opened the door. "The memorial will be held back here after the funeral, which will be held at Woodland Park Cemetery. Programs are available in the foyer. The procession leaves in approximately half an hour. Mr. Brandt can answer any of your questions."

Vale thanked him, felt a flurry of anger at himself for doing it, a bird snapping its wings against a cage.

The foyer was marble and beyond that the rest of the house was blond hardwoods or pale ceramic tile depending on where you were. High ceilings, and panels of sunlight fell everywhere from skylights above. The rooms themselves were dense with low-slung furniture, everything done in clean lines, neutral. A painting on the dining room wall was easily eight feet tall but little more than an abstract collision of aquamarine panels. Clearly Richard's influence. Right? Candice had loved *his* work, or people like Barbara Kruger, her faux-clumsy earnestness. Did she actually *like* this stuff?

People stood in their dark clothes, murmuring in small clusters, holding bottles of water and cups of coffee. Marvin stood next to Vale with his hands clutched behind his back, nodding at the funeral goers looking at them, of which there were more than a few. Even for Hollywood, they stuck out. Their dishevelment, Vale felt, bordered on obscene here. Casper stood near him with his hat pressed to his stomach, gazing at the floor, looking like he'd flinch at a cough.

They stepped out to the enormous backyard. Another green expanse battling the turquoise pool, the top of it dappled in sunlight. Between Richard's copyright work and the Janey books, the two of them had done very well. There was a buffet table and waiters walked rigidly among the guests with carafes of coffee and trays of bottled Evian, appropriately solemn. Casper, with a wince of apology and a slap of his hat against his leg, beelined for the buffet table as discreetly as he could.

Vale caught a glimpse of someone across the lawn amid all the faces staring at him. He stopped, his breath seizing in his chest. The world around him seemed to freeze, turn crystalline.

Fifteen steps away? Twenty? He started moving.

Behind him, Marvin said, "Hold up, Mike. Wait."

Twenty steps on the grass at most and there in front of him was Jared Brophy, his ex-agent, he of Paris, he of Mindyfrompratt, he of the contract that ruined Vale's life. It'd been years, but there he was. Older and clearly ill. Brophy was sick, anyone could see that: he looked like a skull wrapped in tanned, liver-spotted burlap, with a pair of obviously false teeth pressed into the mess. He looked like dog shit in a dark blue suit, honestly, like he would be dying soon. But the eyes were the same. Liquid, searching, darkly mirthful. "Mike Vale," he crowed, "long time, no see," and his voice had become terrible, like he was trying to speak while slurping up the last dregs of a milkshake through a straw.

Vale's fist pistoned out, caught him beneath the eye.

Brophy tumbled to the grass like a puppet with his strings cut.

6

Excerpt from the Transmittal Foundation for Eternal Life pamphlet, *From Static to Signal: Discovering the Almighty's Resonance in a Time of Sin*:

And we ask you IS IT COINCIDENCE that such specters have appeared THERE and nowhere else—the very viper's nest of amorality and liberalism that is HOLLYWOOD, CALIFORNIA, home of the GOD-HATING ENTERTAINMENT INDUSTRY; and south of that, where the once-vibrant border towns of MEXICO are now run by narco-traffickers who deal in MASSACRE AND HUMAN SLAVERY, who publicly DISMEMBER judges and policemen and fling their severed body parts from bridges.

Ask yourselves if it is coincidence that the specters of the dead—the lost ones, the unclaimed—have appeared in the very same place where so many have TURNED THEIR FACES AWAY FROM THE LORD GOD?

Ask yourselves, brothers and sisters, if we really have the TIME and LUXURY of believing in coincidence any longer.

And will you be ready when He comes?

And will you be diligent?

And will you hear and act when God SINGS OUT His Commandment across the airwaves and AROUND THE LIP OF THE WORLD?

• • •

The old man toppled and Vale's fist hung there in the air; he looked like he'd surprised himself with it. Looked more than a little aghast, actually. A woman in the crowd screamed, high and dramatic, a horror movie scream, and a man near her brayed laughter. The two doormen appeared as if they'd been teleported there, just like that, and one of them pulled Vale's arms behind him while the other jabbed him in the kidneys, just once but hard enough to make him gag.

People went to help the old man up, but he waved them away, his other hand pressed to his eye. Casper stood wide-eyed at the buffet table, a three-inch tall sandwich of crackers, cheese and cold cuts poised in front of his mouth.

The kidney-jabber drew a fist back and laid his hand flat on Vale's chest, as if looking for the perfect spot.

"Do it," the man holding him said. "Go."

I stepped forward in the hopes that some half-memory of combat would serve me like it had in the Tip-Top, but Casper was there first. He grabbed the doorman's fist and then awkwardly leapt on his back. Half of his pale and substantial ass hung out the back of his jeans as the two of them spun into the table, a pyramid of bottled waters falling and scattering on the patio. There were more screams.

Vale reared back and rammed the back of his head into the face of the doorman still holding him. "Goddamnit," the man said almost conversationally. He let go, his hands rising to his mashed lips.

Casper reached around the man's head and latched onto his bottom lip with his thumb and forefinger. As Marvin, I'd grown soft: this all unfolded in front of me so surreal, so slow. I shifted this way, that way. Too slow. Too old and timid. Casper pulled on the man's lip like he was peeling the lid off a can and the man screamed and flipped Casper over his back. Casper landed on the cement around the pool, hard, and the man dropped a knee onto his chest and punched Casper once in the jaw. Looked like something from an MMA highlight reel. Casper could've been an appliance he'd unplugged, the kid went out so quick, a pale diamond of belly showing between his pants and his eagle t-shirt.

Vale scanned the lawn, his fists balled, chest heaving, his terrible forehead gored and bleeding again. Finally the doorman, standing behind him with his lips bloodied, just hoisted Vale up by his armpits and threw him into the pool.

7

They stood in a spare bedroom somewhere in the labyrinth of the house. It was quite the little vignette. Casper and Brophy sat on opposite sides of the king-sized bed with ice packs pressed to their faces, and Vale held a wad of toilet paper to his ruined, disgusting forehead. Richard stood next to the bureau and beside him were a pair of policemen, their thumbs hitched in their belts. There was a quilt on the wall, flowers in little ceramic vases.

Did Candice actually *like* this room? Did he know her at all? The doormen had traded some secret handshake or ball-tickle with the cops and were somehow excused from the proceedings, and Marvin was lurking out back with the rest of the deliciously scandalized crowd. Vale couldn't stop looking at Brophy—he'd seen scarecrows with healthier physiques. His fury was tussling with the mortification that he'd struck a senior citizen who looked about fifteen minutes from tumbling into a grave.

Richard pointed at Vale, who stood in his wet clothes, holding his wad of toilet paper.

"I want him arrested," Richard said.

The cops shared a look. One of them shrugged. "We can do that, sir."

"Richard, no," Brophy said with that death-rattle voice of his. He took his ice pack away from his mouth. "It's not necessary."

Richard spat, "Bullshit it isn't."

For Vale, any guilt and sorrow about Candice had been tucked away; he'd dreamt of hitting Brophy for years. Literally dreamt of it. His fantasy hadn't included Brophy looking like he'd been pulled from a hospital bed, but an admittedly ugly part of him was still savagely happy he'd knocked the fucker down.

"What are you even doing here, Jared?" Vale said. "What is he doing here, Richard? How could you invite this guy here? After everything?"

Richard's eyes settled on Vale with a terrible brightness. That stare just glittering with fury. A chilling grin. He snapped his fingers and pressed his hand to his forehead. "That's right, I forgot I was supposed to have you okay who I invited to my fucking *wife's funeral*. Sorry, Mike. I missed that memo."

"After all this guy did—"

Richard took a step forward. "Listen to me, you fucking alcoholic *waste*—"

"Sir," one of the cops said, putting two fingertips of Richard's elbow.

Richard paused, exhaled. He bit his lip and then spoke in a measured, even tone, a voice positively cloying with condescension. Vale could imagine him using the same voice to some low-level office assistant who'd got Richard's coffee wrong in the morning.

"Listen to me, Mike. My wife is dead. Candice. Remember her? Her funeral is supposed to be taking place right now. Right this minute. And it's being held up because I'm *here*. We're all *here*. We shouldn't be, but we are. And why are we here?"

Vale pointed at Brophy. "This man—"

"Why am I here, Mike?"

"That contract ruined my life. It ruined my life."

Richard ignored him. "I'll tell you why. I'm here because you came and fucked everything up. Because that's what you do. That's your whole schtick. You fuck everything up." He threw his arms out. "Some guys do impressions, some guys can, I don't know, make balloon animals. What sets Mike Vale apart? What's his secret power? Oh, that's right. He's rolling chaos. It's all about him. It always has been."

"Richard, please," Brophy said, staring at the floor. "There's no need. This is all ancient history."

"*Not ancient enough!*" Richard roared, and the cops traded

glances again. "It's not ancient enough, that's pretty clear, since we're here right now."

A policeman said, "Sir, please. Let's keep this calm."

"I want this asshole arrested."

"I'm not going to be pressing charges, Richard," Brophy said. He took his ice pack away and looked at each man in turn around the room. Even miserable Casper, who still hadn't said a word.

Vale sneered. "You're just the great white knight, aren't you, Jared? Coming to my rescue again, right?" He took a step forward, couldn't help himself.

A cop put a palm on his chest. "You just don't know when to quit, do you? One more comment like that and you're going to jail."

"Officer, really, it's fine," Brophy said. He held his ice pack at his knees, pressed into it—the packaging the same impossible blue as the pool outside—with his bony, withered fingers. "Mike," he said, "whatever happened is in the past. Bygones and all that. I mean, I haven't thought of you in years. It's funny, because someone actually asked me at a party last week, 'What do you think of Mike Vale?'" Brophy looked past the cops and out the window, as if lost in the memory. "I had to think about it. God's honest truth. I had to think about the last time I remotely considered you. And that's what I told him."

"You asshole."

"It's true. I said, 'Why, I haven't thought about Mike Vale in years.'" He shrugged. "Not in years."

Vale leapt at him. Brophy fell back on the bed, his arms raised. One of the cops drove Vale to the floor and pepper-sprayed him. Everyone grappling and tumbling.

Casper somehow wound up at the bottom of the dog pile and howled as he caught some pepper-spray as well. Limbs flailed. Grunts and curses. A vase fell, shattered. The floor was scattered with flowers, ceramic shards. Vale lay at the bottom of the pile, bellowing and thrashing, snot pouring out of his face. It was a sound an animal would make, high and then low. Someone broke wind during a flurry of exertion. One of the cops stepped on Vale's hand during the disentanglement of limbs and broke two of his fingers. Then Vale's scream went high and stayed that way.

"*Now* we're arresting you, dipshit," the cop said, gasping.

FRIDAY

1

From the journals of Marvin Deitz:

I went back once. In the life before this one, during my Bill Creswell days. I went back to France.

It was 1960 and I flew from Brooklyn to Paris and from there took the train to Rouen. I was not surprised to find there were guided, Joan-specific tours in the city. I paid my money and stood among a clutch of other tourists and listened to the guide, a mousy woman with a faint, dusky mustache. Her earnestness charmed me; she loved Joan, anyone could see it.

I seemed to be both the only American and the only single man among our group, the rest talkative housewives and restless husbands, bored children with rings of chocolate around their mouths.

Every single adult was smoking, including the guide. Germans and Italians, most of them. The sky continually threatened rain and that at least felt familiar. I thought distractedly of fucking the guide, what that would be like, and the baselessness of it made clear to me that there would be no epiphany for me in Rouen.

"Joan the Maid's body was burned three times," she said, "and her ashes were cast in the Seine. She was later martyred, of course, and the court proceedings leading up to her execution were rendered null in a new trial in 1456."

I stood at the back of our group. "And what of the executioner?"

I called out, my hands cupped around my mouth. I couldn't help it. An armada of beehives and flattops turned, frowning.

Our guide's eyebrows rose, lovely little caterpillars. "Joan's executioner?" She smiled sadly. "Little is known of her executioner, actually. They were frequently drunkards or prisoners, as few citizens were willing to do such work."

Later that day I rented a car and drove to Moineau. My little village. I took the freeway, of course, a modern wonder, and got lost for a time. When I finally arrived, the sky was deepening to the color of a bruise and everything, of course, was different.

There were few landmarks I recognized. What had I expected? Much of the place had been charred and ruined by battles between Allied and German forces decades before. Roads were paved in new routes, streetlights brightening everything.

Our plot of land, as near as I could tell, had become nothing more than a clutch of brambles behind the cracked parking lot of a bakery. I found what may have been a stone pillar that was perhaps our chimney, or perhaps simply rubble deposited there during the war.

I drove back to Rouen, dropped off the car, flew back to Paris. Then back to New York.

It had always been unknowable, the Curse, and always would be.

There would be no defining it. There would be no answer. The greatest fallacy: looking continually for an answer in things that are unanswerable.

• • •

Casper and I sat in the van across the street from Men's Central Jail in downtown LA. It was nine in the morning and we drank coffee and watched the steady stream of men be discharged from the doors. It was like watching a high school let out, if all of the students were bedraggled, weary adults who squinted balefully at the sun and shook their heads at the weight of the previous night's misdeeds, their coming futures. Casper's eyes were still red and swollen from the pepper spray.

The police had let Vale hand off his keys to me. Casper and I had found a motel the day before, deciding to share a room again—finances were certainly a part of it, but there was also the simple fact that Casper seemed fragile in a way that neither Vale nor I were. He was a kid. I liked him. I wanted him to stick around.

There had been little of note about our room save for the constellation of dead flies in the ceiling fixture and the fact that our neighbor was either watching pay-per-view porn at a hefty volume or had choreographed a sizeable orgy.

But I'd charged my phone and after that managed to perform what little detective work I could manage in regards to Lyla. I called the *To The Point With Jesse Pamona* information line and after various transfers spoke to a studio representative. She told me what I'd already assumed: no, she could not give out any personal information about previous guests of the show. Such a thing, she said, would not only be dangerous, but glaringly illegal.

No, she could not forward messages to previous guests of the show. No, she could not forward messages, or pass on anecdotes or prayers or threats or rhyming couplets to Ms. Pamona herself. These were all answered in the deathly chipper tone of someone who had fielded these questions countless times before.

"What exactly can you do?" I said.

In a bright and chipper voice, she said, "Well, sir, I can give you our website and email address, our time of airings in your region? I can give you our upcoming schedule of topics if you'd like to be considered for a guest spot on the show?"

"But you can't help me. You won't give me the last names of either of the guests from that particular show?"

As brightly as ever, she said, "Not a chance on earth," and hung up on me.

An hour later, we were watching a nature documentary—sharks and their ceaseless ministrations—when my cell phone rang. I didn't recognize the number, but it turned out to be Vale calling from jail. He'd be spending the night, he said, but would be getting released the next morning. He gave me the address of Men's Central, and Casper shook his head, a wet towel over his eyes, as I listened and wrote the address down.

"We'll be there in the morning," I said. Vale thanked me, sounding tired, wrung out. I wondered distractedly what kind of physical price he'd be paying for a full night without a drink. On the TV a great white burst through the rippled surface of the ocean, pink maw sluicing seawater and blood.

So now, the next morning, nine a.m. Casper not looking so hot with his still-red eyes, the knot on his jaw. Personally, I'd slept well once the calisthenics next door had quieted down—we'd all just been run ragged.

But it was all taking longer than I thought it would; I had to find Lyla, but things kept getting in the way. When had this sense of stupid *loyalty* to everyone cropped up inside me? There was the common feeling of expecting death at any minute—I was closer to it now than I'd been in centuries. I'd never made it this far along in the Curse.

But I was focusing on the wrong things. Lyla's trail was going cold. I had this allegiance to these two and it was throwing me off.

Casper sat in the passenger seat. He blew on his coffee and frowned. "He's flat-out crazy, Marvin. He's nuts."

"I feel like I owe him," I said, tapping something out on the steering wheel with my thumbs.

Casper rolled his eyes at that. "You seriously do not owe that guy one thing, man."

"I just need to stick around for a bit. I can't explain it."

"He's got issues, Marvin. He's a guy who gave us a ride, so what? That old guy had cancer or something, did you see him? And Vale just lays him out. What's next, pushing kids in wheelchairs down stairs? You know what I mean? The guy gives Dunk a run for his money."

Casper was right. I knew it. In my mind, I'd left Vale and struck out on my own a half dozen times by then. And yet he'd been my portent, a sign when I needed one. When I wanted one, desperately. My one-way ticket to Los Angeles.

That was the hassle about trying to divine symbols, about resolutely looking for answers in things: who was to say these roadblocks weren't part of the journey itself?

"There he is," I said, raising my chin. Vale walked down the steps of the jail looking old and hunched over in his blood-dotted t-shirt. A wind came along that sent scraps of trash skittering down the street. His hair blew over his eyes, and God, he just looked like an old man.

Casper pursed his lips and pulled his hat low over his eyes. He put his hand on the door handle. "Guys like Mike Vale and Dunk? They just keep running until they run out of room."

We both got out. "What's that supposed to mean?" I said through our open doors.

The shrug of a resigned kid. "Guys like that just run until they're cornered. I think it'd be real stupid of us if we're there when it happened."

• • •

"My hand's killing me," Vale said. It looked like it. The whole thing was wrapped in a lumpy bandage the size of a loaf of bread, a wedged metal splint poked out the end of it. "You guys got a cigarette?"

"How you feeling?" Casper said. He was leaning against the side of the van with his arms crossed. Mike dipped his chin, gave him a flat, wordless stare.

"About what I figured," Casper said.

Vale opened the sliding side door of the van, his bandaged hand curled to his chest. He lumbered in, clumsy and bearlike, and pushed his way through the boxes. He lay on his back, his arms on his chest, legs bent. Feet still on the pavement. His sigh was weary and drawn. His beer-gut mounded out of his shirt, and his forehead still looked like someone had dragged him along the road by his skull for a few blocks.

"I want to go see Candice," he said simply. "And then I want a drink."

Casper hooked an arm onto the roof of the van, leaned down. "Seriously? No thank you for either of us? We *waited* for you, man."

"Thank you," Vale said dully, his eyes closed.

Casper looked at him a moment longer, like he was expecting more. But there was nothing forthcoming from Vale. "I swear," Casper said, "you and Dunk were probably conjoined twins or something. Two shitheads separated at birth."

2

Culver City again.

Holy Cross Cemetery was two hundred acres and within spitting distance of a half dozen movie studios. The parking lot was massive but reasonably empty that early in the morning.

Vale slid the door open and stepped from the van like an old man, stiff and slow. His hand throbbed and there was the constant and maddening itch of his forehead as well.

He'd spent half the night in the ER next to a hatchet-faced cop, waiting for his fingers to be X-rayed and splinted, and then he'd gone through booking. He'd been placed in various cells as he was processed, fingerprinted, interviewed by an EMS guy about his hand, the pepper spray. Twenty dudes in the holding cell with him and if anyone slept, he wasn't one of them. Before they let him go, the releasing officer had told him some lawyer had talked to the prosecuting attorney and gotten the assault charges dropped.

Brophy.

One phone call from Brophy, and that had been that.

The need for a drink was like some animal, nerve-deep thing way down inside him that yammered a single relentless note over and over again.

The Holy Cross office was a whitewashed stucco building capped with a roof of red tiles. The sign on the door said it wouldn't open up for another half an hour. Marvin and Casper offered to get coffee nearby while Vale wandered the grounds. He could not remember being this tired before, this heartsick.

There were innumerable graves, some little more than flat marble slabs flush with the grass, while others had been carved from massive blocks of stone, voluminous marble-hewn crosses. Stone cherubs lounged pensively, chubby fists on chins. Robins hopped nervously on the ground and sang in tree limbs as he passed. Flowers dotted the sloping lines of gravestones, and for something to do, he went about righting those bouquets that had been toppled. He leaned over and a wave of dizziness gripped him, shimmering black starbursts in his periphery. His hands were freezing. Thousands and thousands of graves here, just in this one place. All these interred bones. Just to think of it. Had they all been afraid to die? Terrified of it, like he was?

Melville Wright. 1908–1978. Loving Husband & Father.
Daniel Astor. 1919–2000. May Your Light Always Shine.
Angela Parsons. 1944–1988. Beloved Mother.

He found Bing Crosby's grave and, near it, Bela Lugosi's. He passed a funeral and gave it a wide berth, and later turned his face away as he walked past an old woman reading a book in a lawn chair in front of a grave.

He saw, on a hill beyond, what may have been either a ghost or a man trying vainly to find a particular marker. And why not? There were two hundred acres here, so many square miles of the dead. It was one or the other.

Inside the office there was a stack of brochures on the counter: *Celebrity Graves! Find Famous Stars at Holy Cross Cemetery! Five Dollars!* A white-haired woman stood behind the counter tapping on a keyboard. Her customer service instincts kicked in, but her face froze when she registered Vale's appearance.

He tried to give his most reassuring smile and rested his good hand on the countertop. "Hi there. My, uh, my ex-wife had services here yesterday."

She softened a little. "I'm sorry for your loss, sir."

"Thank you. Thanks. I wasn't able to make it, but I was hoping you might be able to help me locate her gravesite."

"Certainly." She turned to her computer. "We can do that. Her name?"

"Candice Hessler."

The woman peered up from the computer and looked at Vale over the tops of her glasses. "You're the husband," she said archly.

"Ex-husband."

She took her hands from the keyboard. "You're the *ex*-husband of Candice Hessler. Candice Hessler, the writer. Just to be clear."

"Yes."

The woman raised her chin, her lips quivering. "Five dollars."

Vale realized, suddenly, that the woman was furious.

"Excuse me?"

She pointed at the stack of brochures on the counter next to him. "We charge five dollars for a map of the celebrity gravesites, sir. For looky-loos such as yourself."

"For what?"

"Looky-loos. People come here for the celebrities? Fine. We generate a fair amount of revenue through tours and such, the maps. But someone comes in and *lies*? To my *face*? Saying they're the *husband* of that poor woman? Looking like he just rolled out of a garbage can?" There was a small brooch at her neck and she touched it with her finger. Inhaled sharply. "Well then. Five dollars for you, sir."

Vale knuckled his eye and laughed quietly. "Listen. I really am her ex-husband."

"Oh, clearly," she said.

Vale opened his wallet. "You already put her gravesite in a map? That's crazy. Her funeral was yesterday."

With mock sincerity, the woman said, "Oh *no*, sir. Mrs. Hessler isn't in our maps yet. That *would* be macabre, wouldn't it? No, I'll be providing you with *personal* directions."

• • •

Her grave was at an end plot and he knew it was hers, even as he crested the slight hill, because no other one nearby was mounded and stacked with so many blazing bouquets of new flowers. He was half a dozen rows away when another burst of nausea and dizziness gripped him and sent him retching in the grass, his hands on his knees. Spitting up nothing, nothing else left inside him. When was the last time he'd eaten?

Nearby, palm trees leaned around a ring of stone benches. As he topped the hill he saw a woman rise up from Candice's grave, the mounded flowers, and for a moment his heart leapt, but it was just some celebrity-hunter, some woman who'd been crouching down photographing the headstone. He kept walking, saw the grave a rectangle of freshly laid turf, so new it looked like a doorway in the ground. He cleared his throat and the woman turned and looked him up and down, tucking a length of hair behind her ear.

"I didn't even try to show up yesterday," the woman said. "I knew it would be a madhouse."

Vale stepped to the other side of the grave, the headstone between them, the flowers. He didn't want her there.

"Mike Vale, right?"

He looked at the woman. She wore a thin corduroy jacket over a t-shirt, her hair tied back. Worn blue jeans, tennis shoes. Pretty. Mid-thirties, maybe. "How'd you know that?" he said, and she smiled and ran a finger over her own knuckles. "Oh. Right. Yeah."

"Valerie Sands." She held out her hand, saw his splint, and gave a little laugh. "Sorry," she said, and held out her other one instead. "I'm doing a piece on Candice," she said. "She was a really amazing woman."

"She was," Vale agreed.

"So unexpected, it's terrible. I'm really sorry."

Vale nodded and stared down at the flowers. "Thank you," he said.

"Listen. It's in incredibly poor taste, I know, but my editor would kill me if I didn't ask. I don't suppose you'd be up for doing an interview?"

"Look," Vale said, "I can't really . . . I'm not really well right now." He jammed his hands in his armpits and let his breath drag out loudly. "I'm not doing very good right now."

Her eyes widening, she reached in her purse and handed him a wad of paper napkins.

Vale gave a bitter little laugh, held up a hand. "I mean, I'm done with the crying, thanks. It's not *that* bad."

She pointed at her face. "No, your nose. You're bleeding."

Bright rose-red blooms on the napkins, a hot color like some of the flowers at his feet.

"Listen," he said, "you don't want to talk to me. We haven't hardly talked in years, Candice and me. I don't have anything new to add."

Valerie tilted her head. He could see her wanting to lift the camera, wanting to point it at him. Quietly, she said, "Do you really think that's true?"

Vale balled up the napkin and looked at her. "I do."

"Anything would be great, Mr. Vale. Anything you have to say." She took a small notebook from her pocket, held a pen above it, ready. Her camera hung there in front of her. "There's no wrong answer."

"You sound like a shrink."

She laughed and pulled a string of hair from her mouth, turned her face into the wind. "Not me. Just a fan who messes with journalism on her days off. I mean, I get paid three cents a word. I'll be able to buy a cup of coffee after I write it."

How would I paint this, he thought. This woman standing next to me, the flowers tiered, furiously bright before the headstone. He rubbed his eye with his thumb and hoped she would leave, and when she didn't, when he looked up and she hadn't magically disappeared, he said, "Look. You want to save someone, and you try and try, and they won't let you. You can do everything for them and they just turn away from you. How crazy is that? Even if it kills them, there's no way they're going to let you help them."

"Is that what happened? Were you trying to save her?"

Vale laughed, scrubbed his hand down his face. "What? No. God, no. She wanted to save me. She tried for years, man. I destroyed a marriage, walked over her, *stomped* on her kindness, right? Threw it in the trash. And still she tried to help me. Again and again."

He turned away from her, realized he was afraid of what he would see on her face. See his own self-loathing reflected back at him. Looked at the sad, withered palm trees instead, leaning around those gray stone benches.

"That should be on her fucking tombstone," he said, biting his lip. "*She loved insistently, in spite of great and continued disappointment.*"

He chanced a look at Valerie's face then, her tight-lipped smile, and saw it: it wasn't loathing, it was something parked way too close to pity. Seeing it was like someone using his heart as a strike-strip for a match, *whoosh*. He said, "Can you please leave me alone now? Seriously."

She gave him a last look and seemed poised to say something but finally turned and walked away. Was she pissed? Hurt? Vale stood there among the flowers, the napkin still in his hand.

He looked for the first time at Candice's gravestone. There was her name, the dates of her life and death, *Loving Wife and Daughter* below that. This summation. A life encapsulated. Candice, bracketed.

An ugly, wracking sob loosed itself in his chest. This was all he seemed able to do anymore: cry and bleed. He slowly banged the heels of his hands against his forehead, once, twice, mewling like a child. Mike Vale, little more these days than a storage facility for self-pity and rage. He stood in front of Candice's grave and the world wheeled relentlessly on and he just felt so tired.

3

From the journals of Marvin Deitz:

My lives went on and on as I sang the same endless refrain through the centuries:

I'm sorry.

I'm so sorry.

I saw a man beat a child nearly to death beside a clapboard building on the outskirts of some dusty town. Oklahoma somewhere. I trudged by with my sore-shanked mule, so thirsty, my lips chapped to the point where they bled. I was dying. We were all dying there. Drought, starvation. And I said nothing, simply raised a fist as I passed, too weak to do anything else even though the man himself was so tired he took great pauses between kicks to gather his strength.

Still I had the presence to think: *Damned again, then. For my inaction.*

I once crossed a stream with a hundred other men somewhere in the glittering Malaysian noon, all of us festooned with rifles and clearly defined intentions. Murder in our hearts. I saw a small burr on the pant leg of the man ahead of me, my friend, while the river itself gleamed like a writhing snakeskin. I knew full well what I was about to do. I ran toward it.

Another time came the rich stink—garlic, horseradish, a chemical bite—of mustard gas as it wafted across the lip of our trench.

Seconds later the burning began, and a thought skated like a flare across my mind: *You've earned it. Whatever happens next, you bought and paid for it a hundred times over.*

Even watching Coltrane's long skittering runs in the Blue Note, sweat lit like tiny jewels on his face, his face limned in light and then darkness again as he bent and rose, propelled by his own visions, the sound itself arching like an animal in the room, his perspicuity of movement and sound and how I felt pure joy unfurl inside me like a flag watching them all, these men move in tandem through song. The wonderment of it, the gift of it. Riding on the back of this respite was the knowledge I didn't deserve it.

And through it all I saw the cords in Joan's neck pull taut as the flames touched her, as they took hold. Saw my father lay the spike below an eye, rest it there, felt my own feet rooted to the floor.

My God, who was I to know *joy?* To allow myself that?

Me of all people?

I've long ago grown tired of asking myself these questions. I've wanted to end this for so long now.

• • •

We found a coffee shop a few blocks from the cemetery. Pumpkins and squash sat in decorative clusters on all the countertops. Techno music played just quietly enough over the speakers to be subconsciously irritating. The barista had a tribal tattoo on his neck and called me "bro" when he handed me my coffee, then he grinned and told Casper his eagle shirt was "totally meta." Sometimes I thought of the world now, this particular time around, this life—with its internet sites centered around public sex, and Hollywood gore-porn films that raked in millions at the box office, the metronomic eradication of endangered species and civil rights, conservative politicians' refusal to acknowledge global warming and on and on—and I felt like we were inevitably rocketing toward something, some final collapse that would put Rome's toppling to shame.

Then again, I'd been moaning about the exact same thing for centuries.

Sometimes I just felt like what I was: six hundred years old or so, and exhausted.

We sat at a corner table, the place bustling, traffic passing outside the window in front of us. Casper took a sip of his drink—something orange and mounded with nutmeg and chocolate, more of an art piece than a beverage—and said, "Can I ask how you lost your eye, Marvin?"

I drummed my fingers on the table. "I got shot, actually."

Casper reared his head back. "Seriously?"

"It was an accident. One in a million chance."

An armored police vehicle trundled down the street in front of the shop, something we'd already seen more than once in just our short time here. How such a thing could possibly help or hinder any ghost sighting, I had no clue.

"Listen," Casper said, frowning and lacing his hands around his drink. "I've been thinking. We need to get serious. We need a plan."

"A plan?"

"Yeah." Casper took his hat off and ran his hand through his hair. The lump on his jaw was purpling. "I mean, I came here for a reason, you know. Didn't you?"

"I'm trying to find someone."

"Someone from that show, right? *To The Point?* I heard you talking about it when we were in the motel room."

"I was talking to myself? Like in my sleep?"

"Oh yeah," said Casper.

"Huh."

"Lyla? Is she your daughter or something? Your wife?"

"Just somebody I knew a long time ago," I said, and looked away, Joan's face right there in my mind, vivid. Lavendu holding the cross so she could see it from the crowd. The pity she'd looked at me with.

"Okay, then. There you go. I mean, I'm *here*, you know? We made it. We've arrived. I'm all for making some contacts here and then heading back to Roseburg and getting my shit and moving, you know? Moving here for good. I don't know about you."

I didn't even know how to respond to that. Did I just say, *At best, I've got about seventy-two hours to live, buddy?*

Casper was on a roll. "We should stop dicking around and

start getting stuff done. We need a plan. I say if you want to head to the studio where that show's filmed, we should do it. We might find some answers."

I squinted, tilted my head: *I don't know.*

I was afraid, I knew. For the first time in a long time, I was afraid of failing. Of wanting something and not being able to find it. Of *losing,* when it seemed that I'd already lost so much. I was freezing up. But Casper was right. I was here, and I had so little time left.

"Okay," I said.

"Awesome," Casper said as he jammed his cap back on his head. He stood up, gingerly explored the knot on his chin. "Let's go see if His Lordship is done."

4

Vale sat trembling in the driver's seat of the van. He'd be struck with them occasionally, these flurries of cold like he'd been flung in an ice locker. He couldn't predict it. It was like a thing totally separate from him, outside of himself. Whatever it was, it was a pain in the ass. He held onto the steering wheel, watching people tread the grass of the cemetery, and even with the ignition off, half-expected the van to start shaking. Sweat dotted his face, slicked his arms, his thighs.

Vale and Casper rounded the corner and walked up to the van and Vale rolled down the window and called out, "Let's go."

Casper and Marvin stepped up to his door. Casper frowned when he saw Vale. "You're done? Everything okay?"

Vale tilted his head toward the passenger seat. "Let's go. I need to get a little hair of the dog and all that, you know? Get in the van."

Casper scratched his neck and said, "Actually, Mike, what do you think about going to a movie studio instead? Marvin's trying to find someone there, and I wouldn't mind checking things out."

Vale leveled his gaze at Marvin, who could clearly read the need in Vale's face. Marvin quietly said, "Or, maybe after you get a drink, how would that be?"

"I don't care about after. I need cigarettes and I need a drink. Right now."

And it wasn't even anything anyone said. It was just a look that Casper gave Marvin, this deft little look, and piled on top of everything else—jail, his fingers, the fact that he'd wanted to do one important thing and somehow managed to fuck it up—it was just too much. One little look that said: *See? Told you. That's Mike for you. Dude just pinballs between chaos and ruination.*

"You know what," he said, throwing the door open and stepping out of the van. Casper and Marvin backpedaled. "Fuck you. Get out." Vale stomped around the side of the van and threw open the sliding door. The van rocked. Vale grabbed Casper's backpack and hurled it into the parking lot. He felt the sour-battery taste of adrenaline and was at least grateful for something he recognized. Casper was right, of course. He leapt from tragedy to tragedy. People turned to watch them.

"Mike," Marvin said.

"You too," Vale said, flinging the passenger door open, throwing Marvin's bag out, a journal slapping to the pavement like a shot bird.

Casper said, "What the hell, Mike." He trotted over and picked up his backpack.

Mike reached into the back of the van and grabbed a box. "And take your *shit* with you," he yelled, which admittedly made zero sense, and hurled the box as far as he could. Since the box was empty, it was pretty far. He rammed the sliding door shut, closed the passenger door.

Stalking around to the driver's side door, he felt more warmth running down his septum. His knuckle came away bright red after he ran it beneath his nose. Casper and Marvin were staring at him. A lot of people were staring at him.

"*I* picked you up," he said, pointing. "*I* did you a favor. You *and* you."

"What?" Casper ripped his hat off. He pointed at his jaw. "Are you kidding? I got punched by a bouncer, dude. A *funeral bouncer* knocked me out. Don't tell me what you did for me." Marvin, Vale saw—and it was such classic Marvin—had picked up the box, breaking it down. God forbid someone make a mess with Marvin Deitz around.

"I didn't ask you to do jack shit for me."

Casper shook his head. "You have a drinking problem. You have a serious problem, dude."

"What did you say to me?"

"You are an alcoholic, Mike."

Vale stomped toward him, chin down, loose-limbed, feeling heat spread through his guts. Casper dropped his hat and bounced on his toes a few times, holding his backpack by one strap. Vale took another step and Casper swung his backpack like a mace. He missed. There was easily ten feet of empty space between them. Someone in the parking lot trilled laughter.

"Guys, come on," Marvin called out, tucking the folded box beneath his arm. "We've got to stick together."

Vale got in the van, extended his middle finger out the window, and drove out of the parking lot.

5

Excerpt from CDC (Centers for Disease Control and Prevention) pamphlet:

DO NOT ENGAGE WITH APPARITIONS!

The Centers for Disease Control and Prevention urges you not to engage *with an apparition should one appear.*

<u>If a sighting occurs:</u>

- Remove yourself from the area.
- Do not attempt to verbally communicate with the apparition.
- Do not attempt to touch or threaten the apparition.
- Notify police or emergency personnel immediately.

If an apparition appears on a street or freeway, *do not slow down your vehicle*—this will cause congestion and increase the possibility of accidents and you may be charged with a crime.

Research has shown that there is little to no concern of infection, disease or physical danger from these entities—but long-term effects still remain unknown. Again, citizens are urged to *keep their distance* and immediately report sightings to police or emergency personnel.

• • •

We watched him go.

"Seriously?" Casper said, squinting, his backpack held by a strap and scraping the ground. "That really just happened?"

We walked. What other choice did we have? Past the cemetery, a furniture outlet store, its windows soaped white, an office park. Another office park. We kept walking and the street was eventually cordoned off and we stood for a while and watched—with many, many other people—as a ghost flailed his arms and beseeched the sky. An old, white-bearded man in a suit, the smoke, ringed by a line of police while one of those tanklike vehicles of theirs told us all to move on over its loudspeaker.

The man next to me held up his phone, elbowed me and grinned. "Smoke City, man. *Love* it."

"What's that?"

He gestured with his phone. "The smokes. The *ghosts*. Started out with like, what? Fifty sightings a day in all of California? Pulling in a hundred a day now, just in LA. There's more and more of 'em. People say they're sticking around longer, too. Smoke City, baby. End of the world."

He winked and went back to his phone, hooted, bouncing on the balls of his feet.

It was true. The ghost looked like that: smoke drifting but held still in the shape of a man. A thing continually peering around, lost, abandoned. Entirely uninterested in us.

No, not that. Blind to us.

• • •

Further down the street we came upon an unlikely blending of commerce, something I would have thought more likely to find in Portland rather than some bland section of Culver City: a hair-salon-slash-yogurt-shop, with the truly unfortunate name of Cool Bangs. As terrible as it sounded, the place was surprisingly busy.

We grabbed a booth near the windows and Casper decided, with the air of a man who truly did not know what to do next, to go ahead and get a haircut. His number was called and I sat there for a moment until the panic gripped me again, the sense that time was running out, had already run out. I went outside.

I looked at my phone, pulled up Julia's number, thought about dialing. But what would I say? What was the point?

I put my phone back in my pocket and watched Casper through the window. He was sitting in the chair with a bib shrouded over his body, his hair wet and combed. He said something and the woman cutting his hair titled her head back and laughed loud enough that I could hear her through the glass.

I stood outside watching traffic. The panic, the sense of uselessness, was like a low current thrumming through me, making me edgy. I watched cars pull in and out of the parking lot, idly wondered where Vale was, how I could help him. How he could be helped at all.

When Casper came out his hair was cut short, combed over to one side, faded. His beard trimmed. He was beaming. I'll admit he looked pretty good, even with the t-shirt.

"Looking sharp," I said.

"Thanks." He winked—he did, he actually winked—and held out a business card between two fingers.

"What's that?" I asked.

"Oh, this? Nothing." He ran a hand over the helmet of his hair. "This is just Casper getting Ananda's personal phone number, is what this is. Boom."

"Ananda?"

"That would be my hair stylist."

"Really," I said. "Well. Nicely done."

Casper inhaled slowly, gazed at the car park with his chin raised toward the sun. "LA is shaping up nicely," he said. He admired his reflection in the window for a moment and then clapped his hands, all business. "Where to now, Marvin?"

6

He drove without purpose, his anger wavering like smoke, and everywhere he looked saw neon signs that clamored OPEN in red, blue, white, yellow. Could not unsee them. Bars and taverns and liquor stores seemingly on every avenue he passed, places that suddenly appeared to make up the bulk of the city.

Everywhere he looked he saw placards and posters in windows, fluttering above awnings: airbrushed, hyper-detailed photos of chilled bottles of beer, pint glasses kissed with frost, bottles of liquor backlit with golden light, as if imbued with holiness. Women reclining on beaches wearing bikinis and sea-foam, bottles of beer suggestively placed between breasts. He drove, turned, drove, saw tavern windows dark as eyes.

He passed a shuttered movie theater, its marquee proclaiming *SMOKE CITY—ALL YE ROUND HERE ARE DEAD. WE PRAY FOR THEE!*

He reached a stretch of roadway where left turns were not permitted and so he circled the same five block stretch a half dozen times, biting the inside of his mouth until he finally found street parking between a cell phone store and a take-home pizza place, both with their entrances shuttered.

He took a wad of bills from his shoebox, shoved the box under his seat and walked into a bar he'd seen around the corner. Thinking the entire time that he should go back to the parking lot, to the cemetery, go find them. Go apologize. The bar seemed to have no name, but above the door, a martini glass tilted left and then right—more neon—and Vale stepped inside.

It was dark and cool and the foot of the bar was lit in runners of lights. On a large television he saw a clown punch a horse in the face and then jump over a fence. The bartender sat below the television, reading a book. A scattering of bar vultures sat on their stools, their shoulders hunched toward their ears as if they expected blows to start raining down at any moment. Wood rot, beer, decades of cigarette smoke embedded into the ceiling. No one spoke and the only sound was the wet rattle of the air conditioner.

The bartender stepped over and raised his eyebrows. He was a thin man in a button-up shirt, pale as something pulled from beneath rotted wood. Mustache as narrow as a pencil lead.

"Whiskey and a beer back," Vale said.

"Well?"

"It doesn't matter. Sure."

The drinks arrived and the whiskey went down burning and Vale exhaled like a movie monster. The other men eyed him sourly. The beer helped settle things a little.

He raised his bandaged hand and ordered another round and drank the whiskey. It sloshed around hot and searing in his guts. Minutes later, and the problem was his hands were still shaking and yet he seemed suddenly drunk, *stunningly* drunk, more drunk than he had possibly been in years. His legs kept wanting to slide out from under him, spill him out on the floor. What was happening to him? What was this?

An old man a few stools away lifted his craggy head as if on some swivel and gazed at Vale, a look as if he knew exactly what was happening. He had a yellowed bandage on the side of his neck and Vale, weak-kneed, touched the scab on his own forehead. The man belched then, a sound so wet and horrific and possibly internally damaging that Vale felt his gorge rise. Vale opened his mouth and the whiskey and beers came back up on top of the bar, a burning, foamy mess that he tried to cover through his cupped hands. Tears poured from his eyes.

An explosion of cries from the vultures, hands slapping the bar top in merriment, caws and laughter and mockery directed at the bartender to mop it up, Jonesy, mop it up, here's a fella can't handle his drink anymore.

Vale held up his hand, gestured uselessly. *I'm sorry.*

"Get your ass out of here," the bartender snarled, and Vale left on shaking legs.

7

Excerpt from *Recent Spectral Sightings in the Western Nest of Fornication and Their Relation to the Approaching Armageddon: An Evangelical Primer:*

Do we as THE FAITHFUL believe in coincidence, brothers and sisters? We do not. God does not deal in coincidence! He deals in MEANING and SWIFT and RIGHTEOUS ACTION!

So we ask you, brothers and sisters, you who seek a holy and righteous life, is it coincidence that such specters have appeared where they have? Is this coincidence, or is such a thing HEAVY and FRAUGHT with THE LORD'S MEANING?

That such specters have appeared THERE and nowhere else—the very vipers' nest of amorality and liberalism, chiefly within HOLLYWOOD, CALIFORNIA, home of the GOD-HATING ENTERTAINMENT INDUSTRY, and south of that, where the once-vibrant border towns of MEXICO are now run by narco-traffickers who deal in HUMAN SLAVERY, who publicly DISMEMBER judges and policemen and fling their severed body parts from bridges!

Ask yourselves if it is coincidence that the specters of the dead—the lost ones, the unclaimed—have appeared in the very same place where so many have gleefully TURNED THEIR FACES AWAY FROM THE LORD GOD?

Ask yourselves, brothers and sisters, if we really have the

TIME and LUXURY of believing in the foolishness of coincidence any longer.

• • •

The plan wasn't complicated. Get grounded, hit the *To the Point*
studio and see what we could see. Most importantly, *move*. Even
if it felt like we were treading water. But first, before all of that, we
needed a base, a grounding.

Everywhere we went, places were full—hostels, motels, everywhere. California was packed, LA sardine-tight. Everyone wanting
to bear witness. We finally found a motel on Slauson Avenue.
Serviceable was a generous term for it, especially for what we
were paying: double beds that would look like a surrealist horror
painting under a black light, a winding trail of cigarette burns in
the carpet. A barred window with a view of the parking lot, traffic
beyond that. The TV remote hung from the nightstand on a chain.

I heard the sad rattle of old pipes as Casper turned the shower
on in the bathroom. I turned the TV on and there it was, the same
episode of *To The Point*. Like time itself was grabbing my skull and
shaking it. I couldn't escape.

There was Lyla on the screen, somehow both meek and con-
frontational. I looked for Joan again, buried there somewhere
inside her countenance, but I couldn't do it. I couldn't see her.
The bodyguard sat next to her, big veins curling along the backs
of his hands, into the cuffs of his suit. And there stood Jesse
Pamona, looking at that moment very skeptical as she panned
toward her audience.

Turning back to Lyla, she said, "So it's like a split personality
thing?"

My phone rang. Julia. I put my phone back in my pocket.

Lyla shook her head. "No. We're . . ." She squinted, raised her
head. I saw the tracery of a tattoo beneath the collar of her shirt.
"We're in here together. She's in here." She tapped her breastbone.
The rattling of the pipes stopped in the bathroom.

Jesse tucked her chin down and purred into her microphone,
"Tell me something that only Joan would know," and I felt my heart
clang like a stone down a well, like I was about to be found out.

"Hey, Marvin?" Casper called from the bathroom, his voice muffled through the door.

Lyla smiled. "Come on, Jesse. A girl never tells." The audience whooped, laughing. Some men in the audience stood up and pumped their fists.

"Just a sec," I said.

"Marvin," Casper said. "Seriously. Can you come in here for a second?"

Still staring at the TV, I said, "Gotta admit, I'm really not that interested in seeing you shower, Casper."

"Yeah. Funny. Just come in here."

I dropped the remote on the bed, stepped into the bathroom. It wasn't a large room. At all. A tiny window inset high up in the wall, milky glass gridded with wire. Blue floor tile, grout embedded with grime. A reasonably sized bathtub made for tight quarters. Steam clouded the room, made the mirror above the sink purl and run with condensation. Casper stood in the bathtub, a towel around his waist. He pointed at the sink.

Which was, of course, entirely unnecessary.

"You believe this?" he whispered. "And me with no camera, God dang it."

A ghost woman.

Weeping in front of the sink, imploring the air.

She was like pale smoke trapped under glass. Her form shifted, took hold, shifted again. I saw the sharp collar of a dress, hair in a tight bun and then a hand, a sleeve cuff. Shifting, shifting. The honk and blat of traffic outside, the world resolutely moving on. I caught a glimpse of her seamed face in the mirror, a brooch at her throat. She was oblivious to us, her hands gesturing in front of her as if she were explaining, petitioning.

"Holy shit," Casper said. "Holy *shit*. Where is my camera? Why do I not have a camera? What is *wrong* with me?"

I couldn't look away. "Casper, be quiet."

At the sound of my voice, the woman turned, her eyes widening.

I knew *recognition* when I saw it. It was obvious. Like she had *discovered* me. She turned to me, her hands now clasped together in front of her belly, knotted into each other. It was one of my stranger moments, yet mostly heartbreaking for the anguish so evident on her face.

And she spoke. The sound of her voice was like her form: a shifting, coruscating breath with words half-buried within. I could've sworn I felt it tousle my hair slightly. A breeze, a hushed river of words.

"What is that? Is she *talking?*"

"Chinese," I said. "She's telling me . . . about her son, I think. Her husband."

"You know *Chinese?*"

"A little bit," I said, still not looking away from her. "Learned it a long time ago."

"I should be getting footage of this. Still photos even. Can I borrow your phone? Sweet Jesus I'm an idiot. Who doesn't have a phone?"

"Casper. Just be quiet for a minute."

She spoke of her husband and son. I doubt it even took that long, her story. The three of us in the cramped bathroom, the wan light through that high-set, milky window. It only took a few minutes maybe. But how long, I wondered, had she waited for the telling of it?

A simple story, probably common enough. Irrevocably entwined, I imagined, with Los Angeles itself, and most certainly with America. Her name was Suyin. Her husband and son, Kim and Xan, were hired as laborers for the Southern Pacific line from Goshen to LA. Good money, great money, for the times. Worth uprooting their lives for. And by the spring of 1830, they were able to send for her. Kim and Xan, the totality of her life, her summation, but only two of the hundreds of men hired to bore the nearly mile-long San Fernando Tunnel, the last significant obstacle for the rail line before it reached LA.

I translated for Casper, never taking my eyes off the woman. This litany of heartache as she stared at me, her form dimming and sharpening. This rawness in her voice drifting throughout the room. I'd lived lives as desperate as Suyin's, yes. Been the one to bring anguish to someone like her, too. Now, here, I listened.

The mountain was heavy with water, she told me. Mud mired their shovels, weighted them. The work was slow-going and brutal.

Backbreaking. They worked six days a week, but her husband had proven to be a diplomatic man, a man who frequently calmed disputes between the laborers and the white line bosses and, as such, the family was allowed the rare privilege of living outside the work camp.

They were allowed to move to a rooming house in Chinatown, the three of them. She would spend most of her time alone there until Saturday night, when Kim and Xan hitchhiked or got rides from the line bosses back to LA.

Xan, her boy, was twenty. He was young and strong and was quick to make friends. The money, compared to what he could earn in Chengdu, felt like untold riches. Kim worked alongside his son most of the time but coughed and walked stiffly and seemed to shrink each week she saw him. But he was honorable and recognized their fortune and didn't complain, not even to Suyin.

On Sundays Xan would leave to go walk around Chinatown with his friends and she would put balm on Kim's muscles, bathe him in their tin tub with water she boiled on their small stove. Later, the three of them would sit in the small room on their mats and talk and drink tea as if they were still home, as if nothing had changed, as if even the light here was not different from what they were used to.

Kim and Xan would wake early Monday morning, before dawn, to make it back to the job site before daylight. Kim would sigh, putting his clothes on, and speak of their torches hardly burning in the tunnel, as if there were no air to feed them. He spoke of the frequent shifts and groans of the earth, the dustings of soil that fell on their shoulders as lines of men stood silent, waiting to see if the mountain would bury them. She held her tongue during these times, which was a hard thing to do.

And then the day came:

The Saturday in which they did not come home.

She waited. Cleaned the room, brushed her hair. Drew distractedly in the small notebook Kim had bought her. She didn't sleep that night, waiting for the sound of their voices in the hallway.

She got on the road to the camp before dawn Sunday morning. It was a ways outside of the city but not as long as it had been—they were almost done with the line, after all. But soon she saw that many of the cars on the road were going toward the camp very fast. An emergency, Suyin thought, and felt the skin of her scalp tighten.

When she made it to the camp she looked for Liwei, a friend of her husband's who had traveled from Mukden to work on the line, and a man who had occasionally come and drank tea with them. The camp was in disarray, with many laborers quietly weeping or staring solemnly at the ground as knots of white men stood around yelling at each other and pointing at the mountain.

She found Liwei and looked at his face and knew everything before he said a word to her. She *knew*. How could she not? *It fell,* Liwei said. His mouth looked like a cave, a dark hole falling in on itself. *It fell on them, Suyin. Many men were buried. I'm so sorry.*

And she walked back down the road with the mountain behind her. She walked very slowly. All the way home until sunset sent spears in her eyes and she had to cover her face to shield herself from the glare. She went into the room she had shared with Kim and Xan and lay down on their mat. She had been mending a pair of Xan's trousers and gathered them and clutched them to her chest.

For a moment the silence stretched out between us all until Casper said, "She killed herself, didn't she?"

"Yes," I said. My legs felt useless, blocks of wood. Inside me, sorrow held court, sorrow thrummed a chord of such sadness inside me. A sadness that I hadn't felt in years. Centuries, maybe. Even my time at the hospital hadn't done this to me.

"I'm sorry," I said in my stilted, terrible Chinese. "I'm sorry for your loss."

I stepped forward and touched her hand. She was made of smoke, Suyin, but I reached for her anyway, without thinking. Concerned only with the simple human kindness of it. That ache to somehow absolve another of pain.

Suyin cried out. Casper's feet squeaked a bit as he backpedaled in the bathtub. I pulled my hand back, afraid I had hurt her, but she was smiling. Less a cry, I suppose, than an exhalation.

She didn't dissipate in a cloud—there was nothing so definable as that. There was simply the usual absence of her. She was there and then she was gone.

But I had *heard* her. I had been able to listen to her. There was that.

I stood next to the sink and quickly wiped a tear from my eye. "I'll let you get dressed," I said to Casper, my voice husky. I shut the bathroom door behind me, primly took my glasses off, folded their stems, put them in my shirt pocket. Buried my face in my hands and wept.

• • •

An hour later I'd cleaned myself up the best I could. The desk clerk gave us the address of the closest car rental agency, and Casper and I took a cab there. This part of town: parking lots, office parks, strip malls, all of it so like Julia's part of Eighty-second Avenue as to be interchangeable. Occasional clusters of street corner doom-sayers held signs declaring the End Times. One proclaimed in a nearly indecipherable scrawl DEAD MEANS DEAD FOR GOOD. I carried Suyin's story inside me like an ache, like a blade I kept wrapping my hand around.

We paid the cabbie and I looked around the parking lot and said, "We have to move, Casper. We have to get going."

"Okay," Casper said, giving a little shrug. "That's why we're here." He took his cap off, put it back on.

"I just don't have a lot of time."

He cast me a shrewd look, his eyes dark under the bill of his hat. "Anything you want to tell me, Marvin? Something in particular going on you want to bullshit about?"

I started walking toward the rental kiosk, the wind blowing my hair back, carrying the scent of hot tar, garbage. "No. Not right now, anyways. Let's just get moving, okay?"

Got the rental car and found a copy shop where we printed directions to the studio. Modern phones could do this in seconds now, but my technological prowess began and ended at sending email invoices to distributors at work. I had a landline at the shop and a flip phone with a prepaid card in my pocket. Casper was still wearing the same goddamned shirt we'd picked him up in. We were working with what we had.

I white-knuckled my way through traffic. I was an idiot. Unprepared, and deserving of what I got. I could feel self-pity and desperation settle over me, hook into the back of my neck.

"I don't know how people stand this," I said at one point, my hands locked in rigid attention on the wheel.

"What?"

"The traffic," I said. "The stupid fucking traffic. Is it always this bad?"

"I don't know. It's LA. This is just part of the deal, right? You okay, Marvin?"

"We've managed about fifty yards in the past twenty minutes. People do this every day. Years of their lives, probably."

"Man," Casper said, smiling, "this is the place to be, dude. Are you kidding me? There's a reason why everyone wants to be here." He drummed a little rhythm on the dashboard. The car smelled new, a coffin embalmed in that chemical smell. "You *talked* to that ghost, Marvin. That's crazy. You know that's crazy, right?"

"I guess. I'm trying not to think about it right now." I tried to merge and had a moment of bright, feverish empathy for Vale and his anger.

We eventually found the cluster of studios and soundstages where *To the Point* was filmed, but got lost in the labyrinth of parking lots and connecting roads. Acres of pavement. The tourist section of studio hangars gave way to sad patches of scrub grass and blunted, leafless bushes that stood in ditches between the lots, winding back roads and chain link fences choked with brambles.

The place became quickly charmless. Casper blithely noted that it seemed like we were lost. It was odd to think that so many fantastic and made-up worlds were contained inside all of these buildings, when the outsides were so bland and uniform.

I finally parked in a half-full lot that faced an outbuilding the size of an airplane hangar. There was a line of utility vehicles bracketing the face of the building. No one was outside. I didn't recognize anything. "How did we even get here?"

"Like I said, we're lost."

"I guess you're right."

"We could just walk in." He shrugged. "Let's just try walking in somewhere. Let's just go in that building and talk to someone."

"And then what?"

Casper shrugged. "And play dumb? Try to find, what show was it?"

"*To the Point.*"

"Just ask where the *To the Point* studio is. Say we're late, act like we're in a big hurry. Like we're supposed to be there."

I tapped my fingers on the steering wheel. Pictured an hourglass, me at the bottom of it, buried under sand. My black lens with a funnel of dust falling on it, my mouth filling up. I was freezing up, like I had at Vale's ex-wife's place.

"We'd never find it," I said. "We haven't really thought this out, have we?"

Casper made a little exasperated noise, jabbed his hands palms-up at the window. "Come *on*, Marvin. The studio is *right* there. Fly by the seat of your pants, dude. You need to find this woman, let's do it."

I started up the car. We wound our way through more lots, pulling over to the shoulder once to let a pair of guys in one of those little golf carts putter by.

"You could ask them," Casper said. "Ask those guys."

We came to another lot, this one with a small guard booth and a retractable gate.

"Ram right through that thing," Caspar said. "Jesus, just *do* something, Marvin."

"Casper, please."

The guard sighed when we pulled up. This part of the studio had an air of desolation about it. Like this guard, when she saw people, saw them for the wrong reasons.

She laid her arms on the sill of the booth, looked down at us. "You guys must be lost."

"We're actually looking for the *To the Point* studio."

She pointed a finger back the way we came. "You're about two miles off, guys. Lot 2, Studio F."

"Studio F. Great, thank you."

She smiled wanly. "You know you're gonna need laminates to get in, right? Either that or head on over to the main entrance, and you can get tickets for guided tours at any of the gift shops."

Casper leaned over and bowed down so the guard could see him. "Listen, I don't mean to be a pain here, but you need to get Tom Pugliesi on your little radio there right now and tell him I'm here. Shit's fucked."

The guard nodded, frowning. "Oh, late for an important meeting, huh?"

"Exactly. You're exactly right."

She rested her chin in her hand. "I've heard every name, guys. Every name, every scam you can think up, I've heard."

Casper looked at me, shook his head. "Tom Pugliesi. She thinks Tom's fake." He stared up at her again. "I don't show up, hon? Heads will roll. First yours, honestly."

"Well, I'll get on my radio, friend, but it'll be to call security. You can try your luck at Studio F but they're going to tell you the same thing."

Casper sighed, ran a hand down his face. Took off his hat, put it back on. "Ma'am, do you have an employee number or something like that? Pug's gonna shit a brick in approximately three minutes, and he's an ugly dude when he's unhappy. Did you ever catch the *Treacherous Means* pilot we did last season? About the deaf-mute bounty hunter?"

"Nope."

"That's because the star we got—young kid, boatload of talent, knew jujitsu, all that—was fifteen minutes late to a meeting with the Pug and a bunch of board suits. Fifteen minutes! Pug killed the whole fucking show, ma'am, a pilot and nine episodes. I know I don't want to get on his bad side, how about you?"

She looked at Casper with dead, eternally patient eyes as she keyed the mike on her radio. "Dispatch, this is two-five. I've got two douchebags at Gate T-1 here. Repeat, two d-bags at Gate T-1. I'll get you their plate number in just a second, over." She took her thumb off the mike.

I sighed. "Thanks for your time."

"Be sure and buy a ticket for the tour. They let you guys ride on those little carts. It's cute."

"Douchebags?" Casper said as I drove away. He sounded hurt. "Two *douchebags?* That's cold."

• • •

I started to head to yet another lot, another nondescript patch of pavement that would undoubtedly lead to the same exact answer that we'd already gotten. It all just came tumbling down on me. The weight of it. I'd run out of time.

"I am *fucked*," I said, and gunned the engine, veering through the empty lot and pulling snarling cookies, the stink of rubber trailing behind us. Casper grabbed the handle above the door.

"Marvin?"

I jumped out of the car and slapped the hood. I bellowed, spun around in the empty lot and bellowed again. Flung my arms out, felt my voice crack. There was nothing around us besides a few panel trucks and nondescript vans and another closed-up soundstage the size of an airplane hangar—even the guard's booth was a good half mile away.

I was out of ideas.

I was dead. Any time now. It was a matter of hours.

It had seemed possible, for a moment there. Finally, some kind of answer. Joan suddenly cutting through the endless dark. But no.

Casper got out and laid his arms on the top of the car, resting his chin on his forearms. "Dude. The position of freaking-the-fuck-out-guy has already been filled. Vale's got it, and he's been great at it. *What* is your deal?"

I shrugged, and kept shrugging. I looked ridiculous, I was sure. "I'm out of time," I said. "I'm just out of time."

Casper ran a hand over his new haircut. "Why?"

I let out a big sigh. There was nobody here. I had tried to find the *To the Point* soundstage and happened upon the most remote, desolate area within the entire studio. In all of Hollywood, probably. It was ridiculous. The whole thing was ridiculous. The Man Who Couldn't Find a Building.

"I have to tell you something," I said.

"Okay. Good."

"It's kind of a lot to take in."

"That's what she said."

I just shook my head.

Casper held his hands up. "Trying to lighten the mood. Sorry, Marvin."

"Get in," I said, and we got back in the car. I turned around and headed back down the road we'd come in. To Lot 2, Studio F,

I couldn't even say. Didn't know. I was just going to drive and see where we wound up.

No more time. No more plans left. I couldn't remember the last time I'd felt—and this was saying something, considering—as lost as I did right then.

"Okay, so."

"Hit me," said Casper.

"I was born in Moineau, France," I said.

"Cool. Sounds fancy."

"In 1381."

8

Information gave him the address of Brophy's agency. He wrote it down on the back of Casper's cult pamphlet, his handwriting shaky. Afternoon traffic was gutted and slow and when he got another nosebleed he held a handful of fast food napkins to his face and bellowed with the uselessness of it all. Alcohol itself had abandoned him. Light at the edges of his vision was wavering and strange.

Brophy's agency took up the bottom floor of a sleek cube right between Wilshire and Santa Monica, a smoked glass exterior and brushed steel cast about at shipwrecked angles. Dying or not, the guy was doing well for himself.

Vale parked and fed the meter and waited. Sat there watching the door, knowing Brophy could be anywhere. Might not have come into the office that day. Was out banging a starlet somewhere. Pulling fresh blood from a teenager and infusing into his own body, who the hell could say?

Vale measured time in cigarettes, kept thinking about Marvin, about the idiocy of hurling Casper's backpack in the parking lot, throwing that empty box like an asshole. Another bridge burned. Candice was like a door he kept walking past without looking at.

After three hours, Brophy came out of his office, yammering into his cell phone. Again, the shock of it: he'd lost so much weight, his stork legs scissoring along as he walked, two sticks swaddled in the excess fabric of his slacks. He keyed the door to a white Jag and Vale pitched his cigarette out the window like some ridiculous private eye.

Left, right, left. South on the 405. Then the 10, the 101, past West Hollywood, up in the Hills.

Geographically, some of it was coming back to him. He tried to keep a few cars behind the Jag. When he rolled the window down, he smelled wood smoke; the dry hills surrounding them going up in flame. Inevitable this time of year. Vale followed through canyons punctuated with gated driveways, flashes of multimillion-dollar homes tucked behind ragged-ass copses of pine. Up in these switchbacks, it was pointless to try to hide his efforts.

Finally, on a stretch of roadside with the promise of dusk just beginning to blue the carved canyon walls around them, Brophy pulled onto the shoulder. Vale pulled up behind him and they sat like that for some time, the night's first insects starting to bat themselves against his headlights. Brophy's brake lights in the dark ahead of him like a pair of sentient red eyes. What is this feeling, he thought. Nothing ever happens the way you plan it. He had fantasized about this moment for years and in his mind it was nothing like this. This was hollow, imbibed only with a sense of inevitability. He shut the van off and listened to the ticking engine for a moment before stepping out, the thin scree rasping at his feet.

Brophy the ghoul. Brophy the Halloween mask. His face was sickly and wretched in the green light from the dashboard, gnarled veins bunched at his temples. Skin stretched tight on his face and bunched loose at his throat, like someone had grabbed the flesh and pulled down hard. Vale wordlessly got in the passenger seat, the door thunking behind him, the night sounds outside immediately hushed. Brophy sat rigid with his hands on the wheel. He had a tiny butterfly bandage above his eyebrow from their scuffle.

Finally, he said, "So what's going to happen now, Mike?" That drowning, rattling quality of his voice was better, but not by much.

Vale looked down at his splinted hand. "I don't know," he said. "I haven't gotten that far."

"Do you have a gun? Is that what's next?"

"No."

Brophy rolled his shoulders. A car filled the inside of the Jag with light, moved on.

"You think I fucked you over, right? This is the big showdown. You've had this in mind for years. If it wasn't for me, everything would've been wonderful. Your whole life"—he coughed wetly, curling into the steering wheel before righting himself—"like a goddamned music video. Am I right? Am I in the ballpark?"

Vale didn't say anything.

"Am I close?"

"Come on, Jared. The coke? The crate of booze? The poor, innocent stripper paying her way through college? All that *bullshit*? You had that contract ready to go. That shit was *prepped*. You screwed me over."

Brophy shook his head. "Right. Paying you a million dollars for your work was screwing you."

"Two or three paintings go for that much now."

Brophy turned to him then, wolfish, grinning. "Because of *me*," he said. He jammed a thumb against his own chest. "You couldn't even put your fucking pants on without falling over. Drunk all the time. Blackouts. Screwing around on your wife. Your paintings were turning to shit, Mike."

The thing about Candice cut. "You know what I was doing last week, Jared? Making hot dogs. I wore a hairnet on my beard. Before that I was at a car wash."

Brophy shrugged. "I don't know what to tell you. What's your point? You had a boatload of talent, opportunities guys would kill for, and you pissed on it. Pissed it away."

"You ruined me," Vale said, and Brophy's laughter was brittle and clipped, like gravel flung against glass. It turned into another cough and he pulled a handkerchief from his sport coat and put it to his mouth.

"Spare me," he rasped. "The hell do you *want*, Mike?" He tucked his handkerchief back in his pocket. "You want me to say I'm sorry? You want *closure*? I can't give you that. I don't traffic in it, I don't believe in it."

"I'm trying to remember if you were always this much of a prick."

"Get out of my car, Mike. We're done."

"I want that contract nullified."

"Done," Brophy said. He turned the radio on, some teen pop with bass throbbing like an embolism under it all. "Get out."

Vale looked at him. "Seriously?"

Brophy's head jittered in exasperation as he shrugged. "What'd I say? If it'll get you out of my car. Get a lawyer, draft something in writing, send it to me. First rights to your shit from here on out are yours. Starting now. If you ever pull your head out of a bottle and paint again, which by looking at you seems pretty unlikely, you'll own them. If you want more than that, we can keep it in court for fucking years. Now *get out*. I've got to get home. I'm sick."

Vale stepped out. The night was warm, crickets doing their thing around them. Brophy took off, the taillights of the Jag painting the canyon wall red until he rounded a turn and everything was full dark.

• • •

In the dream, the van was scorched with smoke, the plastic features of the dashboard melting like taffy from some unknown but terrible heat. It felt like the rendering of his own body, seeing the poor van like that. And when he touched his own body his ribs cracked brittle as pasta—this was a terrible dream—and Vale snapped his whole ribcage, he couldn't stop, it was like scratching an itch, he wouldn't stop until his whole body was shattered, and then someone rapped on the window next to his head again and Vale lurched up gasping.

Doused in sweat, the catty stink of himself suffused throughout the van. A cop stood at the window, his flashlight at his shoulder, roving the beam around the interior. Vale had parked across the street from Richard's house. It was nearly midnight.

He rolled the window down, wincing against the cop's light. His lips separated with an audible tearing sound.

"Hi there, officer," he rasped, resisting the urge to cover his face.

The policeman thumbed the light off. He had a skull full of gray stubble and a cleft chin. "Do you live in the neighborhood, sir?"

"What?" he said.

"You can't sleep in your vehicle, sir. I need to see your license and registration."

"Officer," Vale said, and couldn't finish. He looked down at his hands.

"How much have you had to drink tonight, sir?"

Vale shook his head, still looking at his lap.

"Sir," the cop said, "I need you to step out of the vehicle."

Vale nodded and started to roll his window up—this seemed like the right thing to do—and with surprising gentleness the cop put his fingers on the edge of the glass and said, "Stop." He put his other hand on his holster, and Vale pressed his palms against his eyes.

You fling your wreckage in an ever-increasing arc, he thought. Don't you? You fling your shit like an animal.

In the darkness, someone called out, "Excuse me, officer." The cop turned, and they saw Richard crossing the street in a robe.

"Sorry to bother you, sir," the policeman said. "We're fine here. You can go back inside." Vale began weeping unceremoniously. Still the smell of burnt plastic and old piss hung in the air, and it was his own terrible scent, coming out of his pores or something. Richard just needs a sleeping cap, Vale thought. He just needs a lantern, and if Norman Rockwell ever needed to paint a millionaire entertainment lawyer he'd know exactly where to go. Val's hands would not stop shaking and he made them into fists and jammed them into his armpits and still he cried, cried, cried.

"Officer, I know him," Richard said.

Vale saw variants of his future, the summation of his choices. They'd run the plates on the van and it would be stolen. He'd be found guilty of menacing Richard, of transporting hate literature, something. He'd had any number of opportunities to do the right thing. He'd had *endless* opportunities. Prison would not be kind to him. Richard and Brophy would high five and do bumps of coke off the ass-cleavage of hookers. Casper would become famous and revile his name on cable television and Marvin would do . . . whatever the hell Marvin had come here to do. Meet his friend. And Candice would still be dead, still and forever be in the ground. *This is me saying hi. Call me when you discover fire and the wheel.* He put his hands over his face, a distant part of him amazed at the ungodly sounds he was making.

"I know him," Richard said again.

No one said anything for a moment. He heard the cop sigh.

"We can't have him sleeping in his vehicle, sir. We've received complaints. You want to take him inside?"

SATURDAY

1

Vale woke as if he was being pulled from some sea: wakefulness came incremental, borne slowly from darkness to light. He saw swaths of sunlight in unfamiliar patterns in an unfamiliar room and in a strange way that confusion itself was a feeling like coming home.

He recognized, after a time, the bedroom the police had originally arrested him in. The signs of violence had been removed. The broken vase had not been replaced. He was in Richard's house. Candice's house. Outside would be the pool he'd been thrown into.

There was a photo on the dresser he hadn't noticed before, Candice lithe and angular in a white tank top, a bottle of beer held in one hand, leaning against a paint-chipped picnic table. Sexy in that offhanded, casual way she had; a mocking sneer on her face. A canopy of trees stretched green and vibrant behind her.

He realized—the thought arrived as distinct as a snapping branch—that this place was the culmination of her life. She had loved him once, but by the time she had died, their life together had been little more than a back chapter in an older, sadder book. This was her home.

Did I ever know you at all? Did I ever let you know me?

If I didn't know you, how it is that I'm losing you so ferociously now? So fiercely?

He rubbed his face and his hand came away with flakes of dried blood. Rusty pool of red on the cream pillowcase. His broken fingers ached. He took the pillowcase off, scrubbed his face with it. It was already ruined. Blood had soaked through the pillow itself and Vale felt an unnameable twist of shame at that.

He drank *beer*, for shit's sake; he'd hardly ever even touched liquor anymore. What was happening to him?

He opened the window and felt the breeze against him. Saw the backyard, the pool. He had little memory of coming into this room, only a vague recollection of the cop at the van window, Richard propping him up, the smoke-infused nightmare, burnt plastic.

Stepping into the hall, he heard the sizzle and clatter of pans in the kitchen. He smelled bacon and coffee. Nausea rolled in his guts like someone throwing dice.

He veered into a bathroom on the way to the kitchen, pissed. Spat up a few dark wads of something and quickly flushed without looking too closely. Shame curled on itself, wrenched itself into a tangle of fear inside him in this jangling, searing arc. He ran his hands under hot water, scrubbed his face. He was afraid to see Richard, afraid to look him in the eye.

The kitchen was bedecked in black marble and chrome, a wooden island the size of a king-sized bed in the center of the room. A constellation of copper pots and pans hung from hooks above, the counters done in the same pale wood as the island. Magazine-quality shit.

Richard stood at the stove wearing a bathrobe and slippers, his jaw dusted with shadow.

"Mike," he said without turning, gave a little wave with a spatula.

"Hi," Vale said, his voice ravaged. Ravaged and timid; unsure.

Two days ago Vale had walked soundly over Richard's grief with his own agendas, his own resentments and furies. *What would you have done*, he thought, *if the positions were reversed?* Richard turned the bacon, scattered a handful of onion into another skillet, stirred that. The two of them stood there silently like satellites. Orbiting each other's grief, the one commonality of their lives.

Finally, Vale cleared his throat and said, "I want to say thank you."

"Don't mention it," Richard said. "There's coffee if you want some."

"Really, though. How I've acted . . ." he started, and couldn't finish.

Richard turned and pointed the spatula behind Vale. "There should be some bread behind you. Christ knows there's everything else. People brought so much *food*, you know? Can you slice some of that up?"

Vale turned and saw the counter behind him was indeed piled high with food. Pies in plastic wheels, pies in tins. Salad bowls topped with foil. Stacks of cold cuts, plates full of gourmet cheeses, crackers, garnishes he couldn't name, half a dozen bottles of wine. Who in Christ's name would bring a bottle of *wine* to a wake? The bottles gleamed dark and bullet-like, an armory of sleek shells.

He found a loaf of olive bread dusted with flour amid the stacks and took down a knife from the magnetic rack on the wall. He began sawing the bread into slices. Candice's name was shockingly vibrant on his pale hands, the black marble counter.

Richard chopped, drizzled olive oil, stirred, pushed things around with his spatula. He threw what looked like a handful of pink salt into the skillet, his eyes on his work. Vale's nausea slowly dissipated, the smell of the food unlocking something inside him.

He dropped the bread into a toaster. A sliding glass door led to the patio and Vale saw how the sky and the bottom of the pool were almost the exact same unreal hue. An eye-watering blue. For a moment he wanted to paint that, to find that color and bathe in it, cover his body with it. Fill his mouth, his insides. Live inside it.

"I was furious at you all day yesterday. Last night even, with that cop." Richard said. "God, I was so pissed." He was motionless, only the hem of his robe wavering as he stirred.

"I can understand that," Vale said.

Richard turned and looked at him, then wagged his spatula over his shoulder. "No, Mike. Nope. Here's the thing. You don't *get* to understand. You don't *get* to know what it's like. Sorry, but that smacks of sanctimony."

Vale stared at the glowing coils in the toaster. "Okay."

Shallots, garlic. Richard walked to the refrigerator and removed a crate of eggs. Broke a half dozen of them into a bowl. Whipped them. He was the type of guy that could break eggs one-handed.

"I apologize for what I said to you the other day. I feel like, for the last week or whatever, I've just been holding on," he said. "Like I've just been hanging onto the skin of the world. I'm just waiting to fall off." He poured the eggs in the skillet. "But I realized last night," and here he spoke brightly, as if he were telling a joke, a story, "like literally right before I looked out and saw that cop outside your van: I realized that I'd eventually need to do more than that. That just breathing and hanging on wasn't going to be enough. For now, sure.

"But Candice, we—one of our things was to never let each other rest on our laurels. Right? To never sit still. She challenged me so much, man. We never got in each other's faces, it wasn't like that, but she had high expectations. For both of us. That's how we did it. 'What's the bare minimum you'll accept,' Candice would say. 'And what about after that? What comes beyond that?' We pushed each other."

He turned and looked at Vale then and his eyes were red-rimmed and haunted in a way that Vale had seen in his own mirror hundreds of times over the years. A look steeped in sadness, regret. "She still loved you, in her way. Never stopped. In spite of herself, maybe."

The toast rose. Vale stood there locked onto Richard's terrible gaze.

Richard said, "She defended you to her last fucking day, man. To me. To everybody. She always believed in you. She always thought you'd get your shit straight at some point." He stared at Vale almost defiantly, as if daring to contradict him. "So I decided I needed to do more than the bare minimum here. For her. Do you understand me?"

"Okay, Richard," Vale said.

The two of them. Christ. Graceless with pain; Vale's voice clotted, Richard wiping at his bloodshot eyes, holding a spatula.

"I'm sorry about Brophy," Richard said. "About bringing him here. He does a lot of work with my studio. And I'm trying to, I don't know . . . forgive people their trespasses. But it was stupid of me. I shouldn't have had him here. Candice *hated* that guy because of what he did to you."

"I talked to him," Vale said.

Richard turned back to the stove. "You did?"

"Yeah." Vale gave a weak little laugh, sheepish. Stacked more bread in the toaster. "I followed him. Got in his car. It was a pretty anticlimactic showdown."

A pause. "Did he tell you he has cancer?"

"I figured it was something like that."

Richard nodded.

"Pancreas at first," Richard said. "Now it's starting to spread. Doctors gave him a year, year and a half. His agency represents a lot of people we work with. We've had a drink or two together. I'm trying to give people second chances. But still."

"Thirds, for some of us."

Richard turned and looked at him. A ghost of a smile there. "For you? Shit. You've had more chances than a cat gets lives, Mike."

Vale looked at the countertop. "I know it."

They ate standing up. Richard poured Vale a cup of coffee and Vale held it until he was able to will his hands still. They ate in silence, their allegiance to Candice the fragile salve between them. Vale looked at that blue sky outside and swore to himself that he would never drink again, and immediately recognized it both for its familiarity and its unlikeliness.

2

Excerpt from National Public Radio's *All Things Considered* program:

And it's not as if we're talking A-list celebrities here, Robert. Nobody is witnessing Elvis, or John Lennon. In almost every account, these are regular people, from all walks of life and a host of different periods throughout history.

So no one's claiming to see Davey Crockett. Benjamin Franklin. Jesus.

Exactly, Robert. There was the one alleged case of Abraham Lincoln on the San Francisco pier, but so many of these are impossible to verify. But they seem—these apparitions—to run the gamut of ethnicities, social strata, gender, time periods. They're all over the map. It's very *democratic*, actually. You'll have a pioneer-era soldier in Beverly Hills and a, say, Depression-era housewife in Compton.

But all attempts at contact have so far failed, isn't that right?

Correct, all attempts at contact have failed *so far*. We're still trying. But there's just a disconnect going on.

Doctor, let me just . . . So, you're a Professor of Bioethics at Stanford University. There've been a host of federally sanctioned committees formed since these apparitions appeared a few months ago. The Centers for Disease Control is coordinating the investigations. A multitude of research has been done by a variety of scientists, hundreds of millions of dollars have already been spent, the global economy has taken a hit, and we still have virtually no concrete, factual information as to what these things are. So let me just come right out and say it: Are these ghosts? And why are they here? Why now?

Well, that's where the continued attempts at contact and study are so important, Robert. Because if I had to answer that right now, I'd have to say I don't know. But if they *are* ghosts, think of what that says. For the world, for humanity. For our notions of God, and spirituality, and all that entails.

But what do they want, Doctor?

Like I said, we don't know. We're trying. But what do most ghosts want? In all the stories we listened to as kids? They want to go home, they want justice. They want to be heard. They want to be allowed to move on.

• • •

Casper sat in the passenger seat, his arms folded. He'd taken his hat off a few times, ran his fingers along its filthy band, bent the bill into a crease. Hadn't said a word the entire time. We hadn't seen a car enter the lot, either. No movement, just me telling my story that at times sounded ludicrous even to me. Maybe it was the circumstances—I was a long, long way away from Julia's couch—or the simple fact that the entire thing *was* ludicrous. The Curse, defined.

"And that's it," I said. "I've got until Monday to find her. I'll probably be killed any time between then and now." My laugh sounded strangled, silly. "Any second now. Who knows? And even if I do find her, I don't know what any of it means."

Casper ran his tongue over his teeth and nodded once. "Well. I guess we better find her then. Soon."

"Just like that, huh?"

Casper shrugged, pulled his shirt down over his belly. "Listen, Marvin. You and I, and the whole world, man—we've seen, like, ghosts literally wandering around. Literal *spirits*. I saw you talk to one in the bathroom of a shitty motel." He shrugged again. "So what do you do when the whole world pretty much jumps the shark?"

"I don't know."

"Me neither. But I know this: the shit that I've seen since we got here goes a long way toward making me believe you. I mean, I was already inclined, but still. So, yeah. I don't know if I fully *get* all of it, but I'm a long way toward getting there, dude."

And it was ridiculous, how that made me feel. The gratitude I felt. This weight lifted off me. Like netting being pulled from around my lungs. I could breathe again. I thought of the priest who had me drowned in the Tisza. Of Julia's humoring smiles.

It was a ludicrous story, yes. All of it.

But we lived, finally and irrevocably, in ludicrous times.

3

He was in the spare bedroom gathering up his things. In the mirror, his forehead was still marred with quarter-sized scabs, the flesh surrounding it shiny and pink. Here, he realized, was the culmination of a lifetime of choices. Right here, Christ, in front of this sun-shot window in a bedroom in Candice's—*Richard's*—house. The end result of every supposedly good idea he'd ever had had brought him here.

"Hey, Mike?" Richard knocked quietly on the door. Vale opened it and they stood there awkwardly in the doorway, Candice's inevitable *thereness* filling in the room. This man in front of him the one she had chosen to spend her life with. Not him. Not Vale. Vale had squandered it all.

Richard's eyes found the pillow and bloody pillowcase on the bed. "Shit," he said.

"It was from last night. Sorry. I didn't get any on the bed."

Richard sighed, frowning. Vale's mortification was complete. "Listen," Richard said, bouncing his car keys in his hand. He wore a sport jacket and a white shirt with the collar open, faded jeans. The tan, chiseled looks of some retired athlete. Even headlong in his grief he looked more presentable than Vale had been in years, had ever been, maybe. "I was thinking I'd go to the office for a bit," he said. "Just to get out of the house."

"Of course, sure. I've got my stuff here, just packing it up."

"No, no. You're welcome to stay. I thought I'd give you the alarm code in case you wanted to leave the house before I got back. But you're welcome to stay."

He was speechless for a second. *He* wouldn't trust himself in this house alone. But then again, that was one of the differences between them: Richard was a man capable of being uncompromising with himself: his wife had loved Vale at one point, Richard reasoned, and thusly he would treat Vale with kindness. In spite of Vale's missteps. And even though he was, by Richard's own admission, a drunk and derelict. *This* was the weight of Candice's beliefs, right here, and it showed in the buoyancy of Richard's love for her. Here was Richard in the tangible act of honoring her memory.

"No," Vale stammered, unable to meet his eyes. "I should get going."

Richard bounced the keys in his hand again. "It's up to you," he said softly.

"Thanks for everything."

"Of course."

"And again," Vale said as he ran a shaky hand through his hair, "I'm sorry about everything. The funeral, Jesus. I can never make that up to you." He let out a little chuckle as he burned a hole in the floor with his stare. "Ruined a perfectly nice pillow."

"It's fine," Richard said. It wasn't, and both of them knew it, but it was done and they had come this far.

"I'll be going," he said. "Thank you again."

"I was thinking I could give you directions to the grave. If you wanted."

"I already went," Vale said.

"You did?"

"Yesterday."

"Okay then," Richard said. He pushed himself from the doorframe, his jaw working.

• • •

They stepped outside and the brightness of the day was searing, seemed almost artificial. Vale squinted as the two of them shook hands and Richard gave a little wave as he pulled away in his car. Vale went and sat in the van across the street. He felt no sense of resolution, only that exhaustion that he couldn't shake. The neighborhood was quiet; he could hear the blat of a lawnmower somewhere nearby.

He counted the money in the shoebox and then just sat there with the ignition off and his hands resting on the steering wheel. Stared at the constellation of dead bugs on the windshield. He took out his wallet and there in a compartment was Marvin's card. *Sounds Good,* with a phone number for the shop, as well as a cell.

It was a curious moment, and one he would remember: how the notion arrived fully formed—that salvation was possible, or at least worth trying to attain. Maybe nothing as dramatic as salvation. But the feeling that bridges burnt could be built again over time. That apologies meant something, carried some kind of weight, and so did not doing the same endless shit over and over again. He'd come to this conclusion before, but somehow after speaking with Richard, it felt different this time.

It occurred to him that he could drink tomorrow. If he could knuckle through today without succumbing to whatever was happening to him, his tremors and sickness, his terror, then tomorrow he could *bathe* in alcohol if he wanted to. Swim in it. Save it for tomorrow: it was nothing he hadn't heard before by the self-helpers and the AA people, nothing he hadn't thought himself countless times before, but somehow at that moment with the ghostly growl of the lawnmower outside, it fit inside him like a piece in a jigsaw puzzle.

With Marvin's card in his hand, he looked up at the street, buoyed. Hopeful. He resolved to find a pay phone somewhere, to call Marvin and Casper. To help them, somehow, because really, what else was left for him? He had nothing else. This was it.

And across the street, on the grass, there was Candice. Candice—her shape wavering like smoke in the brutal light of day—stood in front of her home, her house, turning and turning.

• • •

Vale stepped from the van and everything remained the way it was, bright and still, a bird twittering in a branch somewhere. The lawnmower stopped, started up again. It was undeniably her.

She wore jeans and a collared blouse and her hair was longer than it had been that day in the restaurant three months before, and pinned above her neck. He didn't know what any of that meant—if they were the clothes she had died in or what forces decided such things. But she stood in her yard and took one step this way and back, as lost as any of them were, stepping from grass to gravel and back again.

He stood in the gravel of their rock garden and said, "Hey, Candice. It's me." His voice so timid, cracking on the last word.

She pivoted on one foot and turned, but away from him. Roved her head around like she was somewhere else entirely, some great and depthless expanse of darkness. He stepped closer and touched her—her arm half-translucent, the color of old newspaper—and it seemed to do nothing; she seemed not to feel it. Neither did he.

"Can you hear me? It's Mike. Candy?"

It was exactly as he had imagined: she had come home to the place that rooted her to the earth. Her home with Richard. This was where she had chosen to return. And he was right about the rest, too: his touch did nothing. She did not recognize him.

"Okay," he said. His voice cracked again. "Okay. I'm gonna get going now." He swallowed, thumbed tears away with his good hand. "I am really sorry I fucked everything up, Dee. I mean, even before any of this. Our lives together. *Your* life. I am so sorry."

Candice turned toward him and he thought that she may have finally heard him, but no—she put her arms out in front of her as if she was navigating through a dark room. Her mouth moved and with a flat crack of heartbreak he realized she was speaking and he could not hear her.

Again he said, "I am so sorry. I hope you find what you need. I don't . . . I don't know what else to do, Candice." The look on her face was not of terror—he didn't know if he could have withstood that—but one of vast confusion, of worry, so different from how he remembered her in life.

He turned and headed back to the van, across the rock garden and the grass, and all the while, the impossibility of the day's brightness bore down on him, the clear delineation of shadow cast from the roof of the van to the pavement. He practically ran back to the van, because his heart, really, just couldn't take anymore.

A big red Cadillac turned onto the street, roving like a blood clot on four wheels. The driver saw Candice in front of the house and Vale watched as it slowed, then stopped. The smoky windows rolled down. Both the driver and passenger took out their phones and began filming.

Vale thought, *She's lost. Poor Candice is alone and lost and this is what we're doing? This is what we do to them when we see them? Gaze at them and film them?*

The car was stopped in the middle of the street. Vale walked up and stood in front of the passenger window, blocking their view. The man and the woman were both gray-haired, older. The man had a big gold watch on, a straw hat that touched the ceiling of the car. Leather-everything inside the Cadillac.

"What the heck," the man said, trying to aim his phone around Vale.

"Move," the woman said, frowning. "What in the world is the matter with you?" She looked back to the driver for help. "Morris."

"Don't," Vale said, his voice thick. "It's not right."

"They can't even tell," the woman said, casting a doubtful eye at Vale's face, his cast. "Morris, tell him to *move*."

"We're not asking you again, son," the man said, and Vale took the passenger side mirror in his good hand and broke it off and threw it down the street, sunlight throwing a single knife of light into his eyes before it landed in someone's lawn.

"Get out of here," he said, and they did.

When he looked back she was gone. Maybe she went inside somehow, he thought, maybe she was safe, looking at her paintings and waiting for Richard to come home. He got back in the van and leaned his head against the wheel and wept as that terrible sunlight fell in his lap and across his hands.

4

Spectral Sightings Continue to Plague the West Coast
—Newsweek

Congress Convenes for Emergency Session Regarding Enforced Curfew in High-Impact Spectral Areas
—Los Angeles Times

Homeland Security and Department of Transportation Consider Freeway Reroutes Due to Increased Apparition Presence
—LA Weekly

Governor under Pressure to Claim California a Disaster Area, President Threatens to Send in National Guard under Executive Order
—Time

• • •

So in spite of my big revelation, Casper and I were still out of ideas. We had the rental car, we had the home base, and the desire to act. That was about it. I had the panicky, dry-mouth feeling that my death would be coming at any minute; it was making me skittish as hell. And that was it, our sum total. We drove around aimlessly, eventually passing an ornate sign that said *Welcome to*

Brentwood—it seemed like a nice part of town, certainly nicer than where we were staying—and we talked very little.

When my phone rang, I didn't recognize the number. Casper eyed me, waiting to see what I'd do.

"Hello?"

"Hey. It's me."

My eyes widened. "Hey, Mike."

Casper faked his death, splayed out in the seat next to me.

"What's up?"

"Listen," Vale said. I could hear traffic noises behind him. "Listen, Marvin, I'm at, like, the last pay phone in America here, man. I just wanted to apologize to you. To you and Casper."

"You want to apologize," I said, more for Casper's benefit.

"I do," Vale said. "You guys deserve that. I was wrong, and an ass. I screwed up. I'd like to help you guys if I can." He gave a jagged little laugh. "I mean, I don't know how—but I don't really have much else going on. I'm kind of at a loss here."

I pulled into the parking lot of a fast food restaurant and turned the car off. "Hold on a sec," I said, and put my hand over the phone. "He wants to apologize. He wants to help."

"Are you kidding me?" Casper said. "Tell him to go throw someone else's shit into the road."

"I'm not going to tell him that."

"Is he sober?"

I put the phone to my ear. "Mike, have you been drinking?"

He seemed prepared for it. "Not today. No."

"Not today," I said to Casper.

"I just want to talk to you guys," he said. "I have some money. Maybe I can help. You know?"

Casper looked at me and shrugged, palms up. *Up to you.* *Look for portents and signs.*

"Okay," I said. "We're at a fast food place. What are the cross streets? Casper, can you see where we are?"

Casper got out and trotted to the corner. He came back and gave me the cross streets, which I gave to Vale. "It's in Brentwood," I said.

"Okay."

"We'll be in the restaurant getting something to eat," Casper said. I repeated it.

"What's the restaurant?" Vale said.

I told him and he laughed.

"What's so funny?" I said.

"Never mind. It's a long story. I'll see you guys soon."

"Okay, Mike." I couldn't keep the doubt out of my voice. And always time running away from me, time dwindling down. This place could be my last meal for all I knew. Jesus.

"Thank you, Marvin. I'm heading your way now. I appreciate it."

I folded my phone.

"Well," Casper said, "this should be interesting."

5

Vale drove, thinking of the Ace High. The vast hours he'd murdered there.

He'd attempted a few times to tally the actual number of hours he'd killed in that bar and those like it; the number eventually became staggering enough that he'd get close to a rough figure and try to stop thinking about—which usually meant going to drink at the Ace High or a place like it. It was just unfathomable. It hurt his heart, that number. Sitting on a barstool, bellowing nonsense in Raph's ear, night after night after night.

He did it for years and years.

The same forty songs played on the jukebox every night, the same ghostly film coating the inside of the pint glasses. Everyone armored with indifference. The bartenders who knew his name and could rarely be stirred to address him by it. The bathrooms dense with misspelled graffiti, the reek of piss. After enough drinks, the women in the bar grew or shrank to become little more than the recipients of his contempt and sadness and—by their proximity, the simple fact of *being there*—the cause of it. Fucking ridiculous.

Vale hunched like a golem on his barstool. Watching a female bartender somewhere bending over to retrieve a tallboy from the cooler. Her very shape causing an ache inside him, this jumping electric desire flaring inside him like a current, causing him to leer like a fucking teenager. And then he would buy another beer and would be moved into actually tipping her that time, would be shamed into it. Not for the looking; he was paying for the want itself.

Years and years like that.

The bluster of pop music from a dead age, those same songs again and again as Vale chased the Moment throughout the room, up and down an emptying glass. What could he have done with those hours had he not spent them in the Ace High and places like it? Who would he be now?

Years he'd squandered. Among spitting neon and felt-worn pool tables, bathroom floors grown slick with vomit, men like him gazing silently up at televisions mounted on the walls. His own ghost continually bounding inside him like a loosed animal. His failure like a coat of ironwork that grew heavier as the night wore on. Years doing this.

And for years he'd blamed Brophy. A face to pin his failings upon. He lifted glass after glass, bottle after bottle, always with the burning hope that Brophy's ruination would somehow rest in the bottom of one of them. Years spent with blame as a useless currency while he let whatever meager talent had been afforded him seep out and grow soft with rot. And beneath the blame lay a constant, heated loathing, a self-hatred like topsoil laid across the poorly tilled fields of his heart.

He'd grown old in there, in that place. Places like it.

All the dead hours. The years cataloged by jobs quit or fired from, by eviction warnings, fights, arrests, by blood spatters in the morning sink. Hands studded in scrapes, knees blown out of his pants from falls on the way home. By the teeth grown loose and bloody in his mouth.

He made it to Brentwood, found the place with little trouble and parked on the street, gazing up at the winged burrito rising from the roof of the building. He crossed at the crosswalk and stepped into the busiest Bean There, Bun That he had ever seen.

It was a massive building, easily three times larger than the one in Portland. Populated by a half dozen cashiers. Potted ferns and faux-marble counters. The staff wore white long-sleeved shirts and dark vests and crimson visors. Where were the paper hats? The suffocating sadness? Where were the old men in trench coats with their newspapers and cups of water, rationing out their little boats of Chili King Fries?

In Brentwood, a basket of Total Taters cost eleven dollars.

He found Marvin and Casper seated in the back, glumly picking at their food. Neither of their faces changed all that much when they saw him, maybe a cloud of guardedness coming over Casper. He reminded himself that he was the one that owed them; it wasn't the other way around.

He sat down across from Casper. Casper was eating a Fishwich Dee-Lish and stared at him impassively as Vale put his hands on the table in front of him. He looked down at the tattoos on his fingers—those four letters, C-A-N-D, the other hand covered in a dirty cast—and when he raised his eyes to meet Casper's gaze he felt suddenly tethered. He felt like he knew, for the first time in Christ knew how long, which way was up. Knew what he needed to do, at least in that moment, that second.

"I'm sorry for leaving you guys like that. It was wrong."

Casper chewed, looked over at Marvin. Finally, he saw whatever he needed to see in Vale's face and he put his sandwich down. "Don't worry about it. Are you really sober right now?"

"Yeah."

Casper frowned at Vale. "How do you feel?"

He felt more awake than he had in years. More present. "I feel good, actually. Tired. But good."

Casper sucked at his teeth and moved a finger back and forth between Vale's eyes. "Well, that's kinda weird then."

"What?"

"Your pupils are two different sizes."

6

From the journals of Marvin Deitz:

When I was Bill Creswell—in my pre-Marvin life—I died one sweltering August night by injecting what felt like seventeen tons of heroin between the webbing of my toes. This was New York, 1961. It was all Ginsberg and uppers and jazz jazz jazz. Beat shit was blooming. This was less than a year after my trip to Moineau, which I'd never really shrugged off. The ensuing disconnect. That sense of being adrift.

I was in my apartment on Avenue B when I did it. It was scorching hot inside, and it could be considered a suicide in the sense that I had grown willfully careless. You just reach that point where you hit a wall. My will had been drawn up for months, all of those stupid records arranged to be shipped to Portland, Oregon after my death.

I fell out of my chair and onto the gritty, filthy floor, the spike still dangling between my toes. I didn't feel it at all. Something like a pale white roar all through me, this heavy drift, this wall coming down. My head hit the floor, felt like concrete wrapped in lace. Mingus's "Flamingo" started in on the stereo, and that was the last song Bill Creswell ever heard.

• • •

Vale, it could be said, was on fire.

In the parking lot of the Bean There, Bun That, the three of us took up our usual spots inside Vale's van and talked. We didn't tell him everything—Casper and I had agreed to as much—but we told him enough to get the immediacy across. The three focal points being: Lyla, *To the Point,* and we're running out of time.

And just like that, he was on it.

He seemed shaky and looked pale and ill-used, but he also looked *inspired.* I don't know how else to explain it. Like a sick man who'd found religion, maybe.

We followed the van in the rental car, and I counted no less than three specters as we drove, the first one just starting to gather a crowd and the other two with the police blocking streets with their huge tanklike vehicles, cordoning the areas off. Soon enough, we'd have cops out in there in riot gear. And then, the National Guard, a curfew. Guns on the street, checkpoints.

It all seemed inevitable and sad—you live long enough and you'll see it plenty of times, even in one life. The curtailing of simple, civil things. The quashing of it. I wouldn't have believed it a week ago, but the ghosts were almost becoming commonplace. Even if I suspected they all had a story as heartbreaking as Suyin's, we were acclimating. It was the military presence that was becoming more unnerving.

We followed Vale out of Brentwood, went to another copy shop, where we did possibly the most archaic, old-man thing possible and rented a computer for an hour. Vale scowled and stood over our shoulders, watching the video with Casper and I as we sat hunched in front of the screen. "*This* is who you have to find?"

"It is."

"Yeah."

"Should I buy a phone? Just go buy a phone somewhere? So we have the goddamned internet?"

Casper spared a glance over his shoulder. "Do you actually know how to work one?"

"What? It requires an engineering degree?"

I printed some stills from the video. I watched the cursor vibrate on the computer screen. Vale took the pages from the printer, handed them to me: his hands were shaking again.

We followed him on the freeway and when we exited—our

little convoy of two—began passing through sections of the city where the luster had clearly faded. Vale would've known what part of town we were in. I didn't ask. Faded trash lay flattened at the curb. Weeds tufted from slats of broken concrete. Banners in convenience store windows broadcast items in three or four different languages. Vendors set up tables on street corners, lining the sidewalk. Sunglasses, jeans, tourist t-shirts. We passed tattoo shops, discount jewelry stores. Pawn shops hawked guns and gold, electronics. Every window was grated.

We parked, and Vale started walking into strip clubs with the stills, passing out twenties to hulking, monosyllabic bouncers, their necks pocked in steroid-induced acne. We followed, timidly. No luck anywhere, but I marveled at Vale's ease. A bartender in a place called the Engine Room watched boxing on the TV over Vale's shoulder. He had a stick and poke tattoo—*KET*—on his cheek and bounced a toothpick from one corner of his mouth to the other. The dancers wouldn't start for another half an hour, he said. Vale passed the bartender the picture with one hand and a twenty with the other, pushing them across the glossy wood. The man looked at the picture for a few seconds and pushed it back, pocketing the twenty. "That chick could be half the bitches in here."

"That's nice," I said, and he looked at me, eyes like pinpricks in black paper. Dead as anything. The toothpick stopped moving.

"Thanks for your help," Vale said, pushing me out the door.

And on and on. Sun arcing across the sky. The city so massive we'd hardly dented it. Like flinging water at a skyscraper on fire.

Tomorrow would be my last day at the latest. Or tonight, or right then. Any moment. What we were doing was idiotic; it spit in the face of odds and logic alike. But it also made room, I supposed, for grace, for something extraordinary to happen.

I *needed* something extraordinary to happen.

What else were we supposed to do?

It was in a club on Pico, with the unfortunate name of Pud's, that something did. It was five in the afternoon and a pair of women in thongs soaped each other from a bucket of suds on the stage. A line of men sat at the rack. The women laughed and blew bubbles at each other, stomped in a kiddie pool. Light refracted. The bass drum kicked me in the stomach. Casper tried not to stare; his jaw was practically hinged to his shirt collar.

"I don't know the chick," the bouncer said, yelling and leaning toward Vale as he pocketed Vale's money, "but this dude goes to my gym."

"Where's the gym?" Vale yelled back.

The bouncer cupped his hand behind his ear and said, "I can't hear you, man."

I said, "He asked where that gym was." The bouncer didn't even look at me.

Vale handed him another twenty.

The bouncer shook his head, sad. "You're mumbling," he said. "Speak up a little."

"Christ," Vale said, and handed him another twenty.

"Wilshire and Wilton," he said. "Ground floor. Dude's always, like always, doing dead lifts. If you've got a beef with him, I'd be careful. He's a monster." He cast a glance over the three of us. "I mean, for you guys."

Rush hour. Bass strobed from open car windows as they zipped past us. Stunted trees rose listless and dry, moored on traffic islands. Whiffs of piss and burnt plastic. Sidewalks thronged with pedestrians, people at bus stops leaned wilting in the heat. We passed a ghost girl on the sidewalk, her hands over her face, and I watched a teenaged boy pretend to grab her by the hips and grind her from behind, his friends cawing rough laughter. She was gone before anyone could take a picture. We got back in the rental, Vale pulling out in front of us.

The Maxxed Gym took up the ground floor of an office complex. White tower of a building. Parking was a nightmare, so we followed Vale into the garage and paid. Our footfalls echoed under the fluorescents. Dim and cool in there, cavernous.

The gym may have literally taken up an acre. Grunts, the clanging of metal muted by air conditioning. Towels and spray bottles of antiseptic hung from pins every twenty feet. The cries of the room reminded me of various darkened chambers I had spent time in. We wandered as discreetly as possible—which was probably not very—but none of us found him.

Vale showed the picture of the bodyguard to the girl at the front desk.

"We're just wondering if he works out here," Vale said. "That's all. Maybe you know his name?"

The girl shrugged, *Get Maxxed!* in arching military stencil across her chest. She chewed gum, seemed wholly unconcerned with their appearance. "Lots of people come here. Like, hundreds a day."

"He dead lifts a lot. Heavy weights."

"Are you guys members?"

"Well, we're thinking about joining, that's the thing."

"I just work here part-time," she said.

Vale leaned forward and tapped the photo, putting his elbows on the counter. He smiled. He did not look well. "Listen. I'm a producer. Okay? I'm working on a new fitness program for FitTV. You know it?"

"I think so," she said slowly, making it sound like a question. I could see her vacillating between wanting to believe his story and gazing directly at the truth—the scabby, dirty, unwashed truth—that was leaning across her desk. "Yeah."

"Great. So believe me when I say this guy is going to be *very* happy if you could help us out."

Behind us, someone said, "Hey, Katrina. How's everything going here?"

I turned and faced a man so frighteningly sculpted and huge he'd need to use his opposite arm to put his phone up to his ear. His vascular system laid out in stunning relief along his arms, into the slabs of his pecs. He looked like someone had an extra bag of suntanned muscle lying around and decided to put a little ponytail on it and make an extra person. A shirt marked SECU-RITY stretched tight across the mountain range of his tank top. Katrina pointed her pen at Vale and said, "These guys want me to give them a customer's name, Levi. They say they're TV producers."

Levi smiled. "I bet they are. Unfortunately, that's not our policy, gentlemen."

Vale looked up at him—the guy had him by a few inches—and said, "It's very important, Levi."

Levi laughed. His biceps jumped like little pets leaping for treats. He leaned down toward Vale and said very slowly, as if speaking to a child, "In five seconds I'm going to bend your arm up behind your back and walk you out the door. It will hurt very, very badly."

Vale put his hands up. "No need," he said. "We're fine. Thanks for your time."

The sun had crested the skyline, the sky awash in purples and blues. The howl and trundle of the city all around us. It was beautiful.

I realized I didn't want to go.

I didn't want to leave this time. I wanted to stay here, in this life.

I was hanging on fiercely, as fiercely as I could, to the skin of the world.

7

They hit another half dozen strip clubs with no results and by then the sun had fallen. In order to save money—and as a gesture of good will toward Vale—they spent another hour returning the rental car and the three of them got back in the van.

They ate at a Thai place in Santa Monica, unsure of what to do next. Vale stared longingly at the beer menu and drank glass after glass of water while Marvin kept sighing and leaning back in his chair. Gazed off into the distance, his eye unreadable behind his good lens. After dinner they stepped out into the warm night and paused: a ghost had appeared across the street.

It was a man, on his knees on the sidewalk in front of a real estate office, his hands clutched together in front of his face. Even across the street in the dying light they saw he wore a robe torn and frayed at the hem.

"Looks like a monk," Casper said.

"He looks homeless," Vale said, and lit a cigarette.

"Do you want to go talk to him, Marvin?"

Vale looked between them. "Talk to him? What do you mean?"

"One of them talked to Marvin. In the bathroom," Casper said.

"*What?*"

"Yeah."

"Bullshit."

"It's true," Casper said. "You want to, Marvin?"

They crossed the street. A small group of boys stood there as well, three or four of them, loose-limbed and fearless in the gloom, one of them straddling a bicycle that seemed too small for him. "Watch this," he said, and rode his bike through the specter, skidding to a stop, turning around and doing it again. The other boys hooted, and then one of them stepped forward. "Can I help you with anything?" he said, in a quavering falsetto, the same words first spoken to the Bride, and then spun and delivered a sloppy, snapping kick at the ghost's face.

Through it all, the ghost registered nothing, his form dissipating and tightening back into focus, a bad picture on a television correcting itself.

Casper stepped toward the kid on the bike. "That's enough. You guys need to get going now."

The boys seemed emboldened by their youth, the anonymity of the night, Casper's own inherent weirdness. "Fuck you, dude," the boy on the bike sneered. "They don't even feel it. They don't even know we're here."

"You don't know that," Marvin said, and the ghost ratcheted its fogged and shaggy head toward him.

"Oh," it breathed among them, its voice like a sheet of glass being scoured with grit. It held its hands out toward Marvin. So obviously a look of recognition on its face, Vale realized. He remembered Candice standing in front of the doorway of her house earlier that day. The blazing sun above her, yet she held her hands out in front of her as if testing the confines of a darkened room. Gingerly navigating her way through the blackness. But this? This look on the specter's face? This was recognition. This was what happened when someone turned the light on.

"No way," one of the boys said, each word drawn out slowly.

Marvin got down on one knee—it took him a bit of work—and the real estate office's neon CLOSED sign pooled like blood in the dark lens of his glasses.

"English?" Marvin said. "Françaises?"

"Nederlands." Again, its voice sounded as if some vital interior machinery had grown ragged with misuse or carelessness. But the look of rapture, of relief, was obvious.

"Oh my God," the boy on the bike said, and pulled out his phone. He started filming. Marvin stayed there on his knee like a suitor as traffic began to slow and the apparition spoke tentatively at first, and then with a growing enthusiasm, a blooming intensity.

"We met a Chinese lady in the bathroom," Casper stage whispered next to Vale, who was suddenly struck with a moment of strange collusion: an inertia coupled with a dizzying wonder at the largeness of the world. The strange vastness of what a single moment could hold. He felt warmth on his lip and touched the back of his hand to his face and it came away bloody. Just a little.

"Dude," one of the boys said, "they're speaking *Dutch,* man. I know it."

"How the hell do you know that, Garrett?" another one asked. "You failed Spanish twice."

"Because my grandma's Dutch, shitneck."

They kept on. Marvin with his sweat stains in his shirt, his dusting of gray stubble, his shirt tucked into his khakis. That black lens. The ghost gesticulated, his voice the windy rattle of pebbles dropped in a glass jar. Marvin nodded, occasionally murmured something in response.

"Two million views by tomorrow," the boy filming said. "I guarantee it." He looked at his friends and shook his head, grinning. "Dude just talked to a ghost in Smoke City, man." Vale looked behind him. People were gathering. When he turned back, the ghost had seized Marvin's wrists, seemed to be really holding them. The specter's face seemed painted with wonder and loss in equal measure. And then it let go of Marvin, clasped its hands together as if in prayer, or gratitude, and then disappeared.

"Just so you know, man," called out the kid with the phone. "You just broke the internet."

Marvin walked between them, Vale and Casper gently pushing past the scrum of people that had formed. "Two million by tomorrow," the kid cried out again somewhere behind them.

"Let's get Marvin out of here," Casper said, putting an arm over his shoulder.

"I'm okay, Casper," Marvin said, his voice husky and drawn.

"You should be milking this," Vale said, holding his cast out as if to ward people off. "Footage for your show."

Casper shook his head as they crossed the street again. "No

way. That was about to turn into a mob scene or something. Plus those kids were dicks."

"And you don't have a camera."

"And I don't have a camera."

Inside the van, Marvin sat in the passenger seat with his fist pressed against his mouth. Vale lit a cigarette and was a little surprised when Marvin said, "Can I have one of those?"

Vale lit one for him, handed it over. "Listen, can I ask? How did you do that back there? I thought they didn't talk to people." He felt strangely ebullient, light. He was sweating like mad. But for the most part, he felt good—and he realized with a start that he'd made it twenty-four hours without a drink. It had been years since that'd happened. His nosebleed was gone, just a tiny one.

Marvin shrugged and rolled his window down. Night sounds filled the van: traffic like an ocean. "I don't know." His lens caught all of traceries of the city night: neon, streetlights, glows from the dashboard.

"I mean, why you?"

Marvin sighed and looked at his cigarette. He ran a hand across his stubble. "Because I've had a long and interesting life, Mike."

Vale laughed. "And a humble one, too."

"Ha," Marvin said, staring at the glowing point of his cigarette. "You know, you're not a terrible person when you're sober."

Vale's chest went loose. He felt like a teenager these days, so quick to anger or weep, sober or not. So at the mercy of the world. He felt himself go flush with simple, animal gratitude. He said quietly, "I think it's a little too soon to tell for sure, you know what I mean? But thank you."

Casper, cross-legged in the back, had opened another box, was peering through it. His phone rang and he cast a bashful look around the van before answering it. "Hey, Ananda," he said. "What's up? How's it going?"

Vale jammed his cigarette in the ashtray and said, "Look, Marvin. I just wanted to tell you—I've got plenty of cash left. Enough, anyways. For gas and hotel rooms for a while. I don't give a shit what happens to the money. I don't care. I'm totally up for helping you guys out. Though I do think you might want to consider a more long-term approach if you and Ken Burns back there are going to try to make it in Hollywood. You know? It's not really a 'Let's pop in for the weekend and get a TV deal' sort of place."

A sad, rueful little smile on Marvin's face. "Thanks, Mike. It's appreciated. I wasn't really planning on staying long."

"Oh, man, I'd love to hang out tonight," Casper said, "but I'm, uh, kind of busy right now. What're you guys doing?"

Vale said from the front seat, "Who's he talking to?"

"He met a girl."

"Really."

"She cut his hair."

Vale laughed. "That's awesome."

"Wait," Casper said, "*who*'re you hanging out with?"

They hit a red light and Vale said, "One among many of my questions, Marvin, is just how is it that you happen to know Dutch?"

The light turned green and they passed beneath it and Marvin's lens flared red and went as black as some dead star. "You know, you pick things up here and there. I was just in the right place. Just have to be available, right?" Speaking so quiet Vale could hardly hear him.

"Wait," Casper said. "Hold on. Our night's just opened up, actually. We'd *love* to hang out. Yeah, totally. Is it cool if I bring my friends? Can you hold on a second while I grab a pen?" Vale eyed the rearview mirror and watched as Casper pressed his phone against his chest and leaned forward between their seats.

"Holy shit, you guys. Holy *shit*. Ananda's at a bar in West Hollywood. And guess what?"

Vale, dutifully, said, "I don't know, Casper. What?"

"She's getting drinks with her friends, Lyla and Louis, who she says were on TV last week."

8

From the journals of Marvin Deitz:

All Manners in Which I Have Died, or at Least as Many as I Can Remember:

(10+) Virus/disease
(10+) Stabbing/disembowelment/hand-to-hand combat
(5?) Gunshot wound/weaponized combat
(5?) Drowning
(5?) Blood disease/bone disease/cancer (some only assumed as such, as diagnoses varied from century to century and were frequently given vastly different names. They all, every last one of them, hurt indescribably.)
(3) Fall from heights
(3) Asphyxiation/smothering
(3) Fire
(2) Blunt trauma (beaten by mob, etc.)
(1) Drug overdose
(1) Hypothermia

• • •

Casper got the address from Ananda and Vale hung his head in mock defeat when he heard where it was located. He predicted we'd arrive, Saturday night traffic being what it was, in approximately three months. I was still stunned, thinking there must be some mistake. Some vast coincidence.

"See you in a bit," Casper said before he hung up.

I said, "There's no way it's them."

"It's them," Casper said. "It's them. Who else would it be? Look for signs, remember?"

"What, specifically," Vale said, pulling into the parking lot of a McDonald's so that he could begin the arduous task of getting us across town, "are you guys talking about?"

Down Santa Monica Boulevard we went, past what seemed like miles of boxy storefronts, fast food joints, tourist boutiques.

Finally, finally, we slowed beside a squat stucco-roofed building, some kind of converted warehouse, that thronged with people sitting at tables out front, a knee-high fence lined around them. The street thrummed; so much movement, sound, lights on the periphery.

What I was feeling, I couldn't put into words. I had been so long imagining this, or something like it, that now that I was here I felt weighted down.

It had been so long since I was afraid of something.

Vale slowed past the building, stopped. "This is the place?"

Casper craned his head to catch an address. "It must be. Wait, there's the sign. Visions. Yeah, this is it."

The name of the venue brought a wry smile. Of course. The Curse, playful as ever.

Someone behind us honked. Vale rolled his window down, motioned them to go around the van. "Parking's gonna be a nightmare," Vale said, lighting a cigarette. "You guys get out, I'll find a spot."

• • •

Even as strangers, or near-strangers, they all greeted us merrily enough—Casper had the ticket of youth as admission but there was no other way around it, the ridiculousness of it: Casper was wearing the same clothes he'd worn for days, and I was a balding old man with one eye. I could have been Casper's father, his just-a-bit-off uncle. It was ridiculous.

And yet there were smiles all around, the three of them clearly a little buzzed (I could picture Ananda getting brave enough to call Casper after a few drinks and some encouragement from her friends), and Lyla and the bodyguard, Louis, seemed entirely unaware or uncaring that I was brazenly staring at them. Night sounds continued to unspool around us—music, a car alarm, traffic, laughter from nearby tables. The tang of cigarette smoke hung like a veil in the air. Bass thundered inside the bar loud enough to vibrate the window glass. It was them. It was *her.*

Louis was as imposing in real life. Hulking in a dark jacket, his face was more seamed in person, more worn. Older than he'd looked on-screen. Lyla's face was thin, sculpted, with almond-shaped eyes that were wide and knowing and more than a little sly.

Again, I felt that stirring of fear when introductions were made and I reached out to shake her hand—what was going to happen? Some starburst of recognition? Our interconnectedness spelled out for us in a flash of light?

Her hand was cool, smooth.

"Nice to meet you," she said to me, and that was all.

They made room for us at their table, and there I was, sitting down next to her.

I still saw no Joan in Lyla. None at all. But what did that even mean? I'd never *known* Joan the Maid, never conversed with her. I'd simply been the instrument that ended her life. There'd been no *knowing* to begin with.

A waitress came and Casper and I ordered beers. He couldn't stop grinning. He kept glancing at me, his gaze heavy with meaning. *All of your lives have brought you here, Marvin.* What was it about Casper that made him so willing to believe my story? "You will not believe this," he said, "but we just saw you on TV. Like, today." The three of them leaned back—Lyla's arm brushed against mine—and roared with laughter.

Ananda pointed a finger at Lyla and Louis, cackling. "You're never living it down. Reruns forever. Into the grave. Job interviews. Everywhere you go." Louis grinned into his cocktail, shrugged those massive shoulders.

Conversation among the four of them, someone laughed at a

nearby table. I put my elbows on the table, leaned forward a bit. "Listen, um, Lyla? I was hoping to ask you something."

Lyla turned to me, smiling as she tapped a cigarette on the iron tabletop. She took a slow sip from her drink—it glowed blue under the lights, the edge of the glass rimed in sugar. She seemed more than a little drunk, her eyes glassy, unfocused.

"What was your name again?"

"Marvin."

"Hi, Marvin."

"Hi. Uh, it was about Joan, my question. I was just hoping you could answer something for me."

Lyla grinned at Ananda and looked back at me, lifting her chin as she blew a jet of smoke. "What do you want to know?"

What did I want to know? This was the crux of the matter, wasn't it? What, after everything, did I want to know?

Countless lives lived, all of them weighted in some measure of pointless heartbreak and hurt. Wandering lost down the backbone of six centuries, searching for meaning. For penance.

And here's Joan? Here's Joan, drinking a blue cocktail, smoking a cigarette, drunk and happy, asking me what I want to know?

I said, "Well, just . . . Is it real? About you and Joan of Arc? What you said on the show?"

This moment. Spanned out the length of years. As soon as I spoke the words, I wished that I could live in that moment, that moment when she opened her mouth to speak but before things moved irrevocably one way or the other.

Even that moment stretched out for eons would be better than what was to come.

Because I could tell, as soon as I asked, what her answer would be. By the set of her jaw, the way her eyes quickly—just for a second—shifted away, some physical tell she had when reminded of a lie she'd told. I'd seen enough of them in my lives, those tells. I knew what she'd say as soon as my own words left my mouth.

She tapped her cigarette into the red plastic ashtray and took a sip of her drink. "No," she said brightly. Eager to talk about it. "No way." I felt the bottom drop out from beneath me, this door beneath my heart that opened up, sent it tumbling down. "It was kind of a joke between me and Louis. To see if we could do it, you know? They put us up in an awesome hotel, comped us a bunch of free shit." She shrugged. "I put it on my CV."

"Dude," said Louis, chewing on a mouthful of ice, "it was hilarious."

9

Richard wasn't really watching TV. He was mostly just letting the light from the screen play across his eyes, letting its sound fill the empty room. He'd fired up a joint earlier that night, smoked little more than a few puffs before realizing it was probably a bad idea. He'd gone through the house afterward, a little high, and turned on all the lights and then sat in bed and tried to watch television. He stared at the joint resting on a saucer on his bedside table and finally unfolded himself from his bed, threw it into the toilet in the master bathroom.

When he shuffled back into the bedroom, the program he'd been halfheartedly watching—a reality show in which a disparate group of longtime vegans had to competitively manage various barbecue and hamburger joints throughout the country—had cut to a news bulletin.

All of the lights in the house burned. Every light in every room. He could not stop thinking of her, of course—was he expected to? Was there anything else to do? This would not change for a long time, this feeling—that Candice's memory was like a barb hooked inside him, something his skin caught on every time he moved. He was just beginning to understand the great and wretched notion that you bring your dead and your love with you wherever you go. You carry it around inside like a stone in your mouth.

He gazed at the TV, turned the volume up to a deafening level. It was a theater-worthy sound system that he wished would envelop him like the lights in the house did. The television reporter, her dark hair shellacked and unmoving, her lips bee-stung, said that the bottled water representative, the man who had filmed the Bride back at the beginning of summer, had committed suicide on the ninth green of the golf course in La Jolla, the very spot where he filmed her. He'd hopped the fence, shot himself.

"A note was left," the reporter said, "but investigators are not divulging its nature or contents." There was the familiar footage, again, of the Bride, her concentric circles on the grass, the jostling of the rep's camera, and then a cut to the golf course at night and from a distance, murky in the dark, police walking among yellow evidence tape.

Richard pressed his palms into his eyes and simply lived in it, lived in that moment, in that ache, because there was nothing, absolutely nothing else to do.

10

Lyla sat smiling in front of me as my hands went cold. As the bottom of the world dropped out from under me.

"So . . . the whole thing was just made up?"

Lyla shrugged. "I watched a documentary about Joan of Arc. That's where I got the idea. Everybody knows that *To the Point* show is full of shit. Half the stuff we said, her assistants gave us scripts for."

"The whole thing was pretty much planned out," Louis said. "Jessie Pamona was totally in on it."

"That whole show's fake," Lyla said. "It's like wrestling or whatever. Totally made up."

Over Lyla's shoulder, Louis smirked. "You thought, what? That she had, like, a split personality disorder with Joan of Arc, dude? Seriously?" He turned to Ananda. "Where do you find these guys, Andy?"

"Excuse me," I said woodenly. "Really nice to meet you all." I tapped the table with one finger as I stood. My smile was rigid, felt glued on. The night wheeled around me in a screaming palette of colors, a cavalcade of sound.

"Hold on," I heard Casper say. "Marvin, wait."

I could hear him murmuring apologies behind me. "Thanks, Ananda. Uh, I'm really sorry? We've just . . . that episode really affected him. It was really moving." Ananda laughed, confused.

"You're leaving? Uh, it was nice to meet you?" she called back.

"Yeah, sorry," Casper said over his shoulder. "It's weird, I know. I'll call you."

"Don't bother," Ananda called back. I could hear Louis laugh.

My legs were numb as I walked along the sidewalk. Just one foot, then the other.

Up the block I saw Vale coming toward us. I put my head down, looked at the flattened trash, the cigarette butts, the capillaries of cracks running along the sidewalk.

"What the hell?" Vale asked as I walked past him. "What happened?"

If I could've spoken at that moment, I'd have told Vale that I'd been led to one person out of millions—the odds of it were still beyond belief, really—only to be shown that most brutal, intractable rule of the Curse:

There is no reason why you are here.

11

Vale gently took Marvin by the elbow and led him off Santa Monica Boulevard after Marvin, his eyes downcast, ran into a drunk college kid in a t-shirt that read *I'm Here About the Blowjob*. The kid wanted to fight until he looked at Vale, who stared back from his ruined face as if he was already regretting the ruination he'd visit upon the kid.

"It means the same to me either way," Vale said sadly, shrugging his shoulders once.

"Keep your friend in check," the kid mumbled, turning around.

Vale had parked a few blocks down a side street bracketed by apartment buildings. Palm trees shrouded the sidewalk, bent toward the street like thugs. No one spoke. Whatever the hell had happened with Marvin, he clearly needed space. The van sat in the dark beneath a stunted little tree, and they could hear the traffic on Santa Monica Boulevard behind them, but this street was relatively quiet. Vale heard two women laughing in one of the apartments above them, but the sound was far away and still in the air.

Vale put his hand on Marvin's shoulder. "You want to just go back to the motel?"

"Yeah, I think so," Marvin said, leaning against the passenger door of the van.

"Are you guys possibly interested in telling me what's going on? Maybe?"

"It's a long story," Casper said.

"It's not even worth telling," Marvin said. He took his glasses off, pinched the bridge of his nose. His eye socket was wrinkled, sagging, the lid dropping over a hollow red pocket.

Vale would never be sure who saw the man come from the mouth of the alley first, come from that small crooked lane between two apartment buildings. Certainly not Marvin, who still had his head tucked down, his glasses in his shirt pocket. It was Casper, most likely.

In Vale's periphery, Casper slowed down a step and Vale himself flinched: the man was big, hulking, and smelled terrible—even ten, fifteen feet away Vale caught the scent of him as he lurched from the mouth of an alley. Big, shrouded in grime, wearing a tight-fitting Lycra jacket and gray jeans with the knees blown out. Cheeks carved gaunt in the wan lamppost light.

"And God will judge," he thundered, and stopped in front of the three of them. The pale wounded glint of his eyes. Like a linebacker on hard times. "God will judge," he said again, sounding heartbroken this time, and he unzipped his jacket and took a small pistol from the inside pocket and passed its barrel over the three of them. Seventeen million people around them and yet the street right then was silent as a morgue. Deathly still.

Marvin looked up and put on his glasses and in a weary voice said, "Here it comes. You're looking for me." And the man settled the barrel back on him as if the matter had been decided, and he shot Marvin twice in the chest.

PART THREE

SMOKE CITY

SUNDAY

1

BREAKING NEWS: Video of man interacting with ghost in "Smoke City" goes viral, receiving over two million views in twenty-four hours
—CNN.com

• • •

The world flared and dimmed, and after some period of interminable darkness, I saw things within it.

I saw dust hovering in a string above a red clay road, the remnant of someone's passage.

I saw worn leather boots beneath a wooden bench.

The crooked figure of one of my fathers as he gathered stones for a cairn for one of my mothers. Bees trundled among the wildflowers, the grass knee high, green as paint.

I saw a loaf of bread dusted with flour.

A rusty hacksaw gelled with drying blood, half its teeth broken.

A fly perched on the lip of a milk jug.

A little girl jumping rope.

I smelled the earthy pong of a muddy field, yellowed bones pressed into its surface, a killing ground.

I heard the fattened pause where the needle found the groove but the music had yet to start.

I saw one of my sons, a boy centuries dead now, naked and

laughing in a jeweled river, splashing his little fists against the skin of the water that ran headlong against his dusky knees. His teeth like little white stones in his mouth. I smelled the river, felt the breeze stir the hairs on my arms.

I saw some faceless man lashed to a rafter and hung upside down. Blood unspooling from his hair as he screamed.

A loaf of bread rimed in mold.

A wooden puzzle of a blue dog sitting outside an orange house.

The corpse of a seagull in the wet sand, lines of mites leaving its body like retreating soldiers.

The mournful ache of a bow skating against a violin string.

A thatched hut wearing a crown of flames.

My husband in an officer's hat.

The heft of my wife's breast against my hand.

A thimble of ink spilled on a tablecloth.

Cornmeal in a blue bowl.

A chorus of rats skittering in the walls.

A fogged window spattered with beaded rain.

A dancing man on a stage.

Joan's body embraced in flame, crowned in a curtain of stinking smoke.

Joan's poor little cross laced in twine.

And my father's yellow coat there in the marketplace ahead of me as I rushed to keep up, the people parting and stepping aside for us.

2

Middle of the night sometime. Maybe even morning. Hours had passed. Sleep pulled at him. He wanted a drink and felt like he shouldn't want a drink right then but there it was regardless. Gnawing at him. He knew the sweating made him look guilty of something.

"Mike, I'm just trying to understand," the detective said. They were sitting across from each other, the pocked table between them. The detective had introduced himself by his first name, Dave, and had offered Vale coffee, a sandwich.

Vale still had blood on his shirt, but good old Dave was acting like they'd gone to college together and spent the last two decades tipping a few back on Friday nights. Pals. But the cops had also separated him and Casper, and the fact was not lost on him: he was sitting in a room that held a table and two chairs and a window with one-way glass, and even Vale could see there was a camera mounted in the ceiling. He wasn't handcuffed, but were there other cops watching his good buddy Dave interview him about Marvin's shooting? Was he being recorded? Oh, probably. That all seemed very likely. That was worth betting on.

Dave smiled and leaned back in his chair. He was maybe forty pounds overweight and had bright red patches of eczema lacing his hands. Vale watched as he reached a thumb into the cuff of his other shirtsleeve and scratched. Dave said, "It's just a weird set of circumstances, Mike. We're just trying to get to the bottom of it all. Unravel everything. For Mr. Deitz's sake."

"There's nothing to unravel. My friend got shot."

Dave nodded, rubbing his knuckles into his palm like some schoolyard tough about to throw a punch. He closed his eyes for a second—the relief of it. The eczema was bad.

"You should see a dermatologist," Vale said.

Dave smiled again, but his eyes went cold. "We found his body a few blocks away. In an alleyway."

Vale started. "Who?"

"The shooter. Guy named Donald Jarvis Smith. Suicided out, looks like."

"Jesus."

"Yeah. Forty years old. Marine. Honorably discharged twelve years back. PTSD, VA assistance was a mess. Spotty. History of mental illness, history of bouncing on and off meds. Got a pretty substantial record after his discharge. Got hardcore into a cult once the smokes started showing up. We found some cultist material on his person. Bunch of pamphlets. Guys like this fall through the cracks sometimes. Because the cracks can be a mile wide, you know?"

Vale went to bite his thumbnail and instead tucked his hands in his armpits. "Why are you telling me this?" His leg was going a million miles an hour beneath the table.

Dave snuck into his sleeve again and looked down at the paperwork in front of him. "Because I'm trying to give you a break, Mike. I'm trying to believe you when you say you're in the clear."

"What's that supposed to mean?"

Dave held up his hand and ticked off each item on a stubby finger as he went. "You've got a shoebox full of thousands of dollars in cash in your van. You spent the night in Men's Central, what, three nights ago? Assault charges that got lifted? And no disrespect, Mike, but you look like you're sick. I mean really sick. As in not healthy."

"Are you a cop or a life coach?"

Dave laughed. "That's a good one."

"Thank you."

He held up another finger. "And Marvin? Mr. Dietz? You know he's wanted by the police in Portland, Oregon for psychiatric pickup?"

"I did not know that, no. But personally, it's irrelevant."

Dave opened another folder, frowned. "Something about Joan of Arc? He knows her? He thinks he *was* her? Something like that. But they were supposed to pick him up if they found him."

Vale shrugged. Still with the knee jittering relentlessly under the table. He thought of Marvin, sighing as he said *Here it comes. You're looking for me.* As if he hadn't been surprised in the least. "And that's weird to you?"

Dave looked up from his paperwork. "Is what weird to me?"

"That he thought he was Joan of Arc, or he knew her, or Albert Einstein, or any other famous dead person. Or that this Smith guy gets off his meds and joins a cult and eventually loses it. Whatever. I mean, there are ghosts walking around within a hundred yards of this room. Fucking straight-up *ghosts*. Right? The whole concept of what's sane or reasonable seems like it should be pretty seriously reconsidered at this point. The old rules don't apply, you know?" Vale swiped a hand across his forehead.

"Why were you in Los Angeles again, Mr. Vale?"

"Oh, I'm Mr. Vale now?"

"Why were you in Los Angeles, Mike?"

"My ex-wife's funeral."

"And what about Mr. Deitz?"

"You'd have to ask him."

Dave folded his arms across the table and sighed. He frowned, as if he was just so sad to see Vale digging his own hole. "Cooperation really will go a long way here. Okay? We're just trying to understand the situation."

Vale said, "That's the situation, Dave. It makes no sense. The dude just walked up to us right off of a busy street. Hanging out like he'd been waiting in that alley for someone to come by. Looked at the three of us like he was eenie-meenie-minie-moeing it, and he picked Marvin and *boom*. Now, am I under arrest? Because I've got my lawyer's number ready to go. I apologize if I'm coming across as uncooperative, Dave, but I find that being held unjustifiably by the police? While my friend's in the hospital, dying or already dead? It's a little fucking irritating."

Dave slowly closed his folder and put his elbows on the table.

Steepled his knuckles beneath his chin and stared at Vale with those hound-dog eyes above his red, chapped hands.

He sighed, hooked a thumb at the door over his shoulder. "He's not dead yet. Thanks for talking to us."

• • •

Vale stared at an issue of *Wired* that was two years old. He was wrecked on bitter cafeteria coffee and cigarettes inhaled practically three at a time outside the emergency room doors. His eyes felt like ossified shit pellets rolling around in his sockets. Sleep? What's that? He and Casper had been camped out in the waiting room for hours, Marvin still in surgery. They sat beneath a television showing women's tennis. There were no windows in the waiting room; they'd have to go down the hall, the elevators, out the doors for that.

"Screw this," Casper said, swiping his hands down his face. "Let's go have a dip."

They wended their way through the hospital. It was morning. A haze of smog already colored the sky. Casper thumped his chew can against his leg and leaned against the wall. They'd gone out to partake in their particular vices so often that they already had their usual spots.

Blood had dried to the color of rust in the creases of Casper's t-shirt from when he'd cradled Marvin. He looked terrible in the morning light, pale and haunted and tired, and Vale figured he looked about the same. He felt a wave of dizziness come over him and leaned against the wall, rolling the back of his skull along it. A wedge of the rising sun reflected itself in the hospital's windows, made him squint.

As if someone had flipped a switch, a ghost appeared in the parking lot between two cars. The smoke-form took shape as a young girl in a dress. She spun in circles. Lost. Ceaselessly turning.

"Jesus," Vale said. "It's just a kid. Hey!" he called out, hands cupped to his mouth.

She kept turning, precise only in her confusion.

"We can't do anything. They don't hear us, man. Smokes, remember? They hear Marvin, but not us. We're just white noise."

Casper watched for a moment then and leaned over and spit, tucked his arms over his chest.

They watched the ghost for a time. Vale was looking at it when he said, "I saw her."

"Who?"

"Candice. Dee."

"Your wife?"

Vale dropped his cigarette, ground it out. "She was just like that," he said, and nodded toward the girl in the parking lot.

"Wait, you mean you *saw* her?"

He pointed at the parking lot. "When she was like that. I tried to talk to her. She didn't see me. Like she was looking past me."

What else needed to be said?

He put a hand over his heart. *Poom poom poom* beneath the fabric. "I think I need to go back inside," Vale said. "I think I need to sit down."

"Mike?"

He pushed himself off the wall and then all feeling stopped at the legs, ceased somehow. So strange, the ground rising up to him. The pavement sounded loud as a pistol crack against his jaw. The taste of metal shavings in his mouth and Casper's face peering down at him from miles above. Darkness like tendrils of cotton at the edges of the world. The roaring of some sea in his head.

3

From the journals of Marvin Deitz:

In the city of Svalöv, in a country called Skåne. Part of Sweden now. Maybe a hundred and fifty years after Geoffroy died, a hundred and fifty years of pretty ferocious living. It had been a busy time, a terrible time of testing the parameters of the Curse, slowly piecing together the Rules. Finally, this time, I was born into circumstances that allowed me some respite. A calm after so long in a rough and bitter sea.

I was born Martin Gormsen, a noblemen birthed into a family of both measurable prestige and wealth. My disfigurement in that particular lifetime, a small and stunted left arm, the fingers smartly curled into the palm, was one I was born with.

When I was twenty years old I met Lise; we were introduced at a banquet held by Tycho Brahe, the famed financier and astronomer. Tycho, deservedly, has gone down in history as a glorious madman. The man was wonderfully nuts, downright brilliant. He was friends with my father and was one of the richest men in Europe at the time. (He'd also had the bridge of his nose sliced off in a duel with his third cousin some years before and wore a gold prosthetic at dinner parties and would on occasion bring a moose to dinner events and feed it liquor.)

Our families had done business together for many years, and perhaps sensing something strange about me, Tycho had taken a liking. I was admittedly an odd young man; a hundred and fifty years of the other shoe dropping—in the most horrific of ways—will do that to you.

To be honest, Lise had been no traditional beauty, but Jesus, neither was I. In all my lives, gender had hardly been an issue, as hard as that is to believe. I bounced between male and female throughout the years, there was a fluidity there. And really, physical relations before Lise had been rare anyway; I felt (and frequently acted) a monster, regardless if I'd been born man or woman. But with Lise we fell into it, into each other.

Oh, she was beautiful to me. Beyond our physicality, she nourished me with her kindness. She soothed me with her expanses of easy silences. She was someone I could sit next to without being reminded of the weight of my own horrors, my ravages wrought upon the world. She blessed me with the easy cadence of her love. My heart calmed when it neared her.

Her father dealt in shipping, and while well off, he was more than happy to marry his daughter into the Gormsen bloodline. We were married a year after meeting and Brahe, as a wedding gift, commissioned our portrait.

The day of the ceremony the priest intoned rites and prayers before us, and we stood on the opposite sides that tradition dictated so that my whole arm and hand should be able to hold hers. I allowed myself a sliver of hope, a glimmer of it. My mother wept to see us standing there; my father, in a rare show of emotion, put his arm around her.

If I could not tell Lise of my past, I thought at the time, this dark and calamitous secret I held, could I still not be happy? At least a little? At least this time? It seemed possible. Perhaps, I dared to think, I even deserved it. Time stretched before us: I was only twenty-one! Even with the Curse at work, we would have decades together.

I might as well have been smote right there, daring to think I *deserved* anything.

Lise birthed us a son within a year. Robair was born without complications, a rarity then even for families of great wealth. I can still remember Lise's howls of pain as handmaidens and midwives gathered around her. My dear Lise, my little mouse.

Where Joan had held her head high, imploring mercy from God and piety from man, Lise had held out our tiny, bloodied, bundled child to me with no less power or grace. I can still see the two of them there: Lise's smile, her hair damp, Robair's little bleat, his spasming fists.

I have survived for years on that image. Nourished myself from that. I have trod through unspeakable events, been buoyed by it, sustained by it.

And then came the inevitable, of course.

Every gift given with the Curse is done only so it might be taken away.

Robair, at five months old, died of influenza. Nothing creative: a rattling cough that took root in the little engine of his lungs. He had been real, I sometimes have to remind myself. This tiny boy.

Lise became wraithlike after Robair's death. A pale, grim-socketed shadow of herself. It was understandable. It was summer when he died and golden light seemed to spill from every window and fall in swaths on the parapets. It was macabre, that sunlight, a mockery. Our home hung heavy with silence.

One morning I stepped into our chambers where Lise lay amid her quilts, moored in the canopy of our bed. Blue veins swam up her throat, the backs of her hands. I stood over her.

"You must eat," I said. Plaintive. Begging.

The Curse, I had come to realize by then, was brilliant in its precision: I would live and live again, would feel life's pains—or growing numbness—at every turn. But Lise, my love, had just one life, and this was what she had chosen with it. Me. Robair.

A disfigured husband and a dead child.

"We can try again," I said, and she made a sound like an animal with a bone in its throat. She turned her face from me, covered her eyes with that blue-veined hand.

I lay next to her on the bed and laid my whole arm across her. She beneath the covers, me above.

The physician would pronounce her barren shortly hereafter. There would be no more children for us, and she would be dead anyway in less than the time it would have taken to bring another child into the world. Pneumonia.

The day after her funeral I went into a tavern in Malmö and taunted a drunken bondsman until he beat me to death.

• • •

After some indefinable time, the darkness retreated to a thin wash of pale light. I was in a bed in a room and if there was a window anywhere I couldn't see it. The room was full of hidden machinery, though; I could hear it all chirring away, and the light, the light had to come from somewhere.

The room seemed formless save for the bed, the chair beside it. But I also saw my hand on the sheet, even the hair on my arm silvered in pinpricks of light. This was a hospital, surely. Surely.

I thought of little Mellie in the children's ward, and her brother. How she had told me something was wrong with his little bones. Would that boy wander Smoke City someday? Was he even now trundling around the alleyways here, a little boy crafted from smoke and sorrow? Lost, looking eternally for his mother?

I turned my head to see Joan sitting in the chair next to me. Her hands were folded in her lap, her hair was shaggy and poorly cut and darkly beautiful, the color of coffee. She wore jeans and a faded red Esprit t-shirt, a brand I hadn't heard of in years. There was even an odd pink shape on the sleeve, a bleach stain. And a white scar on her forearm shaped like an L. Such details! I tried to rise from the bed but couldn't. She blinked her eyes in tandem with the beeping machines.

"Joan?" My voice sounded like a needle running across a record.

She smiled. *Marvin.*

I trembled; the breadth of my regret left me speechless. It flooded me. I gaped and she smiled and touched me on the arm. There was a moment then where I smelled flowers, lilacs, and that detail among all of them seemed the most unlikely.

Marvin? she said. *Or Geoffroy? Do you have a preference?*

"I don't care. I . . . There's so much I've wanted to say to you." I mewled it, tears tumbling down my whiskered cheeks from my good eye, the other socket loose and sunken, tearless. My glasses were gone.

Joan looked at me with her dark eyes. She leaned forward and put her warm hand over mine, and I felt something like a song walk up the ladder of my ribcage. A warm, wordless chorus inside me.

She held my hand and I saw a golden chain around her neck, the pendant resting there between the shallow valley of her breasts. A small figurine there.

Not a cross, or a crucifix. Not what I expected.

It was a little man!

It was a little man wearing a coat. A yellow coat.

Joan tucked her chin down and held the talisman between her fingers, looked down at it. She turned it around and there it was—a little sword on the back of it.

I said, "It's my father's coat."

Joan looked at me and a sadness fell across her features like a slow and inevitable storm. She let the pendant fall against her chest and shook her head.

It's not your father's coat, Marvin.

"It's not?"

You wore it as well. It's yours.

I took my hand away. Shame burned through me. "This is a dream, isn't it?"

It's not a dream.

"No?"

No.

She smiled sadly.

Marvin. This is your reckoning.

4

Marvin's surgeon was a tall, red-faced man named Dr. Torrance. He had a boyish, unkempt shock of gray hair and had been kind enough to drop by Vale's room to fill them in on Marvin's progress—Casper was pulling double duty after Vale's seizure in the parking lot.

"Dr. Torrance," the doctor said—he said this every time he'd spoken to them—and everyone shook hands. Vale had an IV loaded with a saline solution for dehydration and they'd given him, according to the doctor, a round of Xanax and an anti-seizure medication. Vale would have been embarrassed about it all, or afraid, or something, but just couldn't seem to drum much up by way of the negative. He felt better than he had in weeks. He felt awesome, actually.

"He's a little out of it, still," the doctor said, smiling at Vale.

"I am," Vale agreed, grinning.

And then he frowned. Dr. Torrance telegraphed everything with his face. You'd never need to worry about what Dr. Torrance thought about your health. "You know, alcohol withdrawal is a serious matter, Mr. Vale."

"I just drink beer," Vale said. "I don't even get what the . . ." He gestured and then spent a few moments watching his own hands gesturing while the doctor and Casper waited. Finally they understood he wouldn't be finishing his sentence and the doctor cleared his throat and examined his clipboard.

"You're both friends of Mr. Deitz."

Casper nodded. "We all came down here from Oregon together."

"We've done what we can for him in surgery. He's stable at this point. It's a question now of monitoring, of waiting and seeing."

"So you got the bullets out?" Casper asked.

Dr. Torrance nodded vigorously. "We did. One entered his shoulder and shattered his clavicle. But that one exited, which is good. With the other wound, the prognosis really isn't ideal, I'm afraid. As much as any gunshot can be, I mean. There's a high risk of complications in a situation like this."

"Why's that?" Vale managed to ask.

Dr. Torrance shrugged. "Like I said, we got the bullet out. Issues of concern now are hemopnuemothorax and hemostatic shock. He's suffering from peritonitis as well."

Casper said, "We don't have a clue what that means."

Dr. Torrance held his pen up and traced the flight path of the bullet in front of his own chest. "The bullet entered in the left side of Mr. Deitz's chest at an angle, okay? Like this. It missed the heart—amazingly—and glanced off the spine, where it also missed severing his spinal cord. In that regard, he's incredibly lucky. But then the bullet traveled down and hit the left lung. That's what hemopnuemothorax is: blood and air in the chest cavity from a pierced lung."

"Jesus," Casper said.

"Right. Hemostatic shock is, simply put, when there's severe concussive force received by organs within the body as the bullet passes through. The body puts itself in a kind of lockdown." He held a hand up in front of his chest and squeezed it into a fist. "The bullet ran down the length of the lung, opening it, hit the wall of the lower abdomen and ricocheted off of his left hipbone, which is where it exited. Peritonitis means that wall, the abdominal wall, has become inflamed."

Vale flung his hands up. "Jesus Christ. Is he dead? He sounds like he should be fucking dead."

Casper frowned at him, turned to the doctor. "So what does that all mean? Where does that leave him?"

Dr. Torrance looked at his watch. "At this point? It's anyone's guess. He was intubated but now he's breathing on his own. He's got a fever. There seems to be an infection that might be taking root. We're trying to stem that before it gets a foothold. Mr. Deitz's age and physical health aren't necessarily in his favor." He seemed to read their looks then, and said, "Still, he's relatively stable right now. And you never know about these things. The body is an incredible machine capable of salvaging itself, of repairing itself after a lot of trauma. Right now, we're waiting and monitoring."

Vale pulled at Casper's shirtsleeve. "Doctor-speak," he said behind his hand.

Dr. Torrance smiled. "I'll keep you both posted." And here he bowed down slightly and raised his voice, as if Vale was slightly hard of hearing or possibly in another room. "Mr. Vale, we're going to need this room in a few hours, but in the meantime, you just rest. And I'd like to have one of our clinicians come and speak to you about your issues with alcohol. Would you be willing to talk to someone?"

5

From the journals of Marvin Deitz:

I was born Marvin Deitz in Milwaukee, Wisconsin. The fact that I had been born twice in a row within the United States, especially after arranging to have Bill Creswell's record collection shipped to Portland, was something I considered to be a very good sign. An indication of something positive. (It does amaze me that after six hundred years I still look for things to be grateful for. Every time, it's as if the Curse cackles and rubs its claws together. *What a chump.*)

I was the youngest of four children, all of us boys. My parents had met at a beer hall in South Milwaukee. We were raised in an apartment complex on Wisconsin Avenue that took up the entire block. Milwaukee, even more than New York, was a city that seemed built entirely of stone. But beautiful, ornate; even our two bedroom apartment, with its clusters of rat shit in the hallways and its clanging pipes, buckling floors, contained crumbling stonework of such caliber that it left me openmouthed.

I remember that most about my boyhood: the iron-gray sky limned against the buildings of Milwaukee as I stared up at them. It was an analogy I could comprehend. Milwaukee was an industrial town then, and a robust one, but it was also a dirty, bustling city full of crime and corruption. It was, for America, an old and ravaged city even then, but one bursting with hidden beauty—all of those cornices and gargoyles and gilded stanchions.

I had never seen such things in my previous lives, which simply meant that I hadn't been looking. It jolted me. As a child, my mother's standard admonition would start with, "Watch where you're going!" I walked gazing up at the tops of buildings, enmeshed in the details of place.

Also of note: I was born whole and unblemished, which meant only that my disfigurement was forthcoming, expected.

There were a group of boys that roamed the neighborhood. Hard-nosed boys, tough boys, with my brothers soon enough joining their ranks. It was the late sixties, and they idolized the low-level mob men who stood smoking outside the betting parlor across the street.

Milwaukee had heavy Chicago mob ties in those days and the men across the street, with their muttonchops and suede jackets, their twenty-five cent cigars and hip flasks, their Polish jokes, were typical of numbers men, punch-men of the era. The butts of their revolvers sticking out of the back of their chinos. Men willing to break a guy's arm or swing a blackjack against his skull.

My brothers and the rest of them would run errands for these men, bring them their sandwiches from the deli down the street, shine their shoes. The men tolerated it, laughingly called the boys Krauts and Polacks, occasionally shared their flasks with the older ones. I knew trouble courted trouble and that when my ruination came, it would probably come from there.

I checked out books from the library about Portland, Oregon, gathered whatever information I could. I dreamt. I wondered if Bill Creswell's records really were waiting for me or not, if the will had been executed. If things had gone according to plan.

Our parents worked hard. I admired their tenacity: they were first-generation immigrants and decent people run ragged with the needs of four boys. I was almost always left in the care of my brothers, or occasionally by Mrs. Rackowski down the hall, when my mother had to work late at the laundry and my father got overtime at the bottling plant on State Street.

Our mother, in a rare show of exhaustion, sent us outside to play; she had a headache, the fumes from work wracking her.

She shooed us out the door, told us to come back in an hour. My brothers, of course, headed straight for the hard boys on the corner.

"I don't want to go over there," I said, and my brother Henry, the kindest of my siblings and three years older than me, grabbed me by the collar and said, "Come on, Marv. Mom said you gotta come with." We were in the hallway outside our apartment. He put me in a headlock and my hat fell off and Henry picked it up and handed it to me. I remember thinking neither of my other brothers would have done that.

Outside, the air was brittle and crystalline with the threat of more snow. "Ah," one of the men cried in mock anguish when he saw the group of us crossing the street, "it's the Polish army, Joe! Hide your wife, I know how she likes the kielbasa!" He blew into his hands and the men around him chortled like trolls.

I remember the sound of tires through salted slush, the grayed rinds of snow mounded against the base of the buildings. The three men were drunk. I pressed myself against the wall of the building and squinted in the night, looking up at the cornices of our building across the street.

And how do such things happen? Joe took offense. Joe, his wife's honor infringed upon, defended her. The other man responded with a laugh, which is almost always the wrong thing to do, and followed it with *another* joke about Joe's wife's chastity, which was certainly the wrong thing to do. Joe, staggering, his eyes glassy with booze, pulled his revolver from his waistband. It made a sad little coughing noise when he fired it.

Joe's bullet hit the wall at least a foot above the other man's head and ricocheted off the brick. It grazed the surface my eye, severing the ciliary muscle. It shattered the bridge of my nose and then lodged in Henry's throat. The odds of a marksman managing a shot like that on purpose were—I'm sure—astronomically high, though the Curse regularly trafficked in such things.

The other numbers men pulled the revolver from Joe's hands and proceeded to beat him to death. My brothers fled as Henry and I lay on the sidewalk, the old gray snow darkening with our blood.

I tried to staunch Henry's bleeding, my hands at his throat, pressing, but both he and Joe were dead by the time the police arrived. The men had vanished, my face bloodied, my sleeves red to the elbows.

It's an unfair question, not that I expect an answer. (I've been asking it for a while, after all.) But we'll give it a shot anyway. Rhetorically, you understand.

What *is* the point?

To any of it? When every question gets the same answer? When every action ends in the same terrible, hurtful result?

If I learn whatever there is to be learned, will I be forgiven?

• • •

The little yellow coat hung from a chain over Joan's heart. I reached for her and the room washed away and she became this shifting tide, became all of my mothers and my fathers, all of my poor dead daughters and sons. My husbands and wives. Friends and brothers and sisters. Enemies. This sea of faces.

She stood before me and became Time, and Death, and Love, too. The yellow coat swung on a chain.

All of these faces morphed and ran into each other. A tide of them. Joan pulled away from me and she was Casper—and Casper became Cauchon, who became (I knew it without ever having seen him) little Mellie's brother. And *he* became Esme, and Julia, and Luc. And Suyin. On and on and on, this unspooling cavalcade of faces and history that spanned both centuries and a moment.

Everyone was connected—I saw it, felt the expansiveness of it, but also understood that such knowledge needed to be parsed into a necessary blindness: to comprehend the magnitude of it would be too much. As much as I had lived, in all my years, I had seen but a corner of the tapestry. A *thread*.

It was such a large and unknowable thing.

Joan leaned toward me and her lips brushed my forehead like a whisper.

Do you see?

"Yes."

You have a purpose, Marvin. All of the hate and ruination and loss. A reason for it all, finally. Do you know it? Do you see it?

I wept then, bitterly, the yellow coat swinging from its chain in front of my eyes. "No. Please tell me."

I will. But first, I need to tell you something else. Something you've wondered and feared the answer to.

And oh, I knew what she spoke of, and I wept like a child at its mention, these jagged sobs that tore from me. "Yes. Okay."

She pressed her lips to my ear and laid her hand on my cheek. And in a voice like wind, like the ceaseless tide, like the howl of stars, she said, *I forgave you before you laid flame to tinder.*

Marvin, listen to me.

I forgave you the moment I saw you.

THURSDAY

1

From the journals of Marvin Deitz:

"As you can see, Marvin, the place is not gigantic," Avril Noonan had said, all those years ago.

"But the location," I said.

She held up a finger. "The location is nice, true." Randy, maybe thirteen or fourteen at the time, rolled his eyes. He stood there in the doorway with his arms crossed. He had a rattail and his acne was so bad it looked like someone had spattered his face with gore. Just exuding hormones like a fog. He'd been such a hard kid to like, but when I remembered him like that, it made it easy to feel a little sorry for him.

I was twenty-one years old and had recently acquired the keys to the storage facility out in Gresham that Bill Creswell had paid for in perpetuity for over two decades. The storage room had been air- and temperature-controlled, and the albums, all seven thousand of them, were in pristine condition. I'd flown out of General Mitchell Airport with four thousand dollars in an envelope in my jacket—my life savings up to that point.

"So this is okayed for retail space?"

Avril smiled and tucked her hair behind her ear. "My husband left me the building, hon. It's okayed for whatever I say it is."

"I'm thinking of a record store, maybe."

She nodded. "That sounds wonderful. This is a great city for music."

Thirty-five years later Randy would step through those doors with his Boston accent, his mother long dead, and evict me under a pretty impressive pretense. But at the time, dust motes whirled slowly in the windows and I remember hope jangling inside me like a loose wire. Even then, still dumb enough to hope.

Another tumble in the barrel, I thought. Another stumbling shot at the relentless act of living.

"I'll take it," I said.

• • •

Dr. Torrance sighed, unhappy. "This is not advisable, Mr. Deitz. This is not a sound medical decision."

"But it's my decision," I said as I pushed my foot into a shoe, grimacing.

"You were *critically* injured less than a week ago, Mr. Deitz. I mean, the risk for infection or complications are serious. I urge you to reconsider. You shouldn't even be walking, frankly."

I leaned down to tie the shoe and found I couldn't. It wasn't even close—there was a deep, red-edged pulling in my chest by the time I started leaning over. The stitches. Casper took a knee and tied my shoe for me.

I managed to smile at Dr. Torrance. Sweat popped out on my forehead. "I appreciate your help."

"You understand that we've stitched your lung, Mr. Deitz? Your abdominal lining? Your recovery has been impressive, but really, you shouldn't be moving around at this point."

Casper had bought me a new t-shirt in the gift shop, navy blue with the name of the hospital on it. As if people would want to be reminded of the place, like it was a particularly good concert they'd been to. I took my gown off, the starched fabric rustling as it fell to the floor. I stood there in sweatpants, my chest a shaved horror wrapped in gauze and bandages. Casper hovering like a toddler's mother as I started the gymnastics routine of putting my shirt on. Again I needed his help. I lifted my arms and Casper slipped the shirt over me.

I said, "I've really got to go, Dr. Torrance. Thank you for everything you've done. You're a hell of a surgeon." Before the bandages had been changed earlier that day I'd hazarded a look at myself: my torso was bruised purple up to my throat. A bullet had exited above my hipbone, among other places, and I needed a walker to stand up, much less move. My arm was in a sling since the other bullet had shattered my collarbone. I was on a pretty meaningful cocktail of painkillers. Casper joked that Vale and I were keeping the pharmaceutical industry aloft.

Dr. Torrance puffed out his cheeks and let loose a long sigh.

"You're seriously going to go through with this?"

"I am. I need to get home."

He held up a hand. "Well, I'm calling someone down from legal, then. I'd appreciate it if you'd wait until then. I want them down here, preferably with a goddamned video camera, when you triple-sign your release forms."

2

Up I-5 then, back the way they'd come.

Another rental car, some sleek new thing, the van still in some LAPD impound lot. Casper drove with a timidity Vale found both irritating and a little endearing. Marvin lay sweating in the back seat adrift a tide of pain pills.

Vale tuned the radio to a jazz station and got "Round About Midnight," one of the few jazz tunes he recognized. He thought of Basquiat that day outside the gallery all those decades before, the various effluvia that the man had dropped in Vale's hands that day, the random castoffs of his living. Outside the car, the world was full of strip malls and gas stations and parched yellow hills. The sky threatened rain and Vale welcomed it; these stunted dry fields needed some water. The world seemed brittle, ready to light at the slightest random spark.

Marvin cleared his throat and from the back seat said in a husky voice, "Can you guys change this, please?"

"You want us to change it?"

"I hate this song."

Vale turned the station.

"I really do," Marvin rattled, his voice hoarse. "I hate that song with a passion."

Casper whipped his head back as he changed lanes, and Vale said quietly, "You're doing fine, Casper. Chill, man." He tapped his splint against his leg and felt his heart inflate, this thing inside him that threatened to break through his chest. It felt so good it almost hurt. He had pieced together five days of sobriety now. Five days! He had a backpack full of verbose and heavy-handed medical literature about alcoholism that he told himself he may look at someday in the future, and a prescription for Xanax that he wanted desperately to fill but was trepidatious.

And *still* he was struck with this feeling in his heart—like the Moment if the Moment was jacked on steroids—at least a few times a day. It was a crazed, intense feeling of expansiveness. Like anything was possible. Like everything was beautiful. This simultaneous tenderness that paradoxically, when he was in it, made him feel like he could rip phone books in half and French kiss a Doberman and save old ladies and cats from burning buildings. These little half-minute starbursts of savage, leaping joy. They afforded him a gratitude, suffused him with it, that had to be annoying as hell to be around. It was the novelty of sobriety; he knew he was coasting on the high of it but didn't give a flying shit.

Because five days.

Holy *shit*, five days. Man.

The three of them drove in silence save for the radio, pop songs now, auto-tuned and saccharine, until Marvin said from the backseat, "That song. You know, I shot dope with John Coltrane a couple times."

Vale looked back at him. Marvin lay sprawled out in the back seat, his face pale. Sweat ringed his collar. His eyes were unreadable behind the sunglasses Casper had bought him in the gift shop.

"You hurting? You can have another pain pill if want."

"I did, Mike," Marvin said.

Casper laughed uneasily and turned the radio off. He looked in the rearview mirror.

Marvin took off the sunglasses and tossed them in the seat. He palmed sweat from his forehead and Vale saw the drooping, empty eye socket. "I shot a boatload of dope into my foot. Killed myself from it. It was 1961. That summer was hotter than shit, I remember that. I wanted to impress that man so bad. You just meet people sometimes and they're like their own star. Give out their own light. And I just didn't give a damn anymore. Again."

"You're not making any sense, bud. I want you to drink some

water," Vale said, handing him a plastic bottle. Vale, Mister Five Days of Sobriety, was now a big proponent of hydration. Water: his solution to everything. Marvin was clearly beginning to hallucinate, and Vale turned to Casper and murmured, "If he's like this in another hour, we're going to the hospital. I don't care where we are."

Marvin laughed and then winced. Leaned his head against the window. "I've sawed men in half because I was told to. Because it was expected of me. Listened to them beg for their lives. Pleading for mercy! And this song can piss me off more than any of it." He drank some of the water. Some of it ran down his chin. "I was an idiot. I'm still an idiot."

Vale said to him, sadly, "Bud. You're not making sense."

Marvin glared at him, his hair stuck in whorls along his temples. "The hell I'm not."

They passed a string of cars on the shoulder—traffic slowed suddenly and Casper goosed the brakes hard. The inevitable, the now-expected: a smoke.

This time it was a businessman with hilariously huge lapels and equally huge sideburns, feverishly looking at his watch, standing in the brambles beside a fence twenty yards off the freeway.

"Someone's late for the porn shoot," Vale said.

"Pull over," Marvin rasped.

"Marvin. You're *sick*. We gotta get you home, buddy. You insisted on leaving the hospital, fine. But now we gotta get you home. Dicking around in the car is not ideal, okay?"

"Stop the car."

Vale said, "You don't have to get the life story of every ghost you see, buddy. That's not your job. You don't have to save everyone."

Marvin pressed the bottle of water against his forehead, glared at Vale with that one blazing blue eye.

"Just pull the car over," he said.

3

From the journals of Marvin Deitz:

BRIEF NOTES RE: *SPECTER DETECTIVES* OPENING CREDITS:

AESTHETIC: Grainy, jittery camera work, grit on lens. Image: A cemetery in the daylight, bright green grass. Vacillate between hot colors and subdued sepias. Closeup of a weathered stone angel, backlit by the sun.

Somber opening music—*haunting*—single cello or violin piece. Commission something? Casper *demands* guitars, says it's the right sound "according to his guts," but he has yet to prove himself a reliable source musically—especially if his choice of shirts is any indication. We'll see.

VO: *"Los Angeles, California. Home of Hollywood's extravagant entertainment industry, where fortunes are made and dreams come true. But that's not all that makes up Los Angeles. Not anymore. Ghosts—visions and specters—now haunt the city. From the tallest high-rise and most decadent mansion to the seediest back alley, these apparitions have become as commonplace as celebrity sightings. Still, so many questions remain unanswered: Who are they? Who were they in life? Why are they here?*

"And most importantly, can we help them find their way home?"

Casper actually has a good voice for narration. He might have something there. It's a rough draft—especially just focusing on the Hollywood aspect of LA—but screw it. We can work loose and tighten it up later.

• • •

The sky above the parking lot of the Tip-Top glimmered with stars. It was night, and I could hear the crickets chirruping out in the grass. I stood in the parking lot and smelled earth, warmed asphalt, Vale's cigarette. I felt better than I had earlier. We had passed through a late-summer rain and bright pools of reflected neon pocketed the ground here and there.

Casper opened the car door for me and I put my feet on the pavement, looked toward the front window of the Tip-Top. I saw Janelle, the waitress, through the glass. And there was Casper's brother, Gary, leaning across the counter for the sugar container, next to the line of old men.

This all seemed like a lifetime ago, the last time we were here. I could hear Vale rooting around in the trunk, and when he came around to the door with my walker, I was weeping unceremoniously, sitting in the back seat with the door open. It hurt my stitches, crying like that. He and Casper looked down at me.

"Marvin?"

I laughed and rubbed tears away with my palm. I was embarrassed. "Sorry," I said. Vale's cigarette flared in the dark. He crouched down and his eyes were kind, and I thought, *What, a few days sober and Vale's not a shithead all of the sudden? If he lays some pearl of wisdom on me, I'll put his eye out, the sanctimonious prick.*

But he just crouched there before me, nodding.

"It's cool," he said. Not having a clue what he was talking about, of course. And yet, that was when I *really* started blubbering.

"I just realized that I could die in there," I said. Beyond the glass, the men in their cowboy hats sat lifting forkfuls of pie. Janelle poured more coffee for Gary, who looked out and saw us. He said something to Janelle and she turned our way and smiled.

Casper said, "The meatloaf's bad, Marvin, but it's not that bad."

I laughed, a choked, strangled sound. "I just mean, I could die any second."

"Or in twenty years," Vale said. "Thirty. I mean, you took two bullets pretty goddamned well, dude."

"How do you guys *do* this? How do you handle this not knowing? I've never had to do this before. I don't remember how to."

They looked at each other. Vale still didn't understand the Curse, hadn't been told, but the point remained the same, didn't it? How do we live with the time we're given?

Casper looked back at me and shrugged. "It's just life, Marvin. You just do it."

Vale frowned. Something had changed between us after he'd seen me speak to the ghost on the side of the freeway. After he'd seen it reach toward me. The flat relief in the thing's—the *man's*—eyes. A freedom there. Grace. The grace inherent in relief.

"Marvin, you're here now," Vale said. He stood up, his knees popping. "The food sucks. They have severed animal heads in the bar. I don't know if you knew that." His cigarette sparked against the gravel and he ratcheted open my walker in front of me. "But you're among friends, okay, and you're still walking upright and taking solids. You're winning. Anything beyond that is thinking too far ahead."

4

Brophy was dying, and thus was on a great and varied number of medications—pills at mealtimes, upon waking, before he went to bed. He was a storing-house for dope: pills for nausea, for his low blood count, to fight the cancer itself. He kept a little pill organizer in his kitchen and, like clockwork, would forget to take his evening round until he'd already laid himself down to go to sleep, and *then* he'd promptly remember. So almost every night now, he'd get up and hobble into the kitchen, irritated and tired.

Tonight was no different, except there was a smoke sitting cross-legged on the kitchen floor.

Brophy stood there with his heart shuddering beneath his ribs, one yellowed hand on the dimmer switch. The room chock full of electric light and streamlined, laden with modern appliances and all the other physical things, the trappings of modernity that he'd lusted after for so much of life, like a goddamned fool, and now this one other thing as well. Just a black-haired little spirit sitting there next to Brophy's rarely-used Miele dishwasher. Just hanging out. Sitting there.

The smoke's elbows rested on his knees, his head was tucked down, his palms were pressed against his mouth—Brophy had done the same thing himself as a boy, usually during vastly inappropriate times, and he imagined in some spectral realm the kid was making one excellent farting noise. He almost smiled at the idea, and then the boy raised his head up and looked around and

Brophy saw that: a) the kid was cross-eyed, and b) was missing the lower half of his jaw. Where it should be was simply a gored and ruined mess of bone and gristle, a flickering and wavering mess. If Brophy had to guess, he'd put him at seven or eight years old.

"War dead, maybe?" Brophy said, hardly even hearing himself, and the smoke certainly gave no notice, simply curled his hands around his head, tucked his knees in, faded to an almost invisible level and then snapped to opacity like some signal finally coming through.

And what had any of this meant? The last week? Hessler's funeral, seeing Mike Vale. Vale coming back into his life after all of these years, what was that about? The showdown in the car? Brophy had been unable to avoid giving the guy one last dig at the memorial, lying when he said he never thought of him, never thought of the contract.

He'd deserved the punch. He thought of Vale all the time. He had been waiting for the other shoe to drop for years. Waiting to get found out. Waiting to admit to himself that it had been the wrong thing. When Vale had followed him onto the canyon road it had been like absolution had finally jackknifed his fear, finally taken it over.

Vale had given him an out.

He had so little time left, and what was owed?

If a smoke appears and nobody pays attention to it, does it matter to the remnant at all? Does the person that sees it owe it anything at all?

"I'm going to get my pills," Brophy said, and of course the smoke said nothing, gave nothing away, just sat there rocking on his haunches. He walked around the thing, giving it a berth, and opened up his little pill kit on the counter—a thing so like a lady's birth control organizer that he still felt a little weird about using it. Took out his pills, tried not to look at his own hand scooping them out, the knuckles like knobs of hewn wood, pronounced like that, the skin drum-tight and shiny and spotted.

Somehow he had become an old man, sweet Christ. It happened without him knowing.

Vale had released him. It was true. You sit with a bad move like that—even if it makes you rich, and God, that contract had made

Brophy rich—and the fear of getting caught, of litigiousness, of retribution, of some karmic vengeance, it weighs on you. Your life stoops and buckles under the weight of it, conforms to that worry.

So now here he was, with Baby Smoke, the Boy Without a Jaw, some casualty of horrible violence stuttering through the living world and curled like an apostrophe on his kitchen floor. Brophy standing there in his ridiculous silk pajamas like some decrepit, cancer-laden playboy.

But this was the truth: death was in the neighborhood, and it was on roller skates. Zipping around, touching his neck as it passed. Playing with him. But Vale had freed him. There was that, at least. He'd been given the opportunity, the freedom, to correct that long-running error. He could make that right before he went.

He turned on the tap and drank a glass of water with his pills. The night was an ink wash against the window. Brophy saw his own face dim and skull-like in the glass, and on the floor behind him, the smoke rocked itself again and again. Jawless and mute.

Brophy sat the glass in the sink and snapped shut the lid on his pill organizer. He turned.

"So, where you from? What kinda poor kid gets something like that happening to him? Huh?"

And then, with the stiffness and slowness of a man that rarely moved in such a way, unnameable things in his lower back muttering in protest, he sat down cross-legged on the floor next to the smoke, the little boy. As consolingly as someone such as him could be, Brophy sat there on his kitchen floor and waited for the next thing to happen.

OCTOBER

1

Vale stood beneath the awning of Fuel, sipping a cup of coffee and huffing cigarettes. Rainwater fell in jubilant strings from the awning and he watched people pass by with their umbrellas, chins tucked into their jackets against the rain. He felt a flare of melancholy so fierce he wanted to wrap his arms around the world. Rain, at least in the beginning of the season, always hurt him like this. Lovingly.

"Cigarette?"

He looked down and wasn't surprised to see the man in the wheelchair again, his hands still shifting in his lap like errant pets. His teddy bear was gone, but the man himself was the same.

Look for signs, Marvin was always saying, and there was something to be learned from that. Marvin seemed continually poised to tell him something, and Vale kept waiting. He'd be ready to hear it whenever Marvin decided he was willing. And in the meantime, Vale looked for signs. He could usually find them.

Vale handed the man a cigarette and lit it for him as the man's thrumming hands cupped themselves loosely around Vale's own.

The man squinted through the smoke. "Thanks, bud. How about ten bucks?"

Vale laughed. "Give me a break."

The man cackled and pushed off. Still this odd amalgam, the Pearl District: a clutch of kids passed by wearing hairstyles that were embarrassing when Vale was young and yet had now become modern and fashionable. The world ate irony for breakfast. Disheveled kids who walked past—and looked like children to Vale—were in tech, finance, pulled in six-digit incomes. The world was moving on. For good or bad, its relentlessness was the one reliable thing.

Behind him, he heard Fuel's door being unlocked. He turned and saw a different assistant, an emaciated Asian kid in skintight black jeans and with purple highlights in his hair. He eyed Vale warily. Even with the scabs on his forehead healed to pink scars and his beard trimmed to something less animal-like, there was something ragged about Vale. There would always be something ragged about him.

The kid opened the door a bit. "Help you?"

"Is Jacob in?"

"He's working in the back. May I tell him who's visiting?"

Vale said his name and the kid's eyes bulged.

It didn't take long for Burfine to come tearing ass from the back room, again dressed as if there were a fashion photographer somewhere gravely disappointed by his recent absence.

"Mike, goddamn, so good to see you. This is great, so glad you're here. How you doing? You look good! You look great!" Burfine rocked on his heels, ushered Vale inside, clapped him once on the shoulder.

"I'm doing okay," Vale said. He held his coffee in front of him, a minor shield. Almost two weeks sober now and he'd knuckled through some bad cravings. Tremors still wracked him sometimes. The sheen—that magical awe of simple sobriety—was wearing off somewhat, but still. This, compared to what it was like before? This was worthwhile. Scary as shit, but worth it.

Burfine said, "Listen, Mike, I don't want to jump the gun, but I think I found a buyer for *Unraveling.*" He laughed, shaking his head. "I mean, wow. People are *very* interested. This is exciting, man. I want to thank you again."

Vale's jaw dropped. "You're *flipping* it? You're flipping that painting?"

Burfine took a step back, stricken. "I mean—Yeah. I thought it was assumed—"

"I'm messing with you," Vale said. "Flip it. Make money. Good for you."

"Jesus, Mike."

Vale grinned into the mouth of his coffee cup. When he looked up at Burfine, he said, "Let's do a show."

Burfine froze like that, still with that stricken grin on his face. "What's that?"

Vale took another sip of coffee and nodded. "I want to paint again. I want to do a show. Let's do it."

"Really," Burfine said.

Jittery from the adrenaline dump, the fear of broaching him, of asking for help, Vale said, "I need a loan for supplies and a studio rental. You can take it out of sales. Let's drum up a contract. In writing. I'll give you exclusive representation in North America."

Burfine tilted his head, measured him. "You're serious."

"I'm totally serious. North American representation. And I want the name of an entertainment lawyer here in town. Brophy and I are working things out."

"Really. You and Jared Brophy are working things out."

"We are," Vale said. "So what do you say?"

SIXTEEN MONTHS LATER

1

Specter Sightings Decrease for the First Time Since Initial Appearances, Reports CDC
—The New York Times

Interview excerpt from *scifihorizon.com*:

SFH: So, Marvin, you've had a pretty amazing year. The first season of Specter Detectives *was by far the highest-grossing show on the SyFy channel; they've signed on for another ten-episode season, and you're purportedly in talks with some studios about a movie deal.*

MD: Casper and I are, yes. Everything's still up in the air, but things seem to be moving along pretty well in that regard.

SFH: And the ghosts still haven't left Los Angeles, have they?

MD: And we're thrilled about that. (Laughter.) I'm kidding. But yeah, you're right, they haven't left. There's been a marginal decrease, but that's about it. We've made some big leaps on the show, I think, in regards to making contact with the spirits, building a kind of baseline understanding. *Hearing* them, most importantly. But as a whole, no, they don't seem to be going anywhere, at least not anywhere fast.

SFH: Big leaps? I'd say that's putting it mildly. The episode where the crying woman touches your face, or the man who lays down his sword? I've never seen anything like it. I totally teared up.

MD: Me too. (Laughter.)

SFH: It literally chilled me. Because they don't acknowledge us, do they? They ignore the rest of us across the board, but you they react to. They communicate with you, Marvin. To the point where you're now working with some research committees.

MD: They react to me, you're right. Maybe it's the eyepatch! (Laughter.) But yeah, they do seem drawn to me. I feel very fortunate to be able to do this.

SFH: I've wondered, Marvin, after watching the first season—just how many languages do you actually speak?

MD: Um, eight? Seven of them pretty well. But I'm old, remember? (Laughter.) I've had a lot of time to practice.

SFH: That's amazing. Does it ever scare you, being able to talk to them?

MD: No. It doesn't scare me.

SFH: Because you've had a lot more to worry about than a ghost, haven't you? While in Los Angeles doing research for Specter Detectives, *you were critically injured, isn't that right?*

MD: That's true. I was shot.

SFH: What was that like?

MD: Um, unfortunate? It hurt like hell? (Laughter.) Honestly, I don't remember much of it. Bits and pieces. It took quite a while to recover. I *still* feel like I'm recovering, to tell you the truth.

SFH: Well, you seem to be doing great. And on top of everything else, you've gained some notoriety around Hollywood for your philanthropic approach to things, isn't that right?

MD: I guess so. I'm not entirely comfortable talking about it.

SFH: Because you made quite a bundle when the show was renewed for a second season, didn't you? And you gave all that money away, right? To children's cancer research, particularly the ward of the hospital you used to volunteer at in Oregon.

MD: Like I said, Mark, not entirely comfortable.

SFH: It's nothing to be ashamed of.

MD: Still. Let's move on.

SFH: Well, how about this, then—maybe your own brush

with death has enamored you to the ghosts? Maybe, if you'll pardon the pun, they sense a kindred spirit?

MD: It's possible. I'm certainly empathetic. I mean, I know what it's like to be lost, you know? Don't we all?

SFH: The first season finale shows a smoke—

MD: Mark, I really hate that term.

SFH: Okay, sure. Sorry. The first season shows a specter *in dirty rags and this huge dark beard. And he drops before you, weeping and muttering in Latin. Right there on Rodeo Drive! He seemed desperately tired. Just lost.*

MD: Yeah. I think he was.

SFH: And then you placed your hands on his shoulders, and you spoke to him too quietly for the cameras to pick up entirely but (interviewer turns to camera) it was in Latin, people, *and he looked at you and then just disappeared. Just vanished. With what looked like profound gratitude. Where do you think he went? Where do they go after they talk to you?*

MD: I don't know the answer to that, Mark. I really wish I did. I hope they're finding rest, finding peace. But who knows.

SFH: But what do you say to them, Marvin? What did you say to that man?

MD: Sorry, Mark. (Laughter.) We just got renewed for a second season. I can't go giving all of our secrets away.

• • •

"You're sure that you're up for this?"

"Come on, Casper. It's a *cold*. It's not like I'm dead."

First Thursday in the Pearl District, rain or shine: a madhouse. The first Thursday of each month all the galleries in that part of town unveiled their new shows, and tonight was no exception. Fuel was standing room only. More than a few reporters and critics had flown into Portland for the opening.

We stood for a moment in front of the windows. Hundreds of people were gathered inside with hardly room to move, and honestly, few of them seemed to be looking at the art. There was a tended bar, and a four piece orchestra played quietly in a corner.

Jacob Burfine had spared no expense. And why should he? There was a lot at stake. The buzz had been immense.

Vale had been the subject of recent feature articles in the *New Yorker*, the *New York Times*. Word was that Warner Herzog was vying for a documentary. Reporters from *Time* and *Rolling Stone* lurked somewhere inside. Early writings were tinged with the tone of redemption, the sounds of a comeback, while *Art & Artists*—almost singularly—had been vocal in their doubts about Vale's ability to recoup any of his previous momentum from earlier years.

This was something he'd gleefully informed Casper and me over cups of coffee at our weekly "business meetings." Regardless, there was no stopping him. He was on fire with it. The man had paint on his hands every single time I saw him. He told us he painted every day. "I love it," he'd tell us. "I *love* painting, guys. Goddamn. I forgot how much I missed it."

And they were good paintings, I'll admit it. This was coming from someone who still doesn't even care for art all that much.

The lettering in the window:

SMOKE CITY
New Paintings by Michael Vale

The title had actually been one of *Art & Artists*'s supposed signals that Vale had lost it. The show itself had been top-secret before tonight's reception; the gallery windows had been covered in butcher paper while the show was hung. Assistants and handlers had signed nondisclosure agreements. Press materials had been sent out in the form of painting *details*, rather than entire paintings themselves. Still, it had been enough for *Art & Artists* to preemptively call the show "genteel, pandering to the past, full of a yammering, cliché-heavy teen angst, not exactly graceful for a man well enmeshed in middle age."

Vale had brought a copy of the magazine to the coffee shop the day before. He'd been ecstatic. "Now that I'm not blacking out and bleeding into my underwear, the paintings are 'cliché-heavy.' I love it," he'd grinned.

• • •

Our lives are filled with these brief intersections, these unknowable trajectories that never travel in straight lines. Did I ever think I'd be here? No.

I found myself thinking about Donald Jarvis Smith often. The man who shot me. *God will judge,* he'd said, and I'd *known.* I found myself pitying him. His entire life lived, all those years full of hurts and joys and regrets and loves, all leading up to that point.

I found myself, through all of this, wondering not in the existence of God—how could I after all this? That had long since been resolved.

But what of God's intentions? God's leanings?

What about God's willingness to forgive?

I thought about that a lot. In so many ways, it was still the only question I couldn't answer.

• • •

Casper peered in the window, nervously working a wad of chew around his bottom lip. "Lot of people in there," he said.

I pulled out my handkerchief and coughed into it. It was my first bad cold since things had changed, since Joan had come to me in the hospital. Since she'd told me what I needed to do. I was fifty-eight years old and sometimes the fear of it all, the knowledge that this time it was for good, that this was it, seized me with immobility. This was my life.

We'd arrived back in Portland all those months ago to find my store shuttered, the door padlocked. The records were all gone, the room empty. Randy had done exactly what he'd said he'd do: the building was razed, and blocky, pastel-colored condos were thrown up within months. They looked like toys left behind by gigantic, disinterested children. I'd had a hard time caring by then. Music itself had become too full of ghosts, all those records too heavy with memories.

There was no way to fully escape our past. We were all shaped by it, formed by it, but there was such a thing as dead weight, and Bill Creswell's records had become dead weight by the time I got home from LA. Music and memories. Both felt like stones in my pockets, weighing me down, and I had to get rid of at least one of them before I drowned.

I lived in a small two-bedroom house in St. Johns, and Casper and I worked on the show and visited with Vale. The three of us frequently went back to Los Angeles for business meetings, and of course to shoot the show. That was the totality of my life; that, and the ghosts, and most of the time I was content enough with it.

I tried to stay in the moment.

Randy, so said the *Oregonian* last month, had been arrested on charges of racketeering: the bluster about Boston and mob connections had apparently rung at least somewhat true. Litigation loomed. Again, I had a hard time mustering up much emotion about it. I still dragged the past around like an anvil. I don't think you could live for as long—or as fruitlessly—as I had and just magically slough off regret. I was getting better a bit at a time.

We stepped inside the gallery. It was twenty degrees warmer, humid. Casper headed directly to the food platters set out next to the wine, people pausing to speak to him on his way; we made sure that he and I got equal airtime on the show and were both frequently stopped when we went out, especially if we were together.

I held my coat over my arm and scanned the room for Vale. I saw Adam first, and waved. He wedged his way through the crowd. His cheeks were red and he looked uncomfortable in his suit. Mostly he looked shockingly, achingly young, and I was glad things had happened with the store the way they had.

"This show is amazing, Marvin."

I smiled. "I know it. He's good, right?"

Vale's paintings were bright and detailed, like living things snared on the white walls. "It's not even eight o'clock," Adam said. "It looks like almost every one of these is sold. It's crazy."

Adam and I didn't talk about his mother. I thought about Julia a lot, but I was okay not knowing. We lived in the same city, but I was content with her being another ghost in my life. I was learning to navigate among them with at least a minor amount of grace. She had helped me when I needed it so much.

I saw men in tuxedos, in suits, in sleeveless t-shirts with their arms wreathed in tattoos. Women in cocktail dresses, women in paint-splattered smocks. I saw a woman with a shaved head and implants under the skin of her skull to make it look as if she had horns. I laughed at myself as a stutter of envy ran through me, looking around at all the young people here, loose-limbed, happy, talking, their lives yawning ahead of them. And yet, here I was. This was what I'd wanted. *I was here.*

"How's your show going?" Adam asked. He lifted his glass of wine, more than a little drunk, still ceaselessly earnest. Casper had taken a liking to him and wanted Adam to start interning for the show's production team after he graduated. "Let's put that philosophy degree to use," he said.

"The show is good," I said. "The show is blowing up like Vale is blowing up."

Finally, I saw him—Vale—across the crowded room.

"There he is," I said, lifting my chin. "You want to talk to him?"

Adam blanched, nervous.

"He's just a guy," I said. "He's a dick half the time anyway. Come on."

Vale was surrounded by a ring of what I could only assume were collectors, buyers. He'd often insisted to Casper and I that collectors liked to collect artists as much as they liked to collect the art. He sounded good-naturedly bitter about it, playfully put out. Burfine was at his side, hair gelled, in a dark gray suit shot through with silver threads. Bullshitting, elbowing Vale playfully, smoothly transferring the work of the actual sales to his assistants.

Vale hugged me. It was hard to reconcile him with who he was when I'd met him on that sun-blasted stretch of highway a year and a half before. That bloody bandage wrapped around his head. I felt his warmth as he put his arm around me, the scratchiness of his beard against my cheek. He'd lost weight, his face grown thin and hawklike since he'd stopped drinking. He'd become a kind of resolute pit bull in his sobriety, tenacious and unwavering and fierce. His sense of humor had not improved.

"Glad you could make it, good sir," he barked into my ear, and clapped me hard on the back. This lead to another coughing fit, which I tried to cover with my handkerchief. The collectors soured and Vale excused us, steered me away. Adam followed sheepishly.

Vale frowned at me. "Well, at the very least, thanks for getting me out of that, Marvin. But you sound like shit."

"It's just a cold."

He nodded, searching my face for a moment. "I've mentioned that the eye patch is dashing as hell, haven't I?"

"You have," I said.

"Where's the Poltergeist Whisperer? Where's Captain Ectoplasm?" Vale's game with Casper, always a new name.

"He bee-lined for the food when we came in."

"I don't blame him. Who's this?"

I turned. "Mike, this is Adam. He's a friend of mine. Casper wants him to start interning for the show."

"These paintings are amazing," Adam said.

Vale, among other things, seemed to have learned at least a modicum of graciousness. "Thank you," he said. "I appreciate that. I'm happy with them."

He and Adam talked as I looked at the paintings. Vale's work had always been so couched in allegory, but these were all about Candice in some way. I mean, it was about Los Angeles, and our trip, and the things that had happened there, but they were mostly about Candice.

The entire series had been done in grayscale, with one vibrant fist of color blooming somewhere on the canvas. Here, a side-cut of a grave with a skeleton interred in the ground, roots entwining the bones; where they broke the soil, burst forth into a bouquet of orange flowers.

And here, a wolf stood crouched and snarling inside a dilapidated house as water poured from a faucet and flooded over the sink, pouring onto the floor. A swatch of blue dress and bare arm was just visible in the window behind, a snaking drift of curling red hair. Vale seemed to be haunting and freeing himself at the same time.

"They're apologies," he'd told us over coffee. "That's what the magazines and collectors and shit aren't ever going to get. This is me saying I'm sorry."

"To who?" Casper said.

Vale had scowled at him, cracked his knuckles. "Who do you think, Casper?"

He had told me about seeing Candice that day in front of Richard's house. We went back whenever we were in town, Casper and

I, hoping to see her. I would have been happy to listen to her, to free her like that. We'd always park across the street, not wanting to bother Richard. We usually waited an hour or two, those awkward blips of time between meetings.

"They're all about the fact that I can't save her," he'd said to us, "after she saved me a hundred times over. I can't find her, when she always found me." And he'd tapped the *Art & Artists* article with a finger. "So I paint instead. I try to say I'm sorry."

"I bet she forgives you," Casper said.

Vale snorted. "It's unforgiveable, man. I treated her like shit. There's no forgiveness. There's just the act of trying."

"There you guys are," Casper said now. He was holding a glass of wine in one hand, a fistful of crackers in the other. Crumbs scattered on the lapels of his suit jacket, a t-shirt beneath it. He and Vale hugged.

Casper cocked his head to one side, chewing. Snaring Vale with that look of his. So Casper-like. I knew what was coming before he said it. "You sad that Jared couldn't come, Mike?"

Vale looked away for a moment. Squinted at a painting. Nodded. "I am. Definitely." He stared at the floor, scuffed a spot there with his shoe. Nodded again.

Brophy had died two months before. He and Vale had managed to resuscitate a kind of strained friendship once Vale began painting again. Brophy had actually gone ahead and nullified the contract himself; the few originals he still owned all these years later, he had shipped back to Vale. Vale said he had flown out to Los Angeles a half dozen times in the past year and sat with Brophy after his chemo sessions. They sat for hours and, when Brophy was capable of it, talked about art, women, Hollywood. Vale navigating the choppy waters of gracefulness and forgiveness. If it wasn't friendship there at the end, it was something close to it.

Brophy had insisted his new paintings were his best work, the critics could go fuck themselves. He'd also promised to never buy another goddamned Mike Vale painting as long as he lived, which made them both laugh. Vale had gone to his funeral; he'd been buried in the same cemetery as Candice.

For a moment we stood there, this cluster of us. This group. My friends and I. It was a small moment, but I'd come to appreciate them. Then Burfine came back over with a trio of collectors, and Vale squeezed my arm in passing. "We'll talk tonight," he said.

When I am able to stay in the moment, I'm profoundly grateful. I have no inkling of what awaits me beyond this life, what terrors or joys. What promise of ceaselessness. I don't pretend to know a thing about it. A vast nothingness seems likely. But each moment, I've discovered, is my own now—and in my best moments, I am indebted to my history but not moored by it. There is a lot of good to be done.

There are also times—I don't sleep well anymore, thinking that I only have a limited number of nights allowed me now—when I am afraid of death. Absolutely terrified of it, really. When I am kept awake by the failings of my lives before this one, the terrible things I've done. The great debt I will always owe those I've wronged.

And yet, I am able to take small comfort in the grasp and attentions and love of these people, my friends. We are doing the best we can. If we are hurtling toward oblivion, we are doing it arm in arm.

And Joan, you ask? What of her?

I don't know what to tell you.

When you see them, help them, she had whispered to me after blessing me with her forgiveness. That scar on her arm, the bleach spot on her shirt. The pendant with the sigil of my father's coat. *My* coat. After she had given me, truly, my life back. After she'd said, *They'll need you.*

They'll need someone to forgive them. They'll need someone to listen to them.

So what of Joan, you ask?

I only met her once, but I dream of her often. All the time. Her ghost walks the long hallways of my heart. It's not quite as restless a place these days, but I don't think she'll ever go away. And I don't think she should; she's more than earned her residency there.

What of her? Well. I was the dark and terrible mechanism of her undoing. I work now, these last unknown days, to earn her forgiveness.

Acknowledgments

It's been a long road to publication for this novel. I'm grateful to the following people for their support during the process:

Josie Corby, as well as Matt and Sherris Corby—your continued encouragement came at a much-needed time during the writing of this book. Thanks so much.

Sheila Ashdown provided invaluable early feedback on the manuscript.

While researching this novel, Chloe Massarello answered my great number of dumb questions about the general state of affairs of fifteenth century France with measured and painstaking detail, as well as offering some crucial pieces of information about Joan, the ways in which she was viewed at that time, and the brutal lives and societal expectations of medieval executioners. There are undoubtedly errors and inaccuracies regarding this aspect of the book—please be sure to assign them to me, the author.

My agent, Christopher Schelling of Selectric Artists. I mean, I wrote a novel about an alcoholic painter and the reincarnation of Joan of Arc's executioner road-tripping through a ghost-heavy LA and he was like, "Okay, I'm in."

Tricia Reeks and the folks at Meerkat Press for their continued belief in the value of my work. I'm beyond appreciative; with these past few books, you've taken a gamble when few would, and have undoubtedly changed my life. Thank you.

Lastly, to Robin Corbo. For all of it. You're my person.